The Curse of the Dragon Medallion
Series

©2017 All Rights Reserved. At no time should the contents of this book, be copied if done so the person or the persons responsible may be charged under the, Canadian Copyright act. Should you want to copy for such reasons as a TV production, the author must be contacted and notified of such doing. The characters in this book in this book are fictitious and any resemblance to real persons living or dead is coincidental. Publishing House Publishing has published this book exactly how the author wanted it; at no time will Publishing House Publishing make changes without the Authors consent. Publishing House Publishing, High Prairie, Alberta
publishinghousepublishing@gmail.com

ISBN # 978-1-7750736-3-5

Publication assistance and digital printing in Canada by

PageMasterPublishing.ca

To: Hope

TWIN DESTINIES

WRITTEN BY LAURETTA BEAVER

Lauretta Beaver
Nov 25/18

Series and Books written by Lauretta Beaver

Series #1: White Buffalo (New Beginnings)
Book #1: Passionate Alliance
Book #2: Raven & the Golden Eagle
Book #3: (Coming Soon)

Series #2: The Curse of the Celtic Dragon Medallion
Book #1: Dream Dancer & the Celtic Witch
Book #2: Twin Destinies
Book #3: The Seeker & the Shadow Hunter (coming soon)

Cursed

The Prophecy

One female child will be born to each White Buffalo descendant before death claims her!
All shall be blind... **NONE** will have the power!
Many generations shall pass and the White Buffalo prophecy will be all but forgotten… **UNTIL** the unthinkable happens!

In revenge against the Great Spirit, the Celtic Dragon Medallion is hidden away by the last of the Skin Walkers!
Beware the return of the Dragon Medallion… for **THEY** are coming!

I dedicate this book to my husband,
Michel Pelletier
Who had to put up with my constant badgering to read everything I wrote;
I love you to the moon and back my Honey Bun.

APRIL 12, 1872

Quebec

The steady, slow rhythmic beating of a drum; accompanied by the ominous roaring of a bonfire as a loud snap of exploding sparks flying upwards was all one could distinguish in the sinister pitch black night. Not a star or even a sliver of the moon was present in the sky as they waited breathlessly in anticipation unable to glimpse anything beyond the fire.

The five sat in hushed expectation waiting, not knowing what to expect; all were grotesquely painted. They were of age now so after tonight the boys would be banished from the village, for how long was unknown. Come dawn they would all be gone each leaving when the feeling was right for them to find their adult names as well as their spirit guides.

Beside each of them was a small rawhide bundle; inside it was a water bag with an herbal plant they were to mix with water and heat before drinking. A ceremonial pipe was also included given to each in a ritual with a pouch of unique dried leaves to help in their spiritual quest. It also had a medicine bag in case the unexpected happened. A two-day ration of hardtack with a supply of jerky was all the food they would be allowed to take.

A hunting knife plus a bow with half a dozen arrows made especially for them was sitting by the light pack. It would be all the protection they were allowed and their only means for more food if needed. Behind each boy a dog waited patiently; each had a harness so they could pull a small frame that would be made into a temporary shelter when they felt it was time.

Unexpectedly, a dramatic chanting began; where it came from was uncertain. Without warning, a disembodied voice rose high above all other sounds in the inky darkness. Once it began to speak the drums followed by the chanting softened becoming more distant, where or who the speaker was, remained a mystery; the eerie voice sent chills down each of the youngster's spines as they listened raptly, some could also visualize.

"Countless moons have come and gone, how many is uncertain! As each generation passes, more will forget where we came from. Even our tribal name was lost over time; now it is all but a distant memory. Long, long ago a large group of our people were banished from their frozen homeland. They wandered aimlessly or so it seemed, searching for what the people didn't know. All they could remember from before was a black void of nothingness. All that kept them going was a man bundled in a white bear hide; at times it seemed to them the man would disappear then a bear would take his place. In the blinding sleet and snow they trudged through, it was easy to get confused see things not there. Especially when hunger pains, as well as fear, pushed the people onward..."

*****

"Ugh!"

The man leading stopped instantly, he turned at a cry of fear then pain behind him as another fell unable to go on. He hurried back knowing deep down his people were dying. The towering black haired bear of a man in a white hide reached down to touch his friend in comfort before he looked around at his starving, nearly frozen people. "Rest here my friends I will be back shortly!"

The leader turned away and disappeared into the storm, the people watching him go shook their heads in awe. It looked to them that before he disappeared completely, he dropped onto all fours as the storm swallowed him. With no other choice, the people huddled together for warmth waiting. It was hours later but seemed like forever to the ones left behind that a white bear walked into camp; it stood up as their chief returned with a medium-sized seal slung over his shoulder.

The people quickly cut into the meat, pulling strips off they devoured the warm steaming bloody meal raw, too hungry to care; none of them thought to ask where their leader found a seal way out here in the middle of nowhere so far away from the sea.

The man, known to his people as Spirit Bear walked away with a small piece of meat. It was just enough to keep him going, but not enough to stop his hunger. He knew his people needed it more, his visions along with his determination would be his substance it was all he required to keep him going. The leader didn't go far, knowing his people needed to see him. He squatted, then bit off a piece of meat before chewing, enjoying the warm salty taste; making sure he didn't drip blood on his white hide.

It was highly unusual to find a white bear that was not a polar bear or an albino, but he found one in the north. His people called them mooksgmol, they are spirit bears and revered by them. Since the white bear claimed him, his people also chose him as their chief. The other reason was that he was the last of the legendary skinwalkers; according to the stories, hundreds of years ago when they first came into the light a walker could shed his human skin then become the animal they were named after to protect the tribe.

Spirit Bear chuckled in disbelief; he shook his head at his wayward thoughts the most exciting thing that ever happened to him was, HER! The chief sobered before beginning to chant again. Instantly he saw the woman from his visions, she was beckoning him urgently to continue on his way. He didn't know who the woman was but she looked a lot like his people except her skin was white, ghostly looking. Her eyes were a dark colour, really hard to see. If he had to guess, he would say maybe black. Unlike his people, her eyes tilted upwards quite a bit. Her hair was ebony black, it was so long it brushed the ground ever so slightly behind her. He could also glimpse other colours in her hair, which gave her a dark mythical look.

Spirit Bear couldn't help but wonder if he was doing the right thing! She could be leading them anywhere, doubts suddenly assailed him. Who was she, why was she helping them? The chief shook himself in irritation; he had followed her blindly and unhesitatingly at the beginning, so why was he all of a sudden having so much uncertainty. Was he starting to doubt her or himself!

Chief Spirit Bear shook off his unwanted feelings. He shrugged mentally to himself, now they didn't have any choice. If his people stayed here they would all die; he finished his piece of meat then cleaned his hands with snow.

Spirit Bear got up before turning to his people; now calmer, the chief roused them. "Come, we must get over this mountain. I know you are weary, but on the other side we will rest!"

For another week they trudged over snow-covered passes and narrow canyons until suddenly they began descending. Three days later the sun appeared as the storm dissipated; giving the exhausted travellers a needed respite. They travelled south all this time, but now they turned south-west trying to get over another range of mountains.

Once on the other side, enormous trees took its place. Still Chief Spirit Bear continued to lead his people on, obstinately refusing to stop for more than one night at any of their camps. For six full moons, they continued on and even skirted more salty water which sent the people more south than west. Until finally they stumbled upon a valley where there were plants of every description, with an abundance of animals. Spring had finally arrived; the air was crisp, clean with a river two miles to the west. A gurgling freshwater creek fed by an underground spring to the east was half a mile away, giving them plenty of room to expand.

A cry of pain behind Chief Spirit Bear with an urge to halt as the woman in his vision held up her hand to stop him from advancing, had the man turning with a smile of relief. His wife was standing with both hands pressed to her distended belly; she just entered her ninth month of pregnancy and was now going into labour. He knew instantly this would be their new home.

Spirit Bear looked around at what was left of his people; when they started out there was over three hundred, now sadly only two hundred remained. Lots died, but some getting discouraged left to find their own way. Where they ended up or if they were alive, the chief did not know. "My people this will now be our new home, let us begin by rejoicing! We have lost many, but their sacrifice will never be forgotten. We will build the Medicine Man a wigwam first to take care of the sick and the injured. Afterwards, the Shaman's will be next before we see to our own needs."

A great cheer erupted then whoops of joy shattered the quiet of the little valley; they had found a home despite the harsh challenges. With everyone working together by evening the first shelter was built for the healer.

For two days Spirit Bear's wife laboured while he continued to help his people settle into their new homes. On the second day as evening was descending, the chief paced anxiously outside the medicine man's wigwam; he was getting fearful the birthing was taking a long time. He stopped before looking up imploringly, but couldn't see much since there was no moon or stars in the sky only wispy clouds were seen.

A wolf howled eerily in the far off distance, it caused Spirit Bear to frown apprehensively when a shiver of foreboding shook him; as the howl of the wolf faded, a baby crying out lustily from inside had the chief hurrying into the shelter. Forgetting his momentary unease, he rushed inside as a second cry joined the first. He stood there in stunned shock for a long moment, twin boys; now he knew their home was indeed blessed.

*****

Suddenly the youngsters were brought into the present with an unexpected jolt of fright when the fire flared sending shooting sparks flying before the shaman jumped into the firelight.

Dramatically he circled the fire all he had on was a loincloth; draped around his shoulders was a wolf skin with the head of the wolf still attached, so it could be used as a headdress. He was hideously painted with tattoos and piercings everywhere. Shaking a staff, he shrieked then chanted before dancing around until unexpectedly he disappeared into the thick black night.

The five boys caught their breaths in awe when the fire exploded just as the shaman disappeared; sending a burst of different coloured sparks swirling everywhere before the disembodied voice began to speak. Instantly, the youngsters were drawn into the past again...

"Many moons passed as the twins matured becoming big and powerful; the village also grew as our people prospered. A childhood rivalry began between the identical twins as they tried to best each other, but always they were together as one. They needed to be separated though for them to go on their vision quests, only alone can one seek their adult name or spirit guide. Even to this day, nobody knows how it happened or where she came from. Hearing a scream of fear, the youngest of the twins called Ahanu having gone further than ever before rushed ahead. He stumbled upon a woman of beauty being attacked by a rare white bear, not even hesitating with only a hunting knife the young brave attacked the monster. It was a ferocious fight that seemed to last forever, with neither being able to outdo the other. As the two fought, it even looked to the woman cowering against the tree that the bear kept changing colours. One minute, it seemed white before suddenly changing to black or was there two of them? The youngest twin bleeding and hurt killed the strange bear. Standing over his kill in triumph Ahanu watched in shock as the hide fell away from a body, which changed its shape revealing his older twin brother..."

*****

"Aaiihhhh!"

A long drawn out scream shattered the now deadly silence. Wailing in despair Ahanu dropped to the ground in shock. He gathered his older twin brother closer than began rocking him back and forth in remorse; tears streaked his filthy blood-splattered face. It wasn't long before fear set in as he looked up towards the heavens pleading desperately for forgiveness. "I didn't know brother, now what am I to do? I can't take you home they will take my life as forfeit!"

Fearfully, Ahanu jumped up before taking the white bear hide of his brother; he draped it around his own shoulders mumbling shamefully to himself. "So I will never forget this evil deed I am about to do!"

Ahanu turned to the woman who looked exactly like his people, but she wasn't one of them. He tried to talk to her, when she didn't understand he resorted to using sign language to help explain his needs. He stood up before beckoning for her to get up too; he had fought for her, so she was now his. They would marry as soon as he could get her to his home.

Ahanu gestured for the woman to pick up his twins legs needing her help to carry his dead brother the half mile to a fast running creek with a waterfall in the distance. He knew it emptied into a river further downstream; sadly, he allowed his older twin to be swept away. The younger twin never spoke of his brother again, hiding his shame behind a wall of silence.

There was one who did know though since Powaw who was the shaman of this band of Cree watched it all happening in a vision. He took the younger twin into the sweat lodge for his formal naming which also ended in a curse. "You will now be called Matchitehew, which means he who has an evil heart! You will be the last Skinwalker with only one boy child born to each generation; no longer will your line of descendants be able to change as Mooksgmol withdraws its protection from the people! No longer will your ancestors lead the people as our spirit bear disappears because of your evil ways, maybe forever."

*****

The chanting and story halted unexpectedly both on a sharp note bringing about a momentary suspenseful silence; it was followed a few moments later by a scream of disbelief then rage which shattered the night's stillness once more.

"Aaagghhhh!"

The five young males that were fully lost in the tale jumped in shocked disbelief. Rudely they were yanked back into the present by the morbid wailing. It lasted for a long heart-stopping moment before it stopped dramatically; silence descended but only for a short time.

The eerie voice began to speak once again. No chanting accompanied it this time; only the steady beat of the drum keeping them in suspense letting them know the tale wasn't over but was winding down...

"Chief Spirit Bear unaware of what happened to his oldest son soon died of a broken heart. Slowly, the people dwindled over the

Twin Destinies 7

years until all that was left again numbered two hundred. Thinking their homes cursed the new chief took his people away from the valley of abundant richness. They wandered for many moons until they settled here and refused to continue on; now in isolation the people struggled on, waiting for what is still unknown!"

Unexpectedly the drumming quit on a loud explosive sound then the strange voice faded replaced by dead silence, which prevailed for a heartbeat; suddenly, the fire flared with a whoosh as crackling sparks flew everywhere. The wrinkled old shaman jumped into the firelight one final time dancing and chanting he circled the fire before throwing something into the flames making them leap they danced dramatically drawing attention away from him; he disappeared unnoticed.

The morbid voice spoke one last time, but no more did the drum or chanting accompany it. The sad tale of how they had come to be in this hidden mountain range was complete. "Sleep now, when you wake up you must leave here on your own to go on your vision quests. Remember one of you will begin training with the Shaman and one with the Medicine Man. Three of you will become great Warriors... Guardian's to continue protecting this tribe from outsiders!"

The voice vanished before the fire was left to die down.

The five youngsters whispered among themselves in excitement, discussing the spectacular display they witnessed this night before finally, they laid down where they were; obediently, they all slept.

Slowly the shaman and medicine man walked carefully among the sleeping boys not wanting any of them to wake up just yet. They were both chanting softly giving each of the youngsters a special charm to help them find their true paths in life; the two older men stopped as one to stare down at two identical boys... twins.

The medicine man frowned hesitantly; he looked over at the shaman as he gestured down curiously at the youngsters. "Are you sure the time is now, you didn't tell them the rest of the Shaman's curse or the destiny of the twins? You have always done so for all others coming of age, why the difference now there has been twins born before this?"

The old shaman sighed sadly with a decisive nod as he looked up from the two boys at the medicine man. "Yes, I am absolutely sure. They are the last surviving descendant of Spirit Bear our first Chief, the others were not born from his ancestors nor were they identical! I did not finish the curse because even though their destinies are known, they still must choose for themselves what they wish to become. If I told them, it wouldn't be a free choice anymore. The sickness will return they must right the wrong that was done so long ago only then can our people move on. SHE has arrived I can feel it as Mother Earth rejoices. We will not be alive to see the ending, but we are here now to make sure the beginning leads our people to their rightful place in the new world. We have managed to keep ourselves hidden; sadly, as the white eyes expand it is only a matter of time until we are discovered."

The medicine man frowned thoughtfully as the two men turned away from the boys. He could not help remembering the destiny of the twins the shaman left unsaid, he mumbled quietly to himself. "The dawn of a new day will be upon the spirit bear clan when Mooksgmol again tests the Cree people as identical twin boys are born once more. The rivalry will become fierce and a deep bitterness will consume one of them after an accident kills his mate. They must put their hatred aside to heal their people, but an unexpected twist ensnares the twins! One of them must sacrifice their heart's desire to save the other or all will be lost; if the unthinkable happens the people will perish when spirit bear withdraws its protection, this time forever!"

The medicine man wandered back to his wigwam before lying down to sleep, but his dreams were restless. Every time one of the boys got up and left it would wake him so the second part of the curse would play out in his mind. He kept pushing it away not wanting to remember it. Finally, only the twins were left; as one rose to leave, the healer sat up unable to ignore the curse any longer. He began to recite it just as the older of the boys vanished but didn't completely finish the curse until the youngest twin was up then he too disappeared...

"When all seems lost, with only one skinwalker descendant left, another set of identical twins will be born into their line! They will fall in love with White Buffalo, SHE is the one destined to become the Guardian of Aki... the Earth; a healer, she will also give those seeking peace their spirit names! Will the destiny of the twins collide with White Buffalo's causing a catastrophe felt throughout the Earth as the evil is released before its time! Or will one twin's sacrifice heal the rift between Mooksgmol their spirit bear and its people so their twin destinies can entwine!"

APRIL 21, 1872

Ontario

Edward Summerset the three-quarter Cheyenne doctor known to his people as Dream Dancer jumped to his feet, as did the Oriental Guardian Shin. Instantly they both rushed to protect his daughter Cecille who also went by the name of White Buffalo and her nurse Michelle.

Edward known as the former Earl of Summerset cocked his rifle then pointed it at the one on horseback, knowing he was the most important one. The Tianming Monk pulled out the Japanese sword strapped to his back, patiently the Asian Guardian stood protectively in front of his charge waiting. They both looked around grimly at all the Ojibwa Indians surrounding them; there were at least thirty of them, all hideously painted. All were on foot... except one!

Lucky for them the Little Mississippi River was directly behind them, neither of them turned to look knowing nobody could sneak up on them from that direction; unfortunately, it was swollen at this time of year making it unpredictable so escaping across it was not an option either.

How they ended up going south-west, instead of going straight west towards Manitoba for the Queen was Edward's fault. He couldn't help thinking back to his disturbing dream; it ended up causing this detour. The first time it happened to the former Earl, they were still in Quebec City. It was the same night the four of them disembarked from the ship that brought them from England.

*****

As Edward Summerset slept, he heard something unrelated to his dream; it disturbed his sleep enough to make him toss around on the hotel bed before turning violently. It sounded like a sinister hiss of laughter from something. It was the first time since losing his powers to walk in dreams that he felt so much intensity; which told the former earl this wasn't an ordinary dream. The sound he was hearing was entirely different from the evil mist they fought against in England. Relieved, he searched trying to find the source of the threat.

Edward was about to give up when a hillside appeared he saw three white men standing beside a tripod made of wood. It was cone shaped like a tepee with no covering. The men had a rope tied to their right foot; one at a time they lifted their leg before dropping it back to the ground. It turned something connected to the three-legged thing whatever it was ripped open the ground savagely digging deep into the Earth's surface.

   Edward saw the men backing away a few minutes later then hot steam hissed when it billowed all around them forcing them even further away. When the mist cleared, a different kind of contraption replaced the wooden one; it was able to dig a deeper. He saw more of the tripods popping up they were getting larger.

   It was not long before they changed again; becoming huge, towering so high into the sky Edward could barely see the top of it. The contraptions were different now made of black steel or metal of some kind. They continued to dig into the Earth able to go to the very core of the Mother! Piercing the Earth relentlessly a pitch-black liquid sprayed everywhere, causing the Mother Earth to wail in angry defiance. As the black gooey substance settled, he could see animals covered in it. They tried to get away from it but instead died horrible deaths.

   Edward could visibly see an oily substance floating on top of lakes, rivers, streams then well water. He saw children drinking the tainted water, so cried out a warning to them. He watched helplessly, this was only a dream after all; they continued to drink.

   Edward watched the humans on the monster shouting in joy as more of the great beasts began dotting the Earth until the ugly contraptions covered every inch. As they dug further, unknown to the people was that they were stealing Mother Earth's aquifers. Deep artesian oil wells, which had a particular purpose unknown to them, scarring her forever! Even the oceans were not immune; he watched the Earth being covered in them from one end to the other. Dream Dancer cried out in fearful denial when he felt Mother Earth dying all around him.

   Suddenly, a bright light exploded in Edward's head before his dream vanished all he could feel now was an empty void. Instantly, he woke as tears streamed down his face. It was the evil of greed Dream Dancer heard chuckling at the start of the dream as the humans destroyed the Earth; unaware that in doing so they will ultimately kill themselves.

   Edward looked over to see if he disturbed Shin sleeping across the room. He saw the Tianming Monk sitting up watching him sadly the two men had the exact same dream, neither commented as they turned away from each other. It took both men until dawn to fall asleep thankfully with no more nightmares to taunt them!

*****

Edward dreamt about those metal contraptions again; the dream just would not leave him alone. Dream Dancer revised his thinking after the second time it could have been the hiss of steam he heard... not laughter.

The next day at breakfast before leaving for Montreal, Edward asked Pierre if he knew anything about the wooden contraption he continued seeing while dreaming.

Pierre listened reflectively as Earl Summerset described his nightmare to him before nodding thoughtfully. "Yes, there is one at a town not far from the Great Lakes near Sarnia in Ontario called Petrolia; they struck oil earlier this year with it. It's a test model to see if it could work there was a lot of skepticism because nobody figured it would be able to dig deep enough. They call it an oil derrick it is used to bring crude oil up to the surface, which they sometimes call fossil fuel or petroleum. It's collected for things like oil lamps, medicines and other things."

Shin having the same dream as Edward knew about oil, he never heard of a derrick though. He sat down beside the former earl before described to the two men how the Asian people collected petroleum in his hometown. "My people get their fossil fuel by immersing blankets in the petroleum that leaks up to the surface on occasions; afterwards, two people wring the cloth over a pot or tight containers until they are full of the oily substance."

Pierre laughed before nodding giving Shin a knowing smile. "The natives in these parts get their oil in a similar way."

Two days later, Pierre Chiasson stared at Edward in astonishment before sputtering incredulously. "Are you sure you want to go all the way to Petrolia, the Queen left me explicit instructions to get you to Manitoba as fast as possible; do you really want her Majesty angry at you!"

Edward chuckled, but there was no humour in it. It wouldn't be the first time he made the Queen infuriated, it was how the former earl ended up in Canada to start with; he nodded decisively, Dream Dancer felt this burning need to see it, unsure why only that he must go now. "Yes, I must see it for myself!"

Pierre shrugged resignedly; he was not one to argue when it came to making extra money. "Well if you must see it first, I guess we can try to find a river raft going to Manitoba from there. Although, I highly doubt we will find one big enough for all our horses, guess I will worry about it when we get there."

Edward nodded without commenting before Pierre took them south-west instead.

*****

Edward shook off his reflective mood as he stood protecting his daughter Cecille and her nanny; now deep into Ontario, they were surrounded by fierce-looking Indians. He couldn't help wondering if he made a critical miscalculation when insisting on coming south-west. For two weeks they rode steadily, now they were only a day away from a town Pierre called Perth. It was still several days away from Petrolia, which was their goal.

Pierre stood up slower before holding out his hands showing the Ojibwe he was unarmed. Trying to reassure the Indians they were no threat to them not wanting any trouble; the native tribes around here were mostly friendly, but not all it was best to be cautious.

An old man nudged his horse forward, he was the only one riding; he spoke hesitantly in a mixture of English and Ojibwe as he pointed over at the men protecting Cecille and Michelle. "Aanii, I wish to see WIIN."

Pierre understanding Ojibwe frowned in surprise as he translated for Edward; they must be friendly, the shaman wouldn't have given a greeting otherwise. "Aanii means hello, wiin is either her or him."

Edward looked over at Shin grimly guessing it was 'her' the old man meant, the two men were confident they knew who he was referring to; curiously they turned towards the conversation to find out why!

Pierre frowned, thinking of the beautiful English Woman it must be her they meant. It wasn't the first time the Ojibwe tried stealing a white woman. The guide was confused, why would they bother giving a greeting beforehand if that was the reason. He folded his arms angrily, but just in case they meant him he decided he better add a caution for everyone. It had taken him years to gain the respect of the Ojibwe, so he hoped his warning would carry weight among this band. "I am Sleeping Bear; these people are under my protection!"

The shaman full of tattoos with most of his head shaved grunted in frustration at the misunderstanding; being on a quest his face, head, plus his chest were painted quite elaborately. Usually, he would not have warriors with him but because he was dealing with the whites his son insisted this time.

A young man wearing a loincloth, a bone vest, and moccasins with a little headdress of eagle feathers walked up beside the older man.

A quick heated discussion took place before the young man turned to Pierre in explanation. "I will translate because my father does not talk good English, but he understands. He doesn't wish to speak to your woman or the men; he wants to talk to, HER! The one from across the big salt water, she came here in a white man's canoe; a young Shaman being trained by Aki, our Mother Earth!"

Edward knew by the headdress the young man must be significant, either a chief in training or a war chief. It wasn't long enough for him to be the leader since normally their ceremonial bonnets would reach almost to the ground.

The older man Edward knew by looking was either a shaman or medicine man; the tattoos with the combined paint patterns all over him let others know he was no ordinary Indian. If you knew how to interpret the intricate design of the paint, it would tell you a story. He was on a spiritual hunt for something important to his people. The former earl looked over at Shin, his suspicions confirmed.

Cecille with both hands lying flat against the ground listened intently to Mother Earth. The ten-year-old stood up then squeezed between Edward and her Guardian Shin. She turned before putting a beseeching hand over Dream Dancer's arm. She used the Cheyenne name for father which she knew he preferred. "It is okay ni-hoi, he is a Shaman; Po the spirit of the Earth sent him to me! I will speak to him please!"

Shin nodded before putting his sword away trusting Cecille entirely. Besides, he suspected right away this is what they wanted; as a precaution, the Guardian put both hands over his dragon daggers in case he needed one in a hurry.

Edward moved the rifle barrel away from the shaman before turning it he cradled it in his arm, so it was ready for instant use if needed. He nodded permission to his daughter; both men kept the young Cecille flanked refusing to let her go alone.

The old painted shaman dismounted when he saw the girl-child he was searching for coming to him.

Excited whispers were heard from the Warriors after they got a better view of the young blind girl. Cecille was using her cane to walk today since she hadn't gotten a chance to memorize the camp yet; as she moved closer some of them pointed at her before speaking one word, there was an obvious hint of awe in their voices. "Gagiibiingwe!"

The old man walked up then dropped onto his knees in front of Cecille, this is why he had not wanted others to come.

There was shocked exclamation of surprise from all the braves; a shaman did not kneel in front of anyone especially not a child; a white-eyes girl made it that much worse as a bewildered outcry occurred!

Cecille passed her cane to Shin before reaching out she touched the shaman's face feeling the deep crevices over his brows. His character lines also told a story, so she was able to see him in her mind's eye; it helped White Buffalo read his aura. She smiled in satisfaction this was the one she was told to watch for, the Mother Earth even told her how to say grandfather in his language. "You will teach me, Mishomis?"

The shaman nodded in agreement before rising. "Yes; Aki, our Mother Earth she commands me!"

Cecille turned to Edward her expression became beseeching hoping he would understand. Her father had been fighting what she was since she was born; only recently did he come to terms with who White Buffalo was meant to be. "I must go with him ni-hoi, he will teach me the shaman ways."

Edward frowned disgruntled he looked over at Shin for his opinion; the Oriental Tianming Monk was Cecille's Guardian, he would have the final say!

Shin shrugged resignedly in agreement, just recently he warned Edward that he would drive his daughter away if the former earl didn't release his tight hold on her. His refusal to see Cecille as anything but his little girl was strangling her, which had the opposite effect he wanted. Instead of learning openly, the Tianming Monks charge was hiding what she was doing most of the time; it made it a lot more dangerous for her and others! "White Buffalo needs to be taught properly, Dream Dancer! I have no objections if you do not."

Edward grimaced he was aware Cecille would become dangerous without the proper teaching; finally he turned to Pierre. "We will stay with them, but I still want to see the derrick. I need to get my Daughter settled first I will contact you as soon as I can get away."

Pierre frowned in concern, but then shrugged in resignation. "I can wait in Perth."

Edward with the help of Shin got the horses ready to go. Dream Dancer, Cecille, and Michelle all mounted; the Tianming Monk ran with the warriors. They left the guide staring after them grimly as they were led away, back upriver.

Queen Victoria was not going to like this one bit!

*****

Three hours later, Edward's party was led into an Indian village. The braves ran the whole way without stopping once to rest. Dream Dancer was impressed. It took a lot of stamina to run that far. Shin had a hard time keeping up the last half hour; the Guardian's flush of exertion spoke volumes, not being used to running for hours.

Edward looked around with interest. Some of the Indian Braves shaved one side of their heads but kept a long braid of hair on the other side. There were lots of older men who kept their hair; it fell to the middle of their backs. Quite a few wore it loose others were braided. Some shaved both sides of their head leaving only a thin strip of hair at the base of their skull with three small decorated braids only. Dream Dancer wouldn't learn until much later they didn't shave their heads. Instead, they pulled out each hair strand by the root. It was one of the milder tests of manhood for the ones wanting to be warriors.

The majority of them wore a loincloth like Edward did on occasions. The flap on the front and back of the Ojibwe was longer reaching to their knees. Some had bare legs others wore leggings with moccasins. A lot of men were bare-chested; a few wore shirts from the whites, they decorated them with beads or porcupine quills. Dream Dancer could see several wearing buckskin shirts. He could tell the majority were made from deer hide. The men were tattooed with lots of piercings.

The younger women seemed to prefer shirts from the whites with buckskin skirts. Edward saw with approval that the majority of the older ladies were wearing buckskin dresses. Several women were topless, wearing only a skirt and moccasins. Almost all the women wore their hair long, some braided others lose. He did see a few shorter hairstyles in the younger ones though. Ear piercings were popular with the women.

Children under a certain age ran around naked; others wore a loincloth with moccasins.

Dogs were everywhere several horses wandered restlessly in a corral on the left side of the village; Edward figured the horses were for the ones with high standing like the shaman leading the procession, a chief, or a medicine man.

The young man wearing the headdress probably could have a horse too, but with the other braves running he would feel the need to stay with them. That is how Edward would feel anyway; no way would he ride if his men were running, it was a matter of principle and pride.

Edward was thankful to see that everyone looked healthy. The village was clean, which also reassured him immensely. Dream Dancer saw the marks of smallpox in a few faces, but nothing drastic.

Edward immediately identified the chief with his long headdress made of eagle feathers. He was hefty, but not overweight. The man wasn't tall; he had a daunting countenance as he stood there with his arms folded in front of him that said he took his responsibilities seriously. Seeing the chief standing so proud it reminded him a lot of his grandfather Chief Giant Bear. Beside the chief was another man full of tattoos with lots of piercings, Dream Dancer figured he was probably the medicine man; he needed to have a talk with him to see what kind of plants could be used in Ontario for medicines. He was medium height slender not too skinny, with his head shaved like the shamans.

The procession stopped in front of the chief, after the shaman dismounted a heated discussion occurred between them. Edward couldn't understand anything being said; although, a few words did sound vaguely familiar.

Edward dismounted; he went to his daughter first. The former earl lifted Cecille down before he went over to Michelle next. He helped her off her horse too.

The young brave with the small headdress walked over to Edward before beckoning them forward. "Come I will interpret for you, so no misunderstandings occur."

The chief slapped his chest introducing himself when the newcomers halted in front of him. "Niin Ogimaa Waagikomaan!"

The young brave repeated the chief's words in English. "I am Chief Crooked Knife!"

The chief continued to speak; Edward listened carefully to the young brave, ignoring the older one talking. He made sure to keep his gaze on Chief Niin Ogimaa Waagikomaan and didn't acknowledge the one speaking at all. Dream Dancer knew if he looked away for any reason or turned to the one talking, they would consider him rude; afterwards, anything he said wouldn't be taken seriously.

The chief gestured solemnly when he finished introducing himself. "You are welcomed here father of, SHE; you will stay in wigwam beside me, you will be our guests!"

Edward nodded in agreement, but he didn't have a choice since the Mother Earth arranged it without his knowledge. Already having rehearsed his speech, he drew himself up proudly; the former earl introduced himself first. "I am Dream Dancer, a medicine man of the Montana Cheyenne and trained by the whites across the sea in their homeland as a doctor. My Daughter is White Buffalo; she will someday be a shaman of the Native People belonging to no tribe, although she will become one with all people of every tribe across the land. The young Brave beside her is called Shin, he is an Oriental Warrior from across the big saltwater trained to guard my Daughter with his life. The white woman beside him is Michelle... she raised the motherless White Buffalo from a baby since her Mother died to give her life!"

Edward let the young brave translate then smiled inwardly in satisfaction; Dream Dancer knew from growing up with his grandfather's people in Montana it was always best when dealing with other tribes of Indians that you embellish everything. The more dramatic you were, without telling any lies the better one will be received when it becomes known how important you are in the vast complex circle of life. Especially, when it becomes known the tribe you are dealing with will benefit from such a prestigious alliance.

Edward stressed the fact that Cecille would belong to no tribe, but be one with all people. Dream Dancer did so to make sure they would not try to keep his daughter once White Buffalo's training here was complete.

There were excited whispers from the surrounding Indians once the young warrior finished translating. The chief held up his hand for quiet before nodding impressed; he knew the Sioux who lived many days travel further south considered their rivals the Cheyenne fierce warriors.

Chief Niin Ogimaa Waagikomaan kept his face expressionless, waiting for his people to quiet down. When silence finally prevailed, he gestured at a young woman in the crowd making introductions. It was the interpreter Edward listened to again though as he translated. "My youngest Daughter will see to your needs while you are here; come sit by the fire your packs will be put in the wigwam, and your horses will be cared for by my Grandsons."

The chief led them over to his fire then more introductions were made, a pipe was passed around before food materialized; there was the usual native diet of fish, deer meat, corn, bannock as well as wild vegetables.

Edward finished eating before turning to the young warrior inquisitively. He found out earlier that the young man was called

Ma'iigan Niimwin, it meant Wolf Dance in English; he also learned the small headdress meant the young interpreter was in training to be the next war leader of this band of Ojibwa. Hoping his question would not upset the young man, the former earl couldn't help asking about earlier. "When your Braves first saw my Daughter they called her, 'Gagiibiingwe', can you tell me what it means?"

Wolf Dance reassuringly smiled since there was nothing sinister about the name his warriors used. "It means blind, our Shaman went on a vision quest when he was a young man, and he saw her in his vision. Mother Earth, which we call Aki, showed the Shaman she would be blind; because her coming was foretold so long ago, it brought much excitement!"

Edward frowned grimly at the explanation given; the shaman was in his late sixties or early seventies which meant Dream Dancer hadn't even been born when the much older man got his vision of Cecille! He didn't understand why his family was chosen by the Great Spirit or what is expected of them because of it. He didn't like being manipulated by the higher power one bit, but really did he have a choice... does anyone?

CHAPTER ONE

ONTARIO; JUNE 30, 1895

Cecille Summerset heaved a forlorn sigh as she stood over her father, Edward. He was sleeping beside his second wife who was now eight months pregnant. They would have a girl; she would grow up to be beautiful, thankfully there would be no powers in her. She couldn't see Dream Dancer or his wife, but White Buffalo could feel them.

Cecille rubbed her forehead distractedly thinking about how her life until recently was so full of learning; finally, at thirty-one it was time for her leave the village to become all she was meant to be! She had trained with the shaman for the first ten years before being called to the medicine man and trained with him for another ten. While she was being taught the healing and spiritual ways of the Mother Earth; her father Edward Summerset, the three-quarter Cheyenne doctor, was also teaching her everything he knew about being a physician. Dream Dancer as he was known to the natives had graduated with top honours at one of the most prestigious schools in England. Of course, White Buffalo also continued her training with her Oriental Guardian Shin at the same time.

Cecille being ambidextrous was able to use both her hands equally, which meant she could use two sides of her brain. Because of her ability to use both sides she was able to memorize everything. Thankfully, it cut her training with the four most influential men in her life to less than half of what a regular person would need. White Buffalo's mind absorbed new ideas like a sponge she never forgot anything once taught. She always suspected that is why she was born blind; for her to be able to use the power, she could physically feel coursing through her veins there needed to be a personal sacrifice.

Deep down Cecille resented it, she would gladly give everything up to be able to see or so she kept trying to convince herself; although, there were those times when White Buffalo's eyes turned black that she could see just like any ordinary person until they changed back to green.

Dropping her hand resignedly, Cecille reluctantly reached out her thoughts then touched Edward's dream receptor in his brain; every living being had one, even animals will dream. The ones in the Summerset's brain had evolved beyond what most people were able to handle, which explained how they could see inside a vision. Her father lost his ability to seek the dream world years ago in England. Dream Dancer had given up all his powers willingly to save his first wife, who was pregnant with his unborn children.

Cecille knew others were born with this gift if you wanted to call it that. Unfortunately, not knowing what was happening to them they ended up going insane; some could handle it for a while, sooner or later though they would get snared in someone's vision then die or become unresponsive caught in-between worlds unable to escape. Most people who sleepwalk are usually individuals who have an evolved dream receptor, good thing it was not as developed as the Summerset's were.

Cecille shook herself in irritation, White Buffalo needed to quit procrastinating, but she didn't want to go. "Goodbye Father, it is time for me to spread my wings and fly. You will have another Daughter to take my place, please don't be angry or look for me for I must fulfill my destiny as you have done! I will see you occasionally in the dream world ni-hoi."

With tears running down Cecille's cheeks she turned away then slipped out the door of the wigwam; quickly, she went to Shin. All she took with her was her possessions, things she made over the years making them special to her or gifts from others she deemed meaningful; plus some old dresses Edward kept of her mother's. The one she was wearing now was just such a dress; White Buffalo didn't want to wear her native clothes to a white town.

Cecille was riding a ten-year-old mare named Saya the second because the first one died a few years ago. Her first dog Misfit died last year too, but not before producing another that looked just like her, except for the floppy ears; she was so much like her mother White Buffalo couldn't resist naming her Misfit. She was also bringing along a three-year-old filly she had named Precious, a daughter of the mare she was riding now. They were using her as a packhorse to carry their meagre possessions.

Cecille's Oriental Guardian Shin would run in front of her mare, even after all these years he refused to ride a horse. The Ojibwe named the Tianming Samurai Monk from Japan Shadow Stalker for good reasons; he was elusive and soundless like a passing shadow there one moment, gone the next.

Shin turned forty-three at the start of this month. He was rather young to be a master in his monastery, which was on a hidden island somewhere off the coast of Japan; especially since he was living with Cecille's father before her birth, making him a master at eleven-years-old. They were twelve years, six months apart. White Buffalo always considered her Guardian to be her older brother because she never met her twin sibling that was left in England.

Edward had hidden Cecille in Wales for the first ten years of her life not wanting the Queen to know about her. White Buffalo knew her older brother by several minutes was not aware of her at all, neither would he ever be told!

The Tianming Samurai Monks were unknown even to their fellow monks making them very unusual. Cecille learned from Shin that they didn't shave their heads as other monks do; most of them chose to keep their hair in a single braid some coiled into a bun just above the nap of their necks. Nor do they stay in their monastery or even their homeland as others do. They also follow the one true God and Jesus, which surprised most of their people.

Tianming has many meanings; the mandate of heaven, divine mandate, the Great Spirit's or God's will. It could also mean fate, destiny, or one's lifespan; they are Samurai, but not limited to that. They also study Ninja, Subak, Vovinam, Buddhism, Dim Mak, Kyusho Jitsu, and various fighting styles which are all a part of their training from birth.

The Tianming Monks used several names to refer to the higher powers. Mother Earth had two names, so did the devil. God being above both has three names, God is the most formal then Shen second; the Great Spirit was the one they used the most often. The Earth they called Mother Earth when being formal, but they used Po most of the time because it was their favourite name for her. Satan they called Kuei or the Devil.

The names Shen, Po, and Kuei were Oriental names. The Tianming Monks were a blend of all their people's it was only natural for them to use names or meanings that reflected the different cultures. It didn't mean it was a different God as some people mistakenly thought.

These unusual Monks were mostly unknown because they were so well hidden, not even the Emperor is aware of them. Right from birth, they are taught many languages since a Tianming Monk seldom stayed in the Orient; it is their destiny to find people with special abilities scattered all over the world to help them or protect them depending on circumstances.

Wisely Shin didn't ask or comment on the visible wetness streaking Cecille's cheeks. He cupped his hand to help his charge mount her mare. It was highly unusual for White Buffalo to show him this side of her; there was just no time to hide it right now.

Shaking off thoughts of Shin's people, Cecille settled into her saddle before swiping angrily at the tears. Her mind turned back to Mother Earth's demands. She would never refuse her of course, only when not touching the ground could she let the resentment slip out. She hated it when it did surface since this is what White Buffalo was supposed to be born for; she must find a way to bury the unwanted feelings she was struggling with recently! When these feelings began to manifest she couldn't say or even why she was bitter about it all of a sudden. It might be the uncertainty of not knowing exactly where they were headed. Who did she think she was fooling with that nonsense if she was completely honest with herself it was because of her feelings for Silver Wolf!

Halting that thought quickly, Cecille refused to bring up bittersweet memories of a forbidden infatuation, which ended in tragedy. Her mind turned back to Po's demands needing to keep occupied. She had no clue why they needed to go, all she knew was she must go north then north-west. Mother Earth needed White Buffalo's help, even being the most powerful woman in over a thousand years she must go where bidden. Shin, Misfit and her mare Saya would make sure she got there safe; they would be her eyes!

Cecille needing to take her mind off her confused feelings towards Mother Earth remembered back to the day Shin pulled out his Japanese carpet. She was taken back in time and shown the three sacrifices made on her behalf in England; not only by White Buffalo's father but also by a great uncle by marriage who was a Baptist priest that her Aunt Raven brought with her from Montana named Daniel. Of course, Shin's father Dao was the biggest shock to them all.

*****

Dream Dancer painted symbols of his Cheyenne people on his face then his chest before putting the Oriental images Dao taught to him around those symbols. Chanting he felt the power inside him surge through his veins. He was having a hard time restraining it; it was extremely intense. Edward must keep it under control; his Asian Guardian had warned him it would be tough to manage at this time. Finished, he picked up the paint and went over to his sister next to put the Cheyenne images on Raven too. He continued chanting rhythmically in his native language through it all not relenting even slightly.

Dao was already painted with all sorts of Oriental symbols around a large cross tattooed on his bare chest. Dream Dancer couldn't help staring when he first saw it there never having seen him unclothed before now; at this moment, the Tianming Monk was in the process of painting Pastor Daniel Brown's chest with a similar cross while chanting his powerful song. When finished, Edward's Guardian added the doves of peace making sure they surrounded the cross on Daniel's chest.

When the two most powerful men in history finished painting everyone they needed for the healing except Edward's wife Crystin; they turned as one then both knelt one on each side of the unconscious countess.

Edward chanting in his native Cheyenne language got a vision immediately of an unusual black cougar cub with a white tip on its tail. He obediently painted the baby animal on Crystin's cheek knowing that now and forever the countess' Cheyenne name would be, Black Cougar.

Normally cougar cubs were gold to reddish brown with spots; most people when they saw a black cougar referred to them as a panther, but it was just a colour variation. They were also much smaller, which is why people thought they were a different breed of cat, they were not.

The Tianming Monk painted a holy cross with sakura blossoms on Crystin's other cheek. These flowers were known in other parts of the world as a cherry blossom. Dao put them all around the holy cross; the same flower was embroidered on the robe he gave the countess. They were also prevalent on his carpet and surrounded a cross with two doves about to perch in the centre.

Sakura blossoms were considered a symbol of beauty to the Japanese; many of their women had the flower in their name somewhere. The Chinese believed the sakura blossom to be a wild part of human nature; to them, it symbolized lions, tigers, even house cats.

Both men finished painting Crystin at the same time; they were just leaning back when Edward's wife shrieked; rising up the countess pointed at Raven then screamed out a Celtic curse before falling back unconscious once more.

Instantly Raven fell withering to the ground in agony.

Devon cried out in fear and despair; he gathered Raven into his arms in agony. When they first arrived Edward told them she was needed for this healing; desperately he tried stopping her as a shiver of foreboding coursed down his spine. Instantly, it brought the nightmare of her death that he received on the ship into his mind. Of course, Golden Eagle's wife wouldn't listen to him after finding out there were twin babies involved; especially, when they were her brother Dream Dancer's children.

Tears streaked Devon's face as he held onto his wife desperately; He screamed out in horrified dread. "Not Raven, please God... don't take my wife!"

The Tianming Monk jumped up before rushing to his carpet; He had placed it off to the right when they first entered the tepee, near the carpet, waiting was his sword. Once kneeling, Dao beckoned to Pastor Brown so he would get on the carpet. "Hurry, I want you to kneel in front of me Daniel, as you do pray to God for guidance!"

Pastor Daniel Brown, confused, disoriented, and afraid got up in a daze before doing as he was told. He wasn't sure what to pray for, but suddenly he felt that he must; the Pastor dropped to his knees on the carpet facing the strange little Oriental man Edward called Dao.

Dream Dancer rushed over to Raven, but he could do nothing to help his sister; he watched the evil fog possessing her helplessly, he couldn't use his healing powers without taking in the grey mist himself. His Guardian Dao warned him not to do any healing in here until he told Edward it was okay to do so or the evil would win. The Tianming Monk vehemently stressed that if it happened all of humanity would be lost.

Groaning in frustration all Edward could do was stare impotently at the withering Raven as she shrieked painfully. He finally turned away unable to watch; with both fists clenched at his sides helplessly, Dream Dancer stared at his Guardian angrily willing him to hurry so he could help his sister.

The Tianming Monk waited until the Pastor knelt in front of him; once the Baptist Priest was on the carpet, Dao raised his arms up in supplication. "Great Spirit, let your servant Daniel see the truth!"

The Pastor gasped out in awed wonder as the Holy Spirit all of a sudden entered him. He knew immediately it was the real spirit of God, having felt it many times since becoming a Baptist Priest; it is how Jesus spoke to him wanting Daniel to teach certain biblical passages to his congregation.

This time was different; the Pastor felt so full of the pure Holy Spirit that he thought he might burst from the joy of it. Unable to *help himself, Daniel jumped to his feet on the carpet; he raised his arms to the heavens ecstatically before closing his eyes savouring the sensation. "Lord, let your will be known to me!"*

The Tianming Monk rose to his feet to stand in front of the Baptist Pastor; this allowed Daniel to see the Oriental Guardian fully when he opened his eyes. The monk had a light above his head, and a glowing sword was clenched in his hand. Dao continued to stand there silently waiting patiently.

The Pastor saw a man appear behind the Tianming Monk; was it an angel, he gasped awestruck as the man's name entered his mind. Unable to hold it back another moment Daniel thundered in wonder. "Elijah!"

In the Bible, Elijah didn't die; he was taken to heaven in a chariot of fire.

Behind Elijah was the Pastors wife Pamela also known to the Cheyenne as Morning Star; she died recently giving birth to the daughter she had always wanted. She was beckoning urgently for him to come to her. He stared in shock as another woman materialized beside his wife; she was also waving for Daniel to come to them. It was his mother Melissa also known as White Buffalo to the Cheyenne, the first white woman to ever be named as such. Now the Baptist Priest knew why he was ordered to bring the buffalo hide to Edward here in England. His mother died soon after Daniel left home to come here.

Pastor Brown looked towards Elijah again, two passages in the Bible flashed instantly in Daniel's mind: 'Two Samuel fourteen, fourteen. All of us must die, eventually. Our lives are like water spilled out on the ground, which cannot be gathered up again, but God does not just sweep life away; instead, he derives ways to bring us back when we have been separated from him.'

The second passage made the Pastor tremble, knowing what was expected from Daniel tonight: 'two Kings twenty: four-six. God's sovereign hand is in everything. God is in control of the lives of all people, the Universe, and the course of Earth's history directing it to his appointed ends. God's people should pray like God's son. "I want your will to be done, not mine."'

'God's people are challenged to live in harmony with God's will and in the strength that he provides when we live for God's glory; whatever happens, is also for our good.'

The Pastor looked up towards heaven; his face was full of peace, with such a glow of pure love it was almost blinding to see. His arms reached up higher in praise as Daniel began whispering in acceptance, but by the end, he was shouting in joy. "Your will be done, Lord... NOT MINE!"

Instantly Elijah entered Daniel before he prophesied he turned and pointed at Crystin's belly then thundered in warning; it was so loud the Earth shook. "She will be called Cecille Luan Gweneal or White Buffalo to her people. She will bring beauty to Mother Earth as she keeps the evil at bay for another forty years. In the new century evil will begin leaking out of its prison slowly until the mists of Snowdonia are no more. When the last fragment of fog disappears, so too will the six sentient stones. By the end of the next century, it will have begun! Women will kill their children; husbands will kill wives and children. Children will also kill without mercy! Sodom and Gomorrah will return as people turn away, refusing to listen. Wars will prevail as the Earth changes for the worst... storms, fires, plus diseases will rapidly spread across the land. Infestation of flies, grasshoppers, worms then rodents will infest the Earth. The white buffalo will come one last time as the rise of the Dragon begins! Twins will be born to the White Buffalo line once more, but they will be separated at birth, and the last white buffalo hide will disappear. When the sword of truth then the carpet of the Guardians mysteriously vanishes, so too will the Tianming Monks. Once they disappear every last one of the faithful will soon follow, once they are all gone it will be too late! There will be no turning back as judgment draws closer!"

Elijah left the pastor suddenly.

Pastor Brown looked at the Tianming Monk with a serene face; he dropped to his knees before nodding in acceptance; Daniel threw his arms out wide giving his life willingly to save the others.

The Tianming Monks chanting rose higher and drowned out all other sounds before he drove his sword through Daniel's heart; as soon as Dao withdrew the sword, the Baptist Pastor fell to the carpet... dead!

The glowing light of the Holy Spirit left Daniel's body; the pure, untainted nimbus filled the tepee blinding everyone; blood gushed out of the Baptist Pastor's chest flowing over the Tianming Monks carpet saturating it, the first of three sacrifices was given willingly.

Blood soaked through the carpet into the ground pushing the evil mist back to its prison in Snowdonia; everyone alive inside heard a wail of denial as a furious quake reverberated through the Earth. The tepee trembled, shaking angrily it thankfully stayed standing.

The six sentient stones in Snowdonia turned grey once more; as the stones strengthened, they were able to close the portal tight with a loud, vicious snap, it trapped Kuei's minion again as they resumed their guard duty. Once the gate was slammed shut, the fog lightened again to a pearly grey.

The Tianming Monk turned to Devon first then Edward; he pointed his bloody dripping sword at the two men. "Hurry Golden Eagle, pick your wife up; you must lay Raven down beside Crystin. Dream Dancer, I want you to kneel between the women; as you do so I want you to put a hand on each of their foreheads to cure them. Afterwards, your healing abilities will be gone you must give it up voluntarily to save the two women! Your Shaman powers are the second sacrifice that needs to be given willingly so the evil can be drawn entirely out of them both!"

Dream Dancer nodded without hesitation; walking over quickly he obediently knelt beside Crystin.

Devon carried Raven over; reluctantly he put his wife down on the other side of his brother-in-law. He quickly stepped back in shock, too afraid and confused by what was happening to them to argue? Golden Eagle watched horrified as Dao, Edward's teacher and friend killed Pastor Daniel right before their eyes.

Golden Eagle was the only one unpainted; he couldn't see what the others could since he wasn't trained to see with his inner eye so painting him would have been useless. All Devon could do at this point was put his trust in his brother-in-law Edward, in the hopes that he would make everything right again.

Obediently Dream Dancer put his hands on the two women's foreheads before chanting desperately in Cheyenne. He felt his eyes become blacker if that was possible, now no tinge of green could be seen anywhere. The pain was excruciating; he curled up slightly in self-preservation but refused to relent or remove his hands. Edward felt the evil mist enter his palms for the second time in his life.

Dream Dancer sat up knowing that it was time. Screaming in painful determination, he brought both hands with the evil contained in them together in front of him in a prayer-like motion. Unsure why he did so but feeling compelled; Edward lifted them above his head. With both hands pressed together, the most powerful shaman in history sent his power into his hands.

The Tianming Monk continuing to hold out the sword towards Dream Dancer waited patiently. Suddenly, the sword of truth began to glow a deep bluish-grey. He watched in satisfaction as a pure black mist exited the tips of Edward's fingers before the sword pulled it in.

Dream Dancer pushed relentlessly against the evil evicting it from his body; because it contained all of his extraordinary shaman powers it was now ebony black instead of dark grey.

Unsuccessfully fighting to get away, the black mist was reluctantly drawn from Dream Dancer before being absorbed into the sword. Abruptly, the mist escaped its metal prison in triumph by entering the Guardians body instead.

The Tianming Monk threw back his head in pain as he screamed out determinedly. "I am Dao Ba Zevak Hajime, a master of the Tianming Samurai Monks who follows the 'Divine mandate of Shen's will'; we are the truth, way, path, and the flow of the Universe! I am Dao the wielder of the sword of truth. I am Ba; it means third. I am Zevak, which means sacrifice; finally, I am Hajime, the beginning that will lead to the end!"

The Tianming Samurai Monk dropped to his knees in anguish unable to keep himself upright any longer. He couldn't help but scream out eerily again trying to hold onto life for a precious few more minutes. "I am the wielder of the sword of truth; I am the third sacrifice; I AM the beginning, which will lead to the end. I give up my life willingly to buy time for all humanity in the hopes that someday they will hear Shen's message then repent!"

Without warning, the Tianming Monk reversed his sword; holding it by the blade, he thrust it into his heart. After the sword entered his chest, Dao looked up so he could see his Lord. Instantly a look of shock was written on the monks face... in awe, he took the hand extended to him. "Your will is done!"

The Tianming Samurai Master gave up his spirit gladly; once the third sacrifice was given willingly, the blinding white light of the Holy Spirit still filling the tepee disappeared quickly. Dream Dancer and his Guardian dropped to the ground motionless.

The Tianming Monks carpet continued to glow thirstily it drank up the blood of its master and the excess from the Baptist Pastor. When the last drop fell the light dissipated; as it disappeared no blood from either man was apparent on the carpet, but two more symbols joined a hundred others marking the carpet as holy.

*****

Cecille pulled herself reluctantly out of the past when her small party rode into the first town on their journey. It was late afternoon already. Being it was their first day on the road she was hoping to ride further if not the entire way to the next village before nightfall. She was aware for some time they were getting closer to a town because of increasing sounds of other travellers; White Buffalo had ignored the noise too lost in her memories.

Shin seeing a sign let the mare come abreast of him; he looked up at Cecille letting her know where they were. "White Buffalo the town we are coming to is named Calabogie."

Cecille tilted her head towards her Guardian. Shin always stayed on the right-hand side of her so she never needed to guess where he was. "Thank you, I need to get some white woman's clothes. We should get supplies; can you see a store, Shadow Stalker?"

Shin looked around with a thoughtful frown searching obediently. It wasn't a big place; he couldn't help thinking. There was a combined stagecoach, post office, and a telegraph building on the right with a sheriff's office next to it. On the left was a barn with a saloon, straight across on the opposite side beside the sheriff's office was a bank then the hotel with houses passed it. On the other end of the saloon, was a barbershop combined with lawyer's office; thankfully beside it was a store before more houses were seen.

Another building further down the street was being built; Shin could hear the rat-a-tat of the hammers, a few curse words floated towards them on the breeze when the men missed their target. It was probably for the railroad since they passed tracks on their way here. Unfortunate, they wouldn't be able to take a train since the railroad went broke, so nothing was running until a buyer was found.

It was quite busy today with the usual hustle and bustle of people rushing around. The low hum of voices from the ones sitting on the porches gossiping could be heard if you listened closely. There was the customary loud clip clopping of shod horses, combined with the sounds of squeaky wagons.

Trying to drown out the rest of the noise was a saloon with a rickety sign that read, Pete's Place. A loud, discorded, off-key piano was trying to bring in more customers; unfortunately, the nasal voice accompanying it trying extremely hard to sing soprano was actually driving everyone away.

The townspeople gave the two strangers weary looks but continued about their business without smiles of any kind. Some took a second than a third admiring look at the beautiful, unusual looking mares; both were black with white markings, obviously mother and daughter.

The older one's midnight black mane was so long it reached almost to her knees the bottom two inches abruptly changed colour to white. Her forelock between her ears draped past her nose; it was also white. Her black tail almost touched the ground; it turned a silver-white at about three inches from the bottom. She was tall standing seventeen hands with thick black hair around her lower legs.

The English called the coarse hair feather or feathering. It should ideally start below the knee of the front legs and the hock of the hind legs then run down to flow over the hooves. Cecille's mares feathering fell from her knees all the way down to her coronet before it draped over her front hoof. Her back legs had the feathering all the way from her hocks to her pasterns, which is just above the hoof.

It only took one look for Edward to fall in love with the sleek Gypsy Vanner horses. They were a light draft breed popular with his soldiers in England. Not as hefty as a regular draft horse they could carry a man in heavy armour, but still maintain a steady ground eating speed. He wanted to keep the colour patterns; although, he hoped to get a smaller version when he bred the first Saya to his black Montana Mustang Thoroughbred cross stallion. Thankfully, Dream Dancer succeeded too. The ten-year-old Saya the second was just seventeen hands with lighter body weight, she still had the full feathering of the Gypsy horse.

Edward found a white thoroughbred stallion in Ontario to breed to Saya the second, which produced the three-year-old mare following her mother docilely. She was one hand smaller than her mother at sixteen hands. Her colouring was almost entirely black with only some white on her chest, most of her mane was a silver-white except for the bottom two inches it was black. The mare's tail was silver white until it turned black at about four inches from the bottom. Precious' feathering was white and slightly wavy; it was situated halfway down the cannon bone to her hooves from the coronet. She was dainty compared to her mother, but still had the prominent chest of the draft horse.

Shin led Cecille's mare over to the store before he helped his charge to dismount. Lucky for him, her emotions were back in check. He sighed mentally to himself in relief he hated to see her so upset, but he would never tell her that or allow it to show. He always kept a tight rein on his emotions, over the years the Tianming Monk had perfected the Indians expressionless face.

Cecille reached up before taking out her cane, she always carried it inside a rifle pouch she had modified, instead of a gun; White Buffalo had a rifle on her pack mare, which Shin learned to use years ago but only for hunting or emergencies.

Shin learned the art of bow hunting once they were settled with the Ojibwe, which he came to enjoy thoroughly. He kept the bulk of his arrows in a quiver strapped to the packhorse with about fifty arrows in it. He also devised a belt to keep another half dozen arrows against his side within easy reach of his hand. Now he could run through the trees and they wouldn't snag on anything, the Guardian couldn't stand to have arrows flopping around in a carrier. It didn't seem to matter how well a quiver was made either, once strapped to the back the arrows fell out when doing any kind of motion; especially, while showing his warrior skills to others.

Shin preferred to carry his new weapon of choice in his left hand with at least five arrows. This way he could notch then fire an arrow within seconds or be able to grasp a dagger and throw it without having to release the bow. It took a lot of practising to carry arrows, plus a weapon in the same hand. The Guardian having too much time during the day since he only saw Cecille for a few hours had perfected his use of the bow over the years. The sword known as Masamune's Secret was still strapped to his back, but was hardly ever used now.

Shin unhooked the packhorses lead rope from the back of Cecille's mare. Usually, he didn't tie her unless they were nearing or in a town; it was only for her own safety he did so. He tied her to the hitching post before hanging his bow on the saddle horn then put the arrows the Guardian was holding into the carrier. When done, he joined White Buffalo on the porch. He still had the arrows belted to his side with him. He learned a long time ago they could be used in close fighting if need be even without the bow.

Cecille felt Misfit brush up against her in question, she reached down to stroke her dog's fur in pleasure before giving her directions. Not once in all these years did White Buffalo regret saving her mother by taking her away from that cruel man in Quebec when they first arrived. A man had brought a nanny pup from England, which were known as a Staffordshire bull terrier to fight in a dog pit; because once their jaws clamped shut it was almost impossible to open them. What he didn't realize was she was mixed with an English springer spaniel, which made her too loving. Thankfully, the puppy wasn't old enough to fight when the healer rescued her.

Misfit the first then found a purebred black and white Tahltan Indian Bear dog to have puppies with; unfortunately, he was one of the last of the known pure breeds a trader had assured them. He bought six of them from an Indian Tribe called Tahltan in a place further south-west named British Columbia, but only one survived the trek. "Guard the horses Misfit, please!"

The white and black dog gave a little yip of understanding; she lay down then kept watch obediently.

Edward laughed in delight when his daughter rescued the original Misfit; what Cecille could not see was that her dog exactly matched her mares colouring.

Cecille went into the store with Shin following; unfortunately, she couldn't see her Guardian but her father Edward often told her stories of how he met the young monk a few hours after the boy's father died. Dream Dancer described Dao's son to his daughter so many times over the years, it gave her an accurate picture of what he should look like. She always tried to keep it in her mind's eye.

When Cecille's eyes blackened on the ship they were travelling on to Canada that fateful day, she was able to see him. It pleased her when White Buffalo realized she visualized him correctly.

Edward always had such a wistful tone to his voice when describing Dao's son, because he looked a lot like his father who he missed dreadfully. The only differences he could see were Shin's eye-pouches; they were slightly bigger, as well as darker, showing a stronger Korean descent. The young monk ended up short compared to his father, which spoke of his Vietnamese blood. His eye slant, the colour of his skin, plus his nose was exactly like Dao's; it showed the stronger Chinese and Japanese influences in him.

Cecille shook off her distracting thoughts; she gestured around curiously. "Where are the clothes and food, Shin?"

Shin looked around before giving a detailed description to Cecille. "Ladies clothes are on your right five steps, if you want men's clothes they are on the left three strides. The counter is straight ahead about ten steps, staples are on the left side of it; two strides."

Cecille mapped out the store in her mind as Shin spoke before turning right first. She wanted a split skirt, a couple blouses, undergarments plus a ladies hat. She also wanted men's pants, a couple shirts, boots, and a Stetson; if the hats were available here that is, they were still a rare find in Canada White Buffalo knew.

Cecille's father gave her his old hat but she preferred not to use it if possible. The hat was one of the first Stetson's ever made so would be worth something someday. Her Aunt Raven found then brought home a man who broke his leg, John Stetson was his name. He was on his way home to take over his father's business. The young man told Edward he went west for health issues, which thankfully cleared up on its own so now he was heading back.

John was crossing Raven's land in Montana when he stepped into a hole breaking his leg, lucky for him she found him before the wolves did. She cared for him for six months, in that time the young Milliner made two hats. One for her plus one for Dream Dancer because he would read to him for hours, in thanks, John Stetson gave them each a hat. Money was in short supply in those days; White Buffalo knew her aunt would have refused to take money if she was anything like her brother.

Cecille shook off her thoughts. She gathered the clothes she wanted plus a few personal items, before taking them to the counter. Afterwards, the two discussing what they needed in the way of supplies put everything they wanted besides their new garments. White Buffalo knew they would need flour, sugar or honey, coffee, bacon, beans, and whatever else could be used on the trail as long as it wasn't too perishable. They would hunt for meat, fish, or fresh vegetables as the need arose. "Shin you better get what you need too since neither of us knows how far the next town is, it could be several days away. It is too bad the train hasn't started up yet."

Cecille's father set up a bank account years ago in Perth for her under her full name. He promised to put five thousand dollars in it every year, which was her share of Edward Summerset's estate in England. Until he dies, so thankfully money was not an issue. She kept a letter of introduction from the bank manager hidden carefully in an amulet hanging around her neck, with her medallion; because technically there was no record of her ever being born in England; her brother yes, but not White Buffalo.

Shin was paid a small wage even though he protested plus all his expenses were paid for; Edward made sure to set him up a bank account not wanting him left destitute if something happened to them. He also ensured the monk received a letter stating he was a freeman not indentured, included was a certificate that shocked the Tianming Monk. Because the Oriental youngster lived with them since he was twelve-years-old, Dream Dancer always considered him a son instead of just his daughter's Guardian.

Cecille was brought out of her thoughts abruptly by a muffled shriek of shock than pain. "Aiiaaeee, aaugghh... aaah!"

CHAPTER TWO

Cecille paused with a frown of concern as she was grabbing a small bag of salt; she cocked her head listening intently. Again her sensitive ears heard another cry of pain, since she was blind all her other senses over the years sharpened to compensate and became more attuned to her surroundings. Most times she didn't even realize it, White Buffalo turned to her Guardian anxiously. "Is the clerk here yet, Shin?"

Shin frowned thoughtfully looking around there was nobody in the store except them. He didn't hear what Cecille had, all he could hear was an occasional muffled sound from far away; the Guardian went up to the counter then rang the bell.

It wasn't long before a man with blonde hair and brown eyes bustled in; he was sweating profusely, as he rushed in wiping his hands clean on a towel. He had a thick accent but spoke excellent English despite that. "Sorry, folk's wife is having the baby."

Cecille frowned in concern already well aware of that; she gestured grimly. "Your wife is having trouble, is she not? I can hear it in her distressed cries is there a doctor tending to her?"

The clerk snorted in contempt as his accent thickened in disdain. "Not a human doctor, just be the animal doctor in town; I am not let him touch hair on wife's head. Other doctor comes every month from Montreal not be here for couple days."

Cecille turned to her Guardian quickly before gesturing in agitation, she could tell by the woman's cries she needed immediate help; White Buffalo knew the woman couldn't wait two days for anyone else. "Shin can you bring me my doctor bag, please hurry!"

Cecille turned back to the clerk anxiously; she held out her hand in invitation. "Lead me to your wife please I was trained by my father Doctor Edward Summerset who graduated with honours at Harvard in England!"

The clerk sputtered speechlessly in surprise; he stared at the tiny, black-haired, green-eyed woman in astonishment. Finally, he shook himself as he mumbled flabbergasted. "But you are woman and blind!"

Cecille shrugged seemingly unperturbed, but inside she was smiling in pleasure because it gave her a thrill to shock people. She shook off her unexpected thoughts; the thrilling jolt wasn't becoming to a professional doctor. It was also a new unwanted feeling, which sprang up recently at about the same time as her resentment. Doctor Summerset grimaced she could not help wondering what was wrong with her lately!

Cecille brought her attention back to the clerk as she gestured in finality, deadly serious. "Be that as it may I can still help her, without assistance she will probably die and the baby with her! I am all that you have right now she can't wait until another doctor arrives!"

The clerk stared at the determined blind woman standing on the opposite side of the counter in uncertainty. Suddenly, his wife let out another stifled scream; immediately, the clerk shook off his apprehension before walking around the counter. Quickly, he took the unusual woman's hand to lead her into the back bedroom. Silently he could not help thanking God for bringing him this strange woman.

Shin rushed back inside just as the clerk was taking Cecille around the counter; he followed the two of them with White Buffalo's black doctor bag.

Edward had given Cecille his physician bag about two years ago. He officially retired at that time, but Dream Dancer still helped around the Indian village.

Afterwards, with the Ojibwe medicine man's help Cecille collected all the herbs that were inside the bag. She memorized the feel, smell, and taste; if it was at all possible of each one growing in this wild land called Ontario, now White Buffalo could find them anywhere.

Cecille once in the room took her bag from Shin; she gave her Guardian the cane too before shooing both men out after the clerk described the place for her in detail.

Cecille went to the water basin first to wash up; at the same time she chanted softly under her breath, this brought White Buffalo to the surface. Now she could see with her inner eye, it wasn't strong enough yet for her eyes to change to black.

Everything living or once alive had an aura that anyone could see or feel even a blind person if they are trained to see with their inner eye. The humming helped Cecille to distinguish if she was close to any objects blocking her way since sound would resonate off of it. The closer she was to it the more abruptly the sound would be cut off; the further away White Buffalo was, the longer the echo lasted.

Cecille finished scrubbing her hands thoroughly then turned to the bed before bending, she put her hand out to touch the woman on the forehead in reassurance; it helped her to feel the young woman's aura. "I am Cecille Summerset I will help you!"

The woman groaned in agony; she whispered fearfully, knowing instinctively something was wrong inside her. "I Esther, you be the midwife?"

Cecille back to humming put a hand above the woman's belly feeling the aura of the baby. Doctor Summerset spent several minutes pushing on Esther's stomach with her other hand needing to touch the fetus too; she knew by the feel of the nimbus it was a boy, by touch she could tell that he was breech.

Cecille smiled in sympathy as the young woman's belly rippled with another contraction; to distract the clerk's wife, she answered her earlier question. "No, I am a doctor and just passing through your baby is coming feet first, which is why you are having so much trouble delivering. I am going to push the baby back up inside you then try turning the little one around, I will need your help to do that. You must not push when a contraction happens because I can't move the baby up if you are pushing down. You will have to try keeping yourself as relaxed as you possibly can manage, I will give you a mild sedative it should help you fight the need to push."

Cecille turned to the bedroom door once she was sure Esther understood her; she poked her head out knowing Shin, her constant shadow, wouldn't be too far away from her. "I need hot water for tea, and some warm water to clean the two up with afterwards please."

Cecille not waiting for an answer from Shin went back in then opened her doctor's bag. Everything inside was handmade by her, except the medical instruments like the stethoscope, White Buffalo's scissors for clamping the umbilical cord, several scalpels, tweezers, plus a few other things.

All the individual bags inside came from small specific animals Cecille trapped over the years for their water-proof stomachs; all the pouches were different in feel because of the contrasting textures of each animal's stomach sac. Normally, it would be enough to tell her what was in it. A rawhide string was used to tie the top together with a certain amount of knots on each rawhide so no accidental confusion occurred on what was inside. The knots were an extra precaution, since there was that one time... quickly, White Buffalo blocked that memory!

Cecille shook off unpleasant thoughts before pulling out a pair of gold and silver special stork-like clamps, they looked like scissors.

Doctors used them to clamp the umbilical cord after a woman gave birth. They look like storks too; the pointy beaks held upwards were offset rather than straight. They were also rounded instead of pointed, the blades were dull so wouldn't cut fabric. The scissors were given to her father Edward by Queen Victoria herself because he was her doctor for many years. He was at her bedside for the birth of three out of her nine children, each time she insisted on a new pair. He kept all the scissor clamps, so not only did Doctor Cecille Summerset have two in her black bag, but there were two in her native medicine bag. Dream Dancer also kept a pair of clamps as souvenirs of his days when.

Cecille pulled out a razor-sharp scalpel it would be used to cut the strong cord; she reached in and took out two pouches of herbs, she set them on the edge of the mattress in easy reach.

Cecille felt around searching for a chair the clerk said was here; finding it, she moved it to the foot of the bed. Taking the quilt she found off the mattress at the far end of the bed she put it on the floor in front of the chair. She would lay the baby on it while she worked on him. Doctor Summerset turned towards the woman when she was finished and patted the mattress in invitation. "I need you to move down to this end of the bed for me please."

Esther was just getting settled again when her husband walked in with a cup of hot water and a basin of warm water. He cleared his throat loudly so the blind doctor would know he was behind her. "Dr. Summerset I not introduce myself earlier, I am sorry; usually, I not so rude; I be Robert Carey from Ireland, we have been in country for small amount of time. I have pot of water staying warm on stove for washing, but I brought in an extra basin of water in case ya need it now."

Cecille waved away the apology she was not offended at all. Doctor Summerset pointing under her chair with her free hand then at Esther as she turned to Robert before holding out her hand to take the cup of hot water she asked him for. "It is understandable you are worried about your wife, you can put the basin of water under my seat. Afterwards, I need you to get me another basin; an empty one please for the afterbirth, and a couple sheets or a blanket that's no good. When you come back, I will need you to sit behind Esther and hold her so she can't slip away from me as I work inside her. Your baby is backward, so needs to be turned around."

Cecille mixed the herbs while the man put the water under her chair before he went out again. He returned after a few minutes with the required items. She took them from him, the empty basin she put on the edge of the mattress. She ripped the old blanket in half placing the larger part under Esther's hips, so it draped down over the side of the bed to the floor. The rest was put on top of the quilt that Doctor Summerset placed at her feet, to keep it free of blood when the baby was laid on it. The sheet she draped over the woman's legs to spare her husband embarrassment, it also helped to hide what she was doing.

Going around the doctor, Robert sat on the bed; he slithered backward until his back was against the wall. He lifted his wife so he could hold her upper body against him. He draped his left arm across her upper chest holding her tight against his left side. Tenderly the clerk dropped his head down to whisper endearments in her ear and encouragement knowing how scared Esther must be right now. She lost an older sister many years ago from a breech birth.

Cecille counted slowly to fifteen before holding the cup out to Robert; she didn't want the tea to be steeped any longer it would make the expectant mother too weak. "Here, have Esther drink this now please it is only a mild sedative and not strong enough to make her sleep!"

Esther just finished the tea when a violent contraction hit her. She dropped the cup on the bed in surprise before she pushed down, unable to stop herself; the pressure was too much, it caused her water to burst soaking the bed.

Cecille quickly lifted Esther's legs up, she bent them both at the knee then put the expectant mother's feet flat on the edge of the mattress; she parted the woman's legs then inserting her hand inside knowing she couldn't wait any longer. Doctor Summerset grimaced painfully when Robert's wife continued to push with the contraction, unintentionally crushing the healer's hand inside her even as small as it was. White Buffalo moaned in agony she pleaded beseechingly with the woman. "Please Esther you must relax. I can't help your baby if you don't stop pushing against me!"

Esther gritted her teeth hard in determination trying to stop pushing as she heard the plea in Doctor Summerset's voice. It was the thought of her baby that made her stop finally; still, it took her long agonizing moments. She ground her teeth even harder until her breath was hissing out harshly through them as she forced herself to take large fortifying breaths. Thankfully the sedative began working, and the tea helped calm her spasming nerves. The young mother-to-be gave a huge sigh of relief when she felt her pain ease, and her muscles relaxed on their own.

Cecille feeling Esther relax when the tea started to work, was able to push her hand up further inside the woman until she felt the babies feet. Carefully she pushed him up out of the birth canal then back inside his mother's womb. With her other hand, she pushed on the woman's belly trying to get the baby to turn around. All the while she continued to chant, keeping her power on the surface for when she needed it; slowly she was able to manipulate the baby around until satisfied Doctor Summerset withdrew her hand. "Okay Esther, on the next contraction I want you to push down for me!"

Cecille could see the top of the baby's head as he crowned, she encouraged the woman again. "You're doing great Esther the baby is almost out. I want you to push again on the next contraction this time bare down as hard as you can!"

Cecille caught the baby when he fell into her waiting hands. Instantly, she put him on the blanket in front of her so his parents couldn't see what she was doing. Quickly, Doctor Summerset removed the umbilical cord from around his neck. Thankfully, the couple were so wrapped up in an emotional hug of relief they didn't see what was taking place; neither, did they notice the lack of a cry.

Cecille's chanting intensified while she worked; begging Shen our God, who was the Great Spirit of all living things for the power to help give the baby a breath. Feeling Mother Earth's approval at the request, the most powerful shaman/medicine woman in history asked permission before proceeding with the healing. If it was the baby's time, there was nothing White Buffalo could or would do to stop it. Thankfully, a vision appeared of a horse sitting on the ground.

Cecille smiled in relief as she felt her power flaring inside her before her eyes blackened entirely, for a moment she could see clearly. Sighing in satisfaction, she heard the baby take a deep breath on his own as he let out a gusty cry of life; positive he would live now, her chanting diminished so her eyes wouldn't blacken again but the light chanting kept White Buffalo on the surface, just in case.

Cecille left the baby on the blanket still attached by his umbilical cord before turning to his mother; she pushed on Esther's belly when she noticed the new mother was now into the third stage of labour. Her other hand went down between the woman's legs to grab hold of the cord. Carefully, she tugged on it as she pushed down on the woman's stomach hoping the placenta would come away from the womb on its own. Doctor Summerset wouldn't clamp the cord until it did, which was unusual most doctors detached the baby immediately.

Cecille wasn't just any doctor she had a direct link to Mother Earth who told her never clamp the umbilical cord until the afterbirth voluntarily let go of the womb. Once it did, White Buffalo still needed to wait another ten minutes before separation this would give the little one a better start in life because it would strengthen the newborn's blood. Breastfeeding afterwards would be more beneficial since the nutrients were absorbed into the blood better.

Cecille feeling movement reached for the empty basin Robert brought her, she put it between Esther's legs to put the placenta in after it was extracted. Still keeping a steady pressure on the umbilical cord, she went back to pressing on the new mother's stomach carefully; Doctor Summerset tried a bit of a harder tug; not so hard, that it would rip the afterbirth away from the wall because it would cause the mother to haemorrhage.

Cecille grunted in satisfaction when the placenta let go with a loud slurping then a plopping sound; she dropped it into the pan after examining it, making sure it was all there before moving it to the floor beside the baby. A few minutes later, she gave Esther a healing jolt. It helped the bleeding slow down to a more manageable rate.

Cecille sat in the chair before picking up one of the scissor clamps. She snapped it into place after checking to make sure the cord was no longer pulsating about five inches from the baby's tummy. Thankfully, the healer wouldn't need the second clamp this time; she tied a rawhide cord as tight as she could get it about an inch and a half from his stomach. She waited a good five minutes to cut the umbilical cord, severing the connection to the placenta. White Buffalo unclasped the stork clamp attached to the severed cord. She placed it in the basin for safe keeping. The rawhide would eventually dry up which would cause it to shrink, as it did so the excess cord would fall off leaving a stub which would disappear after a while.

Cecille wrapped the baby in the old blanket then picked him up. Doctor Summerset gave him one more shot of healing just to be on the safe side. White Buffalo leaned down afterwards and whispered in his ear quietly. "Sitting Horse, this is the name Mother Earth gives to you. The horse will now be your spirit guide as well as your protector."

Twin Destinies

Cecille kissed the baby on the forehead in blessing before holding him towards his father. "You have a beautiful son Robert; please take him to the kitchen for a wash while I tidy Esther up. Keep the baby wrapped once he is clean, he needs to stay extra warm since he is. A wood stove with an oven would be ideal, after the fire burns down and only coals remain open the door then set a basket with the baby in it on the door; the heat from the stove will keep him warm when not with his mother."

Cecille went to work on Esther after she finished giving instructions to Robert and he left with the baby. Once White Buffalo was sure that the new mother would heal on her own, she stopped chanting; Doctor Summerset's green eyes filmed over causing her to go completely blind. She gestured for the woman to move back up to the head of the bed.

Cecille knowing Esther would want to sleep tried to keep her awake until the baby took his first drink of breast milk. White Buffalo needed to make sure the baby could suckle so he would get the colostrum from both breasts; it was essential to help combat diseases and the many ailments he will be exposed to during his lifetime. "What are you going to name your baby?"

Esther smiled in pleasure as she thought of her new son; she could hardly wait to hold him. "Jacob William Carey."

Esther frowned, she eyed the blind woman curiously; she was not sure if she should ask, not wanting to offend the doctor who saved her baby but her curiosity was killing her. "What language you were singing I not think I heard it before?"

Cecille tucked Esther under a clean blanket; White Buffalo had piled the dirty ones in a corner already. "It is a mixture of Welsh, Celtic, Cheyenne, Oriental, and Ojibwe; even though I have no Ojibwa in me, I lived with them for twenty years learning about herbs. My Asian Guardian has been with me all my life, so I learned his languages when I was a youngster. I am an eighth Cheyenne with several other nationalities, British, Welsh, Scottish, French, as well as a few more I think. Why this is so I don't know, my companion Shin says we are all born for a special reason. He says someday I will learn what the reason is when Shen our God the Great Spirit of all living things wishes me to know. It is like your Son he will be called Jacob to me he will be Sitting Horse. The horse is now his spiritual guardian, I have foreseen that your son will marry and his wife will have a boy. Once your Grandson marries, he will also produce a boy. Your Great-Grandson will produce a special man, who will bring joy to people in the future. Although things can change in the blink of an eye, this is what I have seen for your future descendants. Please keep this between us there is much hatred towards the Indians in this land; it is very disheartening to me."

Cecille was interrupted when Robert walked back in with the baby carefully wrapped in a new baby blanket. White Buffalo waved him over to her then pointed down at the new mother. "You can give him to Esther now so he can take his first drink from his Mother's breast. She should keep the baby against her chest so he can feed as needed since he is small we want him to have no stress if possible; crying right now will only hamper his growth. It will also keep him extra warm too, after a month you can move him to the stove to keep him warm. While she is feeding him, Robert you can show me where the kitchen is I would like to wash up. I also need to boil my instruments for at least ten minutes. You can dispose of the placenta any way you wish; the Ojibwa bury a woman's afterbirth somewhere meaningful to her. Before I leave, I will check Mother and Son one last time, when the doctor from Montreal gets to town have him recheck them both to make sure all is well."

Robert took Cecille's arm obediently, all the while he couldn't help professing his gratitude as he led the blind doctor to the back, where the kitchen was at; once inside the store owner described the room to her in detail then explained where everything was.

Shin followed the two discreetly but stayed in the hallway.

Cecille nodded in thanks before White Buffalo gestured in reassurance. "Thank you; I can manage now."

*****

Cecille and Shin made their escape from the grateful couple before loading their packhorse with more provisions than they expected. Robert insisted they take what they wanted instead of payment, White Buffalo argued it was unnecessary; finally, a compromise was reached. Doctor Summerset agreed to take the food instead of cash. Although, she insisted on paying for the clothes since they were not a necessity.

Cecille lifted her face to the sky with a frown of concern; she could feel a damp heaviness in the air, it was quite disturbing. After she finished loading her packhorse, White Buffalo turned in the general direction she knew her Guardian would be. "It is getting late Shin, and a storm is heading our way, I think we should stay here tonight!"

Shin looked up at the darkening night sky with no clouds in sight; the Tianming Monk knew not to argue with Cecille. White Buffalo was never wrong when it came to the weather. "Okay, I will stable the horses for the night; there is a hotel across the street I will meet you inside when I am finished."

Cecille went to Saya before reaching up she pulled off a harness her father made for her dog; it was always draped on her saddle horn, White Buffalo called her dog to her. "Come, Misfit; you will lead me!"

Edward taught Misfit the second to be Cecille's eyes when she was still a young pup. This way Dream Dancer's daughter could walk confidently around in a town without worrying about running into anything when he was not around. The black and white dog knew as soon as the harness was strapped on it was her job to make sure that nothing happened to White Buffalo. Both floppy ears lifted in alertness, her stance instantly became watchful as the dog led her across the street. Just like her mother, she adored her beloved mistress; she would even die for her.

Shin broke away from the pair heading to the hotel with both horses following; he went up the street to the stable at the other end of town. He had no worries letting Cecille go without him since he trusted Misfit completely. The Tianming Monk took the pup into the woods before she turned a year old, using his Japanese carpet he taught the dog to protect her mistress; even kill if necessary.

Bedding the horses down Shin went over to the stableman after; the Guardian was satisfied when the man with no evasiveness evident guaranteed him the rest of their things inside the horse's stall would be okay. The Tianming Monk satisfied by the sincere vow threw the man a half dollar gratefully.

Shin grabbed two saddlebags one with their new clothes in it the other had food that needed to go into cold storage for the night. Shadow Stalker lifted a trunk onto his right shoulder; he never let it leave his sight for more than was necessary. He couldn't help thinking about the precious treasure inside as he walked out the door. The Tianming Monk used it to communicate with his father a few days ago, although his dad was long dead. Inside the wooden trunk was an intricately designed Japanese carpet, the only one of its kind in existence, it was made after Jesus rose from the dead.

A decade to the day later, the Tianming Monastery was built on a hidden island away from prying eyes. Within a year of being erected, recruiting across the land brought in a dozen students.

The first headmaster of the newly formed Tianming Monk's was said to be the one, with the help of an unknown source, to weave the carpet into existence. It was created on the holy ground, which was in the centre of where the monastery was built. Dao and Shin often speculated that it was Jesus or a representative of the Great Spirits who helped in the weaving. Dream Dancer's teacher had no proof, though. If it was true, the carpet might be a portal or a manipulator of time itself. For what purpose they weren't sure although they had suspicions. Shadow Stalker, believed it was a portal to one of the heavens because the spiritual symbols of the chosen ones are in it.

Dao agreed with Shin in one of their many chats, which spanned a ten year period. At the time, he was using the carpet to communicate with his son who was in Japan, from the castle in England where he was living with Edward. The older Tianming Monk figured it is how he was able to contact his master or his son, even though they were far away in his homeland. It was how the monk talked to Jesus or get instructions directly from Shen our God, the Great Spirit of all living things when needed; he even went back in time on occasions.

Dao also told Shin they were descendants of the first head monk; again there was no real proof to back up his theory. He told his son to keep it quiet in case he was wrong, but why else would his family be the only ones able to use the carpet. The person who controlled the rug was the only one able to use the sword made by Masamune.

According to legend, they used the carpet to make the sword and the two dragon daggers given to Shin before he left the monastery. That meant Dao's descendants were the only ones who could use the blades; because of this, they needed to be returned to his family when it was his time they were useless to anyone else.

Shin sighed in pleasure thinking of his Japanese sword called Masamune's Secret by the monks. It was made in secrecy in a ritual performed by the Tianming Monks, so only they knew its sacred name. There was a mysterious hidden power to it; every time the sword was used to draw in magic or the blood of one of the chosen it became stronger with a bright light shining from it. It also vibrated, or maybe it was singing afterwards with power.

His master at the monastery called it nihonto; it was a Japanese sword that could cut through armour it was so sharp. They used double quenching and up to three different metals. Then a unique folding method was used, which Masamune perfected to get the blade into three distinctive thicknesses. It gave the sword a thin razor sharp edge, but with a wider centre. A soft core gave it flexibility so it would not shatter, still to give it more strength it needed to have a wider back. Masamune also perfected nie, which produces crystal brilliance on the blade; the nie on this sword was a midnight black line running smoothly on the front of the sword. Kinsuji lines were streaks of lightning running through the blade.

When holding the sword, immediately one notices a dragon on the blade. It graced the first part of it going about a third of the way down. Japanese symbols ran down the rest of the length, almost to the tip of the blade. The pommel was wrapped in a red cord giving it a sure grip. The tsuba, a disc-shaped guard between the blade and the handle was designed elaborately with crosses going all the way around; doves were in-between each cross.

Whenever Shin looked at his sword, the disc guard always made the Tianming Monk think of the holy wars.

Shin could hold the sword up with two fingers just below the tsuba it would balance there perfectly. It had a bit of a curve in the blade which made it perfect for drawing before striking your opponent in one swift, smooth motion; that is why the Tianming Monk always wore it blade up, it gave him an advantage.

Shin sighed longingly now he couldn't help but remember his teachers or his last day at the monastery before they sent him to find his father Dao. The Tianming Monk youngster was told he needed to go to England immediately and given the responsibility of protecting Cecille with his life; she was not even born yet.

Shin received a gift before leaving for the shipyard, two dragon daggers both made secretly by Masamune; just like the sword his father Dao carried. The knives had a curve in the blade, hardly noticeable. The thickest part was right at the pommel, once the curve began then it got thinner until you reached the tip. It was razor sharp, and when the Tianming Monk looked closer, he could see serrated grooves on the opposite edge. It would need to be extracted the same way it entered, or it was impossible to remove.

A dragon and Japanese symbols were on the thicker part of the blades, matching the sword. It matched White Buffalo's medallion too Shin noticed, but didn't mention. Both hilts had a red cord wrapped around them giving it a sure grip and a green, black malachite gem was at the end matching Edward and Cecille's eyes.

Shin remembered the long-ago day at the monastery. The Tianming Monk knew when he left the isle he would never return. Because he grew up there, his feelings were a mixture of sadness and excitement; the day would remain etched in his memories.

*****

Shin sitting in front of his master with head bowed in prayer, looked up in surprise when his teacher put two dragon daggers in front of him. "If these blades accept you they are yours! Your journey will be long with many dangers, but we have faith in you. Always remember what your name stands for and be proud because you are Shin, it is Korean it means you have belief, faith, as well as trust. Chien is Vietnamese, meaning you are a fighter or warrior. Eiji it is Japanese because you will be the protector of two. Finally, you are Dao, which is Chinese and means you will become the wielder of the sword of truth! You are young so have lots yet to learn; always seek Shen who is our God the Great Spirit of all living things counsel when troubled, it will never steer you wrong. Go, my son your father Dao is in need of you. I pray you will arrive in time, his passing is near!"

Shin picked up the daggers in awe; he twirled them experimentally. As they spun, the blue from the blade entwined with the green of the gem. It caused a blue-green fire to swirl around the Tianming Monk's hands in acceptance. They will be his for the rest of the Guardians life, until another took his place.

Shin looked over at his teacher deadly serious then smiled half in disbelief; half in awe, as he recited out loud now finished his training. He would be the youngest in their history to leave the monastery a master. "I AM Shin Chien Eiji Dao, a master of the Tianming Samurai Monks who follows Shen our God the Great Spirit of all living things to the appointed end. I will never forget who I am or what my purpose on this Earth is for as I become the Guardian and protector of, SHE; who is yet to be born!"

*****

Shin shook off his thoughts as the hotel came into view; The Tianming Monk never in all these years regretted coming to this strange land, he would follow Cecille to the end of the Earth if need be. Shadow Stalker fell in love with the tiny black-haired, blind girl known to the natives as White Buffalo. She was impossible to forget, especially with the black hair contrasting so strikingly with the silvery-white hair about an eighth of an inch from the bottom.

Not, as long as Shin lived would he tell Cecille how he felt or even admit it. White Buffalo isn't for him he knew. Quickly the Tianming Monk raced up the three stairs to the door of the hotel; it had taken him longer than it should have, he reached for the doorknob to go in.

CHAPTER THREE

Cecille let Misfit lead her over to the counter once they were inside the hotel; she smiled in greeting at the person she sensed behind it. White Buffalo inhaled deeply and knew immediately it was a man, but her smile disappeared as quickly as it appeared. She grimaced in distaste at the unwashed, unwholesome stench coming from the man's aura; instantly, it made her uneasy he smelt wrong.

Cecille could not see the pattern or colours of his nimbus, not unless she physically touched him or was chanting, which would bring out White Buffalo; thankfully she didn't need too, she could sense the wrongness of his aura, even from far away.

Misfit gave a soft growl of warning to Cecille; she didn't like the stench of the man either. She quieted obediently when White Buffalo shushed her. The dog's job of informing her mistress of her danger was now done. She stayed vigilant though, watching the man wearily not trusting him one bit.

The greasy sandy brown haired man with washed out blue eyes grinned down in surprise at the blind, petite black haired young woman. She had a light, almost white complexion, which made her midnight black hair more striking. It also called attention to her vivid dark emerald eyes; even with a light film over them, they drew admiring looks. The white tips on the ends of her hair gave her an exotic look. He allowed his grin to turn into a leer since she couldn't see him. She would make a great addition to his whorehouse.

The clerk heard an angry growl of warning; he looked down at the black and white dog staring at him belligerently. He involuntary took a step back fearfully. He absolutely hated dogs, he rubbed the side of his cheek remembering the last run in he had with one!

The clerks gaze jerked back to the woman angrily then remembered she couldn't see his reaction. He sighed in relief before giving the woman a verbal warning. "Sorry Miss, but we do not allow any animals in here!"

Cecille's smile wavered when she felt the man's fear of Misfit; she could sense his cunning thoughts and his desire to get her alone. White Buffalo now wished she would have waited for her Guardian Shin, not because she couldn't look after herself she was quite capable compared to most other women. If she had waited this wouldn't have happened, she was just to use to the Ojibwa's respect for her as a spiritual and medicine healer.

Cecille's tone conveyed her bitter disappointment that the second white man she came into contact with showed such blazing apparent disrespect for women. "I need one room with two beds in it for one night, please. If you cannot provide one because of my guide dog, please direct me to another establishment where we can stay the night!"

The man laughed snidely before smirking in delight. She had lots of fire the woman would bring him an excellent price, if he could get rid of the animal that is. "Sorry Missy we are the only hotel in this town; now go and tie your dog outside. I won't even charge you for the room this time..."

"Thwack!"

Shin put the two saddlebags down beside the wooden trunk, which he dropped on the floor hard on purpose; in order to warn the clerk someone else was here; it also freed up his hands in case more extreme measures became necessary. As soon as the Tianming Monk walked in, he immediately noticed Misfit's diligent stance then Cecille's angry expression. "What seems to be the problem around here?"

The clerk's stare jerked away from the sightless woman in surprise. He was so focused on getting the beautiful woman into a room alone wanting to taste her sweet innocence, which the hotel clerk could instinctively sense; he didn't hear or noticed anyone come in.

The six foot two mean-tempered man sneered in anger at being interrupted before smirking in disdain as he eyed the slim five foot nothing Oriental standing at the door. He waved his hand at him dismissively. "This is not any of your business mister and Chinks aren't allowed in here!"

The clerk unexpectedly gasped in shocked fear when the Oriental disappeared without warning, within seconds the man was standing behind him with a blade pressed against his throat; how the towering clerk ended up on his knees, he would never be able to figure out.

Shin made sure he put enough pressure on his dagger for a trickle of blood to dribble down the clerk's neck. The Tianming Monk hissed furiously he hated bullies. "You will give the lady your nicest room, or I will cut out your liver than feed it to her dog; I will give you a piece of advice, you should never assume a woman is alone just because she came in first."

Misfit sensing trouble growled almost on cue. The dog moved in front of Cecille before uncertainly crouching with fangs bared in reaction to the violent emotions emanating from the two men; she must protect her mistress at all costs.

The clerk carefully reached under the counter and pulled out a key; the nasty clerk slapped it on the desk hurriedly, he whined fearfully in self-preservation. "Yes sir!"

Shin stepped back; as he was turning away, he sheathed his dragon dagger. When the Tianming Monk passed Misfit, he gave the dog a hand signal to keep her on the alert. With no worries he went back to his trunk; Cecille's Guardian handed White Buffalo the two saddlebags. It would leave one of his hands free in case he needed a dagger in a hurry.

Shin hoisted the trunk back onto his shoulder the Tianming Monk turned back towards the clerk. "We also need food, as well as baths, have someone bring them to our room."

The clerk nodded jerkily then stood up before ringing the bell sitting on the counter.

A tow-headed boy about sixteen ran in; he looked at the woman and Oriental in surprise before turning to his father with a look of fear. The only time his father rang the bell was when the marshal showed up unexpectedly, or the boy did something wrong, which meant he could expect a beating. The boy's eyes continued to look frantically, but he didn't see the lawman anywhere. Only once had he ignored that bell, he would carry the scars on his back for the rest of his life. His voice wavered in apprehension. "Yes Sir?"

The clerk pointed angrily at the two unwanted guests in rage; he made sure a handkerchief was pressed to his neck to hide the wound from his son. "Mark, show them to their room then see to a bath for the two of them and have one of the girls take a tray of food up to them!"

Mark nodded in confusion; they had a bathing room in the back, one for men and one for the ladies. He bit the inside of his cheek to keep from asking any questions, remembering the fat lip he got last time he opened his big mouth. The boy led the two strangers to their room. He paused uncertainly at the door when the woman touched his arm before smiling gently at him.

Cecille knew the boy was hurting; she could feel Mark's pain ran deep even deeper than the scars all over his body. She patted his arm in sympathy hoping he would confide in them. White Buffalo could feel lots of determination emanating from his aura, which was a bit confusing. "I know he is your father, but why do you stay when he beats on you so much?"

Mark frowned apprehensively he looked up and down the hallway before speaking not wanting to be caught talking. The boy could feel the blind woman was different, so taking a chance he answered honestly. "My Father is a mean son of a bi... sorry Miss, I will not continue with that sentence. Anyway, he only works here to prey on women. He runs a whorehouse in the next town, so every chance my Dad gets he steals women who stay here then takes them there. Once in the house, there is no escape. It is my job to foil his plans as often as I can. Thankfully, I helped several women get away the last two years."

Shin growled in rage, the Tianming Monk's hand went to his dagger instantly. "I can stop him permanently for you!"

Mark scowled grimly, giving the offer serious thought before finally shaking his head negatively. "No Sir it is not just my Father involved in this, several townspeople are also guilty even the Mayor is participating; slowly, I am gathering evidence against them all, and I will go to the Marshal when it is time."

Cecille nodded in encouragement; White Buffalo could feel the Mother Earth's approval when Mark spoke so knew they were not to interfere, there was a reason the boy must stay here. "When you come with the tub, I will ease your pain since I am a doctor. I can also help you find your spirit guide it will help you to stop these evil men from preying on the innocent."

Cecille turned to her Guardian after entering their room once Mark left; White Buffalo couldn't help gesturing angrily. "Shin maybe we should leave after I'm finished with the boy, I don't trust the clerk at all, he is pure evil!"

Shin sighed thoughtfully before the Tianming Monk reached out to pat Cecille's arm in comfort after thinking about it seriously for a moment. "No White Buffalo, we both need a bath; it has been quite a while since either of us had a hot one. Only Shen, our Great Spirit knows when we will find time again; besides, if you are right about the storm it would be more dangerous out there, I will keep watch and Misfit will sleep at our door!"

Cecille frowned unhappily; finally, she nodded in agreement when the tub arrived. It didn't take long for White Buffalo to give Mark his new name and heal him since Mother Earth already told her his spirit name was Spitting Badger. The boy left to get the hot water before helping Shin to put up a partition to give the doctor some privacy. Once the boy left their room, she took a quick bath then got ready for bed.

Cecille sat on the end of her mattress then picked up her necklace, which she had put on her pillow before her bath; this was a bedtime ritual she did nightly. She pushed her Indian medicine pouch out of her way to get to the Celtic medallion. She put them together because it made it easier for her while travelling; even though it looked bulky, the necklace was the lighter of the two. White Buffalo couldn't help the feelings of amazement when handling the large pendant since it felt so light considering all the detail and extra pieces making up the cross.

The Celtic necklace had two distinctive layers of different silver entwining circles, each one ended with a knot you could see right through them.

There were four connecting points where a cross is attached to the inside of the Celtic circle. It looked like those four connecting points were the only thing holding the cross inside the centre of the medallion. Two dark green gems were the main connecting points. The arm of the cross called a patibulum by the holy church was where Jesus' hands would have been nailed; it disappeared under both of those gems. The gems were so deep a green they appeared black when not in the light.

Cecille was told many times by her father Edward that the Summerset eyes were also so dark a green they appear black when in certain lighting. Was it a coincidence, White Buffalo didn't think so. Entwining the centre base of the cross was a red and black dragon; it was the other two connecting points holding the cross to the Celtic circle.

The dragon's horns were partially embedded into the top of the Celtic medallion. Both wings were spread a bit so hid the patibulum where Jesus' hands would have been nailed. The upper stipes, which was the base of the cross, was under the dragon's head and neck. Only a little of the pattern running down the stipes was visible. The dragon's stomach hid the centre of the cross and was prominent, which hid the fact that the stipes wasn't attached to the patibulum. All four legs were extended a bit, and the talons were open as if it was trying to land on something beyond the necklace.

Entwining the lower part of the stipes was the dragon's long tail; the tip of her tail was embedded into the bottom of the Celtic circle, the bottom of the stipes showed way more of the pattern running down it.

Shin described the dragon as quite delicate and dainty looking, so he figured it was probably a she plus because her stomach was so prominent she looked pregnant. The dragon was mostly red to a dark red, with some black throughout her armour. The legs were opposite being mostly black with red to deep red around the leathery skin; there was a bit of black on the head, but it was mostly dark red.

Cecille was only able to see colour when her eyes changed to black, which was rarely so needed to rely on her Guardians descriptions. The colour red to the Tianming Monks represented fire or blood, so he always connected the dragon to energy, war, danger, strength, power, determination, as well as passion and desire; surprisingly even love. Dark red Shin associated the deeper contrast with vigour, willpower, rage, anger, leadership, courage, longing, malice, as well as wrath. The colour black to him was about power, elegance, formality, death, and evil... plus there could also be a touch of mystery. White Buffalo always felt the dragon was an ending to something whereas her white buffalo hide represented beginnings to her native Cheyenne family.

Edward always told Cecille the dragon was about to perch on something, but White Buffalo disagreed; when handling the cross, she always got the feeling the dragon was trying to get a hold of something to get away as if it was held against its will.

It was beautiful; the Celtic circle plus the cross in the centre and the chain were all made of pure silver, which should have made it heavy. The silver chain holding the medallion was made of intricate Celtic knots too, but thicker and tighter what the dragon was made of was a mystery!

There was another tiny deeper green gem for the eye of the dragon; Cecille was told by her Guardian that when it caught any light, it made all three stones flare, so the dragon looked as if it were aglow.

The gems were real and were a dark green to black called a malachite gemstone. They were rare because they were only found in the dense mists of Snowdonia in England, which was impregnable to most; only a select few were ever allowed entry, and most of them never made it back out.

Cecille turned the medallion backwards then sideways. She held the Celtic circle tightly with her left hand. The healer put her right thumb on the other side of the thick stipes below the dragon's tail in the gap. Her index finger she pushed between the cross and the right wing, now she was holding the dragon and the stipes. She twisted the centre; White Buffalo heard a soft click as the base with the dragon turned. As it moved, the first set of knots above the cross opened. Turning they entwined again to form images of doves.

Fascinated by the birds, Cecille wondered how the person who made the medallion accomplished it; once the dragon was fully turned, it opened two slots where the gems were situated. Unless the pendant was backwards, you wouldn't even see the slots. Underneath hidden by the two malachite gems was the bottom and top of a key. The wings of the dragon helped to hide it, this way nobody would notice the patibulum where Jesus' hands should be nailed was separate from the thicker base. Once the key was taken out, only the thick stipes with the dragon entwining it remained in the centre of the medallion.

Cecille pulled out a single skeleton key; White Buffalo's father took it to a locksmith then had a duplicate made before they left Wales. Her twin brother needed it to be able to get into Edward's old rooms now that they were his.

Cecille sighed in pleasure; it was nice to be able to do this out in the open. She hid her nightly ritual for years because it hurt her father to see the medallion. The reason White Buffalo did this every night is that it was the only direct link she had to her Welsh mother and ancestors. Through the pendant, she could see them in her mind's eye. Shin gave her a clear picture of what the necklace looked like as he described it in intricate detail for her. That is how she knew about the birds; of course, she could feel them too.

Smiling in contentment, Cecille snapped the key back into place on her medallion; White Buffalo twisted the thick intricately designed circle so that the slot holding it in place was again hidden. The doves mysteriously disappeared, becoming regular Celtic knots. Now it looked like any old Celtic pendant with a dragon on the cross in the centre. The cross proclaimed to other witches or warlocks that White Buffalo's family followed the one true God and Jesus, not the Celtic Gods of old.

Cecille put the cross under her pillow with a sigh of relief before lying back on the bed; she needed to do that tonight it seemed to calm her emotional upheaval, as well as the resentment niggling at her. Why these feelings won't go away was a mystery she couldn't figure out. Sometimes it got so bad she wanted to stamp her foot like a fifteen-year-old girl then yell... 'No, I don't want to'! Now able to relax, it didn't take White Buffalo long to fall asleep.

Shin took Misfit to the door and commanded her to stay on guard. The Tianming Monk feeling his charge sleep also took advantage of the water to bathe. When he finished, he moved his bed over to the double doors leading to the balcony before crawling in; anyone trying to get inside by the balcony would have to crawl over him first, even in deep sleep the Guardians eyes never closed completely.

*****

Several hours later Cecille jerked up into a sitting position on her bed in shock; she grabbed at her chest trying to calm her racing heart down. White Buffalo couldn't remember everything about the dream only a sense of urgency to go north-west then north, which would take them to the border of Ontario and Quebec.

Cecille remembered seeing two dark faces she couldn't even say for sure if they were human or animal; both were covered in bright red blood hiding their body shapes as they stared in hatred at each other with dead bodies lying on the ground everywhere. Who they were or what killed the ones lying there sightlessly, she had no idea; White Buffalo sensed it was not the two antagonists who killed all those people, not directly anyway. Finally, calming herself down she lay back on the bed then went back to sleep. Thankfully, she slept dreamlessly afterwards.

Shin instantly aware of Cecille's fear laid there and waited, if she needed to talk White Buffalo would do so knowing he would be awake. When she went back to sleep, the Tianming Monk settled with a frown; he listened to the thunder crashing around the hotel.

Shin's charge was not the only one having disturbing nightmares tonight; Shadow Stalker was also having bad dreams, one that had haunted him since before they left England. It troubled him right up until they settled with the Ojibwa then the dreams ceased until now.

In all these years it never varied even once, Shin frowned grimly remembering the feelings of helplessness he had felt; he was lying on the ground unable to move looking upwards at a forest of huge trees calling Cecille's name desperately, but his charge was gone. Search as he might he couldn't find White Buffalo anywhere; the Tianming Monk would then see himself die with his duties unfulfilled. A hole in the carpet appeared soon afterwards before all the other Guardians in his homeland as well as the ones all around the world began perishing. Within days of his death, they too were all dead.

Shin shook off the dream impatiently he didn't have time for such nonsense. The Tianming Monk eventually went back to sleep with no more dreams to haunt him.

*****

Shin woke again; he knew instinctively that something wasn't quite right. The Tianming Monk held perfectly still waiting for the threat to materialize. He could see a hint of an orange glow in the window. He knew they were facing west so the sun must be coming up already. Thankfully, he didn't hear any more thunder or rain beating against the window either.

Misfit whined in concern; uneasily, she sniffed at the bottom of the door. Suddenly, she turned with a sharp bark before sprinting to Cecille's bed. The dog jumped up clawing at the blankets, trying to wake her mistress up.

Shin bolted out of bed quickly as he to smelt what was upsetting the dog... smoke! The hotel was on fire it wasn't an orange light of dawn the Tianming Monk was seeing but the orange of flames licking at the old dry wood of the hotel. Shadow Stalker jumped out of bed before rushing over to Cecille. "Wake up White Buffalo; hurry, we need to get out of here!"

Cecille hearing the panic in her Guardian's voice sat up in confusion, she pushed her dog away in aggravation. White Buffalo was still fuzzy-headed from lack of sleep, which always gave her an irritating sinus headache with a stuffy nose that would take a while to clear. The smoke was not even registering yet. "What's the matter with Misfit, Shin?"

Misfit jumped off the bed; barking sharply, she ran towards the door before spinning around she raced back to Cecille. The dog barked again at her mistress insistently trying to get her to hurry.

Shin threw the saddle pack with their clothes inside on Cecille's bed; the Tianming Monk turned away giving her privacy as he gathered his wooden trunk as well as the other saddlebag. Shadow Stalker put them on his bed in easy reach. "Hurry and get dressed White Buffalo, the hotel is on fire!"

Cecille needing no second urging rolled out of bed when her nose cleared enough to smell the acrid scent of smoke. She pulled out of the right side of the saddlebag men's pants plus an oversized checkered shirt before dressing. White Buffalo didn't bother getting out of her nightclothes or gathering last night's clothes piled in the corner. She pulled her pants and her shirt over her nightdress.

Cecille did remember to reach under her pillow to grab her medallion with the Indian medicine pouch attached; quickly White Buffalo put it around her neck then stuffed it inside her shirt out of her way.

Shin already dressed put the harness on the excited Misfit then took her over to his charge. Promptly, he went back to gather the small trunk and the saddlebag with food; thankfully, he had decided not to put it in the cold room because he didn't trust that clerk any. The Tianming Monk turned around; when he saw Cecille with their other saddlebag draped over her shoulder he nodded relieved before rushing towards the door.

Shin reaching for the doorknob suddenly stopped half-way before snatching his hand back, the door was red hot! The Tianming Monk turned, instantly he sprang towards the balcony; as fast as he could the Guardian pushed the bed aside then called to Cecille's dog. "Misfit come, bring your mistress over here!"

Cecille was almost jerked off her feet when Misfit hit the end of her harness at a dead run; White Buffalo managed to right herself as she raced after the dog.

Shin looked down in satisfaction once he was on the balcony, lucky for them they were only one floor up. The Tianming Monk put his trunk and the saddlebag down before picking up Misfit; he stared into her eyes intently. "Okay girl, down you go first. It is a bit of a drop, but you should be alright. Wait for your mistress then take her away from the fire!"

Misfit whined before licking Shin's nose.

Shin smiled in pleasure before putting the dog over the wood railing. He was just glad the rain earlier stalled the fire enough it had not gotten this far yet. The Tianming Monk held onto the end of the long leash connected to the harness and lowered Misfit as far as he could go; he began swinging her just a bit so she would drop away from the building. Satisfied that she would land far enough away, Shadow Stalker released her.

Misfit hit the ground then raced away; she only went a few feet before turning back. The dog began barking insistently up at Cecille, trying to get her mistress to hurry. The flames were still below the balcony, but beginning to climb faster without the rain to hold it back.

Shin went back inside before quickly returning with two sheets; he tied one on each railing as far down as he could get them. He turned to Cecille next and took the saddlebag off her shoulder then dropped it beside the other one. The Tianming Monk grabbed her two hands he squeezed them reassuringly. "Okay White Buffalo, I will lower you by your arms as far as I can go. When you are ready, release one of my hands. You will find two sheets hanging off the balcony, grasp them before lowering yourself as far as you can, it should only be a three-foot drop from there. Remember you will be facing the building, you will need to swing your legs to build up enough momentum to hurtle yourself backward away from the fire."

Cecille nodded in understanding; she let Shin help her over the railing. Turning she retook his hands then allowed him to lower her, White Buffalo could feel the heat as she hung there searching for the sheets. Finding them promptly, she let go of the Tianming Monk and scurried down as far as she could before swinging her legs to build up a sufficient motion.

Every time Cecille got close to the building, she would feel the flames reaching for her. Letting go of the sheets, the healer spun backwards one full rotation then the dexterous doctor dropped into a crouch. White Buffalo rolled to keep the concussion from the fall to a minimum.

The rotation only sent Cecille a few feet closer to the hotel. Thankfully, not enough for her to feel too much heat, now she sure appreciated the many years of vigorous warrior training White Buffalo's Guardian put her through.

Cecille crouched there until suddenly she felt a ball of fur attack her as Misfit licked her face ecstatically in greeting. A moment later she heard a thunk beside her; she knew Shin's trunk was now safely on the ground. White Buffalo was aware that what was inside the wooden box was the most precious thing on Earth. Instantly, she reached out to gather it close to her before getting up. The healer let her dog lead her away from the heat, dragging the trunk with them.

Cecille heard two more thuds behind her hit the ground, but White Buffalo ignored them. Her Guardian would gather the saddlebags.

A minute later Shin joined Cecille; he looked around cautiously, they were in an alley on the left side of the hotel. The Tianming Monk handed his charge a saddlebag. He knelt to open the trunk to take out White Buffalo's walking cane and gave it to her. Shadow Stalker re-locked the trunk then picked it up and put it on his shoulder then rose. "The sun won't be up for four hours. We will gather the horses then be on our way, someone set the fire deliberately. I want to leave fast before anyone looks for us."

They were just about out of the alley when Shin stopped suddenly and hissed a quick warning to halt Cecille. The Tianming Monk could see two long lines of people on the street passing buckets of water from one person to the next. The ones in front threw water uselessly on the flames engulfing the building.

Shin knew there was no way anyone would be able to put out that fire. He remembered smelling a heavy scent of coal oil when he got close to the door of their room; it is how the Tianming Monk knew it was deliberately set. The heavy rainfall throughout the night helped to keep it under control until now.

Shin couldn't help but wonder where the hotel clerk had gotten too. The Tianming Monk was positive he was the one who set the hotel on fire. As if his thoughts conjured him up the clerk came trotting around the corner with a big bandage on his neck; much larger than the nick the Guardian gave him warranted.

The clerk stopped when he saw the two he hated making their escape. Instantly staring into the Orientals eye's in satisfaction, he bellowed for help. "See, I told you I heard a dog barking! The culprits are over here Sheriff getting away; the ones who held a knife to my throat and beat my Son up until almost dead, before setting the hotel on fire!"

Shin spun around rapidly; the Tianming Monk grabbed Cecille's hand. "Let go of the dog White Buffalo, hold on tight to me we need to run!"

Cecille did as she was told. They raced up the alley before going around the buildings. White Buffalo could hear shouts of outrage behind them; desperately, she tried to keep up.

Frantically Cecille began chanting she needed to do something to help Shin get them to safety. Knowing her cane was useless to her now she crooned under her breath letting White Buffalo come to the surface; she felt her eyes changing to black, suddenly she could see. Letting go of the Tianming Monks hand, she picked up more speed knowing that her Guardian wouldn't need an explanation. They raced in and out of the shadows until they reached the far end of town.

Shin held Cecille against the telegraph building for a moment listening for footsteps; when he didn't hear any the Tianming Monk left her there, cautiously he went into the street. Not seeing anyone, the Guardian returned then the two of them rushed across to the opposite side. Once safely pressed against the barn, he looked around guardedly, but everyone was trying to put out the fire. Shadow Stalker leaned close to Cecille before whispering instructions in her ear. "White Buffalo give me your cane and stay here I will get the horses!"

Cecille nodded but didn't speak so she could continue to chant, this way White Buffalo could keep watch for anyone approaching. Shin disappeared inside; feeling her dog brush up against her, she bent and found her dogs leash before standing back up.

Misfit growled a warning as Cecille stood up; it wasn't until White Buffalo moved that the dog noticed a hand materialize around the edge of the barn, but it was too late!

Cecille tensed grimly in fear. Her muscles bunched instinctively readying herself to attack whoever was holding her; she stopped chanting promptly once her mouth was covered, it would no longer do her any good, anyway. Her eyes quickly changed back to dark green. Instantly, White Buffalo went blind!

CHAPTER FOUR

Spirit Bear, the medicine man of the hidden skinwalker tribe of Cree, sighed dispiritedly; he lifted the fur then draped it over his father's face. He stood up wearily before looking around sadly at the other five lying in his wigwam dying. It didn't seem to matter what he did they all died!

Only a few years ago Spirit Bear's people numbered over three hundred, now they were lucky if two hundred remained. What the sickness was he couldn't figure out. The medicine man tried meditating; pleading desperately to the Great Spirit... he received no answer.

How was Spirit Bear supposed to help the people if Misimanito. God, the Great Spirit of all living things, refused to show him what he needed to do to cure them!

Spirit Bear leaving his wigwam flagged down two braves the medicine man gestured toward his home in explanation. "Come with me you must take my Father over to the Shaman; he needs to be readied for burial!"

Spirit Bear holding the door opened for the two men watched in extreme sadness as they picked the fur up underneath his father and took him outside. He closed it after them but continued to stand outside the wigwam waiting. After only a few minutes the shaman came out, the medicine man heard his brother cry out when he looked down at their father lying there dead. Not budging an inch, the eldest of the twins stayed where he was; he knew his brother Powaw would not welcome him.

Spirit Bear couldn't help remembering the night everything changed between the brothers. It was not long afterwards that the sickness resurfaced. It had been dormant since the first identical twins; once the new chief took them away from the valley of abundance it seemed to help for a time.

The twins were inseparable until the fateful night that they had to separate in order to go on their personal spiritual name quests. The older boy had not gone far so was the first of the twins to return. He was extremely excited when he had received a powerful vision of the first chief in their recollection who also happened to be his ancestor, Spirit Bear.

Spirit Bear having recognized the medicine man's voice when he was reciting the story of their people that long ago day had went directly to the older man's tepee. The impressionable older twin was so affected by the story told he asked to become the healer's next pupil, wanting to know more.

When Powaw returned, the younger twin went to the healer's wigwam only to find out his brother beat him there and was now the next pupil. Leaving in angry disappointment, he went to the shaman's tepee then became his student instead.

The younger twin had to change his name to Powaw once his spiritual training was completed; he also had to denounce all ties to any personal, emotional, or physical bonds. Not only did the younger twin take the customary name of every shaman, but he also changed for the worst. He always seemed to be angry with Spirit Bear. Why the medicine man didn't have a clue, everything became a competition between them.

The older they got, the angrier Spirit Bear's brother became. Three years ago, Powaw married the beautiful oldest daughter of their chief; it calmed the shaman down and he even seemed his old self, until...

A year after the marriage, Powaw's wife now eight months pregnant with a dozen other women decided unexpectedly to go upriver to gather food for the upcoming winter. Most of the braves and the shaman were out hunting they wouldn't return for at least two days; so it was decided two older retired braves would go with the women for protection. They were also accompanied by Spirit Bear, along with his father.

Where the storm came from none of them knew, it hit suddenly with no warning; lightning with severe high winds caught them unprepared then a lightning bolt struck a tree crushing Powaw's wife under it. Desperately they tried to help her, but were unsuccessful! Spirit Bear making a quick decision cut his brother's wife open trying to save the baby. Unfortunately, he was too late the baby never took a breath.

Spirit Bear full of his twin brother's wife and son's blood stumbled back carrying her in his arms. He refused to let anyone else touch her; when the medicine man saw his younger brother running over to them, the older twin gave the shaman's wife to a brave to carry knowing what was coming.

Powaw attacked Spirit Bear screaming in hatred; he blamed his brother instantly without even asking one question. Their father dragged the younger twin off the medicine man then tried to explain what happened. The enraged shaman refused to listen to anyone.

Still to this day his brother hated him for not saving his wife and son!

Six months later a sickness spread through the people; the chief abandoned their village thinking it was cursed. Now they were hidden away in this mountain range. How long they would stay here was anyone's guess, even the chief couldn't tell them for certain. It hadn't helped them at all, within a month their people again began dying. Almost as if the evil spirit they called Macimanito-w was feeding off the younger twin's hatred, nothing could seem to stop it! Dispirited, Spirit Bear went back into his wigwam to tend the others then pray again to Misimanito their Great Spirit for some answers!

*****

Spirit Bear stood on the other side of the funeral pyre as far away from his brother as he could manage. The younger twin lit the wood under the platform. With a powerful whoosh flames greedily engulfed the father of the twins as they said their final goodbye. They sent his spirit to the happy hunting grounds of Misimanito, God the Great Spirit of all living things.

Spirit Bear could feel Powaw's heated stare, but he ignored his brother the best he could; thankfully, it did not take long for the fire to burn down enough that the medicine man could turn away from the shaman's accusing gaze.

Spirit Bear knew that Powaw would now blame him for this death too. The older twin sighed grimly as he shuffled tiredly back to his wigwam, sleep was all too elusive lately; neither did the medicine man see any relief coming his way not in the near future anyway.

Spirit Bears shoulders slumped in defeat there had to be a way to stop the spread of this disease. Feeling an urge, he turned then went towards the river but seeing the sweat lodge he changed directions going to it instead. He undressed to go inside, with only his loincloth on the medicine man built up the fire that was always burning in here before sprinkling water on the hot rocks; he continued to add water until the steam was so thick, he couldn't even see two feet in front of him.

Spirit Bear reached over pulling a decorated pouch towards him it always sat beside the fire waiting for a spiritual leader to open it. The medicine man reached in and took out an ornately decorated long pipe then some specially prepared leaves his people used for vision quests.

Spirit Bear also pulled out a spiritual root that he cut a small piece off to chew on. Knowing it was probably more powerful this way

Twin Destinies

the medicine man did not take much, but he was in too big of a hurry to take time to prepare it properly. Usually, they made this root into a tea, which made it more palatable. He grimaced in distaste at the foul taste; he chewed it to a pulp though. He chanted as best he could while chewing and reluctantly swallowed the juice with a shudder; afterwards, he took the root pulp out of his mouth. Thankfully, he threw it into the fire. He was quite surprised when the chewed up root caused the fire to flare up before hissing for several minutes then died down again.

Spirit Bear finally lit his pipe; he drew deeply on it before blowing some smoke towards Misimanito, the Great Spirit then down at the ground for the Mother Earth. He blew more smoke towards the four directions chanting he rocked himself going deep into meditation as the root juice and pipe smoke took hold as the sweat lodge spun violently...

*****

Spirit Bear's vision took him on a journey. He saw himself with his brother they were walking together through the woods; both of them were chanting as they walked searching for something. They were on a vision quest together. All they had with them was the same items given at a boy's vision quest when he came of age. The medicine man could feel his brother Powaw's anger beside him he ignored it.

Abruptly an enormous old silver grey bear attacked them, where it came from neither could say. The twins reacted quickly; both pulled out hunting knives there was no time to use their bows as they fought back ferociously until the old silver bear dropped dead at their feet.

The twins covered in blood stood looking at each other before they grinned, both instantly feeling the old pull of being one they shared years ago. Chanting, the two knelt together to skin the silver-grey behemoth; it took them quite a long time since the once blonde bear weighed over a thousand pounds. Surprisingly, she was bigger than most grizzlies… standing well over eight feet.

Once done skinning the monster a hunk of the haunch was cut away to eat later. Spirit Bear after building a fire in front of the bear went further away to dig a hole before filling it with wood. He walked back to get a burning twig out of the main fire, returning he lit the wood in the ground oven. Meanwhile, Powaw was opening up the bear's stomach to cut out the liver. The medicine man threw the haunch on top of the smouldering wood he added leaves from his medicine bag which would give the meat a sweeter taste; he covered the hole up so the haunch would slowly roast.

The twins finished their appointed tasks turned as one; together they put a tepee up around the old silver grey bear, now she would be directly in the centre. This way they could sit one on each side of her facing each other so she would be the main component of their vision quest.

Spirit Bear shuddered in uncertainty; now that it was darker with only the light of the fire to see by, it was a little disconcerting since a bear skinned looked similar to a human's carcass. The head was still attached, so the medicine man tried to concentrate on it instead. The hide was cut in half before each draped a bloody piece on their shoulders. The healer shivered distastefully feeling the bear's blood dripping down his body; Grimacing, he tried to ignore the gruesome feeling.

Powaw cut the liver into four fragments before holding two out to his brother Spirit Bear. While the shaman was busy with that the medicine man cut up four bite-sized pieces of the hallucinating root; he passed two to his younger twin, exchanging them for his two fragments of the liver.

The shaman dealing with the spirit world chanted to Misimanito, the Great Spirit of all living things. When he felt spiritually ready Powaw buried a piece of the liver with a fragment of the root together in offering; visibly shuddering, he ate the other two pieces.

Spirit Bear took his two bite-sized fragments, chanting he buried one with a part of root in offering to the Mother Earth; the medicine man always dealt with all things pertaining to the body or the physical healing aspect whether it was the Earth, animals or humans.

Spirit Bear looked at his liver in uncertainty for a long moment then his throat closed up in protest; he tried hard to ignore the need to throw up, closing his eyes he popped the piece of liver raw into his mouth with a shudder of revulsion. Thankfully, when the medicine man added the spiritual root, it overpowered the metallic salty taste of the fresh liver. Afterwards, they lit the pipe before passing it back and forth making sure to follow the proper rituals as they chanted powerfully. Waiting for what, was unknown.

*****

Spirit Bear's vision quit. Instantly, he got up before banking the fire for the night. Leaving the sweat lodge, he put his leggings and shirt back on thoughtfully then headed back to his wigwam. All the medicine man could think of was why? He never heard of a shaman and medicine man going on a vision quest together. There are several occasions when a ceremony calls for both to participate with people of their tribe, but not a vision quest. Why not, because dreams were a personal experience; although, on occasions a shaman needed to help someone with a vision. The spiritual leader usually doesn't see what the other person was envisioning.

Spirit Bear as a child listened raptly to the old storytellers tell many tales of dreamwalkers from their past life, these stories were passed down from generation to generation; they were from a time long gone though, just like the skinwalkers the medicine man heard so many tales of; although, even he found them really hard to believe.

Spirit Bear had never heard of anyone else having to eat the liver of a bear raw to get a vision either. There were a few hunters who would eat the organ of a buck raw because they hoped to absorb the spirit of their prey; deer were not meat eaters or scavengers though. Obviously, there was a reason the twins had to eat it with a raw piece of the spiritual root. Usually they made it into a tea and used it to visit the spirit world. Had they been using the plant wrong all this time or was this just a onetime thing they needed to do together, to get the images of what was needed. Could it be a vision on how to heal their people, the medicine man didn't know but he hoped so. Why the twins were required to do this together was a mystery that would only be revealed when Misimanito, their Great Spirit decided they needed to know.

Spirit Bear sighed grimly as he entered his wigwam; the hard part would be to convince Powaw he must put away his anger then go with him. How he was to convince the shaman would be decided later, he was too weary to try figuring anything out tonight. After checking his patients, he crawled into his sleeping fur. Sleep though was hard to come by as he tossed and turned with nightmares of the ancient bear killing his brother instead. The medicine man cried out in alarm before jerking awake at the hollow feeling which would haunt him forever if that occurred. It would leave a hole he would never be able to fill as his people continued to perish around him! Slowing his heart down, he finally fell into a deep untroubled sleep.

****

"Shh, not scream Dr. Summerset!"

Cecille inhaled deeply before wilting in relief at the distinctive liquorice smell of the store owner Robert. White Buffalo never in her thirty-one-years used her powers to harm, only heal; lucky for both of them she hesitated which just saved the store owners life.

Robert feeling Cecille relax removed his hand; he stepped around the building so he could see her.

Shin came around the corner leading the horses, but stopped short; the Tianming Monk reached for a dagger at the sight of the shadowy man standing beside White Buffalo.

Cecille, sensing her Guardian put up a hand to halt the Tianming Monk; White Buffalo knew he would react first then question later. "It's okay Shin."

Shin released his grip on his dagger when he got a better look at the storeowner. The Tianming Monk wouldn't hesitate to kill if he thought Cecille's life was threatened. White Buffalo was the most precious thing in this world to Shadow Stalker, even his carpet took second place to his charge; she meant everything to him.

Misfit quieted as soon as her mistress relaxed.

Robert stepped away from Cecille and gestured hurriedly for them to follow him as he whispered urgently. "Quickly we hide horses in back shed is big enough, it still empty since supplies late. I have cellar under store, is used to keep vegetables fresh with deeper hole for meat, you can hide tonight. Mark hid already, hotel clerk's Son because Father beat up on him bad this time is barely alive. My Esther sent me to looks for you when we heard what happened; she not believes a second you would hurt boy. Besides is not first time she doctored him after Father beats up his Son!"

Robert quieted, stealthily he led them past the saloon then the barber shop; thankfully, it wasn't long before the three were behind his store and walking to the shed. They tied the horses inside but left them saddled just in case they needed a quick getaway. Both helped put up a screen the owner used when he didn't want anyone to see some of his merchandise. Standing in the doorway the screen looked like the back of the shed it hid the horses effectively. They only took Cecille's doctors bag and cane, Shin's trunk plus the perishables with them.

Cecille kept her cane because not only did it help her walk, it was also a weapon; hidden inside was a rapier that White Buffalo was an expert in handling, with it she could help protect them if it became necessary.

Cecille instantly felt the boy as they entered, not even hesitating she rushed down the stairs before going straight to him. She knew he wasn't dead, but close to it! Since she gave Mark his spirit guide, she now had a link to him; if he were to die it didn't matter where she was, she would know. White Buffalo wouldn't know how or why he died, only that the spirit guide was free to be given to another person worthy of its guidance. If she wanted to know more, she had to meditate then spirit walk to find the answers.

Esther was sitting beside Mark; Robert took Cecille's advice, the store owner fashioned a sling to keep his baby against his wife's body so his son could feed when he wished. "Thank God, Rob found ya, I was worried!"

Cecille held out her hand towards the voice she felt Esther take it; White Buffalo squeezed it gently in gratitude. "Thank you so much for your belief in us we would never be able to do this evil deed!"

Esther snorted in exasperation. "Of course we not believe it there is no way you save me then baby before beating up boy; sides, I tried many years now get Mark away from bad Father, boy will listen now."

Cecille smiled in encouragement, confident the couple would succeed; White Buffalo knew the young man lying there half dead would produce a girl who would be important to the baby boy now nursing at his mother's breast. "Yes we can hope, but you two better go back to the store in case anyone comes looking for us; I will look after Mark."

Robert stepped forward to help his wife up she was still sore and fatigued from the birthing; hopefully, Esther would listen to him now. The store owner looked over at Cecille. "You right, I will get ya soon as it's safe to slip away."

Shin nodded, he bowed deeply with both hands pressed together in a show of gratitude; it was the Tianming Monk way. "We are in your debt, thank you both for your help."

Cecille began chanting as soon as the couple was gone. Releasing White Buffalo, she was now able to see; Dr. Summerset gave the boy enough healing energy to mend his broken bones, which should bring him back to consciousness. She held back not wanting others to become suspicious.

Cecille was thankful she never got light headed like her father did when Edward was able to heal. White Buffalo figured it was because she never used her own energy as Dream Dancer use to do; instead, the most powerful shaman/medicine woman that she became drew her healing energy directly from the Mother Earth. This way it never drained her energy, and it gave her way more power than her father ever had.

Mark opened his eyes. He looked up at the beautiful doctor who tended to him earlier in the evening before smiling sweetly in hello. Carefully, he stretched testing his body. Except for a headache and a few minor aches where he thought his bones were broken, Spitting Badger felt fine now; he must have been mistaken. Although, he was almost positive!

Misfit growled a warning; everyone froze instantly at a loud commotion at the doors.

Cecille hushed her dog quickly; she heard Shin draw his sword in preparation. White Buffalo reached over grasping the cane that she propped against the table Mark was laying on before moving it closer. She wouldn't pull out the rapier unless given no choice.

A moment later Robert called down cautiously, the store owner never moved a muscle until he was sure he was heard. "Is only I; Esther sent food, hot water, as well as tea."

Shin sheathed his sword in relief; the Tianming Monk rushed over to help Robert.

Cecille quickly turned back to Mark; she held a silencing finger to her lips before White Buffalo put her hand over his eyes making him close them.

Mark nodded against Cecille's hand; keeping his eyes shut he pretended to still be unconscious.

Once Robert released the tray, he turned back to the door instantly. "I not come back till safe; there is blankets back on shelves, Oíche mhaith… goodnight."

Cecille put her cane back against the table when it was all clear; White Buffalo looked down at the boy in approval. "How do you feel Spitting Badger?"

Mark grinned in bemusement up at the beautiful Cecille, he was utterly smitten. "Much better Doctor Summerset, thank you!"

Cecille nodded in satisfaction; she rummaged inside her doctor's bag until she found the appropriate stomach of a rabbit. She undid the rawhide tie with four knots in it before opening it. She had four of them, but this salve was the most powerful of them all. While she was getting the ointment and ingredients for the drink ready, White Buffalo explained everything as she worked. "Good, I will make you a tea it will help your headache plus it will soothe your pain. Please stay at the store until you are healed, your bone is badly bruised it might even have a fracture or crack. It will be extremely weak for about a month, so susceptible to breaking easily. I am using the same salve I used earlier on your bruised back. I will leave you enough for a while; put a small amount on your leg three times daily. My Father's people make it in Montana; it's a secret recipe few are ever privileged enough to know. When I showed aptitude towards being a doctor, it was one of the first formulas my Dad taught me."

While Cecille tended to the boy, Shin explored their hiding place. He found where the clerk said they kept their meat quickly enough it was a deeper niche in the back. He was glad to see it was big enough three of them could hide in it if someone came to search the store for them. The Tianming Monk made up pallets close to the niche then helped Mark over to the sleeping area before they all settled down.

*****

Shin woke immediately; he wasn't sure what disturbed him this time. He cocked his head listening intently. Quickly, he rolled out of his blankets when Misfit growled low in her throat. The Tianming Monk rushed over before promptly he knelt. He put a hand over Mark's and Cecille's mouths, bending close the Guardian whispered urgently. "Get up both of you, back into the hole behind me as fast as possible. Take your blankets with you then wad them up in front to hide behind. Keep Misfit between you and make sure the dog stays as quiet as possible."

Shin felt the two nod against his hands, so he backed away to let them manoeuvre inside. Once in place, he followed them in as the arguing men standing at the entry to the cellar became louder. The Tianming Monk pulled out both daggers; Shadow Stalker positioned himself in front of the other two with his blankets around him just as the trap door finally opened. The monk heard the store owner arguing heatedly then two other men's voices, one he recognized as the hotel clerk; the other was probably the sheriff, a few minutes later his guess was confirmed.

"I swear to ya Sheriff ain't anybody down here!"

"If that is so you shouldn't mind if we check to be sure, did your supplies come yet?"

"Storage empty, I get wagon any day it'll fill cellar and shed."

"Mark has to be here Sheriff this is where he hides when he gets into trouble; I tell you I should never have taken the boy in, he has caused me nothing but trouble and aggravation all these years!"

Cecille felt Mark stiffen beside her; White Buffalo having given the boy his spirit name was aware the clerk was not the boy's birth father but she hadn't known he didn't know it. She bent close to his ear in reassurance. "Shh Spitting Badger your day will come, it might even be sooner than you think!"

Mark relaxed and nodded; he suspected for some time of course, but could never prove it.

Robert raised his voice angrily; the storeowner made sure he was loud enough so the Oriental would know where they were. "Sees, told you not here probably miles away by now; the boy with them."

"No way Robert that boy was too close to death, with at least one broken leg. It wouldn't make any sense for the fugitives to take him with them after beating up on him so badly. Unless they are trying to hide the evidence or use him as a hostage; he would have to be put on a stretcher. I highly doubt they would want to be slowed by a cripple, so he must be hiding in this town somewhere Sheriff!"

"Well, obviously they aren't here everyone go on home and try to get some sleep. We will form a posse tomorrow then go after them."

Shin heard the hotel clerk arguing some more, but thankfully they heard the bang of the doors before the lock clicked in the silence that followed. The Tianming Monk waited a good ten minutes longer. When nothing else happened, he crawled out before helping the other two. "Cecille, sleep as long as you possibly can; we will try getting out of town as soon as it's safe to do so."

Shin turned to the boy inquisitively knowing how upset he must be at finding out the man who raised him wasn't his birth father; especially considering how abused he was all these years. The Tianming Monk was aware of how fortunate he was to have Edward as a father figure. "You can come with us Mark if you wish we have an extra horse?"

Mark shook his head emphatically in anger. "No, I will stay here; I need to find out who my real parents are!"

Shin nodded not surprised he beckoned the boy to come with him so he could at least help Mark learn to defend himself. The Tianming Monk led the boy away from any object which could injure either of them. Shadow Stalker aware Mark wasn't healed entirely found a sack of flour and a small bag of sugar to make into a figure; the monk used it to show the boy on instead.

When it was ready, Shin demonstrated the moves while he talked. Hoping the visual lesson would have more of an impact, compared to just talking alone. "I will give you some pointers on how to protect yourself using pressure points, be aware most of these can kill. Unless it is the outcome you want, don't use them if another way is possible. The Chinese call pressure point fighting dim mak which means death touch. The Japanese like to call it kyusho jitsu or one-second fighting. The easiest target is the front of the head; if a person were to strike the flat of an opponent's forehead, it would force the head backward. There is only a tiny resistance here because the neck isn't muscled enough in most people, if done right it will move a person's brain within the skull; this will cause a concussion, or worse. Use the heel of your palm rather than a fist because the skull is exceptionally hard, without the proper training you can break your hand instead. Another good one is to use the flat of your palm with your fingers curled up to hit someone in the nose at an angle, push the nose upwards so it will break. Remember if you push it too far, the bone in the nose can enter the brain causing death. Next is the temple area, a good blow here can cause a concussion, hemorrhaging or again even death! It can be achieved using a punch, which involves extending the index finger or middle finger so your knuckle will hit the temple first. The throat is another easy target, curl your fingers into a half moon and grab the Adam's apple before squeezing. Afterwards, give it a good yank downwards to dislocate it making breathing impossible. This one is quite lethal so only use it if there is no other alternative. The sternum is another sensitive place. It's in the middle of the chest area. If you hit it with your index knuckle extended, you can break the sternum because there is not much muscle or fat around it, so it is quite vulnerable. Breaking the sternum can cause a punctured lung or worse. Then there is the solar plexus which is down slightly from the sternum it's a bundle of nerves deep within the centre of the abdomen. Striking the area just below it where the ribs join will cause the breathing muscle to contract violently. It is an easy target it will cause the other person to lose their breath long enough for you to get away."

Once Shin was satisfied the boy knew how to defend himself; the Tianming Monk led him back to his sleeping pallet. Quiet descended as they all slept.

CHAPTER FIVE

Shin jumped up in suspicion at the sound of the cellar door unlocked from outside; the Tianming Monk reached back to grab the hilt of his sword just in case, but didn't draw it from the scabbard he waited.

The stairs creaked ominously as two legs came into view first before the store owner squatted so he could be seen; Robert beckoned for them to get out of the cellar. "Come it's time to go! Mark is nice seeing you up and moving around again. If feeling better you can go help my misses in the store while I'm away but hide if father shows up."

Shin released his sword he reached down to lift his trunk onto his shoulder before gathering a saddlebag. The Tianming Monk draped it on his left shoulder; next, he picked up Cecille's doctors bag.

Mark kissed Cecille on the cheek in farewell, grateful for her help. "I will never forget you, thanks for everything; bye Dr. Summerset."

Cecille cupped the boy's cheek fondly for a moment before releasing him. White Buffalo gestured towards the sky then down at the ground in emphases. "May Shen, our God the Great Spirit of all living things guide you Mark; always remember Mother Earth is only a touch away."

Shin had continued Mark's lessons in the art of self-defence throughout the long morning, mostly to take their minds off the passing minutes then hours; he even included quite a bit of the Oriental philosophy this time.

Mark turned to the Tianming Monk before bowing with both hands pressed together as if in prayer. This is how warriors greeted or said goodbye to each another; something the impressionable Mark learned. It was also how the Orientals showed respect in their homeland. "Thank you for the lessons I will practise them every day, Teacher."

Shin bowed back before grinning at the earnest youngster; the Tianming Monk knew that Mark if given a chance would grow into a fine young man. "May Shen our God, the Great Spirit of all protect and guide you in your quest for justice."

Mark turned without comment; he disappearing quickly.

Shin was followed closely by Cecille carrying the other saddlebag plus her cane; Misfit was leading her mistress. Quickly, they exited the cellar with relieved sighs. Both of them were beginning to feel closed in and vulnerable before anxiety replaced it. Time was creeping by, way too slowly.

Once out, Robert handed them porridge. "Misses say eat."

Robert thoughtfully even brought out a bowl of dog food for Misfit; he set it on the ground for her. "Horses fed, watered, ready to go. I tie rain slicker on back of saddle it not raining yet, but start again anytime. Waited until posse decided where going before coming get you, there is a dozen in total. Told them I sure horses are going to newly cleared Murphy's Road at dawn, they go check to see. I lead you to trail not used much it gives you some time before they figure out I not hear right then comes back. Shin says you headed towards Quebec border road I take you to the west of here little ways it will take you north before goes north-west; always take a north-west trail until it goes directly west or south, take a west road to town Eganville. Trapper friend says is about thirty miles so should be there by nightfall if ya hurry. When you're there ask for Brandan Reid tells him I sent you, he can take you through Algonquin wilderness to Quebec border."

Once done eating, Robert gathered the bowls and put them with Misfit's on the ground; he turned before beckoning them to follow him, he would retrieve his wife's dishes later.

Shin helped Cecille mount; afterwards, he took Misfit's harness off then hooked it around his charges saddle horn. The Tianming Monk put her cane back in its beaded holder before tying the packhorse to the back of the older mare, wanting to keep Precious close for now. Shadow Stalker restored the small trunk; the two saddlebags, and White Buffalo's doctor's bag on the packhorse. He took out five arrows from the holder on the mare, he also lifted his bow off the packs, done he walked to the front of Saya. Now ready the Guardian gestured for Robert to lead on.

Robert frowned perplexedly; he looked at Shin from the back of his horse; the storeowner was uncomfortable since he didn't sit on a horse much, he used a buggy most of the time. "You no ride?"

Shin snorted in contempt; the Tianming Monk used his bow to point back over his shoulder, indicating the mare behind him. "I have two good legs, so I don't need to sit on top of a four-legged beast to get where I am going!"

Cecille couldn't help laughing in amusement. She waved in the general direction of the store owner's voice then interrupted before Robert could comment. "Shin doesn't like horses; don't worry he can run for hours."

Shin harrumphed irritably at Cecille's comment as they began walking; Tianming Monk's never used horses until they became too old and were unable to keep up. "I will have you know young lady that I do like horses. We had several of them at the monastery, so I learned to ride quite well. Someday I'm sure I will be riding again, but until I am too old to keep up I will continue to use my own two legs."

Robert shrugged when the two began bickered back and forth like siblings. He wasn't sure if he believed the Oriental could keep up with trotting horses; the store owner kept his opinion to himself though. He took them west around Calabogie Lake. It took them about an hour to get to where they were going; the clerk gave Shin a few additional instructions as they travelled.

Robert stopped at the Ferguson Lake Trail then gestured down it before turning to go back to his store. "I know is not much, but passable by the horses, once new railroad station finished they talk of widening trail into the road but it will be awhile before it happens. Thank you, Dr. Summerset for saving Wife and Son; may God bless ya and keep you both safe!"

Cecille smiled sadly she hated goodbyes which is why White Buffalo told her father in a dream she was leaving. "You take good care of Mark for me please, he is destined for big things one day as is your Son; may Shen our God, the Great Spirit of all living things watch over your family."

Shin saluted the store owner; he turned away before picking up a fast trot now that the horses were warmed up. The Tianming Monk led Cecille towards the small trail quickly they disappeared.

*****

Cecille grumbled irritably, she reached behind her then pulled the rain slicker from the back of her horse as it started to rain again. White Buffalo was getting upset the further they went she needed to get off her horse to see why the Mother Earth was calling to her. It started about two hours ago; the longer it was taking her to see what the problem was, the more aggravated she was becoming.

Cecille remembered her younger years as she pulled her slicker on before replacing her hat. It wasn't an issue in those days if she wasn't touching the ground. The healer could talk to Mother Earth anytime it didn't matter if she was in the rigging of a ship or on the back of a horse. Now White Buffalo needed to be physically touching the Earth to communicate directly with Po; she couldn't even recall when it changed or even why!

Cecille knew Shin could feel something wrong too, but they needed to put distance between them and the posse before they could stop for any length of time. Unfortunately, with all the rain they were getting hiding their trail was impossible the horses were sinking up to their hocks in the mud. It was so bad the horses were having a tough time with the trot the Tianming Monk was forcing them to do to keep up with him.

The trees were too thick on either side of the trail to try weaving through them, they would be impossible to negotiate around; once they got past the lake, White Buffalo hoped they would thin out or disappear.

Shin slowed down he looked up at Cecille to give her a report knowing she would want to stop soon. The Tianming Monk needed to rest too this thick mud was making it difficult for him to maintain the speed he always used when travelling long distances. "Robert said once we get past the tree that is overhanging the path we should be close to the lake, the tree if it's the right one is ahead. Not far from the lake the store owner said we will turn west for a bit. The trail should curve heading at an angle going north-west. Once we get around the lake, we will stop for a needed rest; hopefully, the rain will quit by the time we get back on the trail."

Cecille grimaced grimly; White Buffalo lifted her new Stetson then pushed her wet hair back underneath it, she jammed it back on in frustration. "I need to get off my horse for a bit Mother Earth is in lots of pain I have to find out why as soon as possible."

Shin grumbled fretfully in agreement he could also feel something wasn't right. They needed to eat too and rest the weary horses. The trail is just too open here and the trees too thick the horses wouldn't fit if they needed to hide; the Tianming Monk didn't like it. "I will keep an eye out for a spot to leave you in, while I double back to make sure the posse is not close. Wish this rain would quit, but at least the lightning hasn't started again."

Cecille frowned in frustration hoping it would stop soon; White Buffalo suspected though that whatever was causing the Mother Earth so much pain was also the reason for this foul weather.

It didn't take them long to reach the overhanging tree; Shin called up in warning. "Duck down White Buffalo you are too tall."

Cecille laid on her horse's neck until Shin gave her the all clear, now they were going down an incline. White Buffalo frowned; she could hear the whooshing of waves hitting rocks, it was quite a violent sound.

They were halfway down the embankment when Shin stopped grimly. According to Robert, there should be a trail at the bottom of this hill. The lake having overshot its banks covered up any trail that had been here and trees were lying in the water, having been uprooted by the savage lake; never having been to this area before the Tianming Monk would need to investigate to find safe passage for the horses. He looked up at his charge in frustration. "White Buffalo stay here I'm going to see how deep the lake gets and how far we need to go to get around it."

Shin looked down at Cecille's dog; the Tianming Monk hated to leave them on their own but didn't have a choice. "Guard your mistress, Misfit!"

Misfit gave a little yip of an agreement, both her floppy ears perked up in alertness. She watched Shin trot down the path uneasily before turning the dog went to touch noses with Saya in reassurance; she sat in front of the mare keeping watch faithfully.

*****

Shin tentatively stepped into the crashing waves that quickly rose to his ankles; he cautiously continued walking forward until he was up to his knees. Thankfully, the water rose no further as the Tianming Monk slowly walked forward. The water level dropped again when he skirted a downed tree. One step at a time, he went carefully around it. No longer going downwards, he stayed even for quite some time. Water again rose up to his knees, but only until he was far enough past the trees, he could see around the lake. Thankfully, the Guardian turned west then followed the edge of the tree line. The water got shallower here now back to his ankles. Every few minutes, Shadow Stalker would use one of his arrows to check the depth as he continued walking.

Shin felt himself angling downward again as the water rose back up to just below his knees, but only for a few steps before it lowered once more. He saw another tree lying in the water ahead; it was the same as the last two, so he veered to go around it. The only difference he saw was that on the opposite side Shadow Stalker could see trees thinning out as a trail opened ahead. In excitement not paying enough attention, the Tianming Monk rushed towards the tree when suddenly his feet went out from under him as an unexpected drop off made him floundered in deep water. Going under he desperately kicked, trying to find the edge of the drop-off.

The rough lake pushed Shin towards the tree until abruptly he stopped dead when he got tangled somehow in the branches. He reached back trying to grasp the trunk, but he was too far away from it. It took him several long moments to realize that what had him snagged was his sword. Lucky for him it was also holding him upwards enough it was keeping his nose, mouth, and part of his forehead out of the water. His chin with the rest of his body ended up submerged in the lake. The Tianming Monk couldn't move at all, or his face went under completely. A wave swished towards him. Quickly, he took a breath just before the water covered his face for an agonizing minute. He sputtered as the wave dissipated; desperately he tried again to get loose.

Another wave rolled towards Shin. Unfortunately, he didn't see this one coming. He swallowed the musky tasting water then gagged as the brackish liquid slipped up his nose, seeing stars he relived his dream from last night. It flashed through his mind as he stared up at the towering trees ten feet away. He saw himself die a hole immediately materialized in the rug where the symbol of his house should be; this was what would happen if the Tianming Monk's purpose on Earth went unfulfilled, without warning everything went black as he passed out.

*****

Cecille still sitting on her horse began fidgeting her Guardian was gone way too long. About to dismount to consult the Mother Earth; White Buffalo froze in fear instead at the thunder of horse's hooves and a shout of victory behind her.

Misfit jumped up with the hair on her nape bristled. She growled so deep in warning her whole body shook with the vibration. The dog crouched readying herself to spring at the horses coming towards her; she was prepared to die protecting her mistress.

Cecille hearing the cocking of a rifle yelled down at her dog; White Buffalo knew they would kill her first. "Run Misfit, go find Shin... RUN!"

Misfit whined plaintively taking a step backwards in indecision. The dog wanted to protect Cecille, but she never disobeyed a direct order from her mistress; not in all the years they were together. She tucked her tail when a bullet hit the dirt where she was standing a moment ago; instinctively, she bolted for the trees.

Cecille unable to go anywhere without her dog or Guardian stayed on her horse and waited. She could use her power to see or protect herself. Although with the Mother Earth in so much pain she wasn't sure if she would be able to and if she did what then? White Buffalo would still be at a disadvantage she couldn't keep her eyes black overly long, besides she knew they wouldn't kill her. The sheriff would insist on having a trial first; hopefully, Shin would rescue her before it happened.

The hotel clerk reached the blind woman first; promptly he pulled Cecille from her horse onto his before whispering in her ear in warning. "Keep your mouth shut or I will break this pretty little neck of yours, do you understand me?"

Cecille hissed in rage, her hat tumbled to the ground releasing her long black silver tipped hair; White Buffalo knew who was holding her by the familiar unwholesome stench of the man. "You will not get away with this, I promise you!"

Donald snickered in pleasure. Affectionately, the hotel clerk nuzzled the woman. "Oh, but there you are wrong; I already have!"

The sheriff rode up quickly, he pointed at the hotel clerk in anger; he never cared for the man and trying to kill the dog intensified his dislike. "Donald put the woman back on her horse this instant!"

Donald grinned unrepentant; he turned to the sheriff before giving a small prearranged signal. "As you wish!"

Unexpectedly, gunshots exploded; eight out of the twelve men fell dead as three of Donald's accomplices sat there holding smoking pistols. The sheriff and the seven unsuspecting posse volunteers from town never knew what hit them.

Donald chuckled in pleasure; he looked over in approval at his three friends. "Good work boys, this little lady will fetch us quite an excellent price in our whorehouse. We will put her up for sale to the highest bidder. Her innocence combined with her exotic look will draw men from every corner of Ontario."

Donald's buddies all cheered at that, quickly they gathered all the horses; already competing for the rights to have one of the beautiful mares or even a horse from the former posse riders. Turning they went up the trail as they headed towards town with none of them sparing one regretful look at the dead men.

Donald stayed where he was ignoring his three accomplices; he squeezed Cecille hard before looking around suspiciously. "Where is your friend? I was hoping to give him a going away present."

Cecille shrugged with a grimace of fear before answering honestly, she knew there was no use hiding it. Besides, it could even prove beneficial if White Buffalo was wrong. "I don't know he disappeared well over an hour ago. I suspect he probably drowned since he wasn't aware of how to swim; Shin would never abandon me except in death, I don't expect him to return… ever!"

Donald sighed in disappointment before kicking his horse into a gallop to catch up with his partners. He couldn't help breaking out into a delighted smile, his patience finally paid off. With the pesky sheriff and deputies now dead, he would take over the town; if he got himself elected sheriff fast enough even the marshal wouldn't be able to stop him. The hotel clerk had been waiting a long time for the opportunity to get the sheriff away from interfering busybodies to kill him.

*****

Misfit whined plaintively from behind the thick underbrush as she watched the others take her mistress away. Once they were gone, she slunk out into the open then sniffed at the men all laying on the ground but they were all dead. Turning the dog trotted down to the lake sniffing as she went; finding the scent she needed fairly quickly, she turned west into the thick trees. Trying to stay as close to the open water as possible, Cecille's dog slunk around thickets then jumped over dense underbrush and weaved around the trees along the shoreline. Constantly, her nose was twitching as she searched diligently.

Misfit stopped dead in her tracks when her sensitive nose picked up a stronger familiar scent. He was here somewhere close she could smell him; it didn't take her long to find the tree that was partially submerged. Carefully, she walked along it as her nose continued to tell her she was getting closer to the dominant male of her pack. Going as far as possible, Cecille's dog could see the head of her second favourite person, but she wasn't able to get to him.

Misfit whined pleadingly, it didn't help any because she got no response from him at all. The dog settled down on the tree then put her head on her paws dejectedly... what, was she to do now?

Misfit's head jerked up several minutes later when the wind unexpectedly shifted, her nose twitched frantically trying to catch a scent. Cecille's dog lifted her floppy ears, she caulked her head trying to hear better. She smelt the smoke first then heard a childish laugh far off in the distance. Jumping up the dog raced back to solid ground before weaving in and out of the trees as she again manoeuvred around thick underbrush, under shrubs, or vaulted over deadfall; running as fast as she could manage towards the people in the distance.

Misfit stopping a little ways away sniffing cautiously before wearily she stepped out of her hiding place; she could smell a male dog, it was an old smell though barely discernible, still it made her hesitant. Cecille's dog whined fretfully at a man standing close to the cabin then gave a little bark needing to get his attention.

*****

A black haired heavily bearded bear of a man with no shirt on was busy chopping wood. Now that the rain quit he could get a few more chores done while his little girl played with a handmade doll his wife gave her for her birthday yesterday. He was not paying her much attention as long as she didn't wander away. His mind roamed trying to decide what was next on his list; they needed to be prepared before winter hit.

In the background a two-bedroom cabin and a small barn could be seen, he finished building the barn last week. Thankfully, one less thing to do the homesteader couldn't help thinking. Now, he was working on a corral hoping to bring in a few more milking cows.

The man stopped his swing in mid-stroke when he finally noticed how quiet his daughter had gotten suddenly. He glanced her way quickly to make sure she was okay before seeing the strange dog standing beside her. Being preoccupied he hadn't heard the bark. His eyes shifted longingly to the rifle propped against the wood pile, but it was too far to do him any good. He eyed the animal in apprehension then slowly he lowered his arms not wanting to scare the dog or his baby girl. The homesteader called out beseechingly to his three-year-old. "Tania, come over here and see your Daddy; please, my girl!"

Tania stared at the dog in delight ignoring her father, she dropped her doll then giggling toddled over to the puppy. The little girl put her chubby arms around Misfit; her tinkling laugh of pleasure was immediate. She vaguely remembered a similar dog, he had disappeared only recently. She stumbled before grabbing onto Cecille's dogs fur trying to keep from falling. "Puppy!"

Misfit yelped painfully when the girl pulled a clump of hair out to keep herself upright.

The man inhaled anxiously at the yelped; his grip tightened on his axe handle, preparing to throw it if he must. Holding his breath uneasily he exhaled in relief when the dog didn't turn on his little girl. Again he tried to get his daughter away from the strange dog. He took a cautious step forward, trying to be as non-threatening as possible. "Tania come away from that puppy, come to Daddy!"

Misfit stood still waiting for the girl to become more stable, being used to Ojibwa toddlers she waited patiently; she absolutely adored small children, Cecille's dog always joined them whenever possible.

She whined and licked the little girl's chubby cheek before remembering her mistress, the dog nudged the little girl with her nose causing her to let go.

Tania landed unceremoniously on her rump on the ground with another giggle, unhurt.

Misfit once free of the girl walked over to the doll then picked it up in her mouth; she walked partway towards the man with it.

Dumbfounded the black haired homesteader put his beefy hand down to take the doll, but suddenly the dog spun around trotting away from him; she turned back and put the toy down before barking at him insistently for several long minutes.

Misfit quit barking; picking up the toy, Cecille's dog ran towards the man before turning she raced away trying to get him to follow her.

The bear of a man frowned in puzzlement as his daughter cried for her doll; finally, figuring out the dog wanted him to follow he bellowed for his wife. "Sharon, come outside to tend to your Daughter I have to go!"

A brown haired, black-eyed, tall, husky woman came out of the cabin at her husband's call; she looked around expectantly, did they have guests she could have sworn she just heard a dog barking? Not until she walked out did she hear her daughter crying, she ran across the front porch in concern. "What is it, Travis?"

Travis quickly put on his shirt then lifted his suspenders back up into place before grabbing his axe. He turned to his wife as he gestured towards the gun propped on the woodpile just in case this was all a ruse to get him away from his family. His wife was a crack shot, he made absolute sure of that. "I don't know for sure; I am leaving the rifle with you I will be back shortly."

Misfit seeing the man coming dropped the doll; Cecille's dog left it on the ground before turning she trotted ahead, every few minutes she would look back to be sure the man was following. It seemed to take forever with the man having to use his axe to clear a trail through the underbrush, but eventually they did get to the half-submerged tree. Misfit stood up on it then barked insistently staring down its length.

Shin came too when he heard the familiar sound of Cecille's dog barking from a long way away; the Tianming Monk called out feebly from cracked lips hoping to be noticed. "Help me!"

Travis didn't hesitate when he heard a man's weak voice calling for help, he jumped in the lake; carefully he walked forward, knowing this area like the back of his hand the bear of a man stopped short of the drop-off. He turned, trying a swing at the tree with his axe. All it accomplished was submerging the tree and the semi-conscious man more. Throwing his axe towards the shore, the man turned back. Not wavering even a little, the homesteader plunged into the water swimming as fast as he could. Taking a deep breath, the man dove under then untangled the unconscious man before pulling him to shore.

Once in shallower water the bearded man easily hefted the slight five-foot, Oriental up and carried him the rest of the way before laying him on dry ground. He turned to go back for his axe; it had taken him over six months to save up for it, he was not about to lose it now. Without it, he would never be able to finish clearing this land for the crops they needed to survive the harsh winter's way out here.

Misfit ran to Shin before licking his face then nudged the Tianming Monk insistently.

Shin turned on his side, in agony he retched uncontrollably for several long minutes. Thankfully getting rid of the lake water he involuntarily sucked into his lungs, once finished the Tianming Monk inhaled fresh air in relief. Unfortunately, he could still feel a deep wheeze; Shadow Stalker knew there was still some water deep in his lungs.

The big homesteader walked over before sitting down beside the Oriental; he tilted his head staring at the stranger curiously, it was rarely an Asian came way out here on their own. Usually they stayed in Quebec in their own little communities, unless he was one of the indentured working for the railroad and escaped. If he were he probably could not speak or understand French, most couldn't even understand English.

The homesteader knew they were treated worse than slaves, taking a chance he tried speaking in English first. "I am Travis, I live west of here. Your sword got tangled in the tree, lucky for you it kept you upright enough you could breathe; how did you end up in the water, anyway?"

The Tianming Monk sat up slowly, putting his head in his hands Shadow Stalker croaked feebly. "I am Shin; I was looking for a way around the lake for our horses."

Shin instantly forgetting his weakness jumped to his feet in fear. The Tianming Monk looked around frantically; Cecille was nowhere to be seen. "WHITE BUFFALO!"

Misfit whined plaintively when Shin called out her mistress's name before barking in eagerness; she raced back the way she came earlier searching for him.

Shin not saying another word to his rescuer stumbled after the retreating dog. The Tianming Monk had no clue how long he was trapped in the water, nor what time it was now since the trees were too dense to see the sky. It probably wouldn't help anyway with so much cloud cover; did the posse find Cecille or was she still waiting there for him?

Travis shook his head before grumbling about foolish greenhorns racing around the woods when they were so close to death. His curiosity was piqued enough he couldn't help following the Oriental wanting to see who this White Buffalo was. Several times he needed to help the man back up as his weak legs continued to give out on him. Twice he had to make a path with his axe for him. The big homesteader admired the Asian's determination even as close to dying as he was, the man refused to give up; whoever this person was, they must be pretty important.

Misfit kept running back and barking at the slow pair; when the dog was satisfied they were still coming she would turn before racing off. Until suddenly she stopped, a low intense growl rose from deep within her chest making her body vibrate, but she waited for the two men. With hackles raised she tentatively walked into the clearing, nose twitching she searched for any more threats.

Shin instantly pulled his sword; the Tianming Monk lost all five of the arrows he was carrying plus his favourite bow, but luckily his sword was still strapped to his back. Thankfully, both daggers were still held fast in their pouches. The belt around his waist still contained his spare arrows too.

Travis hefted his axe as they followed the dog out of the trees.

Shin quickly rushed around searching the dead, but they were all men; the two mares with their precious cargoes were gone. The last man the Tianming Monk turned over had a star pinned to his shirt on his chest.

Shin heaved a heavy sigh knowing the hotel clerk had to be the one responsible for this. The Tianming Monk turned to the big man who rescued him then bowed in thanks. "Travis, I am sorry, but I must leave you here. My friend is being held against her will, the men who have her are on horseback and they also have rifles. You are not equipped for such a fight as big as you are, but I thank you for saving my life."

Travis nodded, he gestured down the dirt path going towards town in explanation. "Four miles east of here there is a small trail which will take you north before veering west; follow it if you come back this way it will lead you to my cabin, you are both welcome to spend the night if you need shelter."

Shin nodded in thanks, but didn't comment further; he walked over and collected Cecille's hat, he put it on his own head this way his hands would be free. He waited until Travis turned away disappearing back into the trees before the Tianming Monk looked down at Misfit, he dropped to his knees in front of her.

Shin chanting in his native language buried his pain, fear, and the need to cough up his lungs. Finally, the Tianming Monk called Cecille's dog closer to him. He took Misfit's head in his hands as he pleaded earnestly. "Find your mistress!"

Shin jumped up, he followed Misfit at a steady ground eating trot; the Tianming Monk prayed desperately hoping to arrive in time, there was no telling what Cecille would or could do if pushed beyond her limits!

CHAPTER SIX

Cecille frowned grimly she needed to get down off this horse. It had been over half an hour since she got taken, with no sign of Misfit or Shin; something must have happened to the Tianming Monk, but until she could put her hands onto the ground she was blind both physically and mentally. Remembering a trick that she taught her three-year-old mare White Buffalo clucked her tongue before giving one sharp whistle.

Donald squeezed the woman hard. "Shush your mouth!"

Cecille grunted in anger at the tight squeeze; unfortunately, the dirty unwholesome clerk didn't put her back on her horse. Every time he breathed on her neck White Buffalo couldn't help cringing in disgust at the foul stench.

The packhorse squealed in alarm suddenly; Precious lifted her left hind leg in pain before she started hobbling. The mare began pulling back on her lead rope after a few minutes, insistently.

Donald grumbled in irritation before sighing in resignation as his stomach chose that moment to growl furiously at him as well, they had not eaten since dawn; the rotund hotel clerk while not overly fat was not use to missing meals either. "We will rest here, someone please see to the horse then get some beans and bacon cooking!"

"Aaahh... ugghh!"

Cecille squealed in alarm when she got unceremoniously pushed from the hotel clerk's horse. She landed with a surprised yelp which got cut short when she walloped the Earth hard enough to knock the wind right out of her. White Buffalo huffed in indignation once she managed to get her breath back; she didn't complain because on the ground is where she longed to be since early this afternoon.

The men laughed at the blind woman's expression of shock.

Cecille ignored them all then put her hands flat on the Mother Earth; she closed her eyes in concentration, she could feel Po quivering down deep, without warning her spirit was pulled free from her body. White Buffalo heard screams of fear and pain when she got near the vibrations shaking the Earth, she saw in her mind an island but only for a moment. Abruptly, it disappeared in a vast cloud of ash as an earthquake shook the foundation; it caused a volcanic eruption within the mountain spewing lava everywhere.

Cecille got yanked violently away; she flew still further away to another bigger island. One she was all too familiar with, having called it home until she was ten years old. White Buffalo came to an unexpected stop in front of a grey wall made up of a thick, impenetrable fog, inside was a mountain peak… Snowdonia!

The Mother Earth again shook savagely; unfortunately, it was way more aggressive now!

Cecille could see the ground shifting violently, causing crevasses to open all around the mountain leaving gaping holes in the Mother Earth. She saw the fog darken as a few tendrils broke off, trying to escape. Po wailed in pain then denial as the entire Earth shifted on its axis, causing a massive wave to raise heading for shore. Several hundred miles further away three huge whirlpools swirled out of control; luckily the vortexes were far away, only one ship with its crew disappeared never to be seen again.

Cecille's celestial spirit raised both arms, a power previously unknown to her peeked at that moment. Shocked beyond words, she became the Guardian of the Earth… a healer. The first Paladin to be born since the beginning of time, now she could transfer control to or take power from Po directly; giving as much as she possibly could to the Mother Earth the powerful shaman/medicine woman glowed ethereal like.

In rage, the mist squealed as it was pushed back again sealing it behind the wall of dark fog. With a vicious crack the fissures closed, it echoed loudly in the stillness and was so violent it almost knocked Cecille to the ground.

Unfortunately, Cecille knew that the damage was done; the whole Earth physically shifted on its axis. The consequences would be felt for years to come, causing severe weather changes plus landmass alterations. How long they had before the fog dissipated completely and the evil contained within was released was now unknown. Suddenly, White Buffalo's spirit was yanked back to her body. It happened so fast the healer was unprepared, which caused her to convulse in a massive seizure; she fell face first onto the ground shaking severely.

The men eating stopped with spoons halfway to their mouths. They stared in horror at the convulsing woman as she began uncontrollably thrashing around on the ground. It was so violent that it caused her to flip onto her back before foam frothed around her mouth; spittle began running down her cheek.

The killers dropped their plates in panic, jumping to their feet the four men raced to their horses. They did not even check to see if the blind woman was alive or dead. Assuming she was touched by the devil himself, they ran as fast as their horses would go back towards town in abject terror. Not one of them looked back.

Cecille's mind wandered aimlessly, lost in the spirit world for what seemed an eternity. Abruptly with a jolt of nausea, she retched as a tongue licked her face bringing her back from the brink of death with a whine of fear. A few minutes later, a blanket enshrouded White Buffalo before she was lifted up into familiar arms. Safe once more, she snuggled close in relief now able to let down her guard; she fell into a healing, dreamless sleep.

*****

Shin growled in anger when he heard the thunder of horse's hooves; unfortunately, they were disappearing into the distance. Twice on the way here, he was forced to stop unwillingly and kneel chanting searching for another hidden reserve of strength because of dizziness as it tried to overtake him. Now because of his weakness, he missed a golden opportunity to rescue his charge. The Tianming Monk slowed when he heard a horse neigh then stamp impatiently, was he mistaken or did the men split up?

Shin pulled out his sword as he cautiously moved forward. Unexpectedly, he heard Misfit bark sharply and whine plaintively. Not hearing any shots or yelling for the dog to get away from them the Tianming Monk became bolder. He stepped into the little clearing before frowning puzzled. Both Cecille's mares with eight other horses were standing some distance away from a fire. Plates with food still on them were lying on the ground completely forgotten; several saddlebags littered the ground as if everyone left in a big hurry.

Shin hearing Misfit whine quickly sheathed his sword. He rushed forward at the sight of long black hair with silver white tips spread out on the ground in a waterfall of silk. The Tianming Monk going around the fire heard his charge throwing up violently, which halted him.

Shin instantly spun the other way instead, in order to get to the horses. He untied the eight posse horses first before fastening the reins around their necks so they wouldn't trip on them. The Guardian couldn't just leave them here to die, either they would follow him or head back to town; Shadow Stalker didn't care one way or the other at this point.

Shin went to Cecille's packhorse to pull out a blanket before walking over he grabbed the right rein of the older mare, bringing her closer to the fire; her reins were always tied, so he didn't need to worry about that. The Tianming Monk knew her daughter would follow without urging, he tied the packhorses lead rope around her neck too. There were no towns where they were going, so Precious would be okay loose.

Shin had no worries when it came to the older mare, Saya would not go anywhere unless he did. Quickly, the Tianming Monk dug out some dry clothes since he was soaked to the bone; he was unpleasantly chilled most of the day because of the rain. The unexpected dunk in the lake made it worse. Especially now that the sun was setting, the air was even colder; he changed in a hurry before putting White Buffalo's hat back into a saddlebag.

Shin left Cecille's horses by the fire when he was done before rushing to White Buffalo with the blanket; he wrapped her up in it and stood up with her tenderly cradled in his arms. The Tianming Monk kicked dirt on the fire to smother it but didn't bother with any of the murders discarded saddlebags.

Shin whistled for Saya to follow him, he walked purposely east looking for the path Travis mentioned. He didn't understand what happened, but Shadow Stalker needed a safe place to whole up so he could use the carpet to find out. He heard the other horses following too, he ignored them.

Shin turned north an hour later following a partially overgrown path they didn't notice on their way to the lake; six of the posse horses followed the Tianming Monk, two continued on the main trail heading back to town.

Shin stumbling in exhaustion walked stubbornly ahead refusing to put his bundle down or stop even for a moment as his steps became more erratic; Cecille was his responsibility; the Tianming Monk didn't even consider putting White Buffalo on her mare. Two hours later Shadow Stalker smelt smoke so knew they were close. "Misfit go get help, go find Travis!"

Misfit instantly raced away.

Shin dropped to his knees unable to go any further. The Tianming Monk heard Misfit barking insistently in the distance; he waited, praying the homesteader had not gone anywhere.

Travis raced around the corner following the dog; he bellowed loudly for his wife to come help him when he saw the Oriental. Running up the big man tried to take the woman from Shin. Refusing to let Cecille go, the Guardian's grip tightened. The homesteader bent with a whisper of promise that she wouldn't be harmed; the Tianming Monk finally reassured released his hold.

Sharon ran up to Travis, she gave her husband an apologetic look when passing him. She hadn't believed his explanation earlier, but with the proof now in front of her the homesteader's wife could no longer refute him; she helped the Asian up off the ground.

Shin heard a woman talking but was so dazed he couldn't figure out what she was saying. A few minutes later, the Tianming Monk heard the clucking of chickens. His nose wrinkled when he smelt the goats, pigs then the cows next as they were brought into a barn and led to a corner stall. A blanket got put around him; thankfully, he dropped to his knees before passing out. Shadow Stalker landed on his side in the clean straw laid out on the dirt floor.

Travis put the woman down beside the strange Oriental before stepping back; he joined his wife a moment later. "I'm not sure what's going on Sharon! It's too bad we don't have extra rooms in the house, the barn will have to do."

Sharon sighed fretfully; she reached over before taking her husband's hand in comfort. "I don't know either love, but I am sure they will be quite grateful just to have a warm, dry place to rest. Thankfully it quit raining again, but will probably continue later tonight. I will put soup on some tea too I think, while you take care of the horses. Why the man was carrying the woman with eight horses following him is beyond my understanding."

Travis leaned over for a farewell kiss from his wife he stepped back so she could go. The dog squeezed passed him while he was preoccupied with Sharon. He turned back to the stall with a frown of disapproval at the mud caked animal now walking around in the clean stall. The homesteader just finished putting fresh straw on the dirt floor for bedding before the commotion.

The dog settled between the two lying in the straw they both looked close to death to him... sighing in aggravation, he let her be.

Travis turned before eyeing the strange horses thoughtfully. He forgot to shut the big double doors, so the two mares leading when he took the woman from the Asian were standing inside the barn waiting patiently. The six horses outside were wandering around the yard eating grass not paying any attention to the two mares; the homesteader got the impression the two groups were separate so concentrating on the ones inside.

Travis stripped the bigger mare first then put her in a stall. The homesteader couldn't help but admire the black and white mare; if he had one such as her here, it would take him no time at all to clear this land for crops.

Travis shook off his wistful thoughts, going to the smaller mare the first thing he took off was a black doctor's bag, he eyed it in surprise. It was heavy and it also rattled so must have equipment in it. The homesteader looked towards the two lying there, which one was the doctor? He was so tempted to open it he knew his wife would give him a supreme scolding if he did; it was no business of his she would say!

Travis tentatively reached out before jabbing his finger towards what looked like a real beaver. Instinctively, he snatched his hand back quickly when he felt genuine animal fur. He couldn't help laughing at his fearful hesitation, but the homesteader was aware of how vicious these animals were when cornered; he just couldn't help his reaction.

Travis usually trapped beavers in the winter, but never had the man seen one looking this alive! He reached out again to pick it up off the side of the pack it was pretty heavy. The homesteader looked curiously for an opening, how did they get the bones out, the clunking coming from inside was not part of a beaver. It took him several minutes of examining the thing to see the rawhide threaded around the neck; he missed it because it was the same colour as the animal, what the heck could it be for?

Travis sighed resignedly trying hard to ignore his curiosity as he pulled off two saddlebags, he slung them both over his shoulder; he brought everything into the stall before laying them in a corner close to the couple. He went back to the younger mare to pull off more packsaddles with food and of course some clothes. The homesteader continued to pile everything in the corner until the only thing left was a trunk sitting on the mare's rump. It was held by a strap, which went around the packhorses belly up to the opposite side before it got tied with a slip knot.

Travis scratched his chin thoughtfully they even had a rope tied to the horse's tail so the trunk wouldn't move which made him even more curious, what was important in there? He pulled on the main line causing the harness to drop onto the ground under the mare. He unhooked the tail rope before reaching for the handle of the trunk, but unexpectedly the homesteader got a surprise. A little shock prickled his fingers; in self-preservation, he pulled his hand away in mistrust.

Travis chuckled as he remembered a similar incident from last winter when his wife made him a wool sweater; every time he wore it and petted the cat he would get the same reaction. An electric shock would snap. Sometimes, he could even swear he saw a little spark. The homesteader shaking off his fond memories reached for the trunk once again. This time he yelped painfully as the jolt became quite a bit more violent. The mare jumped, sending the wooden box tumbling to the ground.

Travis instantly soothed the horse not wanting her to kick inside the barn; she could hurt herself. He frowned down at the offending box then shrugged and left it there. The homesteader stripped off the packsaddle; he dropped it beside the trunk before putting the young mare into a stall.

Travis went over to a wooden storage bin in the far corner of the barn to gather a bucket of oats then went outside. He shook it enticingly, getting the six horses to follow him into the corral on the right side of the barn; it wasn't big but would do for now. Quickly, he forked in some hay before leaving them there. He also stopped to close the big barn doors. The homesteader finished with his chores left to go have supper, his wife wouldn't eat unless he was there he knew.

*****

Two hours later, Travis carrying a tray full of nourishing broth and tea for his wife, dutifully followed Sharon making sure he didn't spill even a drop; the homesteader insisted on carrying the tray since it was full dark with no moon whatsoever, it was difficult to see.

Sharon lifted her lamp then opened the barn door, but quickly stepped back in surprise.

"Grrr!"

Travis nudged his wife aside when he heard the dog growling inside. "I will go first."

Sharon having forgotten about the dog nodded and backed away.

Travis went through the door first; he called out angrily at the four-legged animal he still didn't have a name for, since there was no time for proper introductions before at the lake. "Stop that Dog you are scaring my Wife, I will not stand for it!"

Misfit caulked her head listening, obediently the dog quieted before putting her head back on her paws at the familiar voice; Although, she continued to watch the two strangers wearily.

Sharon hung up her lamp then walked over before taking the tray from her husband so he could pull a couple milk buckets over for her. She put the tray on top while he went around lighting the rest of the hanging lanterns. "Travis, when you're done can you go back to the cabin for me please; I need the small pot of water I have sitting on the back of the cook stove heating. I was hoping to do this inside the house but they are both still unconscious, I need to try finding out what is wrong with them."

Travis nodded before pausing; he eyed the hound uneasily. "Will you be okay with the dog?"

Sharon nodded decisively before waving for him to go out. "Yes, I was just surprised by the growl I forgot all about her; we still haven't been properly introduced, but now she has seen me with you a couple times she should be fine."

Sharon picked up the bowl of scraps she brought and sat it on the ground before turning to the dog. "Come girl, you need to eat; afterwards, you can go out with Travis when he gets back I am sure you have not moved an inch since we left for supper."

Misfit looked towards the bowl of food; her nose twitched as she sniffed at the enticing scent, but she turned away ignoring it. The dog put her head back on her paws, forlornly.

Sharon angrily snapped her fingers at the stubborn animal; her voice rose in command. "Dog, get over here and eat this instant you aren't going to do anyone any good if you die of hunger. Besides, you are in my way!"

Misfit looked up at the woman's angry tone of voice; she snorted loudly in protest. When the woman's expression didn't relent at all, she reluctantly got up before going to the food dish and ate the leftover stew.

Sharon sighed in relief then walking over she knelt between the two strangers, exactly where the dog had been lying. She put her fingertips on the woman's cheek before checking her forehead with the flat of her palm, but didn't feel any heat.

Next, Sharon bent to sniff the woman's lips. Her nose wrinkled in protest, the woman threw up recently; thankfully; the homesteader's wife smelled nothing unusual in it.

Sharon sat back, she pulled the blanket away before nodding in approval; the woman was wearing practical men's clothes to travel in. Some women would get offended by that but not Sharon. The homesteader's wife usually spends half her time in men's clothes when others were not around.

Sharon noticed a few odd things once the blanket was gone completely. First, the woman's shirt was done up crooked; second, two buttons were missed. Her shirt wasn't tucked in either, she tsked in disapproval and undid the shirt. The homesteader's wife stopped with a surprised frown, there was a funny smell; it was also a familiar one, she scowled in puzzlement for a moment before bending. She sniffed the shirt, just as she thought it was coal oil for burning lamps.

Sharon frowned perplexedly when the shirt fell away. The woman was still in her nightshirt, she could tell by the frills. Because the material was thick, it also told her it couldn't be a camisole. The last thing the homesteader's wife noticed is her pants only had the top button fastened, so she must have been in an awful hurry. All the evidence pointed to someone recently in a fire, but there weren't any fires burning around here; she would have smelt it in the wind by now. The coal oil smell made her think of an inside fire, possibly a cabin or a barn.

Travis came in with the pot, Sharon got up before carefully pulling out one of the clothes inside waiting; the water was a little too warm, she needed to let it cool down some. "Tell me again Travis what happened after you left with the dog?"

Travis dutifully told Sharon everything, one more time.

Sharon grimaced uneasily. "Are you sure it wasn't one of them who killed those men?"

Travis nodded decisively before gesturing in reassurance at Sharon's suspicious look. "Absolutely sure, the man was as shocked as I was; besides, the Sheriff and his men got shot with handguns. I could tell easily enough by the bullet holes, and I didn't see any guns or a gunbelt anywhere around the Oriental."

Sharon sighed relieved by that before frowning thoughtfully. "Well I can smell a heavy scent of coal oil smoke on the woman, so I am pretty sure she was in a fire recently. I will try waking her up now we know the Oriental is okay only exhausted I imagine. He did have the presence of mind to change since his clothes were not wet. I am extremely concerned about the lady since I can find no injuries or any reason for her to be out too. Her clothes are all intact, so I don't think those other men... um, ravished her."

Travis set the pot of hot water down before turning to Sharon. In irritation using the bottom of his palm, he hit his forehead in frustration. The homesteader forgot about this morning because of all the excitement. "That's what I didn't tell you at lunch, early this morning there was a hint of a smoke smell on the eastern breeze coming from town; the wind changed directions soon after, so it slipped my mind when the dog came for help."

Travis kissed Sharon before turning towards the barn doors; with a sharp snap of his fingers, he called the animal to him. "Come on dog you can keep me company it will stop you from getting in trouble with my wife."

Misfit whined plaintively not wanting to leave her mistress; obediently, she turned with tail tucked between her legs unhappily, Cecille's dog followed the man out when the woman scowled at her before pointing for her to go.

Sharon turned back to the woman; she knelt to put a warm cloth on her forehead, she gently ran it down her face. "Come on Lady I need you to wake up!"

*****

Cecille felt something warm touch her face and heard a distant murmur; someone was trying to talk to her. She frowned in concentration, but couldn't figure out who it was. Slowly the woman's voice got stronger before the fog keeping her under lifted suddenly the sound was right above her. White Buffalo grabbed the wrist of the woman trying to wake her. "Who are you, where am I! Shin, Misfit where are they?"

Sharon stared down in fascination at the darkest green eyes she had ever seen. She noticed a film over the woman's pupil; the homesteader's wife couldn't help exclaiming in shocked surprise at the unfocused look the woman gave her. "You are... blind!"

Cecile smiled grimly before releasing the woman's arm. White Buffalo inhaled deeply allowing all her senses to expand trying to figure out where they were; it didn't take her long to realize they were in a barn. Her nose wrinkled at the sharp scent of fresh manure. "Yes, didn't Shin tell you?"

Sharon sighed in remorse; she wasn't usually rude, it just shocked her to find a blind person way out here. "No, if you are talking about an Asian he is laying behind me. He hasn't moved since we put the two of you in here, my husband found him nearly drowned in the lake earlier. If it weren't for your dog finding Travis when he did the Oriental would have died there."

Cecille frowned in worry; she had known deep down something was seriously wrong with Shin. White Buffalo's Guardian would never abandon her willingly. "My doctor's bag where is it I need to check his lungs for water."

Sharon snorted incredulously in disbelief before sputtering in amazement. "You are a doctor too? Unbelievable, a woman doctor who can't see; I never thought it was even possible for a female to become a doctor never mind a blind one! Who taught you, where did you go to school?"

Twin Destinies

Cecille having another anxious moment grabbed the woman's wrist again. White Buffalo ignored her shock and questions; her voice caught uneasily fearing the answer. "My two mares are they here with a wooden trunk?"

Sharon remembering her manners snapped her mouth shut on any more questions. It wasn't her business, but her curiosity was killing her. She pulled away from the insistent woman surprised by the vehement inquiry. "Yes, two mares followed us into the barn. My husband put them in a stall already it's the only room we have in here; the six horses outside are in a corral. Give me a moment I will look for your doctor's bag my husband put all your stuff in the far corner. As for a trunk, I don't recall seeing one."

Travis walking in heard the end of his wife's comment; the homesteader called out in reassurance. "The trunk is over here beside the packsaddle, it gave me quite a shock so I left it where it fell!"

Misfit raced into the stall with a relieved yip of greeting for her mistress. The dog jumped into Cecille's lap when she sat up; she proceeded to give White Buffalo a thorough face washing.

Cecille laughed in pleasure before she pushed her dog off her lap; White Buffalo was relieved that Misfit was here, she was just about to ask the woman about her dog again since she didn't get an answer earlier. "Lay down over there now, good girl."

Sharon got up and went over to the corner to search. It didn't take the homesteader's wife long the black doctor's bag was easily recognizable. She bent to pick it up before walking over she put it beside the woman. I made soup for you both; with a pot of willow-bark tea, I even included mint since it's so damp out. Although, I think they are both pretty cold by now.

Cecille waved away the woman's concern. White Buffalo did use it as an excuse to get rid of her. "The soup will be fine cold, but would you mind getting me more hot water; I need to make some medicinal tea for Shin, something a bit stronger."

Cecille sighed in relief when Travis went with Sharon; the homesteader didn't want his wife out alone at night, bears were a big problem out here most of the time.

Cecille began chanting then hurriedly put her hands over Shin's chest before healing him. He still had quite a lot of water in his lungs, which would have eventually caused sever pneumonia; by the time White Buffalo was finished though, all the water had disappeared.

The Tianming Monk began to come around as the pressure eased. Thankfully, the rattle in his breathing left too.

Shin still disoriented reached up; he stroked Cecille's cheek lovingly. Forgetting where or even who he was, the Tianming Monk couldn't help commenting. "I thought I lost you, White Buffalo."

Shin suddenly aware he was touching real flesh tensed grimly, realizing he gave away his true feeling; the Guardian dropped his hand before sitting up, he was glad Cecille couldn't see his infatuated expression. The Tianming Monk's mask of stoicism got replaced instantly. He fired off questions hoping White Buffalo didn't notice his slip. "The horses, my carpet; are they here?"

Cecille smiled in reassurance; she took Shin's hand before squeezing it consolingly. She had known for many years how he felt about her, but White Buffalo didn't love the Tianming Monk in the same way. She had ignored it all this time not want to make a big deal out of it, which would embarrass her Guardian causing unpleasantness between them. "Everything is here safe and so are we thanks to you!"

Travis followed closely by his wife returned just then.

Cecille sighed in relief as the awkward moment with Shin faded; White Buffalo hoped no repercussions would result, making the Tianming Monk regret coming with her.

Sharon walked over to Cecille before carefully setting her mother's tea set on the floor beside the blind doctor; while White Buffalo was making the tea, the homesteader's wife brought them each a bowl of cold soup.

Travis promised Shin he would go with his wagon to collect the dead posse; thankfully, the temperature was cold enough there shouldn't be much smell. Afterwards, the homesteader would gather all the evidence at the abandoned camp. He would also take the horses to the store owner who would contact the proper authorities.

Sharon eventually got her answers to the hundred questions she had for Cecille, on how she became a doctor. Especially, when the homesteader's wife found out the woman never went to a proper school, all her training was hands-on no book learning. White Buffalo kept a certificate stating she was a doctor hidden in the big wooden box that was always kept locked.

Cecille's training was unorthodox since her father Doctor Edward Summerset took her as an apprentice for twenty years; twice as long as a student who could see. When he felt White Buffalo was ready, he arranged for her to do a practicum at the hospital in Quebec for one year with a senior doctor. All she needed to do was go in for the final exams.

Thankfully braille had been invented in eighteen twenty-four by Louis Braille, to assist the blind in reading. Calling in an old favour from William Moon from Brighten, East Sussex England who had developed a Latin alphabet for the blind which was similar to braille; Edward sent him the questions then William put them on paper for him. Cecille took the exam both orally and by the moon system in front of a panel of senior doctors that also included White Buffalo's father.

They gave Cecille one of the hardest tests ever given to a student; Doctor Summerset didn't go easy on his daughter either. The healer answered every one of their questions without faltering even once. Since White Buffalo's father was an Earl of the realm, they didn't have any choice but to award her a certificate when she passed with honours.

Good nights were exchanged before Travis and Sharon returned to their cabin.

Shin blew out the lamp before listening to Cecille describing her horrifying experience with the Mother Earth; White Buffalo had waited not wanting to share this with the homesteaders. The Tianming Monk told her all about his lake episode. Afterwards, Shadow Stalker gave her a detailed description of what he found at the campsite until finally exhausted, they both fell into a dreamless healing sleep.

CHAPTER SEVEN

Shin turned to Travis in gratitude the Tianming Monk bowed deeply in thanks. The big homesteader insisted on taking them across the lake that was narrowest not far from his cabin then travelled with them another three miles to a shortcut he guaranteed was the better of the two, so they needed to take it instead.

Travis awkwardly bowed back before the homesteader turned to the older mare on his right. He patted Cecille's leg in farewell. "Both of you take care of yourselves. Stay on the Flat trail until you get to a town called Dacre you should get there before high noon. From there take the Scotch Bush path, it will lead you to Constant Lake. There's an Indian who has a barge for transporting goods across the lake to a road which leads directly into Eganville. You can continue on Scotch Bush trail if you prefer, but crossing the lake onto the better-travelled road will save you two hours of travel; and yes, the raft is big enough for your horses."

Cecille reached down then squeezed the hand Travis casually put on her leg. White Buffalo had given the homesteader his spirit name earlier on at the cabin. She also gave one to Sharon before whispering another one in his daughter's ear. "Thank you Black Crow Feather; may Shen our God, the Great Spirit of all living things and Po guide you. The crow will be your Earth's spirit guide from the Mother Earth."

Travis chuckled in pleasure, liking the name Cecille gave him. Once the two were out of sight, he turned heading home. Black Crow Feather still needed to get a large coffin made for the dead men before animals destroyed them. Afterwards, the homesteader needed to get to Calabogie by nightfall; it would be a long day for him, he knew.

*****

Without Black Crow Feather to slow them down, Shin was able to pick up his pace. He settled into a ground-eating trot; thankfully, the horses had no trouble keeping up now that the ground was dryer.

They arrived in Dacre an hour earlier than predicted; Shin looked up at Cecille inquisitively. "White Buffalo they have a hotel here, which should have an eating place do you want to stop to eat lunch?"

Cecille thought about it for a moment before shaking her head negatively; she wasn't hungry enough yet and White Buffalo also felt a need to hurry. "No, Black Crow Feather said the lake wasn't far from here. I imagine we will be on the barge for a while so we should be able to eat there. It will give us something to do to make the time pass faster."

Shin nodded in agreement; he was not hungry either. "Okay."

Dacre wasn't big, so it only took them a few minutes to negotiate it; they found Scotch Bush trail easily enough. Forty-five minutes later, Shin once again slowed as the lake came into view on his left. On the right was a small Indian village with several tepees and no wigwams. He figured it was only a temporary summer camp. The Tianming Monk turned then went to the dock but did not bother going any further when he noticed there was no barge. Turning around, Shadow Stalker went to the village in order to talk to a man he could see sitting in front of his fire smoking a long pipe contentedly, and questioned him.

Shin left the man with a thoughtful frown then walked over to the mare; he put his hand over Cecille's since it was resting on her knee. "Unfortunately, no raft till tomorrow we missed it by an hour. The old man said this Scotch Bush trail goes for another seven miles north. Afterwards, it turns west until we meet up with a trail called Fourth Chute. It will take us another mile and a half north-west right into Eganville. We can be there before nightfall easily he assured me."

Cecille shrugged, not minding at all; she was feeling a need to be on this road, anyway. "Okay, lead on."

Shin squeezed Cecille's hand in approval; he turned from White Buffalo before going around the mare, the Tianming Monk picked up the trot again.

*****

Cecille's belly growled at her causing White Buffalo to sigh in defeat. She was starving since they didn't eat as planned. "Shin I can hear the river; I would like to stop, fresh fish would be welcome for a change."

Shin slowed but continued walking ahead he could see a split in the trail so wanted to look first. He was pretty sure the right fork would lead north to the river. Once standing in the centre of the converging trails, the Tianming Monk looked down a slight incline then saw smoke. It could be a town or even another Indian village they could rest, maybe buy some fish if need be.

Shin looked up at Cecille. "We're at Fourth Chute road; a trail going to the river is on the right. Eganville is to our left but at least two hours away. I agree fresh fish would be nice we have about four or five hours of daylight left plenty of time to make it to town before nightfall."

Cecille smiled in pleasure before grimacing as she shifted in her saddle. White Buffalo needed to get off her horse for a bit both her butt cheeks were numb. Her smile disappeared suddenly she cocked her head to listen; she picked up the sounds of the river loud and clear, but she could also hear someone screaming something in the distance

Shin hearing it too instantly stopped the horses, they had only gone a couple steps; the Tianming Monk looked up at Cecille in concern. "Stay here White Buffalo I need to go check that out before we go any further."

Cecille nodded in agreement; White Buffalo snapped her fingers sharply. "You stay here Misfit."

Misfit whined in agitation hating to be separated again, but obediently sat then waited with Cecille.

Shin trotted back after only a few minutes; the Tianming Monk had a relieved note in his voice. "It's okay it was just a woman calling out for her son. They live in a cabin ahead, seems the boy has not returned home yet. No village anywhere nearby she informed me, but we are free to go fishing there."

Cecille nodded reassured; thankfully, she nudged her horse along. After another excruciating fifteen minutes she was dismounting. She took a moment to rub her aching backside, trying to relieve some of the numbness. White Buffalo turned to her horse before taking the harness from the saddle horn to put on her dog since she wanted to walk down to the river.

Shin touched Cecille's elbow to get her attention; the Tianming Monk lowered his voice. "White Buffalo, the woman is standing on her porch waiting for us she said we could leave the horses here if we want to go fishing. She will watch them because it gets fairly steep by the time you hit the bottom of this hill. She even offered to lend us two of her husband's fishing poles that he made himself just before he died."

Cecille nodded thankful they wouldn't have to make poles; White Buffalo gestured ahead of her. "You can lead me over to her, please."

Shin took Cecille's elbow to take her around the front porch where the woman had both fishing poles waiting. The Tianming Monk knew White Buffalo would want to talk to her first. He looked up at the blonde woman with striking deep blue eyes before introducing the two women. "Violet this is my step-sister Cecille Summerset; her father took me in when I was fourteen, so we were raised together. Cecille is a doctor, but because she is a woman and born blind, she decided to take her skills where it is needed most; there's a lot of prejudices when it comes to female doctors in the cities, but I owe her family a debt. I decided the best way to repay her father back for all the years of love he has shown to me was to become his daughter's protector as she travels."

Cecille smiled up at the petite slightly plump blonde before lifting her hand so the woman would take it. White Buffalo could not see her outer shell, but she could see her aura once the woman took her hand; it told the shaman/medicine woman everything she needed to know. "Hello Violet it is nice to meet you, Shin tells me you have a son who is missing?"

Violet squeezed the blind woman's hand in greeting distractedly, obviously worried. "Yes, he should be back here by now; I keep telling my son to stay away from the rope my husband put up to cross the river. A year ago Henry Senior was coming from the opposite side in a storm but the rope was too wet making it slick, my husband never made it across. I told my son Henry Junior last night we are moving to Eganville. This morning he disappeared, which is not really all that odd because he likes to fish early in the morning. He usually comes home for lunch though. Although, there have been times since my husband died he stayed out till after supper. This time I have a gut feeling something isn't quite right, it is the same feeling I had when my husband never returned."

Cecille smiled up in reassurance trying to ease Violet's anxious thoughts; she could feel the woman's fear. "I'm sure he is probably being a typical boy and forgot about the time, especially now that the days are getting way longer. We will keep an eye out for him I will send him home immediately, I promise."

Violet sighed in relief, not sure why but suddenly her fear eased; she released Cecille's hand. "Thank you, I would appreciate it."

Violet turned before going back inside to continue packing.

Cecille turned to her Guardian troubled; White Buffalo knew a mother's instincts were seldom wrong. "Shin can you go get my beaver medicine bag, please. If we are leaving the horses I would feel much better having it with me."

Shin left, but returned quickly; the Tianming Monk handed the entire beaver hide to his charge.

Cecille tied it around her waist with a sad smile of nostalgia; it brought back fond memories of her father. She trapped the beaver herself with Edward's help. He cut the front of the throat making sure to leave a portion of the back of the neck intact. Afterwards, all its insides... bones, with the meat were drawn out through the neck leaving the skin whole. All that was missing was the tail, they would have left it on too; unfortunately, it made the medicine bag too heavy for White Buffalo once everything was added.

The skin itself was even drawn through the neck so the beaver was inside out, this way it could be scraped before curing. It took more work and longer for the skin to dry properly, but the result was a watertight hide Cecille could store herbs in without worrying about moisture getting in and wrecking her dried plants.

Cecille didn't just have herbs in there it also contained everything her black doctor's bag did. A tough sinew was threaded around the neck opening before being drawn tight and tied; the beaver medicine bag was more convenient when not on horseback, it fastened around the waist which left White Buffalo's hands-free for other things.

It didn't take them long to get to the river; the trail was a little steep but not impassable by horse, Shin couldn't help noticing.

Cecille gestured around curiously. "Any sign of the Boy, Shin?"

Shin frowned before looking around thoughtfully, he found the rope Violet told them about almost immediately; it was hard to miss, but there were actually two ropes. The Tianming Monk left Cecille then walked towards them, but kept his eyes on the trail. It didn't take Shadow Stalker long to find the tracks he was looking for.

Shin returned to Cecille before turning to stare at the churning river in contemplation. The Tianming Monk wanted to give as accurate a picture to White Buffalo as he could. Here there was direct access to the river for fishing there was also a pond to the left teaming with tadpoles, frogs, and small fish. It was even big enough and deep enough you could submerge completely up to the shoulders. There were several huge rocks about thirty feet away, which kept this little pond separated from the river. A small trickle of water seeping between the boulders kept it full of water.

About halfway across the river it dropped into a gorge then became a waterfall, it was not huge nor would it kill you if you accidentally went over it; although, the rocks below could if you were to hit them on the way down.

Shin gave Cecille a detailed description of the river before the Tianming Monk described the only way to cross. "There are two ropes White Buffalo, one for your hands and one to walk on. I think the boy added the lower line because it is newer it's not that far apart either, a man over five feet would find it difficult to use. There is a partial wooden bridge, but it only goes out a few feet. My guess is the boy's father was building the bridge, I can see another rope across the canyon it is hanging down the far cliff face. He probably used it to bring the bigger trees down here that I can see up on the cliff, the trees around here are quite small in comparison; I found fresh tracks leading to the ropes, so the boy crossed sometime today."

Cecille nodded before kneeling; she put her palms on the Mother Earth searching for the missing boy. Instantly she felt anger, determination with a touch of fear, all rolled up into a ten-year-old boy who was determined to stay here. He just needed to find a way to convince his mother. White Buffalo followed the strong emotions across the river which followed a well-beaten path through the thick forest. Suddenly the trees disappeared and she was now looking at a marshy open field.

The boy looked around surprised, there should be water here at least until late fall. Afterwards, he would have to go further east to a smaller pool of water which joined the river it was teaming with all sorts of fish. It was the best fishing around he always boasted to his mother, but she didn't seem to care how he felt.

Cecille kept following the emotions bombarding her; unexpectedly, it vanished! With no warning the feelings she was following disappeared into thin air, halting her instantly. White Buffalo couldn't feel the boy at all now, so she backed up until she found the trail. Again as soon as the healer moved forward or in any other direction, it disappeared. Several times she went back and searched, but she could find nothing he just seemed to vanish without a trace!

Cecille paused listening then detected it again; if she stayed really still a faint sob of frustration and pain could be heard, followed a moment later by terror. Abruptly, a pitch-black hole engulfed White Buffalo. Unwillingly, she was pulled in unable to escape... trapped!

*****

Shin watched Cecille carefully he could tell by her expressive face what she was experiencing as she followed the boy. The Tianming Monk frowned in worry when she stiffened in apprehension; he waited, knowing his charge would be furious if he interfered at the wrong time. Shadow Stalker could see her closed eyes beginning to flutter violently as White Buffalo's eyeballs rolled around searching for something then her cheeks flushed in exertion, still he waited.

Misfit was laying off to their right panting with eyes half closed resting; she was enjoying the sun and the break from travelling. Unexpectedly, the dog jumped up in agitation growling in uncertainty. She looked around wildly searching for a threat, confused the dog couldn't see anything out of the ordinary!

Cecille moaned in terror, she twitched trying to get away.

Shin dropped the two fishing poles instantly, quickly he fell to his knees in front of Cecille; the Tianming Monk grasped his charges wrists before pulling her hands from the Mother Earth it severed White Buffalo's connection to the boy.

Cecille slumped against Shin; the boy's emotions were too strong for her, it pulled her unwillingly into a black void. White Buffalo sighed and sat up before explaining everything to the Tianming Monk.

Shin frowned grimly as he listened to Cecille totally baffled. The Tianming Monk shrugged in uncertainty before looking up at the sky in worry; he looked back at his charge thoughtfully. "White Buffalo there is only about four hours of daylight left, are you sure we should search for him now it might be better to wait till morning?"

Cecille jumped to her feet instantly in anger she couldn't believe Shin would say such a thing. She would never leave a child in danger... ever; not if White Buffalo could prevent it that is. "I must go now the dark doesn't bother me!"

Shin sighed in defeat before picking up the two fishing poles off the ground. He walked over to a tree to lean them up against it. The rods would be fine there until they returned. When he came back the Tianming Monk put a restraining hand against Cecille's arm. He knew she would want to leave immediately, Shadow Stalker just needed to be sure she was aware of the time left. "Okay White Buffalo, but stay here while I run up to the cabin. I have to grab rope, and other things off the packhorse; afterwards, we will go."

Cecille sighed relieved; the boy was in some kind of trouble and a shiver of urgency told her tomorrow would be way too late. Impatiently, White Buffalo paced in agitation waiting.

Misfit yipped in excitement when her second favourite pack member came back into view, letting Cecille know Shin was back.

Shin hurried over, reaching out he took Cecille's arm to lead her to the rope bridge. He uncoiled the rope on his shoulder before tying one end around his waist. Taking the other end he fastened it to White Buffalo, the Tianming Monk wanted to take all necessary precautions; he also brought several essential items just in case they were gone longer than they should be. "I am tying us together, once we are across the river I will undo the rope from around us but we will keep it in hand to keep us connected. From your description I can only think of one possibility, he fell into something! It can't be the river or you would have felt him getting further away."

Cecille nodded; glad Shin was taking this more seriously now. White Buffalo gestured down at her dog not wanting to leave her here before asking the Tianming Monk worriedly. "What about Misfit can she swim across the river?"

Shin looked down at Misfit contemplatively; the Tianming Monk would have to carry her across since the two ropes they would be negotiating went upwards to the top of a cliff ledge, it was pretty steep. The cliff was limestone on the opposite side most wouldn't be able to climb it because the river having eroded it made the surface smooth and relatively impassable. "No, I will thread the rope through her harness, she won't like it but it's the only way."

Shin picked up Cecille's dog. Fortunately, she was all legs very lean; the dog didn't even weigh fifty pounds. The Tianming Monk lifted her up so their noses were close. "You must remain calm Misfit if you wish to come, it's a long way down but I will keep you safe."

Misfit whined before licking Shin's nose; it wouldn't be the first time she was carried in strange ways by the male leader of her little pack, she trusted him.

Shin grinned; he kissed Misfit's nose before putting her down to undo his rope then squatted. The Guardian pulled her against his side so he could thread the line through her harness. The Tianming Monk was careful to make sure the rope didn't restrict her airways or her breathing in any way. He redid the line around his waist then stood back up, which made him realize Cecille's dog was not stable enough. Shadow Stalker reached down to grasp the leash dangling from the harness. He brought it up under her front legs then pulled it around his upper leg before tying it tightly to his thigh. Now the dog's upper body was held snug against him and only her back legs dangled loosely, plus she could still move her head.

Shin reached down then stroked Misfit's head soothingly; the Tianming Monk could feel her trembling a little. "It will not be long girl, I promise!"

Misfit snorted, her lip curled slightly showing her teeth as if she disagreed with the Guardian.

Shin laughed when he looked over at Cecille; he could not help comparing the dog hanging on his left side to the beaver medicine bag White Buffalo had hanging on her side. The Tianming Monk was sure the two of them looked if nothing else, absolutely ridiculous.

Shin reached out to take Cecille's arm leading her closer to the rope bridge. The Tianming Monk put White Buffalo's hand up on the top rope so she knew where it was. "You go first it's a hard upward climb to the top of the cliffs. About a half mile I would say I tied a rope to the two of us to keep us connected. I will add another line to the top rope before attaching it to the cable between us; it will slide as you walk so be prepared for a little tension. If you slip the line between us will stop you from falling too far, giving us stability when my weight contributes to keep you from plunging into the river."

Cecille nodded in understanding then reached up with her other hand she grasped the top rope to steady herself; she stepped up onto the other line. She wobbled at first but it only took her a few minutes to adjust. White Buffalo paused, waiting for Shin's go ahead before proceeding.

Cecille had no fear of heights and remembered fondly the time she had spent getting acquainted with the rigging of a three-masted ship, which brought them to Quebec.

Even today; Cecille could still feel her father's fear on their last day out at sea. White Buffalo did the unthinkable scaring not only Edward this time but Shin too in the process...

*****

Edward heard a tinkle of laughter, so he turned to watch his daughter Cecille in delight as she scurried up the ratlines. Shin, of course was right behind her. The Tianming Monk had a rope tied around his waist with the other end linked to White Buffalo; there really wasn't any need for a line between them since she was as surefooted as the sailors were, but Dream Dancer always insisted anyway.

Watching Cecille a stranger would never believe that the rambunctious ten-year-old was totally blind.

Shin was using the mast as a teaching tool. The Tianming Monk knew from personal experience that Edward's daughter Cecille would learn balance and flexibility; plus how to use her inner eye to see. Here there was nothing around White Buffalo except space, ropes, rigging, and canvases.

Edward was watching when Cecille stood on the arm of the tallest mast with her arms outstretched then she walked forward as if she were on a tightrope; Dream Dancer chuckled in humour, White Buffalo would make a great circus performer he couldn't help thinking to himself.

Edward was amazed by how quickly Cecille adapted to her surroundings. It took her two full days to put her walking cane away that is how long it took White Buffalo to memorize every part of the massive three-masted ship; now, Dream Dancer's daughter didn't need it anymore.

The sailors watching Cecille in awe for two days; now, they made absolutely sure nothing was out of place so the blind girl could walk around freely without assistance. It didn't take White Buffalo long to wrap every one of the sailors around her finger; the captain laughed in utter amazement never having seen his ship so well maintained or clean before, he asked half-joking if he could keep her.

Cecille's uncanny knack for languages amazed them all, even her father. She could speak several kinds already Edward was quite flabbergasted sometimes by her ability. Welsh and Celtic, which was a form of Cornish White Buffalo learned from Michelle, as well as her old nanny who had been left behind. Various Oriental languages she learned from Shin, her Guardian. Cheyenne from him and one of the sailors was teaching her French, with one guiding her through the German language.

Shin was training Cecille to see with her inner eye. At the same time, the Tianming Monk was teaching his charge that when she hummed a tune the sound would reverberate back to her if an object was too close. Giving her sufficient warning to stop and find out what was impeding her way, if the sound continued on there should be nothing around to stop her. Just these two simple tricks were making it possible for White Buffalo to have a normal life; now thankfully most of the time Edward's daughter didn't need to use the walking stick. It wasn't just a cane though, inside was a lethal rapier she was an expert in handling.

Cecille also took to the Tianming Monk Warriors training; White Buffalo could do things with her body Edward only saw in circuses, it just amazed him to watch her; Dream Dancer's daughter even surpassed Raven when it came to flexibility.

Cecille could pop every bone out of joint before wrapping her limbs around herself until she was in a ball. She could roll around like that. Back flips, cartwheels, somersaults, standing on her hands walking around or bending backwards until White Buffalo's feet touched the deck was no problem for Edward's daughter; even on a swaying ship.

Every time Cecille began her exercises the crew members off duty would come to gather around her watching in fascination; before long they were clapping or singing to encourage White Buffalo trying to help her.

Edward shaking off thoughts of his daughter Cecille gave a sad sigh. Dream Dancer missed Crystin dreadfully, even though it was a forced marriage because of the evil mist; he ended up falling in love with his wife before she died. Having a future with another woman didn't appeal to him, maybe never.

Edward's dreams of another woman were all too real lately. Still, he didn't know for sure if he was meant to love her in return. He knew she would fall in love with him since Dream Dancer saw it in her eyes in both dreams. He was also aware he would meet her someday, so she would influence his life somehow good or bad was unknown yet.

What life would throw at Edward next remained a mystery, with no powers he remained blind so to speak; what would be, even if he didn't like it, would be Dream Dancer knew!

Edward learned the hard way on that fateful day, it didn't matter what a person wanted only the higher powers needs would prevail. It seemed so long ago now, but it would forever haunt him because Dream Dancer not only gave up his powers to save his sister Raven and his wife Crystin; he also lost his Guardian, teacher, and long-time companion Dao.

Edward still missed Dao fiercely; although, his son Shin seemed to be taking over but it was still not the same thing. Dream Dancer knew he would mourn for his lost friend forever, always feeling a hole in his life; sadly, even more so than for his wife late wife Crystin.

Edward stiffened in apprehension when a shiver of foreboding shook him; he looked up in dread. Dream Dancer's daughter Cecille was standing on the lookout platform at the top of the mast balanced precariously on the edge of it, with arms outstretched. White Buffalo's face glowed with excitement as storm clouds directly above her start to churn, swirling violently.

Other clouds raced towards the mass becoming an immense purple and mauve storm cloud with streaks of angry black thunderheads throughout. The sky all around the clouds turned a dark orange making it impossible to see what was happening above; it was as if it was trying to hide what was taking place from the decks below.

Edward shading his eyes with his hands moved into the darker shadow of the mast; he stared upward in horrified fascination, even in the shade Dream Dancer needed to keep his hands in place to follow what was happening above.

*****

Shin frantically tried to coax Cecille over to him. He couldn't get to White Buffalo from where he was at. If the Tianming Monk tried pulling on the rope that connected them they would both fall to the decks below; all he could do was watch helplessly as the heavens opened all around them.

Several lightning bolts came straight down then flared around Cecille keeping Edward's daughter directly in the center, but seemingly not touching her at all; it was as if it was teasing White Buffalo or maybe it was fighting her.

Watching Shin gasped horrified as Cecille glowed brighter and brighter. It seemed to the Tianming Monk that White Buffalo was drawing the lightning in; forcing it to enter her body.

As the bolts reluctantly went into Cecille the clouds above them got smaller before disappearing; within seconds, the sky turned a crystal blue allowing others to see the top of the mast.

Shin leaped up ignoring his own danger as he carefully made his way forward. The platform wasn't big, and with the two of them on it; it was even smaller since it's meant for only one person. The Tianming Monk finally reached his charge, but he didn't dare touch Cecille. White Buffalo still had a glow all around her; the Guardian knew if he tried to take her arm he would get a shock which would send him flying, right now the monk wasn't willing to chance it.

Cecille looked up at Shin when she felt the platform shake; she knew it was her Guardian, not her father Edward. White Buffalo gestured towards the deck of the ship. "I am ready to go now Teacher, my Dad needs me!"

Shin looked down, he could see Edward running towards the ratlines so he could climb up; the Tianming Monk knew Dream Dancer was going be furious, it took a few minutes to negotiate the platform before the two of them could go down the rope ladder.

Edward saw Shin leading Cecille to the edge of the lookout so backed away from the rope; he waited impatiently for the two to come down.

Shin reached the deck first. The Guardian jumped down the last few feet before facing an anxious father; the Tianming Monk lifted his hands in caution to stop Edward's advancement. "Don't touch White Buffalo yet Dream Dancer, she is okay!"

Edward frowned forebodingly; Dream Dancer gestured sharply in decisiveness, his voice quivered just a little. "Never again will I allow you to climb that mast... ever!"

Cecille jumped down the last few feet; lithely, White Buffalo landed in front of Edward. Using the Cheyenne name for father she hoped to ease the angry frown on her dad's face. "I am sorry ni-hoi for scaring you! I could feel your fear for me, but I was in no danger. A storm was coming, I needed to stop it since we are almost at our destination and the wind would have pushed us way too far off course."

Edward stared at Cecille in shock that was something new. Dream Dancer watched in fascination as his daughter's eyes now black glowed for another minute; slowly they lightened before going back to their customary deep green with a faint film over them which was the only indication, White Buffalo was blind.

Cecille's hair colour was ebony black unless you looked closer than you could see a silvery-white frosting on the tips about an eighth of an inch on each. Edward cut her hair many times trying to get rid of the white tips. Within a day or two, the different colour again covered the ends; Dream Dancer finally gave up. The only other indication the lightning touched White Buffalo was the tips of her hair were glowing before it too dissipated.

Cecille wasn't a beautiful girl; her face was too long. She was also extremely skinny, but Edward could see potential for beauty when his daughter was older. White Buffalo's face was ghostly white, so her midnight black hair made her... ghoulish looking.

Several unusual gifts were beginning to show themselves the older Cecille got. She had a close affinity towards animals which was uncanny even wild animals would flock to her if she called them. White Buffalo could also coax a flower to bloom or get a seedling to sprout; it was amazing to watch. Edward often wondered if she could get them to grow could she make it die. Not *wanting to encourage the dark half of his daughter to blossom, Dream Dancer never asked her to try it.*

Edward looked around fugitively to see if anyone was watching them with a fearful look; it would tell him immediately if any sailor saw what happened in the mast. Thankfully, most of the crew were in the galley having lunch. It didn't look like the ones on deck saw what Dream Dancer's daughter did, lucky for them.

Edward knelt before he took Cecille's two hands in his; Dream Dancer squeezed them gently but kept his voice firm trying to convey to White Buffalo how serious this was without scaring her.

Edward remembered with fondness a similar conversation that he had with Devon; who ended up marrying his sister Raven, in Montana. Just before Dream Dancer left for England his soon to be brother-in-law gave him a similar speech, but this was more serious since his daughter already surpassed him in power. If he couldn't make her understand some things were just wrong, they would all be in big trouble. "Cecille this is important so listen carefully to me, please! You can't go around changing things, everything happens for a reason. Storms bring much-needed rain for fresh water to drink if you stopped the rain people and animals would die of thirst. Trees and flowers would end up dying too. Shen our God, the Great Spirit of all living things makes things happen for a reason so for us to tamper with nature could cause a catastrophe. We are all born, and we must all die when it is our time to go; only the Great Spirit can make that kind of decision. For you to stop someone or something from dying when it is their appointed time is wrong. Remember even if it hurts us to see it that it's part of our life cycle, there are consequences for every action you do. Think of who or what will be affected in the long run. You are a special girl White Buffalo, but you must hide it from strangers or people will try to use you. I know you wouldn't want or like that, my girl!"

Cecille nodded matter-of-factually; White Buffalo squeezed Edward's hands trying to reassure her father. "I know this already ni-hoi, I would never stop a storm when it is natural but we must make land tonight. This storm wasn't meant to be Dad I'm not sure where it came from. Po, the Mother Earth, informed me she didn't bring it to life nor did Shen it was unnatural. Po asked me to put a stop to it Mother Earth even told me how to do it. She said the storm would make the ship crash against the shore so the sailors would all die even though it isn't their time!"

Edward frowned in surprise; Dream Dancer didn't know about Po. "Mother Earth talks to you?"

Cecille nodded decisively she always figured Edward knew this so never mentioned it to her father since she inherited a good portion of her powers from Dream Dancer. "Yes ni-hoi, all the time; Po tells me when things aren't right or when I'm not to interfere. Mother Earth also tells me when she needs my help with something she can't do herself."

Edward looked at Cecille's Guardian grimly; Dream Dancer gesture sharply angry he was not informed before now! "Shin, did you know about this?"

Shin shrugged unperturbed that Edward was furious; the Tianming Monk nodded. "That Po talks to White Buffalo, yes I did. I was not aware the Mother Earth was asking Cecille to do things for her; I will speak to my master tonight about it."

Edward scowled infuriated he jabbed a finger at Shin sharply in demand. "Do so, and I want you to find out what or who is sending storms trying to stop us from getting to our destination. I am not happy either that Mother Earth is asking my daughter to do things already; White Buffalo is only ten-years-old after all!"

Cecille let go of Edward's hands, reaching out White Buffalo put her arms around Dream Dancer to comfort him. "Ni-hoi, Po would never ask me to do something I couldn't do. She is teaching me many things so please don't worry so much; I was born to help keep the evil at bay. It is my destiny Dad to help the Mother Earth all I can..."

*****

Cecille was rudely brought back to the present by a gusty wind making the ropes sway violently; White Buffalo heard Shin swear as the Tianming Monk's left foot slipped off the line, they were only about eight feet from the top of the cliff. Unexpectedly, she froze in fear.

Misfit howled in panic then fought trying to get loose.

Cecille hearing Misfit cry out in fright moved back down the rope quickly trying to reach Shin in time; knowing if she didn't calm her dog down, they would all end up in the river. Time seemed to stop, all of a sudden. White Buffalo caught her breath in horror and held onto the top cable for dear life when the bottom rope under her feet just disappeared.

CHAPTER EIGHT

"MISFIT... stop that this instant!"

Misfit immediately froze when she heard her mistress scream her name in a fearful, angry commanding tone. The dog's ears perked up she turned her head as far as she could to see White Buffalo; Cecille's dog couldn't turn her head all the way, but it was enough now she was able to catch a glimpse of her mistress who was searching desperately for the rope.

Cecille dangling awkwardly tried desperately to find the rope that had disappeared beneath her feet. White Buffalo was strong enough she could climb the rest of the way hand over hand if she needed to. There was a bit of a problem though, the line Shin attached to the top rope was still fastened to the cord between them. Unfortunately, it would snag continually making it almost impossible to negotiate the last eight feet before becoming too exhausted to continue.

Shin sighed grimly in exasperation as he too searched desperately for the rope; he managed to get one foot on it before eventually the other one, he hoped Misfit would remain distracted long enough for him to become stabilized. The Tianming Monk looked over and saw Cecille also getting back on the bottom rope he deflated in relief.

It did not take Cecille long to get to Shin once she was stable.

Shin took Cecille's hand then put it on top of Misfit's head so she could reassure her; the Tianming Monk needed the animal to stay calm. "White Buffalo the wind is picking up the higher we go it's whistling through the rocks so scaring your dog; hurry, we are almost there."

Cecille nodded in understanding, without commenting she gave Misfit one more comforting pat and turned away to do what her Guardian asked. White Buffalo stayed closer to Shin this time so her dog could see her. Ten minutes later the Tianming Monk yelled out a warning just before she stepped off the rope onto the firm ground; the healer walked far enough away to allow Shadow Stalker some room, but it wasn't long before she dropped to her knees in relief.

Shin, quickly unhooked the rope from the top line, he was just thankful that he had the presence of mind to put an extra cable between them; it had just saved their lives. The Tianming Monk walked over before falling to his knees beside Cecille; for a long moment, they both gave heartfelt thanks to God the Great Spirit, for watching over them.

Shin sighed in resignation when Misfit began squirming around getting impatient to get down. She whined insistently when that didn't produce any results, wanting loose; the Tianming Monk pulled at the stubborn knot. "Shush girl, stay still will ya I can't untie you if you are moving around."

Shin was finally able to release Misfit after she quit squirming so much; the Tianming Monk sighed in relief when Cecille's dog ran off glad to have that done with.

Misfit barking in excitement raced down the trail then back, turning once more she again sprinted down the path. She was so ecstatic to be loose she couldn't help but make one more run before going to Cecille and jumping into her mistress's lap; the dog proceeded to lick White Buffalo's face in enthusiastic greeting.

Cecille laughed in delight before pushing Misfit away.

Shin frowned impatiently at Misfit, but said nothing trying hard to ignore the dog's antics; the Tianming Monk pulled off his water bag he passed it to Cecille. "Here White Buffalo, I brought drinking water and some food we will eat before continuing on."

Cecille nodded gratefully glad Shin had thought to grab something for them, she was starving; White Buffalo had nothing to eat since this morning, the thought of food caused her stomach to growl at her angrily.

Twenty minutes later, Misfit was leading Cecille. Shin followed them closely keeping their rear guarded they were once again going down a fairly steep hill. The Tianming Monk found a footprint not far from where they had eaten; the dog now had a viable scent for the boy, so she was following it.

Shin put the pouch he used to carry the food up in a tree since there wasn't much left, not wanting animals to tear it apart. He put the water back on his belt before coiling up the long rope; the shorter one the Tianming Monk left with his sack, one rope was enough. He put it over his shoulder than slung the gun strap over the long line holding it tight so it wouldn't bounce against him. Shadow Stalker brought the rifle because he hadn't gotten a chance to find another suitable long branch for a bow. Even while walking he continued to keep an eye out for a potential limb that might call to him.

The natives used all sorts of different tree types to make their bows as long as the wood was hard enough it didn't break easily when bent; anything from hickory, yew, oak, Osage orange, cedar, walnut or birch. Some even used bones from an animal if it was large enough the bow-shaped ribs didn't take much manipulating to get them to the desired shape.

Different plant fibres could get used for the drawstrings, they including nettles, dogbane, and milkweed. There were some braves that liked to make them with animal guts, but it took a lot of work to get a strip of sinew or rawhide thin enough; it was worth the extra time because it was way stronger and they also last a lot longer. Arrows were made from reeds or shoots such as dogwood, cattails, birch, oak, as well as the chokecherry.

Shin preferred the yew tree for his bow, chokecherry for the arrows. He also liked animal sinew for the drawstring; luckily, he always made sure to do two or three strings at one time, so he did have an extra waiting.

Having left the monastery so young Shin didn't have time to train extensively with the bow and only got a few lessons from a master. It gave him an edge when learning with the natives here since he was able to implement both teachings into one. It helped him become a master unequalled anywhere in Canada or his homeland. In the monastery, they shot arrows from the right side of the bow, but the natives shot their arrows from the left. It made quite a bit of difference in speed, plus the Tianming Monk could pick up enemy arrows then use them too before they could stop him. There was also the benefit of carrying his arrows in the same hand as the bow.

The Japanese bow or yumi was way different compared to the native bows here in Canada; especially when it came to length. The most well-liked bow when Shin left the monastery was the maruki yumi it was known as an asymmetrical bow, it was seven feet in height. Your hand didn't hold it in the centre, but the nigiri or grip was positioned two-thirds of the way down from the upper tip. The hand holding the yumi would experience less vibration that way. Traditionally the bow is made by laminating bamboo, wood, and leather. The Tianming Monk's used techniques that had not changed since the monastery got built.

There were different reasons offered for the asymmetric shape. Some believed it got designed for use on a horse. The yumi could be moved from one side of the horse to the other with ease, but there was evidence the asymmetrical shape was used before they rode horses. Another clan claimed that asymmetry got invented because it was the best when shooting from a kneeling position; a more straightforward explanation was that they used a single piece of wood at one time, way before anyone invented laminating.

Ontario's thick forested areas weren't friendly to the Japanese Yumi since it was way too tall. Shin modify it, what he ended up with was a cross between the asymmetric bow and the D-shaped heat-treated bow the natives preferred. He added the upper then the lower curve of the Yumi, but less pronounced so travelling through the forests wasn't as tricky and untangling the bow was not needed. The Tianming Monk didn't have the material to laminate his bow; he steamed it in a sweat lodge for two days to get it pliable enough to shape.

Shin borrowed the native's technique of roasting meat in an underground oven. He then built a platform to put his bow on so it wasn't directly in the fire or too close to the heat. It roasted the bow slowly to dry it after it got shaped. The Tianming Monk hadn't been so sure it would work at first; it wasn't long before he realized heating it made the bow a lot stronger. It also became better able to resist the damp temperatures of Ontario's climate.

*****

Shin shook off his thoughts quickly when he heard Misfit growl then back up into her mistress keeping Cecille from advancing any further. He frowned and went around the two so he could see what was upsetting the dog; he pulled the rifle off his shoulder just in case the Guardian needed it as he walked forward another ten steps.

Shin stopped in surprise as the monk looked around at the beautiful scene in front of him; no longer were they surrounded by trees, they were now on the edge of a wet field with spongy green moss that took over the firm ground. Tentatively, Shadow Stalker stepped out, he sank a bit but only a quarter of an inch before firm ground was felt.

Shin walked out a few more feet testing the marshy ground as he went, but it was firm and stable. There was moisture left in his footprints so their feet would get soaked by the time they reached the other side he knew. The only advantage that he could see was the boy's trail was more pronounced here; the Tianming Monk could easily identify the boot prints.

Shin turned to Cecille giving her a detailed description before voicing reassurances. "It's pretty marshy from here, but the ground is still very hard underneath. I found an excellent trail that we can follow; unfortunately, Misfit doesn't like the feel of the moss on her paws."

Shin whistled for Misfit to come then watched her in amusement; the Tianming Monk couldn't help laughing at the dog's antics.

Misfit tentatively put a paw down on the wet moss before snatching it back and whined at the wet, damp feel of the ground. Her nose was going none stop she didn't like it here, there was something not right about it. This place should be full of water, but there was none. The dog again pushed back against Cecille; refusing to let White Buffalo go any further.

Shin frowned in frustration before the Tianming Monk marched purposely back towards Cecille grimly. He wasn't amused by Misfit at all now; she wouldn't let her mistress go past. "White Buffalo, do I have to carry your Dog again!"

Cecille knelt then put her face on the side of Misfit's as she whispered reassurances in her dog's ear; she could feel her quivering in fear. White Buffalo eventually reached over to unhook the harness from Misfit. "You can stay here and wait for us girl I don't blame you at all. I also feel something's not quite right here!"

Cecille stood up she tucked the harness in her belt then reached out her hand to Shin. Knowing her Guardian the way she did White Buffalo had no doubts that he would have what she needed. "Please pass me my cane Shadow Stalker; Misfit knows that this is not natural, there should be water here and fish. I can even smell some in the distance rotting, but most of the wildlife here has cleaned them up already. I'm not sure why or where the water disappeared too."

Shin pulled the cane off his back, he had wedged it behind his sword just in case Cecille needed it, now he was glad he had; the Tianming Monk passed it to White Buffalo. "It is spongy, but firm. Here take the end of this rope then coil it in your hand loosely, I will stay in front checking the ground to make sure it remains firm."

Cecille did as she was told and coiled the rope around her hand, but not too tight. It was only to keep them connected so if either of them fell down the other one would know instantly. White Buffalo grimaced as she walked she was quite uncomfortable here; she could feel and hear a loud sucking sound coming from her feet as she walked forward.

Misfit whined loudly, she paced along the edge of the moss in agitation; the further away her mistress got, the faster she went until the dog sat on her haunches, howling in protest she tried to get Cecille to turn back. Ten minutes later her two pack leaders disappeared from view, it was more than she could stand.

Misfit jumped up, quickly she launched herself into the air; it was not long before she dropped onto the wet ground. The dog barely touched the moss when she once again leapt up trying to keep herself air-bound as long as she possibly could.

*****

Shin hearing a closer bark turned to look back. He couldn't help laughing at how funny Misfit looked as she hopped from one spot to the next; as she did so her floppy ears would lift before dropping with her. The Tianming Monk described what he saw to the baffled Cecille. "She looks just like an over-sized rabbit, especially with those long ears of hers."

Cecille laughed in amusement at Shin's description and waited for her dog to get to them before continuing on; White Buffalo left Misfit free instead of putting the harness on her because the cane was helping her keep her balance better in this damp slippery bog.

For half an hour they cautiously followed the boy's trail; the further they went, the more water was oozing into their footprints. Shin was beginning to get worried; dusk was not far off, soon they would have to go back or find somewhere to camp for the night. The Tianming Monk knew they were ill prepared for that.

Cecille heard water trickling over rocks, but there was no water here except for what was seeping into their footprints; White Buffalo rubbed her forehead in bafflement before calling out to Shin. "Shadow Stalker I need to stop for a moment, I can hear water rushing from somewhere!"

Shin sighed grimly in confusion as an unexpected shiver of foreboding rippled down the Tianming Monk's spine. "Yes I can hear it too, but I don't see any water nearby flowing for such a loud sound; there is definitely something not right, I can feel it now!"

Cecille frowned as she nodded agreeing with her Guardian; she squatted then put her palms on the ground searching for answers from the Mother Earth. White Buffalo eventually stood up with a scowl of uncertainty before gesturing all around her. "This is all part of the river, it gets quite deep at the start of spring and until yesterday there was water here. Usually as spring advances to early summer the water from the river recedes until there is barely any left; unless it is a wet year, the water will stay at that time. It is only June so the water level should be just below our shoulders. When the Earth tilted on its axis from the earthquakes yesterday something happened that caused the water to disappear. According to Po, it's now back in the river how it got there I couldn't figure out. I didn't feel any shifting here nor are we going down a hill, so I'm really confused."

Shin sighed resignedly as he turned back to the trail then lifted his free hand to shade his eyes from the lowering sun. The Tianming Monk could see a glint in the distance about three miles away, so he knew the river was getting closer with still no sign of the boy. Lucky for them, the trail was easy to follow since all the footprints were full of water. "Let's keep going White Buffalo, there is still daylight so I can continue to follow his tracks; once it gets dark we will have to rely exclusively on Misfit. I will tie the three of us together before it gets too hard to see so we don't get separated."

Cecille nodded in agreement; White Buffalo followed Shin dutifully without comment.

Shin stopped ten minutes later with a soft murmur of warning for Cecille to halt; the boy had jumped up onto a large rock it was about waist high. The Tianming Monk studied the indent where the toe had dug in deep, but hardly any heel was visible that is how he knew the youngster had jumped up on it. "White Buffalo there is a rock ahead that the boy climbed over. I'm not sure why he did I don't see anything particularly special about it, so we will go around it."

Cecille caulked her head listening intently before scratching her head in frustration, with a snort of irritation at her inability to find an answer; finally, she gestured towards her Guardian's voice. White Buffalo paused for only a moment then pointed at the ground grimly. "Shin I can hear rushing water again it is coming from the ground underneath us I think, it is way louder now!"

Shin frowned thoughtfully as a suspicion began to form, but he still couldn't see any way it was possible yet; he turned left and skirted the rock without commenting on his charges opinion needing to find proof he was right first before mentioning his hunch. When they got to the other side of the stone the Tianming Monk walked ahead searching, no tracks were visible, so he went further. The boy probably jumped off the rock, being young he would have vaulted as far as he could go which would be a little further on the Guardian surmised.

"Ouch!"

Cecille cried out in surprise before frowning perturbed when Misfit jumped up against her chest unexpectedly with a growl of fear. Instinctively, she grabbed her dog close as they both fell backward. White Buffalo's yelp turned into a scream of horror as the ground unexpectedly disappeared under her feet; falling, she clutched the rope in her hand desperately.

Cecille's arm was wrenched out of its socket suddenly causing her to screech even louder when pain ripped through her shoulder as the rope she was holding tightened. Thankfully it slowed White Buffalo's descent, which caused her to swing to the left; the rope uncoiling from her hand flung her further away.

Cecille's painful outcry died abruptly then a brief silence prevailed for a long moment; allowing her to hear the shouted cry of shock from Shin above. Seconds later she heard Misfit howling in fear as the jerk hurled her dog with her cane away from her. Suddenly, all other sounds were drowned out by the roar of rushing water below. White Buffalo's head hit a rock with such force that the thunk echoed eerily over and over again reverberated off the cavernous rocks, but she never heard that.

*****

"Ugghh!"

Shin yelped in shock when he was unexpectedly yanked right off his feet. He fell flat on his back onto the hard ground and was dragged backward for a few feet but managed to flip himself onto his stomach. The Tianming Monk dug his booted feet into the soft marshy ground before digging his fingers into the spongy moss as hard as he could. Thankfully, he halted at the edge of the sinkhole that Cecille unfortunately just disappeared into. His head was actually inside the hole; he could see it was a thirty-foot drop from here maybe more!

The rope coiled around Shin's shoulder yanked him so hard it almost pulled him right into the gaping hole. He cried out in horrified surprise, it took him several long moments to be able to focus his eyesight when the pain almost overwhelmed him. Finally, the Guardian's sight cleared enough for him to see White Buffalo and Misfit. They were both lying lifelessly on the rocks below but from here there was nothing he could do; groaning in denial, the Tianming Monk pushed himself backward onto firm ground.

Shin quickly jumped to his feet before running to the closest rock, uncoiling the rest of the rope as he went. Lucky for him he had been able to brace himself against the edge of the sinkhole; it helped to keep the line from unravelling from his shoulder. The Tianming Monk looked up briefly thanking Shen for the foresight in keeping the rifle draped over the rope. It had wedged the line between the shotgun, the ground, and his sword. Shadow Stalker knew it was the only reason he had managed to keep the rope from falling in the cave with White Buffalo.

Shin quickly tied the rope tight around a smaller rock that was closer to the hole; thankfully, it was large enough that it would support quite a bit of weight. Shadow Stalker rushed back to the edge of the drop off, Cecille's Guardian threw the rest of the line down then turned. The Tianming Monk lowered himself carefully until he reached the end of the rope.

Shin still had a ten-foot drop to where Cecille was plus there was a deep hole to the right if he miscalculated he could end up in there; the Guardian had no idea how deep it was. Swinging his legs the Tianming Monk managed to get a good rotation going. Satisfied he was close enough to White Buffalo, Shadow Stalker let go of the rope before dropping into a crouch beside his charge.

Shin shuddered in despair as he stared down in horror at Cecille's battered bleeding body; there was blood everywhere, whether it was all hers or mostly the dogs since White Buffalo had landed partway on Misfit he couldn't say for sure. The Tianming Monk took the rifle off his shoulder, kneeling he put it on the ground before removing his sword.

Shin tenderly scooped Cecille up into his arms, standing he turned before taking her to flatter ground. Thankfully, it was close to the cave wall so he could lean back against it if he needed to; the Tianming Monk carefully sat with her in his lap. He put his cheek against her lips in relief, the Guardian felt a faint flutter of air as his charge struggled to breathe.

Shin quickly began chanting in his native language before rocking Cecille; he pleaded with God, the Great Spirit for help. Unfortunately, the Tianming Monk didn't have his carpet here he would have to rely on his charges will to live. Unnoticed, tears made rivulets down his dirt-streaked face falling on White Buffalo's broken, bleeding body.

*****

Cecille could feel herself floating, which kept the excruciating pain a distant memory. Where she was, she couldn't remember or even how she ended up like this. White Buffalo felt helpless, which was an entirely new feeling for her. Never had she ever felt so vulnerable, she began to feel fear... was she dead? No, that was impossible; she was too important to die for some reason. Why she couldn't remember!

Slowly sensations began to be felt and heard; a chanting started niggling at Cecille's subconscious. She couldn't understand what was being said, but she knew that it must be important. White

Buffalo concentrated on that voice slowly it pulled her a little more into the present. She could feel an omnipresence emitting from somewhere, she sensed that it wasn't the one chanting. It was trying to talk to her, but it only caused her pain when she tried to listen.

Cecille's breath caught in wonder when a field of beautiful wildflowers appeared unexpectedly in front of her, with every colour imaginable present. A mountain in the far distance made her giggle like an awestruck fifteen-year-old; she could see everything around her. Slowly she walked forward with both hands opened letting the flowers brush her fingertips in reverence. White Buffalo continued on when the presence became stronger. Without even realizing she was doing it, she searched for whatever was compelling her forward.

Cecille stopping in uncertainty at an image in the distance it was huge, towering so high she had to crane her neck up to see. Still, White Buffalo couldn't quite distinguish what it was she was looking at. The sun was directly behind the entity, which hurt her sensitive eyes so she had to squint; even then she couldn't look at it entirely. The light continued to brighten until she had no choice but to look away.

A light breeze came out of nowhere rippling across the flowers before it fluttered around Cecille. A disembodied voice could be heard in the wind if you concentrated hard enough, whether male or female was uncertain. **"You are troubled my child; I have felt your disquieting thoughts for some time now?"**

Cecille frowned in frustration, she had tried so hard to keep her feelings a secret but White Buffalo should have known it wouldn't stay hidden for long. "I have many questions; why my family, why must we be blind, and will we ever be free from this curse?"

Cecille stopped her rant in mid-sentence in surprise as a laugh floated on the breeze. It reminded her of a gentle trickle of water over rocks or the hum of bees in flight; maybe it was the flutter of hummingbird wings when they hovered over a flower. It had a feminine tone to it, shocking White Buffalo into silence.

"Ah, such dramatics... you are not totally blind are you? If you are, then it is your own doing nobody else's. You can see beyond what any other person alive at this time can. You might not be able to see the different colours of the world but you see the truth, even the soul of the Earth if you wish. People have gotten so used to seeing the outside shell they lost the ability to see beyond, life is a circle that keeps evolving just like the Earth. I

AM never cursed your family, only made sure that because of your sacrifices and devotion to the Mother Earth, your descendants will forever continue in the life cycle. Every time you give a spirit name to a person you are saving their line of descendants from extinction, so choose wisely Healer; I AM as well as the Mother Earth, are counting on you!"

Cecille frowned incredulously now that there was a short pause. She could hardly believe what she was being told. Why was God... the Great Spirit, even telling her this? It must be some lesson or test so she better pay attention what White Buffalo was supposed to do with this information she would have to discuss with Shin. The Tianming Monk's had a special bond with Shen; she shook off her thoughts when words began once more to float all around her.

"Animals even humans can sometimes become extinct, while others evolve beyond expectation. Humankind or people, as they are called now, are the perfect example. I AM created them to be companions, to help take care of Mother Earth. They evolved beyond what was intended, so now they are destroying what they should be protecting. I AM even tried living among them for a time to teach them, it didn't help! Once a full circle is again complete, will the people or humans be the same... possibly! Will they be the dominant species, maybe! All I can tell you is that the truth is out there for you to see, will the people want to know the truth? NO, they do not; the people have destroyed most of the facts leaving only what they want others to know to keep them ignorant, but the time will come regardless of their wishes. Just like the ones that had come before them learned although too late to stop their extinction!"

Cecille cringed at the angry biting tone as it thundered through her skull; it was hard for her to keep following the Great Spirit's reverberating sound. She sighed in relief when the wind softened then it changed portraying a definite sorrowful tone when Shen spoke of the others that were once here. What others, there were other humans before us? White Buffalo was glad when there was another short pause trying to collect her frantic thoughts, but it was impossible. She felt the wind pick up once again as the voice floating through the air continued.

"The Earth has changed countless times since its birth. Lucifer's treacherous reign brought the heavens crashing down, which destroyed the Earth's surface causing a barren lifeless world. No sun, moon, or stars for centuries were visible causing

a freeze that paralyzed Mother Earth for thousands of years; until the re-creation of the dead Earth that I AM brought back to life before it was repopulated in seven days."

Cecille perked up at that revelation, she had read about it somewhere. White Buffalo just couldn't remember where exactly. She remembered talking to Shin about it though... on the ship maybe! Quickly, she shook off her thoughts so she could listen intently; having confirmation to the many unanswered questions was exciting.

"A rebellion by the sons of God or angels as the humans liked to call them, brought the reign of the giants. I AM called them Nephilim, the Giants are the children of the Grigori, half watchers and half human. So again the Mother Earth was sacrificed when floodwaters rushed in causing Noah's flood, which destroyed the offspring's of the fallen angels. Noah's family has always been, plus they will always be not only the catalyst that brings disaster to the Earth but they are also her salvation; they are born to be Paladins, Guardians, and powerful Healers to keep the Mother Earth strong.

"Cecille's mouth dropped open in shock, she was a direct descendant of Noah's that would explain her affinity to the Earth; she couldn't help feeling curious wondering which one of her parents had such distinctive bloodlines, her mother or her father. White Buffalo wasn't sure if she liked the fact that her family would destroy the Earth, but she was glad her descendants will save her in the end. When the wind picked up, she leaned forward eagerly wanting to know more engrossed in the tale.

"There will be one final altercation between the higher powers, sadly the Mother Earth will again be sacrificed... this time by fire; your descendants will be her salvation they will bring her out of the ashes to become glorious as the life cycle comes back full circle. That which was hidden will again be released as I AM leads the people to another beginning!"

Cecille listened closely but the feminine tone apparent in the first chuckle had disappeared; again she couldn't distinguish if it was male or female. White Buffalo shrugged in irritation what did it matter, anyway!

Cecille dropped to her knees before bowing her head; White Buffalo raised both arms in supplication. "I'm sorry Shen, my God the Great Spirit of all living things for questioning you; I am now and will forever be your servant, I will never doubt you again!"

Cecille heard a deeper chuckle this time. It reminded her of crashing waves against a rocky shore or the deep croaking of the bullfrogs. It was definitely male sounding; White Buffalo shook her head in irritation at herself. The creator was a divine or celestial being there would be no gender so why was she trying to put one on Shen. She grimaced it was a human trait to automatically call anything living and even some things that weren't, he or she wanting to humanize it.

"Child I don't believe that for one second, you will always ask questions as well as be defiant when it counts. You have many trials yet to go through before you can become all that you are meant to be. Remember, only you can accept your destiny. Noah's bloodline wasn't chosen for its compliance, but for its strength of will to do what needs to be done; their leadership abilities plus their deep capacity for love and compassion. You will make mistakes along the way, but Mother Earth will always be there if you need to talk. Go now, your Guardian is beginning to think you are dead and he will forfeit his life if he thinks you have died!"

The field of wildflowers disappeared just as quickly as it had appeared; Cecille felt herself floating in nothingness once more. She could feel her body mending itself, this wasn't the first time it had taken over to heal her. Years ago she had broken her leg, but by the evening it was completely recovered. White Buffalo could hear her Guardian chanting. She concentrated on Shin's voice, keeping herself in-between worlds to give her body the time it needed to mend her broken bones.

Cecille's thoughts turned to Shen, the Great Spirit of all living things; she was completely confused by what she had heard... how was she keeping herself blind? When she touched someone she could see auras which gave White Buffalo shapes. Usually, they were white, grey, or black lines that had a pattern to them seldom was there any other colours. Was she supposed to be seeing that all the time or maybe there needed to be colours showing, if so what could be blocking that ability from manifesting fully.

Shin had also mentioned a few times that he didn't need to be touching a person to view their auras only be close enough to see it. Unlike Cecille, who had to touch a person to look at the patterns! The same with Mother Earth, at one time White Buffalo never needed to be in contact with the Earth to feel or talk to Po; now for some reason she did.

'**Nephilim**,' Cecille shook her head perplexed. She would have to ask Shin if he knew anything about them she had no clue who or what they were. As for the reference to others, '**Just like the ones that had come before**', she was quite curious to know who they could be; Shen mentioning them made White Buffalo think of stories her Celtic mother's people used to tell of fairies, trolls, elves, and many other magical or unbelievable creatures. Could they have lived at the same time as the Nephilim that the Great Spirit had mentioned or possibly even in Lucifer's time?

Cecille shook her head in confusion then turned her thoughts to the circle of life; it wasn't a new concept to her since most natives held strong beliefs in it. They believed that life will come full circle and they will once again return to being caretakers of Mother Earth, which the whites had stolen from them. The fact that the Great Spirit wouldn't say whether humans would continue as they are had her a bit anxious; White Buffalo was sure she heard an unyielding note of anger at the people for destroying truths. When or how they had been destroyed Shen hadn't said, she wisely didn't ask either.

Cecille had called God, Shen as well as Great Spirit, with no angry outburst over it. The Great Spirit had used, '**I AM**' quite a few times in their conversation earlier. White Buffalo's nanny had read the Bible to her when she was a child, several names were used in it for God; although, the Great Spirit seemed to prefer... '**I AM**.'

Cecille felt deep down that as long as one believed, the name used wasn't as important as some people seemed to think. Take her for instance, she had several names given to her by Elijah; he named her Cecille Luan Gweneal, so any one of these names she would answer to. Plus there was her native name, professional name then her surname that she would also answer to; White Buffalo, Dr. Summerset, and Miss Summerset were all relevant at any time.

Unexpectedly, Cecille's head began spinning; swirling so fast White Buffalo wanted to throw up... again!

CHAPTER NINE

Cecille, felt her subconscious being pulled back to her body, and it wasn't long before White Buffalo opened her green unseeing eyes.

Shin quit chanting instantly, he couldn't help giving a huge sigh of relief before looking up he thanked Shen; the Tianming Monk kissed the top of Cecille's forehead gratefully.

Cecille reached up and tenderly stroked Shin's cheek; White Buffalo's feelings for the Tianming Monk were strong, but they were for a brother, not a lover. "Thank you Shadow Stalker, will you be alright?"

Shin nodded against Cecille's hand; the Tianming Monk had just a slight tremble in his voice it was hardly noticeable unless you knew him well. "Yes, I am now!"

Cecille paused, she anxiously frowned when she thought back; all she could remember was her dog howling in fright. White Buffalo feared to ask but needed to know inquired with a distinct dreadful quiver in her tone. "Misfit?"

Shin shook his head sadly against Cecille's hand the Tianming Monk was almost positive the dog was dead. "I only saw one leg twitch about a half hour ago I think; I'm sorry White Buffalo, but it doesn't look like Misfit made it!"

Cecille rolled off Shin's lap quickly; White Buffalo's voice wavered uneasily. "Where is she?"

Shin stood then helped the still weak Cecille up; he led White Buffalo over to her dog. The Tianming Monk squinted in the fading light from above, but he could not see any movement at all. He had little hope that Misfit was still alive, for his charges sake he wanted to be wrong!

Cecille dropped to her knees before chanting feverishly. If Misfit were dead there wasn't anything she could do about it but if there was a faint breath in her; White Buffalo could heal her if Mother Earth and the Great Spirit allowed it.

Cecille laid her cheek down on Misfit's chest quickly, a tiny inkling of hope surfaced; her dog was still quite warm. For several minutes, she chanted waiting for any sign of life, sadly there was none. White Buffalo's breath caught in her throat as a sob threatened.

Cecille started sitting back up, but paused instead at a tiny unexpected whimper. Instantly, White Buffalo laid both hands over

Misfit's chest then her chanting intensified as she pleaded to the Great Spirit to allow the healing.

Shin, needing something to do to occupy himself while he waited picked up his sword and sheathed it. He grabbed the rifle then draped it over his left shoulder since the right one was somewhat tender to the touch. The monk got up before walking to the far corner where he had noticed Cecille's cane had come to rest. Shadow Stalker scooped it up, turning the Guardian returned. Kneeling beside her, he held his breath waiting; the Tianming Monk knew how much Misfit meant to his charge. If her dog died now in this way, White Buffalo would never forgive herself he knew.

Cecille felt the power surge through her veins before her healing energy entered the dog's body, it didn't take long for Misfit to want up; White Buffalo quit chanting instantly.

Cecille spent several minutes fending off Misfit's happy, sloppy kisses with a relieved chuckle she had never tried to heal an animal before. White Buffalo was just glad it had worked; she turned in the general direction of her Guardian in question. "Any sign of the Boy, Shin?"

Shin frowned as he stood up looking around speculatively. The Tianming Monk hadn't given the boy a thought since all his attention remained focused on helping Cecille heal herself. "No, and these caverns look pretty extensive, as well as dark. The boy could be anywhere down here. We don't even know where he would have fallen in; I didn't see any other holes in the ground around this area!"

Cecille grimaced in frustration then put both hands against the ground asking Mother Earth where the boy was at. She was taken deep inside the caverns before she felt him scared, shivering in the cold and hurt. White Buffalo stood up and still chanting she reached out for Shin's hand so they would stay connected. She gratefully accepted her cane needing its stability; she kept it held out in front following a trail that only she could see.

It took them at least a half hour as they wound slowly around obstacles with the blind Cecille leading the way. Here Shin couldn't see a thing, so had to rely on his charge entirely; it was a new experience for him, one he wasn't sure he liked at all. The Tianming Monk's respect for White Buffalo grew more profound, especially now that he understood how she felt every single day.

Cecille paused, at a roaring sound in the distance. White Buffalo caulked her head listening intently before turning to Shin. "The river is just ahead over time the water has slowly worn down the rocks making these caverns; they go right to the edge of the river. The Earth shifting on its axis weakened the ground in some areas opening sinkholes, two for sure I don't feel any other disturbances yet."

Cecille went back to chanting she knelt to touch the Mother Earth to pick up the trail again. Rising she took Shin's hand she continued to lead him. The sound of the river was growing louder; it seemed a lot closer once they entered another massive cavern. They only went ten steps inside when Misfit growled then jumped in front of White Buffalo keeping her from advancing further.

Shin able to see better in this extensive cavern, pulled Cecille backward behind him. The Tianming Monk looked around curiously the hole had a ray of sunlight shining directly on it, which was giving enough light for him to see. The Guardian looked up, the daylight was coming from the ceiling but it was too high for him to see the opening. He was still a little unsure; although, it was possible for the boy to have fallen in right here. If he did, Stanley must have dropped straight down into the crevice. "There is a large hole in front of you, White Buffalo!"

Cecille frowned disgruntled; White Buffalo nudged Shin in concern, she needed the Tianming Monk to check the hole. "The boy is here somewhere the feeling is really strong now!"

Shin scowled grimly when Cecille confirmed his suspicion, would the boy be able to survive such a fall was his next unvoiced question. He pulled his rifle off his shoulder before getting on all fours, the Tianming Monk had to push a curious Misfit out of his way; Shadow Stalker crawled close to the edge of the hole. "Hello is anyone down there?"

Instantly they both heard a fearful cry for help. "I am stuck down here!"

Cecille knelt quickly then put both hands against the ground searching. White Buffalo looked over at Shin musingly, describing what she saw. "Stanley is quite a ways below us; this hole tapers getting smaller the further down you go which makes it too tight for either one of us to drop beside him!"

Shin sighed in relief, Stanley was alive; how the boy had managed to fall that distance without killing himself was a question for later. He examined the crevice carefully before looking over at Cecille in speculation it might just work. The Tianming Monk pulled White Buffalo closer to the fissure, wanting her to check for herself. "The hole is large enough that either one of us would fit in there but our best bet would be for me to hold your legs. Hopefully, he will be able to reach your hands."

Misfit went back to sniffing around the hole inquisitively once Shin got up; Cecille's dog could smell the boy but also a strange odour. Suddenly, the dog whined before growling she didn't like the rank foul smell coming from inside.

Cecille gathered her long hair into a bundle then coiled it into a tight rope that she had Shin tuck into the back of her shirt, she had forgotten to look for her hat. Kneeling she spent several minutes feeling around the crevice, in irritation she had to push Misfit out of her way; her dog was trying to keep her away from the hole. Slowly, White Buffalo began inching her way inside. She felt Shin grab her legs, so she slithered down more. "Stanley, I need you to reach up as far as you can and grab hold of my hands we will pull you up!"

"Who are you, how do you know my name?"

Cecille could hear a lot of fear, with a touch of uncertainty plain in the young boy's voice. Thankfully, talking gave her something to concentrate on taking White Buffalo's mind off the wet slimy feel of the walls. She shuddered in revulsion when the mud clung to her then answered the frightened boy. "Your Mother told me your name; she is quite worried about you. My name is Cecille, my friend is Shin, and my ever faithful dog is Misfit... can you reach my hands yet?"

Stanley brightened at the mention of a dog; he reached up trying to find the woman's hands. If she had an animal they must be okay. His mother always told him that a dog would only stay with people it trusted. If an animal didn't like someone, there was usually a reason so he should stay away from them. "I have a dog too his name is Blacky how did you manage to get in here with a dog!"

Cecille felt a light brushing of fingertips against hers, Stanley couldn't quite reach them though; White Buffalo called up to Shin beseechingly. "I need a little more I almost have him!"

Shin yelled down at Cecille grimly, with an unmistakable strain in his voice; the Tianming Monk knew that he couldn't hold White Buffalo like this much longer. "I can't lower you any further there is just no way that I would be able to pull you both up if I did!"

Shin looked around desperately searching there had to be another way; the Tianming Monk was about to give up but then Cecille's dog drew his angry gaze.

Misfit barked sharply; it echoed over and over again as it reverberated through the tunnels. The dog cowered down fearfully looking around frantically for other dogs. When the sound faded, she got up then whined plaintively at Cecille before pacing impatiently. She didn't like her mistress down there one bit.

Shin furiously shushed Misfit, who knew what kind of animals or creatures were down here. The Tianming Monk noticed Cecille's cane lying on the ground when the whimpering dog moved; he looked again at the hole and back at the walking stick in calculation before grinning it just might work! "White Buffalo I'm going to pull you back up I have another idea that will be better!"

"Don't leave me please!"

Cecille heard the distressed cry which caused her throat to close up in a sympathetic reaction. White Buffalo gulp back tears at the desperate sound. She had to swallow several times before she could reassure the boy. "I promise Stanley we will be back as quick as we can; you need to be strong for me now, okay?"

"I will try!"

Shin grunted then pulled back for all he was worth; slowly, he felt his charge move up an inch. The amount of effort it was taking him was tremendous. He knew he was right there was no way Shadow Stalker could have pulled both of them from that hole at the same time. The Tianming Monk dug his heels into the ground to gain leverage as he heaved until Cecille was able to push herself the rest of the way out. They both dropped onto their backs breathing heavily in exertion for several long minutes.

Misfit rushed to Cecille then licked her mistress's face before lying down against her in relief.

Shin eventually stood up and unstrapped his sword sheath before pulling out his arrows. He put them on the ground with his rifle a safe distance away, the Tianming Monk's daggers soon followed. He walked over and picked up the walking stick; afterwards, he went back to the hole to measure its length. Shadow Stalker grinned relieved it should work. To give himself a little extra leverage he pulled the sword that was hidden inside out about an inch then laid the cane across the crevice. "Cecille your walking stick is long enough to go across the hole; I will lower myself using it to keep me close to the opening, this way I will not get wedged in there too. Once inside, the boy can climb up my body to get out."

Cecille frowned in surprise; she sat up slowly thinking furiously. White Buffalo had her doubts that her walking stick was sturdy enough. "Are you sure the cane will be enough to hold not just your weight, but the both of you combined?"

Shin grimaced as he rubbed his chin irritably before he let out a frustrated breath. The Tianming Monk shrugged unknowingly, even though he knew Cecille couldn't see it; it was an automatic movement, usually done without thinking. "I can't be sure White Buffalo, but with the rapier inside I am hoping it will be!"

Cecille scowled thinking furiously; she tucked her long hair behind her ears in annoyance. Several strands had come loose when she was getting lifted up she had lost her hat somewhere. White Buffalo knew they had no choice, but to try it. Although, with the walls so muddy there was still one more alternative she was contemplating. "Well, it is worth a try I suppose; I notice the walls are quite damp so if that doesn't work one of us can brace against the wall before sliding down until we get close to him. Afterwards, we can dig holes in the dirt walls then he can climb if he can manage it. Stanley is hurt, I'm not sure how badly yet. If I can reach the boy, I can heal him down there if I have too!"

Shin grunted in agreement before turning away without comment; he left it up to Cecille to give the boy instructions. When White Buffalo moved back the Tianming Monk sat on the edge of the hole, he leaned forward and grasped the cane then pulled himself over it. The Guardian hung there with his arms braced testing it, but it held his weight easily with only a slight give as the ends dug into the firm soil. Once sure it could take the weight, Shadow Stalker lowered himself down until his arms were all the way extended. "Stanley, can you reach my feet yet?"

Shin thankfully felt Stanley's hand grasp his ankle it was pitch black inside the hole since the Tianming Monk blocked the light that had been shining in. Not able to see what the boy was doing; the Guardian broadened his senses trying to grasp what was happening below him, all he could hear was a frustrated mumble before a sob of fear.

Stanley grunting tried to pull himself up, but the mud all around him kept sucking him back in he couldn't get away from it; giving up the boy let go of Shin with a wail of frustration. "I can't get out of here, please help me!"

Shin heard the panic plain in the boy's tone. The Tianming Monk kept his voice calm not wanting the youngster to start thrashing around he might end up hurting himself more. "It's okay Stanley I can flip myself to make a hole right above you so my feet will fit inside to give me leverage. I can haul you up that way; I promise it will not be much longer."

Shin lifted himself back up then out. The Tianming Monk looked over at Cecille. "Stanley can't get out, so I am going to try your idea of holes dug into the sides. Can you hand me the rifle White Buffalo on your left as well as one dagger please? After I lower myself I want you to sit on the edge of the hole; when I'm ready, I will holler up so you can hold my feet it will give me stability."

Cecille did as asked; White Buffalo was getting concerned with Stanley's ability to cope. She had heard the panic quite clearly from here in his voice but all she could do now was pray.

Shin took his dagger from Cecille; he put it in his mouth backward making sure that the thicker flat side was first. Afterwards, he put the rifle over the hole beside the cane. The Tianming Monk lowered himself until his arms were fully extended. When in position he curled himself in half before lifting his legs through the opening, over the walking stick and the rifle so his knees would hold him! Shadow Stalker didn't hang down quite as far now, but that wouldn't matter. If he could dig a hole in the wall on one side deep enough his two feet would be able to fit inside; he could put his back to the opposite side then slither down as far as the Guardian could go.

Shin could make another hole in the opposite side later if need be, but it didn't look like one was needed; the Tianming Monk was pretty sure he could reach the boy from there. Taking the knife out of his mouth he called up. "Okay, White Buffalo I am ready now!"

Shin, thankfully felt Cecille holding his feet tightly it gave him the ability to move without worrying that his motions would dislodge him from his precarious perch. The Tianming Monk called down to the boy in caution. "Stanley there will be dirt falling as I dig a hole, I will try to make sure the dirt falls as close to the wall as possible; is everything okay down there, you said you are stuck can you tell me how and what is keeping you there?"

"Mud, it is really thick and gooey... deep too, just above my belly button! When I try to move, it holds me even tighter but if I stay still it is less clinging. I think my right leg is broken just below my knee because I hit it on the way down; the muck seems to be helping it cause it don't hurt no more. I keep feeling little pin pricks where the mud is touching me; I'm getting pretty tired too, it is hard for me to keep from falling asleep even while I am talking to you. A voice in my head says I can lie on top of the muck and float so I can sleep, I haven't because it scares me badly."

Shin frowned grimly then his digging became more frantic there must be leeches in the mud weakening the boy. He needed to keep him talking and awake. The Tianming Monk now had his answer on how Stanley managed to survive such a long fall, if the wet dirt was sloppy enough it would soften his landing, as quicksand would do. "Try moving around to loosen the surrounding mud some; it might stop it from clinging. I met your Mother today; she tells me you like fishing. I love fishing too, what kind of fish are in this river?"

Cecille listened to the two talking; she frowned in concern at the boy's comment of pin pricks than something telling him to lay in the mud and sleep. Her first thought just like Shin's was also leeches, until Stanley mentioned the voice that didn't sound like a bloodsucker to her. White Buffalo consulted the Mother Earth. It was not long before her grimace of anxiety turned to one of fear. They needed to get the boy out of there as fast as possible. He didn't hear an actual voice it was his own subconscious telling him to sleep. The mud ticks latched onto his spinal column were sending signals to his brain that sleep was needed. If the boy complied he would sleep all right, but it would be an eternal sleep!

Cecille still in meditation followed the caverns on the left to the river; the Mother Earth pulled her back insistently before taking her further to the right into a different cavern. The healer had to take Stanley there first, they must not leave the cave with the mud ticks embedded in the boy; White Buffalo's healing wouldn't get rid of them either. Most if not all the creatures in these caverns were thought to be extinct, they had never seen daylight.

Shin finished digging, wiped the knife on his pants. He called up in warning to Cecille so she would let go of his feet before putting the blade backward in his mouth again. His stomach muscles rippled when he used them to lift himself. The Tianming Monk grasped the cane with two hands; uncoiling his legs he lowered them. Searching the far wall the Guardian found the hole he had made, the monk stuck both his feet inside. Moving to the far side of the walking stick he pushed himself against the wall. Gingerly, Shadow Stalker let go of the cane. He sighed in relief when the niche for his feet held. He didn't slip down even a little. Thankfully, there had only been a half an inch of soft mud behind it was firm hard clay.

Shin taking the knife out of his mouth, shoved it into the muddy wall as hard as he could beside him. This way he would have a little more stability when it embedded into the hard slimy clay halfway up the blade. Holding the dagger for balance the Tianming Monk slithered down the slick wall before stopping then wiggled the knife until it was loose. He pulled it from the wall; again he shoved it into the mud close to him. Shadow Stalker did that twice until Cecille's Guardian was practically sitting.

Shin pulled out the dagger and reaching down he began digging another hole. Stanley having assured Cecille's Guardian that he was stuck fast knew he would need a lot more leverage. Shadow Stalker quickly finished since this gap didn't need to be as big as the first one. He reached up with his knife so he could reinsert the blade where it had been earlier to pull himself upwards; twice more the Tianming Monk did that until he was almost entirely upright again.

Shin moved his left foot out of the hole that was on the right before sticking it into the slot that he just made; holding both sides of the wall, he bent his knees then slowly pulled his arms in relinquishing his grasp, testing his perch. Luckily there was still no give although his legs were spread a bit far it was not unbearably uncomfortable. The Tianming Monk sighed in relief, bending at the waist he reached down as far as he could. "Stanley can you get a hold of my hands you might have to jump up to grasp them."

Shin not being able to see anything had to rely on his hearing. Suddenly, detecting a grunt and a loud sucking sound he braced himself as the full weight of the boy grabbing hold of him almost caused him to be pulled headfirst upside down.

Thankfully, the small hole prevented that. Gritting his teeth Shin heaved the boy up with him until the Tianming Monk was standing upright; now the youngster was hanging by his arms, his head was above the Guardian's calves. "Stanley, when I lift you all the way up, put your left foot in the hole beside my foot. Afterwards, I want you to push yourself backward to brace yourself against the wall so I can bend down. When ready you can get on my shoulders, it should make you tall enough for Cecille to pull you out of the hole; can you do that for me?"

Stanley nodded his head hard in agreement. "Yes!"

Shin's arm muscles bulged outward in strain, causing him to groan in exertion. The boy not only outweighed the Guardian, but he was close to the same height. Lifting Stanley up by the hands as far as he could the Tianming Monk felt the boy searching with his left foot since his right was useless. The ten-year-old finally lodged it beside his before pushing himself against the wall as instructed. Shadow Stalker sighed in relief when the boy steadied. "Okay, I'm going to swing around first. When I bend down crawl on my shoulders so I can lift you, try to push yourself forward as quick as you can; if you need to grasp my shirt or hair to keep yourself upright, you can."

Stanley bit the bottom of his lip in uncertainty, but what choice did he have; he had to trust a man he could hardly see. "Okay, I am ready."

Shin bending his knees launched upwards; at the same time he twisted one full rotation before grasping the cane up above him. Now facing the opposite direction the Tianming Monk lowered himself back down until his feet once again rested inside the holes.

Holding onto the wall with his back now to the boy Shin squatted as far as he could. He pushed himself backwards positioning himself between Stanley's legs. The Tianming Monk was now up against the far wall, he felt the boy crawl onto his shoulders. He put his hands under the youngster's thighs mindful of the broken right lower leg.

Shin with muscles bulging in his legs groaned in determination as he slowly stood up. Once upright fully, he stayed still for several minutes inhaling and exhaling deeply as his legs followed closely by his stomach muscles, spasmed. Normally, this position would not be a problem for him; the Tianming Monk could lift way more weight than Stanley, it was the awkward way he was standing that was causing the problem. Usually, his legs would not be spread this far apart. The Guardian called up in warning to Cecille, his voice quivered in strain. "White Buffalo are you ready for him?"

Cecille kneeling beside the hole listening intently quickly moved the cane and rifle out of her way when she heard Shin's instructions to Stanley. White Buffalo impatiently had to push a whining dog out of her way again Misfit kept trying to get her away from the crevice; she had not scolded her for it knowing that she was only doing her job by trying to keep her mistress out of danger. She called down in reassurance. "Yes, I am!"

Shin took several deep, steadying breaths. Suddenly, he heaved the boy upwards over top his head, with a grunt of exertion. The Tianming Monk's muscles bulged once again straining upwards he was able to lock his arms into position, trying to keep Stanley above his head. The two almost toppled forward, but Shadow Stalker's quick reflexes kept them upright.

It wouldn't have mattered Shin knew since the tight confines of the hole would have kept them erect; although, awkwardly tilted. "Here he comes, White Buffalo!"

Cecille reached down as far as she could, she was careful not to lean so far over that she was in danger of being pulled into the hole; White Buffalo called down grimly with a distinct urgent tone to her voice. "Take my hands, Stanley."

Cecille stood up from her crouch with a groan of effort as she heaved the boy out of the hole; instantly, White Buffalo sat Stanley down. She turned before picking up the cane then put it back over the crevice. "Hurry Shin you need to get out of there!"

Shin grimaced in aggravation at a tingling stinging sensation where the mud was clinging to his neck and shoulders. Hearing Cecille's plea, he pulled his dagger out of the wall before sticking it back in his sash, crouching the Guardian launched himself into the air. Grasping the cane the monk pulled himself up so he could brace himself over top of the walking stick; now, the Tianming Monk would not be able to fall back inside.

Shin pushed himself backward out of the hole; letting go of the cane he dropped exhausted onto the ground. With his hands free, the Tianming Monk scratched at the mud on his neck in irritation.

Misfit yipped in excitement; she raced around the hole in the ground. She had reluctantly retreated there after Cecille pushed her away. The dog was ecstatic to see her second favourite pack mate out of danger... "MISFIT, stay!"

Cecille turned in the direction of her Guardian once Misfit dropped into a confused crouch obediently; White Buffalo had her cane, Shin's sword, his other knife, the rifle, plus the remaining arrows that he miraculously held onto all in one hand. "Shadow Stalker pick up Stanley, you will have to carry him... hurry! I will take your hand then lead you we must get out of here!"

Shin hearing the urgency in Cecille's voice did as he was told, it was seldom the Tianming Monk heard panic in White Buffalo's tone; he heard it now though, she would explain later he knew.

Cecille grabbed Shin's shirt sleeve tightly, once he was standing with Stanley awkwardly cradled in his arms. The healer pulled her Guardian towards the right quickly, away from the river. It wasn't long before they were out of the vaulted cavern. White Buffalo rushed them down a shallow side passage that gave them barely room to maneuver; for ten minutes they followed it until it began sloping downwards, suddenly it widened out.

Cecille could hear a gurgling ahead so she went straight for it. The cavern they entered had a couple different coloured crystals peppering the walls with twice as many hanging from the ceiling; it lit it up enough for White Buffalo's Guardian to see. It was beautiful with a bubbling pool of water dead center in the room.

Shin took over the lead now that he could see again the Tianming Monk described the cavern to Cecille as they walked ahead. Shadow

Stalker was beginning to feel sluggish now, wanting to sleep. "The water has a pinkish colour because most of the crystals are too, with only a few blue ones; I can see steam coming from the pool so it must be hot?"

Cecille nodded, relieved that they had found it so quickly. White Buffalo gestured decisively with a tone that left no room for disobedience. "Yes, I know; where is the easiest entrance, we must get in it clothes and all... quickly now!"

Shin found a gentle sloping edge after searching for a few minutes then headed for it. He couldn't believe how well he could see in here with those crystals lighting everything up. Gingerly hoping to get used to the temperature slowly, he began tentatively one step at a time to enter the water; the Tianming Monk grimaced uncomfortably. "Cecille it is too hot!"

Cecille standing behind Shin bent before picking up her dog as well as a pink crystal that she had known would be there. Mother Earth had informed her that it wasn't a hard rock like substance when wet the pink ones would melt into a mineral salt immediately; the blue ones would eventually too, but they took way longer to break down. White Buffalo needed to rub them down with the pink one that is why the water was such an unusual colour. It was full of minerals from the hundreds of crystals that fell from the ceiling over the years.

Cecille still holding her cane with all of Shin's stuff too pushed the Tianming Monk towards the water before switching to Japanese not wanting the boy to panic. "You must get in the water; the ticks will continue to eat through your skin if you don't get them off. We can't take them from the caverns or they will multiply quickly in the sunlight, they must not leave the dark cave. The hot mineral salt spring will kill the mud ticks that are now feeding off us. It is the only way to get rid of them I will also heal the boy while we are in the water."

Shin nodded with a grimace of irritation, he was exceedingly itchy; the Tianming Monk was beginning to weave too needing sleep. Now he knew why he was so tired, without further complaint the Tianming Monk walked into the hot water up to his waist.

Stanley clung to Shin whimpering. "I don't want to go, it's hot!"

Cecille took Stanley's hand in reassurance; White Buffalo fibbed just a little, hoping to calm the boy down. "It will be okay, I promise! Shin will not let you go and I will stay with you as well. You need to be in the water for it to heal your leg."

Stanley nodded relieved, the pain was back in full force but now it was worse; if the water will stop it, he would gladly get scalded.

Misfit whined the dog tried to climb onto her mistress's shoulder.

Cecille whispered reassurances to a really upset Misfit, chanting she put her dog into a trance calming her instantly. It seemed to take them forever to get completely covered by the shallow spring. White Buffalo got directions to the closest ledge from Shin then walked over so she could put the things she was carrying on it; she wanted to work on the dog first.

Cecille once back up to her shoulders in the hot spring, dunked down wetting Misfit; afterwards, she rubbed her dog's fur with some mineral salts that she broke off the crystal. White Buffalo made sure not to miss any spots, too bad she didn't have any soap here. Eventually, she let her dog loose to swim to shore now that she was awake and responsive.

Cecille went back to the ledge, she put Shin's sword, the one dagger she had, and his arrows in the water for a quick rinse. She didn't think any of them had bugs but it was better to be cautious; next she pulled out her rapier so she could treat it. Finally, White Buffalo dunked her cane before putting them on the ledge to dry.

Cecille immersed herself before stripping off her shirt, boots, pants, socks then her undergarments. She scrubbed each piece of clothing vigorously as soon as she took them off; squeezing out the excess water White Buffalo put them on the ledge to dry, next she scrubbed herself raw with the mineral salt. Turning she went back to Shin, so he could wash her back. Afterwards, she went back to the ledge to put her undergarments back on.

Cecille once sure she had no bugs left on her went over to Shin. White Buffalo handed her Guardian the rest of the crystal. "Give me the boy so you can stripe, here is the rest of the mineral salt; clean yourself good with it. Make sure you have absolutely no mud left on you at all or your clothes; when you are ready, I will wash your back."

Cecille turned away making sure the sleeping boy was in front of her. White Buffalo kept a supportive hand under his head in case he woke up. The thick salt water would keep him buoyant all on its own; there was so much salt in it that the mass of the water was denser as long as he didn't fight against it he could float here for hours or even days.

Chanting Cecille healed Stanley's broken leg while she waited; White Buffalo was also able to wash Shin's back without disturbing the boy. The healer wasn't worried about the ten-year-old seeing the Tianming Monk naked, the youngster was too exhausted.

Shin walked around Cecille ten minutes later fully clothed. The Tianming Monk helped her undress Stanley; she didn't comment on the fact that her Guardian refused to let anyone see him without clothes. White Buffalo knew it was the same reason his father never let Dream Dancer see him naked until that fateful day.

Once they were all clean, the two adults stumbled exhausted out of the water. Shin put Stanley down carefully before laying down beside the boy; the ten-year-old hadn't roused since falling asleep.

Cecille dropped onto the hard ground with a big sigh of relief; a few minutes rest was all she needed but overwhelmed with fatigue they all slept where they lay.

CHAPTER TEN

Cecille woke to the sound of infectious childish giggles. She caulked her head listening intently, disoriented. Unsure where she was, at first; White Buffalo heard a playful yelp from Misfit before it all came back to her in a rush just as she heard Stanley laugh again at her dog.

Shin, seeing Cecille awake walked over. He made sure to make enough noise that he wouldn't scare her; the Tianming Monk squatted down beside White Buffalo. "They have been playing for about half an hour or so, I think."

Cecille groaned painfully before sitting up the hard ground was way too uncomfortable, she was sure at least two rocks had dug into her side; White Buffalo ran her fingers through her hair in frustration. "How long did we sleep?"

Shin sighed grimly the Tianming Monk handed Cecille his water bag. "Here, have a sip of water. We slept for about an hour, the boy has been awake the longest; we need to get out of here, we have no food, and that is the last of our drinking water White Buffalo!"

Cecille nodded in agreement with a troubled frown before taking a drink of the tepid water. Afterwards, she handed the pouch back to Shin. She hadn't wanted to sleep only rest; White Buffalo stood up then stretched cautiously. She heard a few cracks, but she didn't feel too bad now that the rocks weren't jabbing her in the back any longer. Especially considering what her body had just gone through today.

Cecille frowned thoughtfully, she gestured vaguely towards the tunnel they came through earlier; she was pretty sure she was facing the right way. "Shin we need to go back to the cavern we found Stanley in there is another passage that will take us to the river. I'm not sure if we can get back to the boy's cottage from there, but we should check it first, regardless!"

Shin stood up he went over to get Cecille's cane, pants, shirt, and socks, followed by her boots before bringing them to her. The Tianming Monk had already gathered his things off the ledge. He discreetly turned his back giving her a bit of privacy. "I hope there is a way out it would be easier since we are below where the cabin should be if my sense of direction hasn't failed me!"

Cecille's laughter got muffled as she dressed still there was a strong note of skepticism in it with a distinct teasing quality to it;

White Buffalo couldn't help the disbelief from entering her voice. "I would be quite shocked if it did I have never known you to be wrong when it comes to directions of any kind!"

Shin grumbled good-naturedly at Cecille's playful tone, but he refused to comment. The Tianming Monk gathered up their things before gesturing for Stanley to follow White Buffalo. The Guardian would watch their backs just in case; although, he hadn't seen or heard anything threatening down here yet!

*****

Ten minutes later Cecille skirted the hole the boy had fallen into then took another passageway further to the right; just before entering she knelt with a soft whistle, calling Misfit over to her. She smiled tenderly when the dog stood up on White Buffalo's knees to give her a wet sloppy kiss on her cheek in greeting. She grabbed her dog by the ruff trying to convey how important this was. "Misfit, I want you to go first, lead us outta here girl!"

Misfit whined before turning away, nose twitching she entered the tunnel. Cecille followed her dog, with Stanley behind White Buffalo; still, keeping their rear guarded was Shin.

Shin and Stanley both held three glowing crystals each one was pink with two being blue; since it seemed to the monk, the darker ones held more light. Cecille had warned them they might not stay lit once out of the main cavern, but lucky for them so far they had. They weren't overly bright, but it was enough for them to see the person in front that was critical right now; the Tianming Monk knew neither Misfit nor White Buffalo needed a light that is why they were out in front.

For half an hour they climbed upwards there had only been one fork that had branched off. Misfit had not even hesitated, she followed the left one. Shin was thankful the other one was darker so had tons of cobwebs hanging down, he wasn't afraid of spiders, of course, but the feel of webs freaked him out. The Tianming Monk would never tell anyone that, even his charge was unaware of his aversion to spiderwebs.

Shin was beginning to get a bit worried though, should they have taken the other tunnel it had looked like it was going down? He frowned disgruntled why were they going up? It wasn't a little slope either the Tianming Monk was starting to feel a burning in his legs at the steep incline. He was about to call a halt when the ground levelled off. A curve up ahead had them winding left then right before going left again; finally, it angled downwards steeply.

Cecille started down the slope carefully it was getting pretty slick; she reached out to touch the side of the tunnel it was quite wet, with a slimy feel. She brought her hand back up to her nose before sniffing cautiously, but there was nothing sinister in the smell. It was just water, mould, and fungus all natural in caves. White Buffalo could hear the crashing of waves even louder now, so she knew they were getting closer.

The four continued going down; unexpectedly, the cave floor evened out before it curved right and doubled back on itself. The three entered another vaulting cavern even more vast than the last.

Shin hearing a distinctive squeak put his crystals in a pocket, he whispered for Stanley to do the same; the Tianming Monk quietly called out a warning to Cecille. "White Buffalo, there are bats up on the ceiling hundreds of them!"

Cecille knelt quickly; urgently White Buffalo called softly for Misfit to come to her, but she was too late!

An unexpected squeak from a small brown bat above them caused an excited bark from Misfit. The fevered woof from Cecille's dog reverberated off the cave walls; it echoed eerily throughout the caverns.

A furious explosion of sounds followed from the myotis bats, it also resonated off the cavernous walls when they got involuntarily roused from their roost. It had everyone running back into the tunnel as fast as they could possibly go; as a few hundred outraged squealing bats bolted for the entrance and disappeared into the night.

Misfit tucked her tail in fright as she ran from the chaos she had created. The sounds of the bats echoed for a long five minutes; totally drowning out the bark, causing Cecille's party to cover their sensitive ears from the high-pitched indignant screeching.

Shin waited a good ten minutes before cautiously walking out of the tunnel, he lifted one of his crystal but all the bats were gone. The Tianming Monk turned to Cecille with an amused chuckle. "Well, that is one way to make sure no bats stay around; White Buffalo try to be careful where you walk, the cave floor will be slippery with bat guano."

Shin took the lead now that he could see better than led them to the huge cave opening. It wasn't long before he stopped with a sigh of disappointment at the roar of the waterfalls. There was no way they could get out this way. The Tianming Monk turned in frustration to Cecille. "It is a steep drop from here into rapids with another waterfall in the distance, so we will have to go back the way we came. Dusk is close to being finished I can barely make out the opposite bank; Stanley's mother will be getting frantic. Now that we have some light from the crystals, it shouldn't take us as long to get back. White Buffalo grab hold of the strap on my rifle, I will lead. Stanley stay as close as possible behind Cecille please, try to keep up... let's go!"

   Shin quickly settled into a steady ground eating trot; he tried not to go too fast, the Guardian didn't want to tire Cecille or Stanley out, they had a long way to go. The Tianming Monk kept his crystals up high. Thankfully they shed enough light it took them less than an hour to get back to where the rescuers had fallen inside the second sinkhole.

   Shin called a halt, Cecille and Stanley both dropped to the ground breathing heavily. The Tianming Monk unhooked his water bag before passing it to White Buffalo. "Here, you two drink the rest of this; I will try to find a way to reach the rope I used to get in here."

   Shin reached down, he held out his hand to Stanley expectantly; the Tianming Monk hoped the extra light would help him see better. "I need your crystals too I will return them later."

   Stanley nodded, he handed the three to Shin before reaching for the water really thirsty now!

   Shin turned away; with all the crystals shining he could see quite well. He wasn't worried about Cecille or the boy getting out. The Tianming Monk could easily vault them up into the air so they could climb the rope. It was Misfit that was the problem, how could they get the dog out of here.

   Shin walked over to the hole that was directly under the rope. It was not a large hole but deep enough a person could get wedged in there if they fell in, similar to what had happened to Stanley. He was sure he could hear water further down, but the light from his crystals didn't reach that far. The water might even go directly into the river, where it would come out was anyone's guess. Looking up at the sinkhole above he tsked in irritation, it wasn't a big hole just large enough for the two of them to fall into; he had this feeling that if Misfit hadn't jumped up pushing White Buffalo backward, they might not have even fallen.

   Shin finished planning his strategy to get the other two out began walking back; suddenly his foot struck something that cluttered as it hit the ground again before settling. The Tianming Monk brought his lights down, searching hoping he didn't imagine it.

Shin eventually finding it scooped up his prize before rushing back to the resting pair in excitement. The Tianming Monk held up a dogs leash in triumph. "I just found Misfit's harness not far from the hole; quickly now, both of you follow me!"

Shin showed Stanley the dangling rope first; the Tianming Monk explained as the boy stared up at it grimly, it was pretty far up there. "I will lace my fingers together so you can put your foot inside, when ready I will throw you up as hard as I can. Once you catch the rope climb up then wait for us, can you do that?"

Stanley nodded vigorously ready to try almost anything to get out of this place. "Okay!"

Shin took Cecille's cane away from her before dropping it on the ground, he put all the crystals in his charges hands; the Tianming Monk lifted her two hands up to where he wanted them, he made sure the gems glow was pointed upwards. "White Buffalo I need you to hold these up like this so Stanley can see the rope better."

Cecille did as she was told without arguing; White Buffalo could hardly wait to get out of the caverns. The smells, sounds, even the feel of the cave was foreign to her.

Shin laid his rifle and Misfit's harness down on the floor beside the cane; he laced his fingers together tightly making a solid cup for Stanley's foot before squatting. Holding out his hand the Tianming Monk never said a word just waited for the boy to come to him when he had himself ready.

Stanley nervously looked at the gaping hole behind Shin in trepidation. He was sure the crevice under the rope was even deeper compared to the one he had just gotten out of. The ten-year-old shook off his apprehension there really was no choice, he had to try it. He put his foot in the Guardian's hands tentatively then placed a hand lightly on the Tianming Monk's head to help hold him steady. He closed his eyes before inhaling deeply trying to prepare himself, opening his eyes he nodded quickly so he couldn't change his mind. "I am ready!"

Shin braced himself; the Tianming Monk twisted each foot making sure they had a firm flat purchase with no stones under them that might throw him off balance. "Okay, I'm ready to. Get set... now, jump!"

Stanley pushed himself up as Shin heaved him upwards, the boy airborne for several long moments had no trouble catching the rope, hand over hand he climbed; being young, as well as used to manoeuvring around on ropes he had no problems reaching the top.

He pulled himself over the lip of the hole then rolled thankfully away from the edge before calling down in triumph. "I'm alright now."

Shin took the arrows that he still had strapped to his side out. He threw them away before unhooking his belt, Shadow Stalker kneeling put it on the ground. He picked up the rifle to take off the strap that went over his shoulder; the Tianming Monk put the two separated pieces on the dirt floor beside Misfit's harness.

Shin picked up Cecille's cane next; he wedged it behind his sword before the rifle quickly followed. He stood up and bent then moved around experimentally. Shadow Stalker jump around for several minutes, but the two were wedged in there tight enough they would keep the other from falling out. Hopefully, they would stay there when he jumped for the rope or he would be searching for new ones in the next town.

Shin turned to Cecille and took the crystals from her before putting them on the ground; hoping they would shed enough light for him to see when he was standing up. The Tianming Monk put his hand over his charges arm to convey how serious he was. "White Buffalo, I am going to strap Misfit onto your back. I can guarantee she isn't going to like it much, but it is the only way to get your dog out. You need to make sure she remains completely calm, I will yell when the rope is within your reach. If you miss, I can't guarantee your dog's safety because your life is more important than hers. Whether you will like it or not, I will kill her myself if I must!"

Cecille grimaced angrily, but didn't comment; her face hardened resolutely she knew that her Guardian was right if this did not work, they would have to leave Misfit behind. White Buffalo was determined it wasn't going to happen; she knelt and called Misfit over to her, Cecille gathered her dog into her lap lovingly. White Buffalo whispered soothingly, rocking her gently she chanted rhythmically putting Misfit into a sleep-like trance before giving her to Shin. "She will not fight us now!"

Shin nodded in satisfaction, after putting the harness back on the dog he had Cecille stand then turn. He put Misfit's two paws over his charges shoulders. The Tianming Monk had her hold the dog there before bending he picked up the thick strap for his rifle. He put it as close to the centre of Misfit's back as he could and brought it around using the belt he had utilized for his arrows. The Guardian tied the dog as tight as he could to White Buffalo, without making it so uncomfortable they couldn't breathe. Grabbing the long leash

Twin Destinies

from the harness Shadow Stalker brought it under Cecille's arm; across her upper chest under her other arm before securing the end to the other side of the harness.

Shin stepped back eyeing the pair speculatively, Misfit's head was lying on Cecille's left shoulder with her left front paw relatively close to it; her right front leg was on his charges right shoulder. The Tianming Monk had both dogs back legs straddling White Buffalo's waist just above her hips.

Shin eyeing Cecille's medicine bag speculatively how she managed to keep that intact was anyone's guess. Unhooking the beaver, he turned it so the beaver was now directly behind his charge its legs draped over her buttocks. He positioned the head right underneath Misfit's backside. The Tianming Monk pulled both ties under then over the dogs back legs before tying it in front of White Buffalo around her belly.

Shin backed away the Tianming Monk continued eyeing the two looking for more ways to secure Misfit to Cecille. "White Buffalo I want you to bend, jump do a few twists too. I need to make sure the two of you are securely attached to each other."

Cecille did as instructed; White Buffalo halted when Shin told her to stop.

Shin frowned perturbed, Misfit's head was flopping around way too much; getting an idea the Tianming Monk reached under his tunic and pulled out his Indian medicine bag. He put it around the dog's neck before bringing the ends down and hooked it to Cecille's Celtic medallion. It also contained White Buffalo's white medicine pouch that never got removed except when bathing or sleeping.

Shin stepped back then sighed in defeat; the Tianming Monk had done the best he could, it was now up to Cecille. "White Buffalo that is as good as we are going to get I have nothing left to tie her with. If this doesn't work, we will have to leave her here!"

Cecille pulled away from Shin angrily unable to help envision leaving Misfit behind, White Buffalo's voice quivered apprehensively. "It will work, I refuse to leave my dog here; I won't let her die this way!"

Shin frowned grimly; wisely he kept silent knowing he wouldn't need to say anything. Cecille was already aware that the Tianming Monk would take what action he deemed necessary whether she liked it or not.

Shin bent before cupping his hands, again the Tianming Monk twisted his feet preparing himself; it gave Cecille a few extra minutes to compose herself, she was still pretty upset. "White Buffalo let me know when you are ready!"

Cecille shook off her feelings, now wasn't the time to get distracted. She lifted her right leg, standing awkwardly with one foot securely in her Guardian's hands; she began chanting softly, bringing White Buffalo to the surface. She tapped Shin on the head letting him know she was ready. She sprang upwards as the Tianming Monk heaved her into the air with all his strength.

Cecille flew upwards; reaching up White Buffalo searched for the rope desperately.

Shin screamed at Cecille insistently; the Tianming Monk didn't think she was going to find it. "White Buffalo, to your left!"

Cecille desperately twisted searching; just when she felt herself beginning to fall back towards the caverns below, her left hand closed on the very end of the rope. She hung there for a moment swinging back and forth slowly. White Buffalo gave herself a minute to get her heart back into a normal rhythm then pulled herself up before grabbing hold of the rope with her right hand.

Misfit whined plaintively she was coming out of her trance too soon; the dog began squirming against the bonds holding her in place, she whimpered in confusion.

Cecille desperately pulled herself up the rope another few inches until she was able to wrap the line around her left foot to keep herself steady. White Buffalo quit chanting so she could calm her dog down; with Misfit's frantic movements the rope they were clinging to started to sway faster and faster, it was gaining momentum. "MISFIT!"

Misfit instantly froze as her mistress yelled at her sharply.

Cecille felt her dog settle down; thankfully the rope quit swinging as much, so she pulled herself up further. She was almost out when her head jerked up in fear at a loud crack as one of the braids in the line released with a violent snap. Slowly, as White Buffalo had climbed each of the four strands in the braid that was against the edge of the hole having rubbed a lot let go. Luckily, there were two more braids with four strands in each braid of the rope. It should hold long enough she hoped. She reached the top as quick as she could before she pulled herself over the lip then onto firm ground.

Cecille promptly turned around; White Buffalo yelled down a warning to Shin in Ojibwe. "Shadow Stalker, the rope is breaking!"

Shin already aware of that backed up as far as he could then ran forward. He used the edge of the hole in the cave floor to vault himself up into the air, with both legs churning it looked like the Guardian was climbing stairs; he made it seem effortless. When the Tianming Monk grasped the rope, he heard two snaps as more strands in the second braid let go. Climbing up as fast as he could, Shadow Stalker tried to reach the gaping hole above before the rope separated completely as another strand snapped. There was only one left in the one braid; the other braid would not hold long he knew.

Cecille fumbling desperately got Misfit unhooked; she turned and dropped to the ground on her belly before reaching her hand down as far as she could imploringly. She had a hold of the rope still hooked to the rock with her other hand to keep her from being pulled back in when he took her hand. White Buffalo couldn't see what was happening or where her Guardian was at. All she could hear was the rope breaking as the second braid let go with a salvage snap. "Shadow Stalker!"

Shin now close enough to the unravelling rope to see the last four strands in the final braid giving away lunged up; the Tianming Monk just managed to get a hold of Cecille's hand as the rope fell into the cavern below.

Cecille holding desperately to the leftover rope heaved for all she was worth. Her arm muscles bulged; straining White Buffalo slowly pulled a dangling Shin to safety before they both collapsed onto the firm ground exhausted.

Stanley rushed over then knelt. "Are you guys okay? I need to get home my mother will be so angry with me by now."

Shin groaned in protest not wanting to move yet; finally, the Tianming Monk reluctantly stood up. "We need to cover the holes first so no other person or animal can fall in the caverns, do you remember where you fell in Stanley?"

Stanley nodded vigorously and pointed forgetting it was too dark to see. "Yes, on the other side of the smaller rock when I jumped down the ground gave way beneath me."

Shin helped an unwilling Cecille up; the Tianming Monk switched to Ojibwe so Stanley wouldn't be able to understand what they were saying. "White Buffalo, you will have to ask the Mother Earth for help; there is no way we will be able to move that big rock over this hole by ourselves."

Shin went over to the small rock then retrieved what was left of his rope; he coiled it then put it back over his shoulder before pulling out the four blue crystals he had remembered to pick up. He lifted them high so he could see better, the pink ones were too dim to be any help. The Tianming Monk noticed the lights on the blue ones were beginning to fade too, now that they were away from the cavern. He hope, the light would continue to glow until they were back at the cabin, he would be surprised if they lasted that long.

Shin ushered everyone behind the big rock first; the Tianming Monk turned his back and dug his feet into the mossy ground, pushing backward against the stone.

Stanley just put his two hands out facing the rock he dug his toes into the Earth; pushing with all his strength.

Cecille knelt on the other side of Shin so the boy didn't see what she was doing. Chanting, with one hand against the rock, she pushed it. The healer had the other lying flat on the ground; she brought White Buffalo to the surface then asked Mother Earth for help.

When it seemed that no amount of pushing was going to move the stubborn rock and they were about to give up, the ground heaved. As it rippled, it shifted the rock an inch then two before suddenly the Mother Earth shook violently in a small earthquake; causing the boulder to roll, it settled on top of the hole closing off the sinkhole.

Shin moved Stanley and Cecille to the next rock. Again, it took several long minutes of White Buffalo chanting to the Mother Earth as she pushed against the stone. Lucky for them it didn't take as much effort before that rock too obediently moved over the smaller hole. Now they could leave without any more worries.

Cecille whistled then bent when Misfit rushed over to her; White Buffalo took off her dog's harness leaving her loose.

Shin pulled out his rifle and restrung the strap before putting it on his shoulder. The Tianming Monk strung out his short rope making sure everyone had a good hold. "We need to move fast; Stanley you stay in the middle, Cecille will bring up the rear with Misfit. Hold tight to the rope; whatever you do… don't let go!"

Satisfied Shin turned then they were off. He kept four blue crystals together in one hand; the other two were in his pocket. He was hoping the dark would prolong their glow. An hour later they were hurrying up the path. It took another fifteen minutes before the Tianming Monk was thankfully pulling down his pack and the extra rope he had left behind. The other two were resting up for the last leg of their journey. Shadow Stalker knew that contrary to what the other two thought, this would be the hardest obstacle because they were all physically and mentally exhausted.

Shin found three pieces of jerky in his pack, they each had one. It would give them a little more strength. Cecille shared hers with

Twin Destinies

Misfit; the Tianming Monk frowned grimly, but he didn't comment on it knowing it wouldn't do him any good.

Shin gave them ten minutes then roused them before tying Cecille and Stanley together with the long rope; he used the smaller one to tie Misfit to him. He kept one crystal out then tucked away the rest. "White Buffalo you go first, Stanley will follow you. Remember there is no rope attached to the top line so if either of you slips we will all fall. If that happens nobody will find us until morning if at all, please be careful. I will follow you with Misfit, go on now."

Cecille carefully stepped up then waited for Stanley before proceeding ahead. The trip back was easier in one sense because it was all downhill. In another, it was harder it seemed to take them twice as long. By the time they reached the end their nerves were strung way out, they all fell to the ground in exhaustion. Misfit getting used to being carried this way had quit fighting it; thankfully, their trip across was uneventful.

Shin groaning eventually got up; the Tianming Monk went over and untied Stanley before giving him three crystals out of his pocket. "Here, go see your mother she must be sick with worry by now, we will be along shortly."

Stanley nodded gratefully then took off running without comment.

Shin unhooked Misfit, barking in excitement the dog raced off ecstatically. The Tianming Monk gave his last crystals to Cecille to hold for him before pulling out her cane, he handed it to her so she wouldn't trip on anything.

Shin turning away drew out his sword. The Tianming Monk walked over to the tree that the rope was tied to. In one swift motion, the monk severed the top line followed closely by the second cable; they both fell into the gorge before disappearing. He turned away in satisfaction as he re-sheathed his sword. Walking to where they had put the two fishing poles he collected them, and they headed to the cabin.

Cecille aware of what Shin had done never said a word; White Buffalo agreed with the monk, Stanley didn't need to go back not for many years, anyway.

They were met by a grateful mother who ushered them all to the table which thankfully had a meal as well as tea waiting; after the food was finished, stories were told then pallets made on the floor for Stanley and Shin. Cecille crawled into Stanley's bed gratefully it wasn't long before they all slept too tired to talk or even dream.

CHAPTER ELEVEN

Shin sighed in frustration as he sat on the porch waiting impatiently for the last trunk being packed. They should have been in town by now, but no; Cecille insisted on sticking around until Violet followed by Stanley moments later got up so they could say goodbye, not wanting to be thought rude. Neither Violet nor her son got up till after eight o'clock.

Shin pinched the bridge of his nose in irritation if that wasn't bad enough. White Buffalo had invited Stanley's mother to accompany them to town after hearing they were also going there today. So here it was, ten thirty and still Violet wasn't ready; almost the Tianming Monk got informed in a, don't rush us tone of voice from his charge earlier.

Lucky for Shin, Violet did have a mule which already had one trunk on her. It was docilely waiting for the second chest. The donkey had more patience compared to the Tianming Monk this morning. Unfortunately, Stanley's mom also had a milk cow now tied to the back of the burro. Shadow Stalker would be leading two goats; Stanley would bring the overweight pig. Last, but not least was a crate with four hens squawking inside; it would be loaded on the back of the mule's rump after the trunk was put in place.

Shin leaned forward, he propped his elbows on his knees before bending his head then ran his hands through his hair in aggravation; that wasn't even the best part of the whole morning! The Tianming Monk couldn't help but give another snort of half laugh, half frustration... oh no! The best part of it all by far was the black male hound dog trying his damnedest to mount Cecille's female. Shadow Stalker was beginning to feel sorry for the poor male.

Shin sat up to watch in amusement as Blacky not willing to give up so easily, again tried mounting the teasing pulsing female that kept rubbing against him. The male clamped his jaws on the back of her neck trying to hold her still, but as soon as he got close to his goal; Misfit would promptly sit down and no amount of growling, barking, or whining from the male would budge her. The black hound frustrated again slunk off to lick himself clean to get ready for another try, after a short snooze that is.

Stanley ran out of the cabin with two fishing rods plus a small bucket of worms. He held out one to Shin in invitation. "I asked Mom if I could go fishing one last time, she said it was okay;

Cecille told me to take you with me, your step-sister said we aren't to come back for an hour unless she sends Misfit to come get us."

Shin gladly grabbed a fishing pole before standing up with a sigh of relief; it was way better than sitting here twiddling his fingers uselessly. The Tianming Monk bowed with his two hands pressed together in thanks. "I will be honoured to fish with you, Stanley."

Shin called Cecille's dog over; the Tianming Monk pointed at the door in command. "Guard your mistress, Misfit!"

Shin walked off the porch; he turned back briefly to watch as Misfit now on guard walked over to the door before turning. She promptly put her backside against it to keep the male away from her. As soon as Blacky would get close, the female would snap and growl savagely. There was no playfulness in Cecille's dog at this time now she was all business. She laid there with both floppy ears up watching the front yard diligently.

Shin chuckled as he shook his head in wonder. The Tianming Monk eventually turned away in amusement from the retreating black hound with his tail tucked between his legs.

Shin trotted down the path to catch up with Stanley it didn't take them long to reach the fishing hole; the Tianming Monk accepted a worm from his young fishing partner, he put the bait on his hook before casting it into the little pond.

Stanley looked towards the ropes, but noticed they were both gone; the boy turned to Shin with a questioning tone as he pointed. "The lines must have come loose?"

Shin not looking in that direction nodded solemnly; the Tianming Monk pulled in his line and recast before turning to Stanley expressionlessly. "It is best!"

Stanley gave a hesitant nod. "I suppose so, my Mother only wants to stay in town until we sell everything then we will be moving to Montreal; I don't want to live in a city, it is noisy and dirty!"

Shin shrugged in understanding; he gestured in reassurance before the Tianming Monk gave the young impressionable Stanley some advice. "It is hard when we are young, and our parents will not consider our wishes, but your Mother is wise. There is not much opportunity for school way out here. If you are smart you will learn about the bridge your Father started or find out more information on the crystals hidden in your trunk; with that knowledge, you can come back here someday to continue your Dad's work."

Stanley thought about it for a moment; he recast his line into the water before grinning with a decisive nod. "I might just do that!"

Shin nodded pleased; the Tianming Monk knew Stanley was destined to return someday. The Guardian was meant to encourage him to come back because there was something important he needed to do in the future. They sat back to enjoy a pleasant hour of relaxation both savouring their newfound friendship.

*****

Two hours later, Shin pulling two reluctant goats that wanted to stop to eat everything grumbled in aggravation under his breath so the others couldn't hear. Stanley led the pig, with Cecille on her mare leading the cow. Violet was on White Buffalo's packhorse leading the mule; it was slow going, so would probably take them at least another two hours to get to town at this rate. The black hound did not amuse the Tianming Monk now as he once again half-heartedly aimed a kick at Blacky as the Guardian growled angrily. "Enough already, leave Misfit alone you pesky mangy mutt!"

Cecille snickered, she was well aware Shin was angry at her, but she ignored the Tianming Monk. She knew Misfit was close to her time but wasn't quite in full heat yet. White Buffalo knew her dog wouldn't have pups because in all these years she never let a male mount her, always she would sit so they couldn't.

Cecille taking pity on her frustrated Guardian whistled sharply for her dog before lifting both arms up in front of her waiting expectantly; Misfit loped over obediently, she jumped up in front of her mistress onto the neck of the mare. White Buffalo had no worries her mare would get upset since it had been taught to them when her dog was big enough to jump this high.

Cecille stroked her dog soothingly. "Have a rest, Misfit."

Blacky whined plaintively; he raced around the mare before barking insistently, trying to get the female to come down.

Violet called out loudly in command, starting to get annoyed. "Blacky, get over here that is enough; you stay here beside me."

The black hound dog reluctantly fell back; obediently, Blacky stayed with his mistress.

Shin sighed in relief as quiet descended except for the occasional squawk from the chickens; the Tianming Monk picked up his pace as much as possible hoping to get to town sooner.

*****

Three hours later, much later than Shin had hoped their weary group trudged into the outskirts of town.

Violet took the lead then led them left away from the village, around and up a steep hill to a cottage tucked away in the trees; she rode up to the hitching post before dismounting then tied her mule up.

A woman came out of the house, she stood on the porch eyeing the strangers in confusion but didn't move to see who they were; the only motion she made was to cross her arms in front of her defensively, neither did she say a word to anyone only stared in bewilderment.

Cecille frowned uncomfortably as all of a sudden dark auras began swirling around the outline of a shadowy woman. There were a few short bright strands in the mass swirling, but most of them were dark and angry. White Buffalo wasn't used to seeing auras this far away from a person; she stiffened in reaction before blocking the woman out.

Cecille jumped startled when someone unexpectedly put a hand over her knee. She inhaled searching for a scent that would tell her who it was; the long slim fingers with the smell of violets instantly brought to mind Stanley's mother. Thankfully, it distracted White Buffalo from her unexpected reaction to the woman standing on the porch.

Violet frowned then chastised herself, she should have warned Cecille she was coming. "Sorry to startle you, this is my sister's place so you are both welcomed to stay here overnight if you wish; my sister is a slow and not quite right, but she loves company nonetheless."

Cecille quickly shook her head; there was no way White Buffalo would be able to stay close to Violet's sister even for an hour, never mind all night. "No, we need to find our guide as soon as possible. Hopefully, we can be on the trail for a few hours before nightfall hits thank you for the offer. Just let Shin know what to do with your animals so we can be on our way."

Violet patted Cecille's hand solemnly in sad farewell. "You take care of yourself my friend; thank you for saving my son's life. Hopefully, someday we will meet again."

Cecille squeezed Violet's hand in goodbye. White Buffalo had seen a great future for Stanley's mother; she didn't need a name from the Mother Earth she had already found her spirit guide on her own, without even realizing it. "May our God, the Great Spirit of all living things guide and watch over you."

Once Violet moved out of the way Cecille called out to the woman's son; White Buffalo needed to give him his spiritual name from the Mother Earth. "Stanley, are you here?"

Stanley quickly handed his mother the rope for the pig before hurrying to Cecille. He touched her left knee to let White Buffalo know he was there. "I am here; I want to thank you for saving me, I will forever be in your debt."

Cecille squeezed Stanley's hand affectionately in goodbye; White Buffalo's voice portrayed her sorrow when it deepened solemnly and became gravely serious. "I will never forget you either, the Mother Earth wants you to have the name Red Fox, the fox will now be your spiritual guide in life."

Stanley chuckled, he reached up then ran his hand through his carrot red hair; Cecille didn't know his hair was red unless Shin told her. "Thank you... I will never forget you either!"

With that, Stanley pulled his other hand away from Cecille's before running off to help his mother; he also wanted to say goodbye to Shin.

*****

An hour later Shin was leading the horses down the road once more before turning into town. To the right of them was the river; on the left were the town businesses and behind them going up the densely forested hillside were houses peeking out among the trees. It was a beautiful setting the Tianming Monk couldn't help thinking if he were an artist it would make a beautiful painting.

Violet told Shin the guide they were looking for would most likely be at the local saloon. The Tianming Monk took Cecille to the hotel first her safety was his primary concern; although, he didn't tell her that knowing she would resent his coddling. "I'm going to leave you at the hotel then go find Brandan Reid I want to meet him first."

Cecille dismounted with Shin's help; knowing they would be around a town today she had worn a fancy split skirt with a feminine, frilly blouse. She misplaced her new Stetson, so she was wearing one of her ladies bonnets. The healer couldn't help smirking at herself in pleasure she should do this more often it made her feel good. All she needed was a parasol to complete the ensemble of a fancy lady. She waited for the Tianming Monk to finish putting Misfit into her harness. The Guardian finally took White Buffalo arm and led her inside.

Shin sat Cecille at a table, turning he discreetly took the hostess hand before slipping her a silver dollar to ignore the dog. He leaned closer to whisper in the woman's ear, so she would bring his charge a cup of tea and possibly a scone or biscuit; afterwards, the Tianming Monk hurried out the door.

Twin Destinies

Shin walked down the wood sidewalk purposely, without paying any attention to those veering around him. Neither did he pay no never mind to the ones going so far as to cross the street to avoid him; the Tianming Monk was used to that reaction and it had never bother him one bit.

Shin remembering back couldn't help an unexpected uplift to the right corner of his lip. It was all the amusement he showed as the memory of that evening so long ago came rushing to the surface. It was after they arrived in Montreal; being as it was the Tianming Monk's first experience in a tavern, he could recall every detail of that night as if it happened yesterday.

Sin had stealthily followed Edward when he left to meet the guide taking them to Manitoba; Pierre was meeting Dream Dancer for a drink since it was way too early for bed.

Shin remembered the noise first then the stink of sweat intermixed with the cloying scent of cheap perfume, plus the acrid odour of cigar smoke and whisky; unfortunately, none of those smells could cover up the smell of someone's vomit. The younger Tianming Monk had slipped under the batwing doors, unnoticed he hid in a dark corner keeping Edward's back guarded without his knowledge...

*****

Edward, feeling like a new man now that the grime of the train got washed off walked to the tavern Pierre said he would be waiting at. Entering, Dream Dancer looked around in interest. The bar was made of mahogany; it was against the far left wall. To the right were tables as well as a piano. Seeing the Frenchmen at the bar he went over and joined him, he smiled cordially at the barkeeper. "Whisky please!"

The man serving alcohol behind the bar eyed the stranger suspiciously; after a few minutes, he frowned in anger then made a shooing motion with his hand. "We don't serve Indians in this establishment, now get out of here!"

The barkeeper barely got the words out when Pierre reached across the bar; the massive black haired Frenchman hauled the bewildered man by the scruff of his neck across the bar, so he was staring into his eyes. "You will keep a civil tongue in your mouth Walter when speaking to an Earl of the realm. Now get Edward a drink before I smack you silly, friend or not!"

The unfortunate chubby brown haired five foot two barkeeper choked; he grabbed at Pierre's muscular arm trying desperately to get loose, he nodded hurriedly. "Right away Pierre, sorry for the mistaken identity he looks like a half-breed."

Pierre, letting him go shoved Walter back across the bar. "Edward Summerset is part Indian he is also an Earl; right now he is under my protection so don't forget it!"

Walter hurriedly got Edward a drink without further comment; you didn't argue with Pierre, he could be a mean bastard when he gets riled. Unfortunately, being his friend was no protection when the guide was angry, especially if he was drinking.

Edward chuckled at the byplay but didn't comment as he accepted his whisky. He turned around to survey all the other patrons who had ignored the going on's at the bar familiar with Pierre's quick temper; Dream Dancer nudged the guide and pointed at a group of men playing cards. "How about we go join them for a friendly game?"

Pierre turned around to look at the men Edward was referring to, the guide nodded with a grin. "Sure, maybe I can win some of my money back they are forever bleeding me dry. I swear they cheat, but I have never caught them at it; not yet anyway."

Edward nodded thoughtfully, but didn't say anything; as they walked over he studied the five men carefully, brothers or related somehow Dream Dancer figured by the looks of them. He grabbed a chair at an empty table, Pierre did likewise then they pulled them over before sitting. "Mind if we join you?"

The leader nudged his cousin playfully; he tipped his head towards the guide teasingly. "Well looky here Joey, Pierre is back to lose more money! He brought a friend with him this time too."

Joey chuckled in amusement; he scooted over to give the big Frenchman more room to sit before pointing out each man as he named them. "By all means sit my dear man you remember my brother Daniel sitting on your right I hope. My brother Jason is beside me, my cousin Paul is next, and finally my other cousin James on the other side of your friend."

James was the one who first spoke; he moved his chair over then let Edward sit between him and his brother Paul. "We play poker five card draw, gentlemen. All newcomers are more than welcomed to lose their money."

Edward pulled out his billfold before taking out the fifty dollars he had waiting in it for just such an occasion; he had more hidden away, it was much safer to keep it out of sight when around big towns or cities. Dream Dancer eyed the dealer Daniel who wasn't quite straight across from him he had dark brown hair with brown eyes. Right beside him on his left was Pierre then his brother Joey, the two were the same build, but he had sandy blonde hair with the brown eyes. Jason on his brothers left had the same hair colour as his cousin James but was Pierre's size. Paul who was on the right side of Edward, he had the same features as his cousin Daniel although he was stouter. The leader James was on the earl's left he was the largest of the five, with black hair and blue eyes.

Edward picked up his cards, studying them in interest he threw two away. As the dealer dealt out a card, he watched closely then saw it but he never said a word. Dream Dancer accepted another whisky from James; although, he left it untouched. The earl settled back letting the five shysters rake in hand after hand.

*****

Shin hidden in the shadows watched Edward curiously he knew Dream Dancer had seen the men cheating, how could he not it was so obvious; the Tianming Monk wondered why Cecille's father was letting these men take his money.

Edward never told Cecille he had legal custody of Shin nor did he tell the young Oriental. Dao made sure before his death to have custody papers legally filed so the earl could adopt his son, knowing he was soon to die. The young Tianming Monk had accidentally found the documents while they were on the ship; he never mentioned it since Dream Dancer didn't want him to know.

It didn't really matter Shin would always feel indebted to the Summerset's for taking him in. They both made him feel like part of their family, not like a servant. He never moved a muscle as he continued to watch knowing eventually, Edward would react; the Tianming Monk must be ready to help his foster father.

*****

Edward frowned down at his cards, for three hours he let the five cheat him of his money, now he was on his last five dollars. Pierre had run out of money an hour ago he just sat watching silently. Dream Dancer didn't have anything, but he only threw one card away just to keep them guessing. Paul sitting on his right was dealing, the earl watched him take a card from the bottom of the deck this time; James' brother wasn't as good at that as he was with the cards up his sleeve.

Edward deciding it was time swiftly reached over then grabbed the unfortunate Paul's arm; at the same time, the earl jumped to his feet and pulled his gun from his holster in one smooth motion before pointing the muzzle at the leader James. Dream Dancer knew he was the biggest threat out of the five.

Pierre seeing Edward's small gesture was ready; he jumped to his feet with his revolver out, he pointed his at Daniel's head.

James followed closely by Jason pointed their pistols at Edward; Daniel and Joey had their guns pointed at Pierre's face; they were at a deadlock. The room hushed instantly as everyone froze, you could have heard a pin drop as time stopped for a heartbeat.

James' lip curled up in a triumphant sneer; he chuckled at the earl. "Well, it looks like the game is over boys. Drop your gun Edward before my trigger-happy cousin's blow Pierre's hea...!"

Instead of finishing his sentence, James put up the hand holding his gun then carefully put the revolver down on the table; he hissed in command at his cousins as he lifted his hand away slowly. "All of you lay down your guns!"

Daniel, Jason, and Joey looked at each other in bewilderment unable to see what had caused the fear on their cousin's face; they all looked back at James speculatively none of them moved.

Shin dug his knife a little deeper into the back of his victim drawing more blood but kept himself hidden behind the outlaw. The Tianming Monk didn't want the other men to see him, being short the Oriental was taken for a youngster at first it might give them ideas. He really didn't want to kill anyone if he could avoid it; although, he wouldn't hesitate if given no choice.

James' breath hissed out painfully before he growled furiously at his cousins. "Now you idiots lower your weapons, I said!"

Slowly the three obeyed, still very confused; they all stepped back from the table, gunless.

Pierre moved back, but kept his revolver trained on Daniel's head he sighed in relief.

Edward aware that Shin was behind James twisted Paul's arm; he watched in satisfaction as cards spilled out all over the table. Dream Dancer looked around the room expectantly, making sure everyone could hear him clearly, he exclaimed in a shocked tone. "Let everyone know these men are cheats I'm certain most of you have lost money at one time or another to them."

Edward looked over at Pierre before gesturing with his gun at the table; Dream Dancer wanted to get out of here fast, but he needed to teach these men a valuable lesson first. "Take the money my friend; I am sure they stole more than that from you!"

Pierre nodded without any argument he holstered his gun before gathering up the money on the table; it was not until the guide stepped back that he noticed Shin, he grinned in thanks.

Edward backed away cautiously with his gun still pointed at James; Pierre and Shin joined him a moment later. "Sorry boys but I will be leaving you in the loving hands of the townsmen!"

Instantly all the men in the saloon stood up they angrily advanced towards the unfortunate card sharks; it gave Edward's group a chance to get away before blood started spilling.

*****

Shin returned to the present with a nostalgic chuckle; Edward gave him the custody papers after they settled with the Ojibwe. Dream Dancer waited until he turned twenty-one to present them as a gift. His papers were hiding with the Tianming Monk's carpet.

Shin walked off the sidewalk into an alleyway before reaching another set of stairs that lead up to the saloon. Edward taught him a valuable lesson that night, what goes around comes around, if you're not careful it will even take a bite out of your backside; the Tianming Monk shook off all thoughts of Dream Dancer as he walked through the batwing doors then into the tavern.

Shin looked around speculatively this place looked exactly like the one in Montreal, except it had a cedar bar. The smell of cedar was thankfully strong enough to mask some of the unpleasant odours; even this early in the day it smelt of whisky, old vomit, sweat, and cigar smoke. The Tianming Monk would forever associate these smells with a tavern.

A man stood up angrily his chair fell backward as he pointed at the stranger in anger. "Chinks aren't allowed in here, now get out!"

Shin looked at the man briefly then ignored him; the Tianming Monk looked around inquisitively. "I am looking for Brandan Reid, Robert sent me here!"

A slim, broad shouldered man sitting in a shadowed corner got up; he beckoned for the Oriental to sit with him. "It's good John I take responsibility for him."

John nodded disgruntled, but didn't argue with the Irishman; he righted his chair before sitting back down. He continued to grumble irritably under his breath, making sure it was too low for anyone to hear what he was saying.

Shin walked over and bowed, with both hands pressed together. The Tianming Monk never in all these years of living here forgot his heritage; although, he didn't wear his traditional Asian outfit much anymore unless doing a ritual with Cecille. Now he preferred the typical western outfit; denim pants, flannel shirt, moccasins or boots, and a vest. Occasionally he even wore a Stetson, but the native buckskins with a headband were his favourite. "I'm Shin, thank you for allowing me to state my business with you."

Brandan familiar with the Oriental culture since he haunted Chinatown in Quebec for over a year bowed respectfully back; he gestured for the slender Asian to take a seat, curious to find out what the man wanted.

Shin pulled out a purse; the Tianming Monk set it on the table between them, closer to the Irishman. "We need a guide to take us north-east through Algonquin Park to the border of Ontario then possibly into Quebec. This is half the payment now more will be forthcoming when we reach our destination."

The red-headed, tall Irishman picked up the purse weighing it thoughtfully; Brandan was a little surprised by its weight. "You said we, how many is there?"

Shin shrugged negligently pretending that it did not matter to him if the Irishman was their guide, it was all for show; carefully, he was watching for any evidence that Brandan wasn't trustworthy. "There are two of us with a couple of horses plus a dog."

Brandan frowned in surprise there was enough gold here to guide five families clean across Ontario, according to the Oriental this was only half of it; who did he have with him... the Queen of England? The Irish guide stiffened in suspicion as his overactive imagination evoked images of a tied up Monarch with a gag in her mouth hidden away at the hotel. "Where's second person?"

Shin pointed over his shoulder dramatically; he couldn't help teasing the serious Irishman just a bit. If the Tianming Monk could have read the guides mind, he would have laughed hilariously. "She is at the hotel having a cup of tea."

Brandan grimaced in relief as his hunch was only partially confirmed it was a woman but thankfully not one that was being held against her will; although, females could be hard to get along with at times there was still a lot of gold here even for that headache. The Irishman frowned distrustfully, having entirely missed the amusement in the Orientals voice. "Why would ya take a woman into Indian Territory for are yous missionaries?"

Shin smiled at the mistrustful Brandan before giving a negative shake of his head, he was enjoying this by play very much. It reminded him of his time with Edward, the Tianming Monk was sure missing his adopted father lately. "No, we are not missionaries! Cecille is a doctor, she wishes to help people along the way; she hasn't decided exactly where we are going only that she feels pulled in that direction. She is my step-sister, and I swore to my step-father to keep her safe since he has always treated me like a son."

Brandan nodded at that simple explanation; he eyed the Oriental thoughtfully before pointing at him in demand, his Irish burr became way more noticeable. "Maybe so, I have feeling yous are leaving something important out!"

Shin chuckled when the red-haired, hazel-green eyed Irishman called his bluff refusing to be distracted; the guide was perceptive, he approved of that. The Tianming Monk shrugged dismissively. "You are correct; unfortunately my step-sister is blind."

Brandan's mouth dropped open in shock, he couldn't help it; never in a million years would he have guessed someone would take a blind woman into Indian Territory or expect her to survive such a trek. His Irish burr thickened in incredibility. "Yous crazy, ya can't take a blind woman into Algonquin Park its full of savages, not to mention animals wanting ta tear her apart if gets hold of her."

Shin shrugged, he got up before holding out his hand for the purse; the Tianming Monk didn't mind bickering over price, but the Irishman hadn't even mentioned it. "I will take that as a no, is there anyone else around here that can guide us?"

Brandan stood up as well; he tightened his grip on the purse involuntarily. The Irish guide could really use the money that was in here; could he live with himself if something were to happen to a helpless blind woman! "Only Roger, I would no trust him as far as I can throw him which is not far."

Brandan hefted the purse once more, the burly guide eventually conceded; a woman would never be truly safe with Roger. "I will take ya, but her life is in your hands. I will not accept responsibility if she dies along the way."

Shin bowed; the Tianming Monk grinned pleased Brandan changed his mind, he liked the Irishman. "She will always be my responsibility, so no worries. All we need is a guide to get us to the border, not a babysitter."

The two men shook hands in agreement before leaving the tavern they headed directly to the hotel to collect Cecille. Neither of the men noticed a dark shadowy figure listening avidly to their conversation; he was hidden in the far corner, he also stood up then hurriedly went in search of his comrades.

CHAPTER TWELVE

Cecille sipped her tea in pleasure with a big sigh of contentment as she patiently waited for Shin to get back. The healer picked up her scone; she already spread cream on it before artfully arranging on top a small dollop of strawberry jam. She closed her eyes in anticipation as she bit into the sweet pastry. White Buffalo hadn't had one of these delicacies since leaving Wales.

Cecille groaned in delight savoury the treat when the warm cream and the tart taste of the jam hit her tongue it tantalizing White Buffalo's taste buds.

Cecille finished her scone before sitting back; she took a sip of her tea in pleasure, it was nice to relax and enjoy her own company for a change. It was seldom she got away from her ever watchful Guardian Shin. White Buffalo relished these little respites.

Cecille's mind wandered to her experience with the Great Spirit; now that she had a chance to think she took the opportunity to analyze everything that happened after her fall. The healer learned over time that nothing was by chance, everything going on in our lives good or bad makes us who we will become later in life. Even the people we meet affect us somehow it can make us stronger or unfortunately sometimes weaker. Life is full of lessons you just had to step back from time to time to analyze what you learned.

Most people didn't see life the same way Cecille did since she had first-hand knowledge of the higher powers. Still even knowing that White Buffalo never stopped learning, regrettably a lot of times it was quite a painful lesson.

Cecille knew that the movement of time on Mother Earth was different from God's time; if Po got made in seven Earth years that would mean it wasn't very old; White Buffalo was one of the few aware the Earth was created in Shen's time making it much older than anyone knew.

It wasn't until Cecille's discussion with the Great Spirit after her fall that White Buffalo found out the Mother Earth was older still.

Cecille knew that the time frame of God's was the same as the mist that trapped her parents. They were in the fog only a few minutes, but White Buffalo's mother ended up six months pregnant because time moves faster between heaven and Earth. Contrary to what people believe, there is an in-between part of it was used to keep the souls of the dead in until judgment day. There is a section for dreams plus another one for souls waiting to be born; the healer wasn't exactly sure how many more sections there were to it.

Cecille asked Shin if he knew about the Nephilim before going to sleep at Stanley's cabin. The Tianming Monk reminded her of the books of Enoch; one and two that he read to her when aboard the ship that brought them to Canada. Noah's great-grandfather supposedly wrote them. Once her Guardian reminded her of it, the healer remembered several critical things from the Bible, the books of Enoch, as well as Noah's written account; if White Buffalo went by all three teachings, there were at least five heavens.

The second heaven was supposed to be holding the Angels of Satanii; Cecille wondered if these were the twenty Angel leaders with the two hundred conspirators that are the Sons of God or watchers; they rebelled after falling in love with human women. The third heaven is where the actual temple of God is located. The fifth one mentioned is where the giants whose brothers were fallen Angels are found, those must be the Nephilim. White Buffalo knew there was still the first and the fourth heaven not mentioned at all what could be in them she wondered?

Cecille knew there were four hidden accesses to the heavenly realms scattered around the Earth. Why she wasn't sure the reasons yet. One was in England, Snowdonia to be precise; it housed an evil trapped in it, either Lucifer himself or one of his minions. White Buffalo knew the second one was somewhere between Egypt, Rome, Spain, Turkey, or Jerusalem... hidden inside it was Eden.

The third access Cecille had no idea where it was at or what was inside it; the Mother Earth refused to talk about it at all, which made her a lot more curious. It must have something to do with the magic that at one time prevail on Earth, could it have turned evil forcing God to lock it away? Most of the lost cities like Atlantis, the Mayans, Pompeii, and Tyno Helig in Wales... even Alexandria, had all been able to use magic in one form or another. Was that what the Great Spirit had been trying to tell White Buffalo, did the magic as well as its people evolve beyond control? If so was Shen warning them that it could happen to these humans now as well.

The magic must have gotten sealed away somewhere, it couldn't have vanished entirely and what about the civilizations that depended on it; did they perished because of it or were they hidden away, maybe in one of the heavens not mentioned. If they were waiting, it could be for the circle of life to come back around again so they can be released.

Aware now that there were humans on Earth before the fight with Lucifer, she tried picturing what they might look like but failed. She could only speculate that those people or creatures were made from the magic that the Angels had been able to take advantage of. Cecille knew from the Mother Earth what scientists were starting to discover, some humans evolved from apes which means there is more than one kind of people. For some reason, nobody knew yet or maybe they didn't want to believe it, she wondered if they ever would. The Tianming Monk's hidden on a small island in Japan and White Buffalo's family were the only ones who knew this for a certainty. Surprisingly it was Po, the Mother Earth, who brought about the unexpected evolution of the apes allowing them to become a new species of humans.

God at that time was busy creating his humans Adam and Eve; the Great Spirit even gave his new people their very own garden of paradise in Eden, Shen had ignored all else.

Cecille wasn't sure what happened to bring about God noticing something was not right. Immediately, the Great Spirit left Eden to deal with Mother Earth's betrayal. When Shen arrived back in Eden, the people created in God's image also rebelled by eating the apple that was forbidden. Eden was taken from Adam and Eve leaving them earthbound and the garden disappeared soon afterwards becoming a mythical legend. Shen after a time forgave the people then called them Israelite's and the Great Spirit started encouraging them to produce offspring's.

God being preoccupied ignored the humans that were now evolving on their own, in time they outnumbered Adam's offspring's three to one. Cecille figured the reason the Great Spirit never mentioned Noah or his son's wives names in the Bible was because they were one of the evolved races; making them unclean at that time. Once Shen could no longer ignore the new humans more attention was paid to these people. God named them Gentiles then used them to teach the Hebrews who ended up split into three groups, Jews, Israelites, Judahs.

It wasn't long before they won their own place in Shen's heart. Although they were unclean at the time, a way to cleanse them and bring all people into the Great Spirits loving embrace occurred when the Messiah was born. When Jesus Christ died, all humans became clean through the blood of God's son and Christianity was born.

Cecille's Asian Guardian Shin was an evolved race so too were the people on the English Isle, which included Celtic's, Norse, Scottish,

Irish, and Englishman. People from France and several other people; they were all once considered Gentiles by God.

God's people then were Israelites, Jews, and Judahs, Romans, Egyptians, Spanish, and the Turkish as well as many others. These were all offspring's of Adam and Eve; although, most went their own way and didn't acknowledge the Great Spirit at all, which made them Gentiles to Shen as well.

Cecille was aware that with ships crossing the oceans regularly, intermixing would occur causing the people to become one.

Cecille sighed in annoyance bringing her thoughts back to the hidden entrances to heaven as she contemplated the fourth access. It was a well; it wasn't your typical water well, but one to the core of the Mother Earth. Technically it wasn't even a well only a black hole in the ground. White Buffalo liked to think of it as a well because it made it seem more... special than the black hole. Anyway, the well was continually shifting and hiding so nobody could get to Po.

Cecille's father told her years ago about dreams he had when they first came to Canada of oil derricks covering the Earth's surface in the future; they were even in the Ocean's. White Buffalo believed the petroleum pockets might be where the Mother Earth's wells were situated at one time. When Po moves, it leaves a pocket of oil in its wake to keep the hole available for later use just in case it was needed; if that was true, it could mean once the petroleum is removed it was no longer viable for reuse by the Mother Earth.

What would happen when Po's wells had nowhere else to go? Could that be what will ultimately destroy the Mother Earth in the future especially when the next Earth's destruction would be by fire! Petroleum was prone to burning for hours, look at what happened to the hotel. It ended up burning to the ground even though it rained hard most of the night because oil is almost impossible to extinguish when lit.

Cecille sighed in frustration as she shook her head reflectively; there was more to this than anyone knew and still she felt there was something important to this puzzle hidden from her. White Buffalo frowned thoughtfully why was she learning from the Mother Earth if God was angry with her had Shen forgiven Po or was there another sinister reason; the healer knew the end of days was coming, but not for another two hundred years or could White Buffalo be wrong? With the higher powers nothing was ever sure plus with the Earth shifting the other day, it could have shortened the end by ten or even one hundred years. Maybe even more, there was no way to know for sure!

Cecille should have Shin write a journal for her once they are settled; liking that idea White Buffalo pushed all thoughts of the Great Spirit's mysterious plans out of her mind until she could talk to the Tianming Monk about it.

Cecille's thoughts drifted to earlier, her experience with Violet's sister brought back unpleasant memories. She turned ten-years-old a few months before they left for Canada; living in a huge castle surrounded by friends, family, and servants hadn't prepared her for the realities of the outside world.

The Great Spirit was right it was her doing being entirely blind, it happened when they arrived in Montreal from Quebec City. An incident similar to what happened today forced her to block that ability; why, because of the violence she could see swirling around so many people. It tormented White Buffalo to the point where it made her physically sick. To deal with those people she had to turn off her power to see beyond their physical shell. Once done she couldn't figure out how to undo it, in time she forgot she did it.

Cecille's musings were interrupted by the sound of loud voices coming from outside, since they were faint they must be coming from down the street a ways; White Buffalo's hearing was exceptionally keen making up for the fact that she was blind.

Misfit growled a warning to her mistress when the voices rose louder in anger.

Cecille was just getting out of her chair when two shots were fired; White Buffalo scowled in concern before nudging her dog with her foot impatient to get her up off the floor. "Hurry Misfit let's go outside!"

Misfit needing no second urging jumped up, the dog pulled Cecille to the door; she guided White Buffalo onto the porch before stopping in front of her mistress to let her know there was danger ahead.

Cecille feeling her dog brush up against her remembered the steps, so stopped immediately. White Buffalo, hearing boots thumping loudly on the stairs, knew a man was rushing up to the hotel; she stepped in front of the landing keeping whoever was there from getting past her. "Can you tell me what is happening please?"

"Get out of my way woman I need to find the doctor!"

Cecille put out her hand quickly she could find her way if she absolutely had too, but this would be faster; White Buffalo just needed to grab her doctors bag, which was still on her packhorse. "Lead on, I am a certified physician..."

The man snorted in contempt not even letting Cecille finish. "A woman doctor that is blind not in my town there isn't!"

Cecille frowned in anger, she moved to the left knowing from the tone of his voice there would be no reasoning with him. Seconds later White Buffalo heard a stair creak, but no boot scuffs; she inhaled and knew instantly it was Shin as Misfit's tail wagged furiously hitting her mistress's leg in her enthusiasm. "Shadow Stalker I need my medicine bag!"

Shin took Cecille's hand then led her down the stairs before guiding her left towards the tavern. "Come, White Buffalo, I already stopped and picked up your doctor's bag. We were on our way to come get you when we met up with two arguing men. It seems the founder of this town made some nasty comments about another fellow's character, so got called out to a dual; I left our new guide holding a cloth to the Governors chest he is bleeding pretty bad!"

It only took them a few minutes to get to a crowd of people ringing the downed man. Shin impatiently pushed his way through the crowd; Misfit helped by growling in warning. The Tianming Monk handed Cecille her black doctor's bag before turning away to deal with the crowd of gawking people. He kept a snarling Misfit with him to help move them further back to give White Buffalo room.

Cecille ignored the people as well as her Guardian; kneeling she chanted lightly releasing White Buffalo so she could see briefly, but only long enough for her to get her bearings then she quit. Now working from memory, she put her hand over the man's forehead. Bending down Dr. Summerset listened to his ragged breathing before taking out her stethoscope; she listened again to his chest. She took over pressing down on the wound so she could send the burly guide on an errand. "I need hot water, quickly please."

Cecille went back to chanting, but a little stronger now; the bullet had lodged in the man's left lung, so it was filling up quickly with blood and fluid. White Buffalo needed to stop the swelling before she could safely move the man or remove the bullet.

Cecille heard a commotion behind her then the voice of the man from the stairs; he was trying to get past Shin, Misfit remembering his nasty demeanour to her mistress earlier snapped at him before growling in warning.

The sheriff stepped back quickly in surprise, but it didn't stop him from making loud demands; he pointed passed the Oriental in command arrogantly expecting immediate obedience. "I want that woman to quit whatever she is doing this instant I found a real doctor to tend to our Mayor!"

Cecille ignored him although it effectively stopped White Buffalo's muffled chanting.

Shin angrily eyed the blonde-haired, green-eyed, rude sheriff. He wasn't impressed with what he saw either; his disdain was glaringly obvious. Without moving an inch, the Guardian looked to the left assessing an older doctor with compassionate, warm brown eyes and greying brown hair. He had a black physician's bag that was similar to Cecille's; the Tianming Monk nodded in approval. "I am sure that Doctor Summerset would be glad to have your help, Doc."

The older doctor grinned at Shin then without a word to the angry sheriff brushed past the Oriental; he made sure to keep his distance from the dog. Kneeling on the opposite side of the injured man, so he wasn't in the woman's way he put his bag behind him before laying his hand over the woman's. "I am Doctor McGregor I will take over exerting pressure on the wound for you."

Cecille sat back in relief then nodded in thanks; it gave her an opportunity to open her black doctor's bag. She rummaged inside before pulling out a thick, sterile rawhide cloth. She put it beside her to keep her instruments up off the ground. Pulling out a scalpel next she placed it on her cloth then a long thin reed-like tube with a sharp pointed end was placed beside it. A bone mallet appeared next she had made it herself... a needle with thread, scissors, a bottle of laudanum, and several herb pouches followed. Finally, she added a small bottle of chloroform to the growing pile.

Chloroform was a new drug that Cecille's fathers partner from England shipped to him to try out here. When inhaled it caused a person to sleep deeply making it safe to operate on them. White Buffalo had used it once on a horse that was bloated since it only arrived a few months before she left the village; it is why she also had a hollow tube with a sharp pointy end. She was hoping to use the same method on the founder that she used on a bloated animal.

Cecille looked in the direction of her new helper. White Buffalo smiled distractedly. "Hello, Doctor McGregor it is nice to meet you. I'm Doctor Cecille Summerset; I have to warn you I mumble to myself quite a bit."

Dr. McGregor chuckled knowingly. "Yep, I noticed that."

Cecille finished her preparation just as she heard the guide's footsteps; she pointed for him to put the pan of hot water beside her supplies. White Buffalo had the Irishman take over exerting pressure on the wound then handed Dr. McGregor her needle; plus a fine, thin rawhide strip that she used to sew wounds up with. Dr. Summerset found rawhide to be stronger keeping the wound tighter so scaring wasn't as bad, the tricky part was to get the sinew thin enough. "Can you please thread that for me, while I get the tea?"

Cecille dipped a small cup that she kept in her bag for medicinal teas in her hot water she added herbs and laudanum to the cup; White Buffalo letting them steep cut open the man's shirt, exposing his ribs.

Cecille sat back then picked up the tea; she stirred it before sniffing it, satisfied that she had the right potency White Buffalo lifted the man's head. "Drink!"

Obediently the man took a drink, feebly he trying to push the awful tasting stuff away. "Yuck!"

Cecille chuckled unsympathetically making him drink almost all of it. White Buffalo left enough in so the needle and thread could be soaked in it; she handed the cup to the doctor. "Please put the needle after it is threaded in the solution to disinfect it."

Cecille knew too many people were watching to use her healing powers except a minuscule amount which meant there was no way to move the man without killing him; operating out here would have to suffice. White Buffalo doused a small rawhide in chloroform then put it over the man's mouth and nose for a count of twenty backward. Satisfied Dr. Summerset threw the rawhide cloth into the rest of the hot water it would be used later to clean the wound since chloroform was also an antiseptic.

Cecille bent closer so she could listen to the man's breathing; when she was satisfied it was deep enough, White Buffalo picked up the reed then put the thin tube between the third and fourth rib. Taking her mallet, she firmly struck the tube with the soft, flexible hammer. Dr. Summerset needed it to enter the lining of the lung before embedding inside just a little, not too much or she could disable the lung completely. The hole the healer wanted had to be just big enough to let the fluid flow into the reed, which would help to empty the lung.

Cecille softly chanting felt a bit of dampness on her finger, she sighed relieved it worked! She quit chanting bending down White Buffalo listened carefully; it took several long, excruciating minutes but thankfully she heard the man's breathing steady. "Whisky does anyone have some?"

The old physician pulled over his doctor's bag he extracted a bottle before pulling the cork out; Dr. McGregor passed it to the blind woman with a verbal caution. "Here, I have some I opened."

Cecille nodded in thanks distractedly. The healer pushed the guides hand away from the wound before pouring the whisky onto the scalpel that she picked up.

Cecille made sure to hold the knife over top of the wound, so the alcohol dribbled onto the man's chest to clean away the blood. It would help to disinfect the skin around the bullet hole at the same time; she handed the bottle back to the other doctor to hold for her. White Buffalo, feeling around the injury carefully inserted the scalpel then dug around for what seemed like an eternity.

Finally, Cecille heard the distinct sound of metal on metal then pulled it free in triumph. She threw the bullet into the cup with the cold tea in it. Dr. Summerset closed up the wound; once done she put the needle back into the container, it turned the liquid an even brighter red.

Cecille reached over then pulled out the soft rawhide cloth that was still in the water. She wrung it before she gently cleaned the blood away. White Buffalo gave just enough healing energy that no infection could take hold; it was also sufficient to close the hole in the man's lung, but not the one in his side. Dr. Summerset pulled the tube out slowly; she threw it into the basin of water. Taking the whisky from the other doctor, the healer doused his wounds once more.

Cecille pulled the needle out of the cup to put one stitch in the governor's side, satisfied it wouldn't bleed White Buffalo put the needle back. "Dr. McGregor, do you have a bandage big enough to wrap around this man's chest?"

Doctor McGregor murmured a soft affirmative; he pulled out a bandage before wrapping the man's chest himself. He had watched the blind woman doctor in fascination, he even helped where needed but hadn't interfered in any way. Dr. Summerset had unknowingly taught him several new things the man sighed wistfully. He couldn't help but ask even though he had little hope. "I could use a doctor with your talents, would you be interested in staying here?"

Cecille stood up calmly before dusting the dirt off she needed a minute to compose her expression. White Buffalo looked up with a genuine smile of regret, having seen the doctor's aura when he touched her; she knew he would die soon. The healer wanted so much to blurt it allowed, but it wasn't permitted. "No, I'm sorry; we

Twin Destinies

are headed for the border of Ontario and Quebec, you will look after this man now I hope?"

Dr. McGregor, seeing a few people he knew gestured for them to come to him. "Can you put the Governor in my wagon please, I will take him to my place to recuperate; it will give my wife something to do she loves to spoil my patients rotten."

Doctor McGregor turned back to the woman before reaching out he took her hand in his; he made sure to include the Oriental too. "Godspeed to you both I will be sure to thank the good Lord tonight that you arrived in time to save the founder of our town!"

Within moments the street cleared, Shin helped Cecille gather her stuff then put everything back in her doctor's bag. When they stopped for the night, White Buffalo would boil everything.

Shin introduced the guide to Cecille as they headed back to the hotel to gather their horses.

Brandan pointed out the store, after what he just witnessed the guide no longer had any qualms about taking the blind woman doctor through Algonquin Park; Cecille proved to him beyond a doubt that she could look after herself. "I will meet ya at the store I need to gets me a mule."

Shin nodded before they parted company, the Tianming Monk steered Cecille towards the hotel; White Buffalo needed to change back to her travelling clothes. Unfortunately, her blouse got thrown in the garbage having blood all over it. It took them another two hours, but they were finally on their way out of town.

*****

Brandan kicked his mule to catch up to Shin; he estimated that they had been riding for about an hour or so now. The guide had stayed behind watching their back trail since this road was easy to follow along here. They wouldn't be going far anyway before camping for the night. If they had gotten an earlier start, they could have made it to Alice, which was the next town on this road, it was only eighteen miles from Eganville.

Brandan decided to take them there before deciding which way to go; it was central to the two trails that they needed to take to get them to the north-west border of Quebec and Ontario. "There are other people following us."

Shin frowned, looking around the Tianming Monk pointed out a hill with lots of trees in the distance. "You both can hide there I will go back around to get behind them; they could be just travelling in the same direction as us, but I would rather make sure first."

Brandan nodded in agreement he reached out taking hold of Cecille's horse's reins; the guide swung them left it wasn't long before they began climbing a steep hill, he didn't need to take them far into the thick trees.

Shin turned right; within seconds the Tianming Monk vanished.

Brandan jumped down from his mule before gathering the other two horses closer to him he put a hand over their snouts to keep them quiet; unfamiliar with the pair, he wasn't sure if they would call out. He stiffened in anger when the three rode past their hiding spot then began to quarrel. They were loud enough he had no trouble at all hearing what they were saying."

"I am telling you Roger, they came this way. The woman will bring us a high price across the border the Comanche always pay well. That bag of coins given to the Irishman was heavy; I heard the Chink say that it was only part of the payment."

Brandan heard a grunt suddenly followed closely by a thud; he released the horse's reins before racing out of the trees to help Shin, but there was no need all three men were huddled on the ground. He turned back to retrieve White Buffalo, the packhorse, plus his mule.

Shin looked over at Brandan when he heard him returning. The Tianming Monk gestured down at the huddling men curious to hear the Irishman's answer; it would also give him a good idea what kind of man they had as their guide. "They are from town what would you suggest we do with them?"

Brandan shrugged with an angry frown the guide gestured down grimly. "After what I just heard I think we should shoot them now; it will save the sheriff a lot of trouble."

Brandan let the three stammer, pleading for their miserable lives. All the emotion he showed was a curled lip, which showed his disdain for the lot of them. Having heard enough, he held up his hand for silence. "On second thought shootin is too good for them. Send their horses back to town without them, maybe the long walk will teach them a lesson; if they hurry, they can make it before dark I hear the wolves are pretty hungry at this time of year."

Shin chuckled in approval, liking that idea; the Guardian couldn't help thinking as he walked over to the animals that he had chosen wisely in their guide. One by one he tied the horse's reins around their necks before the Tianming Monk slapped their rumps sending them on their way.

Brandan drew his gun; he shot at the ground behind the horses spooking them more.

Cecille gestured down at her dog in a shooing motion; White Buffalo knew that she would enjoy the pursuit plus she needed the exercise. "Go chase the horses for a bit, Misfit come back when you are tired."

Misfit raced off ecstatically she loved to run, this slow travelling was tedious.

Brandan dismounted, he took all the men's weapons he didn't want them getting any bright ideas, like trying to double back; he waved one of their guns negligently to get them up before pointing towards town. "Better skedaddle or I will change my mind it would be interesting to see what the Orientals sword could do when used to take off someone's head!"

Needing no more urging the three raced off without looking back.

Brandan waited till they were out of sight, he threw the three revolvers into the trees before mounting his mule; the guide gestured for Shin to precede him. "We need to pick up our pace more, they probably won't be back but I want to put as much distance as possible between us."

Shin nodded as he replaced his sword he took over the lead once more; the Tianming Monk broke into a faster, ground eating trot.

*****

Three hours later Brandan called a halt. "I will guide ya from here there is an overgrown path ahead we need to get down to lead the horses in. It goes to an old abandoned logging shack, we can stay there for the night; it will give us some shelter since those dark clouds are getting closer."

Shin helped Cecille off her horse the Tianming Monk pulled out her cane before handing it to her.

It took them another half an hour to reach the camp, but none of them complained as a cold breeze picked up then the rain began to fall. A shelter with a roof was preferable to no shelter at all, especially in this type of weather. They stripped the animals before leading them to a lean-to in the back, Shin fed the horses some grain; thankfully there was hay inside for them to nibble on during the night. Brandan hobbled his mule, but Cecille left her mares loose they wouldn't go far without her or the Tianming Monk, White Buffalo's father taught them well.

Cecille carried the saddlebag with food on her shoulder; her doctor's bag was in her left hand. Shin gave them to her to bring into the cabin; once inside she inhaled deeply before following the smell of burnt wood to the fireplace, making sure to keep her cane out so she didn't run into anything. White Buffalo hummed as she walked, it helped her to find the hearth without incidence. She knelt to pull out two cans of beans, coffee, and bacon.

Shin followed Cecille in a few minutes later; the Tianming Monk dropped an armload of wood he found at the back of the shed beside the fireplace. He took the bucket of water he got from the well to the other side of the fire and left it there so it was out of his way. It didn't take him long to start a fire, finding a pot for water he filled it half full so White Buffalo could boil her instruments. When Shadow Stalker was finished, he knelt beside his charge to give her a description of the one room cabin. Afterwards, he helped her go through her doctor's bag while supper was cooking.

Brandan pulled out sleeping furs since the others were busy with supper the guide made up three pallets; of course being a gentleman the cot had Cecille's white buffalo hide on it.

With the three of them working together it didn't take long for plates to get pulled out they all helped themselves to supper; Shin handed out cups for some much needed hot coffee.

Cecille was about to sit down when White Buffalo heard an excited bark at the door.

Brandan jumped up to let in a soggy Misfit.

Misfit entering promptly shook; water flew in every direction.

Cecille yelled at her dog indignantly when she unexpectedly got sprayed. White Buffalo wiped the water off her face in irritation. "Misfit, stop that this instance; go lay down by the fire, you need to dry off!"

Brandan couldn't help chuckling when he saw a drop of water dribble off Shin's nose.

Misfit whined when her beloved mistress scolded her. She slunk over to the fire obediently before dropping down in front of it. With her tongue hanging, she panted heavily; exhausted from the chase, she enjoyed the warmth.

Cecille fed her dog the leftovers.

Brandan belched in appreciation when finished eating before sitting back the guide eyed the beautiful blind Cecille inquisitively. "If I'm not mistaken, you are Celtic, or Welsh are ya not; who taught ye to be such a good doctor?"

Cecille smiled at the curious Irishman, Brandan spoke good English most of the time; only once in a while when he wasn't paying attention did he drop the 'th' sound then used a 'd' instead. He also used ye, which meant you and most of the time ya was used to describe one person. He didn't use them too often, only occasionally. The guide quite often dropped the 'g' using 'in' instead of 'ing' at the end of a word. "My Father was Earl Edward Summerset my Mother was Lady Mary Crystin Alexandrina of Llannor Castle. Llannor is in the middle of a little jut of land called Llyn Peninsula. It is between Caernarfon Bay and Cardigan Bay; both Bays go out to the St George's Channel which leads into the Irish Sea. There are six castles right on the cliffs that keep watch for invaders, but Llannor is the primary defence of the inlet."

Brandan sat up in interest at the name of her mother and the castle in Wales. "Well, I guess we are related fifth or sixth cousins I think! Oh, that explains why every time I look at ye... ya remind me of Eriu. She is a Goddess or the Mother of Ireland which your mother's people are directly descended from; if ya believe in the old magic of the Irish, Celtic, or Welsh druids that is."

Cecille laughed in amusement; White Buffalo had suspected that there was Irish in her family, it had been discreetly hidden all these years. "It is so interesting to meet others that are related even this far away from our homeland. I believe the Irish, Welsh, Scottish, and the British people all intermingled throughout the years even though nobody wants to admit it; especially, between Ireland and Wales."

Shin went to the fire to refilled his coffee cup; he brought the rest over before emptying the last of it in Cecille's cup when Brandan shook his head then put his hand over his cup.

Cecille smiled up at her Guardian in thanks; White Buffalo turned back to Brandan. "My father is Earl Summerset he graduated a doctor with full honours from Harvard in England. My Dad taught me everything he knows."

Brandan sat forward in interest with a nostalgic chuckle. "Oh, the famous Earl of Summerset three-quarters Cheyenne and a quarter English, my cousin was a Lady-in-waiting at the time. Whenever she came home to Ireland, she would tell us about the wondrous things the Earl would do. It took our minds of our hungry bellies, especially when she came home with treats for us. She was there the night Dr. Summerset saved the Queen's life; someone poisoned her while she was celebrating your father's graduation. He became our Majesties personal physician as his reward. Wish I could have met him, I was quite sad when it became known publicly he died. I thought your parents only had one boy though?"

Cecille smiled enticingly she waved vaguely to the south. White Buffalo had no qualms in telling the Irish guide their secret. "You still can, when you are finished being our guide go to Perth. My father goes to town quite regularly since he lives not too far from there. My parents did have a boy he is my twin; I was kept hidden because they didn't think I would live at first, which is why they never register me with the other royal children. Besides my Father knew he would have to leave my brother in England to become the next earl, he didn't want to give up both his children. The rumour of his death was for the Queen's benefit; he was supposed to go to Manitoba for Victoria, but he got sidetracked then ended up marrying an Ojibwe woman. A Chief's Daughter, now they are about to have their first child together."

Brandan smiled in delight he had always wanted to meet the famous earl; unknowingly, the Cheyenne and English doctor had been a huge inspiration to the young impoverished Irish Lord as a boy. "I just might do that, thank you. I can take a letter to him for ya, I'm sure he will be quite anxious to know how ye are farin."

Cecille nodded in agreement; she picked up her cane before getting up, ready for bed now that her instruments were drying. White Buffalo didn't really need a letter to communicate with her father, but the guide wouldn't know that. "I will make one later, thank you goodnight."

The two men mumbled goodnight, they visited for a bit longer to give Cecille a little privacy before they also went to bed.

CHAPTER THIRTEEN

Spirit Bear sat in front of his fire cooking broth there were four men in his wigwam a woman died at dawn. It seemed to hit the men the hardest, thankfully only occasionally did a woman die of it. Why would the Cree healer become upset if more women were dying compared to men; because they needed the women to produce more generations, without them their people would die out becoming extinct. The medicine man added herbs to the water then sat back with a frown of concentration.

Spirit Bear's thoughts turned to his frustrating inability to trap his brother in one spot long enough to discuss anything. He refused to give up; the medicine man would try again later today to approach his brother. Still, he didn't know what he was going to say to him as of yet.

For four days, Spirit Bear sought to talk to Powaw about the strange vision he had the night their father died; aggravatingly his twin brother would disappear into his wigwam as soon as he saw the medicine man coming.

Spirit Bear took the broth off the fire before pouring it into four bowls the others were still sleeping; hopefully, it would be cooled enough by the time they woke up. The medicine man just finished putting the pot down when shouts followed closely by a woman's grieving cries from outside, had him jumping up... hurriedly, he left his wigwam.

Already a ring of curious onlookers surrounded the chief, shaman, and four others. Spirit Bear could tell by the intricately beaded headbands that the four in the centre were Guardians of the tribe; they were strategically placed around the village to keep outsiders out. It wasn't until the medicine man pushed his way through the crowd to the centre that he saw four others, two were dead. One was a warrior the other one was a white man.

The other two were white-eyes as well but blindfolded both were kneeling with hands tied behind their backs. The man's hair was a strange red colour the white woman had the lightest colour hair he had ever seen.

A heated discussion on what to do with the two captives was taking place this wasn't the first time a white-eyes had been found encroaching on their land. The last time was about seven years ago, but there was no bloodshed.

Spirit Bear, getting an unexpected vision of an old white man in his wigwam from Misimanito a few months before that kept the trapper as a slave.

For five years the old man taught him English; the slave also told the medicine man tales about the land beyond his home, which he passed to his chief. Unfortunately, the trapper succumbed to the disease afflicting the village that unexpectedly resurfaced only after being dormant two years once they settled in these mountains.

Powaw gestured angrily trying to make his point more dramatic; the shaman figured they wouldn't listen to him anyway, but he argued heatedly just the same. "They both must die immediately the white man killed one of our Guardians so we can't let them leave here. If they find their way back, the white-eyes will kill all of our people when they discover us."

The old chief with arms folded in resolution shook his head in finality he couldn't justify taking such a risk. "No, if we start killing white-eyes more will come for revenge then all our people will surely die; with the death of so many of our braves lately from the sickness, we can't afford to lose anymore. They were captured and blindfolded before they entered the hidden pass, the Guardians can take them far away."

The chief saw the medicine man so gestured for him to come forward knowing he was the only one who could speak their language. "Spirit Bear, you will explain to the captives they won't get harmed; they will be taken close to one of their villages before being released, but only if the two take an oath. They must swear never to come back this way again!"

Spirit Bear nodded in relief glad his twin hadn't gotten his way, he agreed with their chief too many deaths had occurred lately; he knelt in front of the captives. Obediently, the medicine man gave the two reassurances from his chief before he added a final warning of his own. "You must never come this way again, or next time I can't guarantee you will live! One of your people is dead, but so too has one of our warriors gone to the happy hunting grounds of Misimanito... a life is given for a life. There will be no retribution from my people, just as I am sure there will be none from yours. Do you wish to keep the dead man or leave him here we will give him a warrior's funeral if you wish."

Both captives wilted in relief and vehemently swore on their lives to never return or come back for revenge. The red-headed man sighed grimly at the death of his friend; he remembered seeing him shoot at an Indian that they stumbled upon without provocation before an arrow entered his chest. Unfortunately, he had a wife and two small children; they tried to leave him behind, but he refused to stay there insisting he too wanted to search the mountain streams for gold. "No, we need to take him to his family so they can mourn for him properly."

Spirit Bear satisfied with their sincere vow got up; the medicine man gestured towards the Guardians. "Take them away they will not return. The white-eyes also wish to keep their dead so you can take him too."

Powaw snorted in contempt before turning away he stalked back to his wigwam; the shaman knew it would not end there sooner or later the two would tell what they knew then more white people would come.

Spirit Bear unable to pass up such a good opportunity, raced after his younger twin; the medicine man slowed before falling into step beside the shaman. "Powaw!"

Powaw swung around in a rage; the shaman held up his hand grimly to stop his brother from advancing any further. He pointed an accusing finger towards his twin. "Spirit Bear you know that they will come back with more of their people, if they do our people's deaths will be your fault!"

Spirit Bear shrugged resignedly, Powaw would find a way to blame him... regardless. The medicine man stopped as commanded before trying to reason with the shaman. "Maybe, but you know we can't hide here indefinitely; if the sickness isn't halted soon someone will have to go to their town to try finding a cure; killing these white-eyes will not help our cause, the whites could have or know a medicine that will work."

Powaw growled before turning to stalk away in anger, he mumbled to himself infuriated that nobody listens to their shaman.

Spirit Bear sighed in aggravation before trying one more time to speak to his brother. The medicine man hesitantly took several more steps than stopped. "Powaw!"

Powaw spun around angrily the shaman stabbed a finger towards Spirit Bear. "I am not interested in anything you have to say now stay away from me!"

Powaw turned continuing his infuriated march to his wigwam.

Spirit Bear stayed where he was the medicine man called out one final time, beseechingly. "Powaw, I received an unusual vision from the Great Spirit; we need to go on a quest together!"

Powaw stopped at the door of his wigwam in surprise, why Spirit Bear would get such a vision and not the shaman only made him angrier; eventually, he called over his shoulder in a rage not even turning to look at the medicine man this time. "NEVER!"

Powaw with that heated statement of finality disappeared inside.

Spirit Bear sighed dejectedly he couldn't force Powaw to go with him as much as he wished he could. He turned to find his apprentice, so be it he would just have to go on his own. He would leave the village once all the arrangements for the care of the sick were seen too. Because the medicine man's apprentice was young; he would need a detailed list of things to do. He couldn't leave tonight since they must send their Guardian to the happy hunting grounds of the Great Spirit first. Hopefully, he could get everything arranged within a couple of days; he wanted to be gone no later than the third.

****

Cecille grumbled irritably under her breath, they had been on the trail for three hours now. She was sopping wet, chilled right down to the bone; luckily, the rain quit about half an hour ago but the sun was still behind dark clouds keeping it cold and damp. Needing to take her mind off her chilled body White Buffalo turned to their guide Brandan. "How long have you lived in Canada?"

Brandan frowned painfully, remembering his youth. "Thirty-five years about, I was just a teenager when both my parents then my sister died in the great potato famine of Ireland; being a Lord didn't help us any. I managed to find a ship soon afterwards, so I sailed with them till we landed here. I did odd jobs for a couple of years, till I met up with an old French trapper who needed someone young to handle chores. It was one of the best decision I made teaming up with him, he died years ago of smallpox."

Cecille listened sadly to his tale she saw in her mind a wolf howling sorrowfully at a full red moon. White Buffalo opened her mouth to give Brandan his name from the Mother Earth; all that came out though was a gasp of shock at the sound of a far off scream of pain and fear. She reined her horse towards the left.

Shin was two steps ahead, lucky for them the trees here were further apart since the larger ones got logged long ago. Neither was there much undergrowth because the soil was so hard, it was also extremely rocky. The Tianming Monk pulled out one of his daggers as he dashed towards the sound of the scream.

Cecille chanted to release White Buffalo so she could see.

Twin Destinies

Brandan streaked passed Cecille's big mare since his mule was smaller he could get around the trees faster. He pulled out his rifle as he came abreast of Shin then caulked it; the Irishman barrelled out into an open field, within seconds two shots rang out since it only took the experienced guide a moment to process the scene.

Shin threw his dagger just as the second shot rang out the Tianming Monk watched in satisfaction as a third wolf halted in its tracks before dropping dead.

Brandan jumped off his mule, within minutes he was standing in front of a woman protectively with a snarling Misfit beside him; two other wolves with tails tucked in disappointment at losing their easy meal vanished back into the trees.

Cecille jumped off her horse before pulling out her cane; White Buffalo grabbed her Indian medicine bag. "Shin, I can smell the wolves from here can you make sure they aren't rabid."

Brandan rushed over then took Cecille's hand before leading her to the woman with blood dripping from her arm. "There are two women one is beyond help because she has her throat torn out, the other ones wounded. She has a knife pointed at us, but hasn't moved; I can't tell how badly she is hurt, both women are native even though they are wearing white woman's clothes. They could be Algonquin I think, not sure where the tribe is most of the natives out here are west of Petawawa on a reserve."

Cecille nodded her thanks when Brandan halted her; White Buffalo gestured over her shoulder needing some privacy. "Please go help Shin check for rabies; for God sake's though don't touch any of them if they have foam around their snouts it's a highly contagious disease, with a painful cure!"

Cecille knelt before putting her cane on the ground. She put her medicine bag down beside it. She switched to Ojibwa; thankfully, out here the native languages were similar except for a few syllables added or subtracted depending on where you were from. The plains, central, or eastern Indian tribes all used the Algonquin language making it possible to understand an Ojibwe, a Cree, a Pottawatomi, a Blackfoot, and others.

Cecille shook off her distracted thoughts. "I am White Buffalo, shaman/medicine woman of the Ojibwe by the three big waters. My companions are an Oriental named Shadow Stalker the tall man is an Irishman called Brandan. What is your name and where is your tribe; why are you two out here alone... you are hurt, will you let me treat your wound?"

The young woman eyed Cecille suspiciously. Finally, the pain was too much and she dropped the knife before holding out her arm then spoke in perfect English. "We are not from any tribe, at least not since I was a child. We were captured by three white men when we were fifteen and twelve; afterwards, we got sold to the Madame in town. Thankfully, she wasn't unkind to us. She died two days ago so they will be selling us again. I convinced my sister to run away with me, now she is dead because of me."

Cecille gathered her close then let her cry out her sorrow and fear, the wound wasn't that dangerous; White Buffalo knew the puncture marks on the girl's arm would mend, but the damage inside was even deeper it might never heal.

Shin trotted up he cleared his throat softly. The Tianming Monk hated to interrupt, but Cecille needed to know. "White Buffalo they aren't rabid, but were starving; one is female with nursing pups."

Cecille sighed in relief at that good news White Buffalo whistled her dog over. "Shin, you can take Misfit with you to help find the den. If the wolf pups are too young to survive the best thing would be to kill them, so they don't suffer for days; starving to death is a slow painful death."

Cecille tilted the woman's head upwards with her finger White Buffalo tenderly wiped the tears away. "I must see to your wound now; what is your name and how old are you?"

The young woman looked down in embarrassment as she shrugged sadly. "Don't remember my name from before, the Madame called me Silk because my skin was smooth and shiny silky looking. I was twelve when they took me; we were at that house for eight long years. Thankfully I served as her personal maid because my older sister agreed to service the men's special appetites if I became a handmaid to the Madame. My sister was fifteen, more beautiful than I was. She always dressed me in loose ugly clothes afterwards to make sure nobody looked too closely she would put paint on my face to make me look even uglier. She also taught me to talk with a lisp, so I spoke dumb, except when private with the Madame. Once sold, my sister would no longer be able to protect me."

While the girl was talking, Cecille was busy wrapping the girl's arm. She bled quite a bit, but it wasn't as bad as it first seemed; lucky for her no stitches were required. White Buffalo finished before repacking her bag. She was just sitting back when she heard a dog howl in the distance as it found the distinctive scent of its prey. "Silk get behind me, quickly now!"

Cecille grabbed her cane; she pulled the sword out a bit but didn't draw it completely. White Buffalo crouched there waiting.

Brandan ran in front of the two women, he lifted his Winchester rifle to his shoulder but didn't pull down the lever. If he did, it would put a bullet in the chamber, and he wasn't sure if he needed one yet, so he waited patiently; it would only take a flick of his hand to arm it. The guide could hear several horses with at least one dog or maybe two.

Misfit suddenly appeared from nowhere then ran into the clearing she crouched in front of her mistress with fangs bared; several tense moments later Cecille's dog jumped up then raced passed Brandan as two massive hounds lunged into the open.

Misfit jumped towards the one in front she went straight for the dog's juggler. Unfortunately, she missed her mark as the other dog barrelled into her knocking her from her intended victim; she squealed in pain.

Brandan pulled down on his lever; he heard the bullet enter the chamber with satisfaction, aiming he tried to shoot. Unexpectedly, Misfit jumped up getting in his way. The big Irishman blinked when a blur of motion streaked passed him, within seconds one dog lay dead with a knife protruding from his eye.

Misfit had the other hound on the ground; her powerful jaws were clamped on the dog's throat waiting for permission to kill him. Cecille's dog was tall and lean taking after her father, but she inherited the Staffordshire terrier's ability to lock their jaws from her mother. If she didn't want to let go only death would make her!

Cecille heard a shrill whistle in the distance; White Buffalo having watched the drama unfold through the Mother Earth's images called her dog off. "Let him go, Misfit!"

Misfit growled again in warning before obediently she released her hold; Cecille's dog trotted over to Shin who was now standing beside Brandan with sword drawn and held out ready for use.

The red and white haired dog on the ground, twice Misfit's size, whined in submission before getting up with tail tucked then ran towards his master.

Three men trotted into the little clearing with the leader out in front. He looked down at his red long haired Nova Scotia retriever dog in relief he had paid a lot of money for her; she hurried past him bleeding and limping, but at least alive. Looking down at the black Newfoundlander dog lying dead with a knife sticking out of his eye, he tsked in regret. He pulled his horse to a halt beside the dead animal then leaned forward insolently before pointing at his dog. "It isn't very sporting of you to kill someone else's animals!"

Shin shrugged dismissively; the Tianming Monk felt no remorse for killing a vicious dog nor for that matter would he feel bad for the ones who trained them that way. "I wouldn't have had to do it if they wouldn't have attacked us first!"

The man inclined his head in acknowledgement then pointed towards the dead woman. "Well, since I wasn't close enough to see what happened guess I will have to take your word on that; did my dog kill the girl they are not trained to do so, but I suppose accidents do happen!"

Shin frowned grimly; he shook his head, the Tianming Monk didn't believe him. "No, wolves got her before we could get here!"

The man nodded affirmatively before giving the Oriental a smirk, he gestured inquisitively. "Is it the older girl or the simpleton?"

Shin scowled angrily not caring the man at all his dislike was instantaneous; the Tianming Monk shrugged dismissively with a sharp tone he conveyed his feelings to everyone. "Does it matter?!"

The man's grin slipped a little he sat up in his saddle in aggravation. "Not from these parts are you; both women are my property, so yes it does matter!"

Cecille had her new Stetson hat pulled down low to shade her face she was just glad she bought one before they left town. White Buffalo didn't want the man to see her they were slavers dealing mostly in women for brothels; she switched to Japanese not wanting them to understand her. "She is the younger simple one."

Shin moved to peek quickly at Cecille with no worries, knowing Brandan had his back; he turned his attention back to the man the Tianming Monk was glad White Buffalo was taking precautions. "I was just told she is the simple one."

The man sighed angrily before reaching up he pulled his hat off as he scratched his head irritably. He couldn't help remembering the last time he had two sisters and one turned out to be retarded. The simple one killed herself after she found out her sister died, so he lost more money in funeral costs than the two girls were worth. He stared past the woman at the girl moaning and rocking herself violently. Eventually making up his mind, he jammed his hat back on his head in finality. "Well, that is too bad; since I don't have time for a simpleton you can keep her."

With that statement of disgust the slaver gestured at one of his men to pick up the dead girl; having claimed her, he couldn't leave her there with so many witnesses. He swung his horse around before twirling his finger at his comrades then whistled for his dog to follow; showing no emotions towards the animal laying on the ground, he left the dead dog for the scavengers. Thankfully, it wasn't long until they disappeared towards town.

Brandan having loaded a bullet into the chamber carefully lower the hammer he put on the safety to make sure the weapon wouldn't accidentally get discharged; later the guide would remove the bullet, but not yet he still might need it.

Shin walked over to the dead dog and pulled his dagger out of its eye before wiping his blade clean then turned back; he walked over to Cecille. He sat in front of the girl, who was still rocking back and forth violently; the Tianming Monk eyed her reflectively when she quieted then stilled suddenly, but spoke to White Buffalo. "She is a bit simple?"

Cecille turned to face Shin; White Buffalo shook her head before explaining everything the girl had told her earlier.

Brandan walked over before squatting beside Shin he frowned in aggravation once Cecille was finished then gestured inquisitively, needing to know in what direction they wanted to go now. "Well, so much for staying in town tonight. Two miles ahead, right on the main road is a fork that goes straight into town or branches north-east. It will take us a day or two to reach the Ontario and Quebec border from there; we can follow it as far as ya need to go. We can also go north-west it cuts through Algonquin Park, but it is tough going. It will take a week if not more to get to the border with lots of rivers needing crossing or finding ways around, which means plenty of backtracking. We can leave the girl in the next town if we can find a suitable place for her."

Silk sat forward with an angry huff of annoyance; she surprised herself when she talked back to the Irish guide. "I am not your property to put anywhere nor will I let anyone own me again!"

The Irishman's face turned red as a beet; Brandan stammered in apology. "I am sorry I didn't mean it like that miss!"

"Ggrrr... ruff!"

Everyone froze for a heartbeat before all eyes swung to Shin's moving shirt as a little whimper escaped from inside.

Shin chuckled at the three identical shocked expressions turned his way; the Tianming Monk reached inside his shirt before pulling out a two-week-old puppy. "There was only one; I just couldn't kill him with those big blue sorrowful eyes staring at me helplessly."

Shin put the pup on the ground; the Tianming Monk watched the little wolf in interest when he started stumbling around, he looked like he was on a mission all of a sudden. He went to Brandan first. The baby wolf sniffed him before turning away then went to Cecille next. He licked White Buffalo's hand, but again he didn't stay. Tripping over his two paws the pup toddled over to the girl; he sniffed her foot first. Afterwards, he tried to crawl into her lap.

Silk pushed the pup away in anger. "Get away from me!"

Cecille picked up the pup before putting him in the girl's lap. White Buffalo took Silk's hand then put it on the baby wolf. "This puppy is meant for you at one time your name was Singing Wolf; the Mother Earth gave you this name as a child. Now that you are marked by the wolf, someday you will sing the wolf-song to the moon your pup will teach you. He will also aid you in healing."

Cecille turned to Brandan with a smile of satisfaction White Buffalo reached over and took the guides hand. "The Mother Earth has also given you the name Red Wolf; the wolf will now be your spiritual guide, as well."

Shin turned to Cecille then changed the subject; the Tianming Monk didn't want to stay here. "Which way do you want to go?"

Cecille placed her palms on the Mother Earth. Closing her eyes, she listened intently for a long moment before White Buffalo pointing north-east. "We will follow the border I'm not sure how far we are going, but there was urgency in the command to get closer to Quebec; a week I sensed was too long."

Brandan nodded thoughtfully he rubbed his chin distractedly staring off into the distance recalculating. A few minutes later he sighed hopefully, the guide pointed back towards the trail. "Petawawa is about twelve, maybe fifteen miles from here. If we pick up our pace, we can still make it before dark barring any more unforeseen sidetracks that is. There is a well-used trapper's trail that is relatively easy going having been used for many years. The town is more of a logging, Algonquin, and trapper's settlement than a family community. Still, they are a friendly bunch. Four years ago they were putting in rail lines; there was a lot of inspiring talks last time I was in the town of finding a way to bring in more families once the train came regularly."

Cecille took the pup from the girl so she could get up. White Buffalo stood up too, she handed the baby wolf to the young woman. "Put the pup inside your shirt close to your heart he will sleep for quite a while there; I will make him some corn meal mush later when we stop to rest. You can ride the filly she is well trained to follow, so just hold on. She will not run unless her dame does."

Once, Singing Wolf, had the pup settled Brandan took her over and helped her up onto the packhorse before vaulting into his saddle. He waited for Shin to tie Cecille's mare to the back of the guide's saddle; the Tianming Monk would keep their rear guarded now. A few minutes later, they were off once more.

*****

Brandan pulled up he waited for Shin to catch up; the guide pointed ahead. "We are about halfway now I think we should be far enough from the town of Alice we can eat. The pup is starting to fuss I can hear him from here, which means other humans or animals can also hear him. There is a camp ahead about a mile that I have used in the past. It always has dry wood all that is required to use it is replacing what ya use."

Shin nodded in agreement; the Tianming Monk fell back to guard their rear. As promised within minutes they were all dismounting.

Brandan rushed over to help Singing Wolf get off Cecille's packhorse; she was such a tiny thing it barely took any effort for the guide to lift her down.

Singing Wolf put her hands onto Brandan's broad muscular shoulders tentatively so she could steady herself; she couldn't help looking into Red Wolf's beautiful eyes. Her breath caught in surprise when a twinkle of laughter lit them up making them change to a hazel green.

Brandan feeling Singing Wolf's body react to his grinned devilishly, but suddenly she stiffened in fear; immediately, the guide set her on her feet before turning away he hurried over to Shin without a word, aware she needed time to get use to him.

Singing Wolf stared after him in vexation; she grumbled irritably at being ignored, but quickly went over to help Cecille. She received a lesson on how to prepare then feed a nourishing mush to her wolf pup before she was allowed to eat her own meal.

Within two hours they were once again in the saddle; just before leaving Brandan gave the camp one more intent look. Satisfied that no trace of them remained, the guide kicked his mule into a trot.

*****

Brandan was grumbling irritably to himself four hours later while staring off to the east in trepidation. Suddenly, the guide reined his mule around so he could call Shin in closer. He looked down at the Tianming Monk in caution; Red Wolf had to raise his voice because the wind had picked up trying to drown out his warning. "We are still an hour and a half to two hours from Petawawa, but there is a big storm heading this way from the Quebec side. Last time I was in one of these, it had blustery high winds, heavy rain, with some hail, and lightning. We can either find shelter or make a run for it. Thankfully, it is easy going from here. Closer to town there is trees to contend with; making the possibility of lightning hitting higher!"

Shin frowned grimly; the Tianming Monk gestured ahead. "We should quit talking then I'll lead since the road is easy to follow."

Cecille whistled at her dog; White Buffalo held up her hands until Misfit settled in front of her. "I agree, let's go!"

Shin unhooked Cecille's mare from Brandan's saddle before grasping the reins. The Tianming Monk didn't need to keep a hold of the horse, but it made him feel better. There was still a lot of daylight if the storm caught them Shadow Stalker would have to slow down or risk injury to one of the horses; for now, running as fast as he could go was the only option.

Forty-five minutes later Shin had no choice but to slow when a fierce wind and blacker storm clouds overtook them making it almost impossible to see; he tenaciously continued at a ground eating trot. A half-hour later the rain was coming down in a solid sheet with lightning flashing in the distance every few minutes. When it settled Shadow Stalker was able to see several tiny pinpricks of lights ahead, he picked up his pace even more.

Brandan raced up to Shin then retook the lead from him; the guide was impressed by how quickly the Oriental had managed to get them to town. Especially, considering the Tianming Monk ran the whole way. "There is a hotel with an eating place just ahead, follow me it also has a barn behind it."

Shin nodded; thankful the horses would be close. The Tianming Monk needed the barn to be next to where they were staying. Particularly after the fiasco in the first town that they stayed in, just in case they needed to leave in a hurry again! Ten minutes later, they were crowded in the stables shaking and shivering chilled to the bone.

Shin helped Misfit down then Cecille; he handed her the cane, a saddlebag with their clothes in it before giving White Buffalo the doctor's bag. The Tianming Monk undid his trunk with his carpet inside then pulled off the packsaddle of food that needed a cold room. Last Shadow Stalker took Misfit's harness off the saddle horn but didn't put it on her.

Brandan waved them on to the hotel; the guide included them all but addressed Shin directly. "I will look after the horses, while you get us a couple of rooms. I believe there are baths for the men in the back with tubs in the ladies rooms."

Shin nodded thanks before taking the lead. The Tianming Monk had to move to the side so Singing Wolf could open the door for him. Cecille took the younger girl's arm again once the young Algonquin woman moved back to White Buffalo's side; they trudged wearily inside.

Shin put his trunk down first, followed closely by the saddlebags. He left the two women to guard them. Cautiously, he walked to the counter remembering his last unpleasant hotel experience at the first town. The Tianming Monk chuckled before relaxing at the sight of an old grey haired man with his chair tipped back; his two booted feet were crossed at the ankles then they were propped on top of the counter. He was snoring softly. "Excuse me!"

A faded blue eye opened immediately. "What can I do for ya?"

Shin pulled a silver dollar he had waiting out of his breast pocket; the Tianming Monk flipped it into the air towards the Innkeeper. "I need two rooms, one for the ladies and one for two men we will also need food then baths."

As quick as you could blink the Innkeeper snatched the coin out of the air. Instantly, he was standing at attention; nobody would guess that a moment ago he was sound asleep, neither was the old man as frail as he at first looked. "Yes sir ladies rooms are over on the west-side, men's are on the east-end."

Shin frowned disgruntled, he didn't like being that far apart from Cecille; the Tianming Monk motioned in demand. "I need a room as close to the ladies as you can possibly get me please!"

The retired trapper turned hotel keeper shrugged; he pulled down two keys before slapping them on the counter in finality. "Unless you are married this is as close as you can get."

Shin nodded dissatisfied; the Tianming Monk took the keys before turning back to the women just as the door opened letting in a blast of frigid air.

Brandan grumbling under his breath walked in; he didn't realize the others had heard him. "Damn weather, it could have waited at least a couple more hours!"

Brandan pulled off his sopping hat with a blush when he saw Singing Wolf staring at him disapprovingly at the cuss word. The guide turned towards the counter; forgetting his embarrassment instantly, Red Wolf grinned in surprise pleasure. "Well you old coot, still around are ya Jim, figured you'd a been dead by now!"

Jim grinned as he stroked his long grey beard reflectively, remembering the last time the two of them had been together. Brandan had saved him from a nasty scalping job. He reached across the counter before shaking the guide's hand. "Nah the Huron tried several more times after ya left, but they never succeeded. Glad to see ya my friend, your rooms are on me; I will rouse the boys and the lassie to see to your baths then food."

*****

Three hours later an exhausted Cecille, followed soon afterwards by Singing Wolf fed and bathed crawled into their beds; even Misfit and the wolf pup were treated to a bath. Within moments both women were asleep worn-out they didn't talk to each other.

Shin hearing a murmured goodnight from Cecille then the thunk of Misfit settling against the door turned away in satisfaction; the Tianming Monk left the ladies wing before heading back to his room fatigued beyond words; he fell asleep to the deep rumbling snores of the Irishman.

CHAPTER FOURTEEN

Cecille stood on the dock waiting forlornly for the ferry to come back across so they could continue their journey into Quebec. They had spent two thankfully pleasant, uneventful days travelling with Brandan and Singing Wolf to the border town of Rolphton Ontario.

The four of them had crossed the border into Quebec about an hour ago, now the two would leave them here before going back to Petawawa. It hadn't surprised White Buffalo or Shin at all when the pair fell in love; she was glad they decided to go back to the hotel to help the older Jim look after the place.

Singing Wolf took Cecille's hand one last time the Algonquin woman bent close to whisper a special farewell to White Buffalo. "Thank you for everything, because of you I have found where I belong in this life; I hope someday you too will find your place, may the Great Spirit guide you."

Cecille squeezed Singing Wolf's hand in goodbye; White Buffalo took her other hand then put it on the Algonquin woman's belly before whispering in her new friend's ear. "May Shen our God the Great Spirit of all living things, watch over you both! I pray that your little one, which was conceived in love, is both beautiful and wise. Her name will be Blue Fox after the aunt that helped keep her mother safe and strong in spirit. So long my friend, may we meet again in this life or the next?"

Singing Wolf backed away in surprise the Algonquin woman put a hand onto her stomach with a hopeful expression; they had only spent one night together how could it be?

Brandan gave Cecille a heartfelt hug of gratitude before Red Wolf said his farewells. He gave a little chuckle of delight at her melodramatic groan of pain. "Goodbye my cousin several times removed; may the Mother Earth with the help of your Great Spirit, guide and protect you. Remember to continue following this logging road, it will lead you straight to Kipawa; a friend of mine assured me the trail was finished early this year, but the last twenty miles might have some stumps needing to be cleared away. He said with no problems it should only take you about three or four days of constant travelling to get there."

Cecille turned away without further comment she let Misfit lead her over to Shin, who was waiting for her with the horses. The Tianming Monk had already said his goodbye's to the retreating couple. White Buffalo stayed on the dock while her Guardian loaded the horses. It didn't take long with the help of one of the crewman then they tied them to the post in the center of the raft; put there to keep animals from getting too close to the edge which could tip the ferry.

Cecille gladly climbed up with Shin's help before allowing the Tianming Monk to lead her over to a bench where White Buffalo could sit.

Misfit lay down at her mistress's feet panting heavily; she didn't like boats the swaying made her want to get sick, swallowing hard the dog closed her eyes before trying to sleep.

Cecille sighed in pleasure; she lifted her head enjoying the feel of the hot summer sun caressing her face lovingly. White Buffalo turned to Shin before giving him Brandan's final words. The Tianming Monk nodded, but didn't comment already aware of that.

The two lapsed into silence they both dozed for a time enjoying the respite from travelling. Twenty minutes later they were both jerked awake as the ferry reached the other side sooner than they had anticipated. Shin groaned in disappointment at the short trip, he got up and helped Cecille to stand. The Tianming Monk took White Buffalo off the barge first before going back to assist the crew in unloading the horses; a few minutes later, he was disembarking from the ferry.

Shin helped Cecille onto her mare before putting the rifle away then gathered his new bow plus some arrows in pleasure. Brandan took him to see an Indian Bowyer after hearing White Buffalo tease the Tianming Monk about his inability to find the right limb for a bow; the experience left Shadow Stalker quite bewildered.

*****

Brandan, hearing the disappointment in Shin's voice that he still hadn't found the right tree limb to make a bow; went straight to Jim and asked if the Bowyer still lived in his wigwam at the end of town. When the guide got an affirmative, he took the Tianming Monk there before they left. Red Wolf told Shadow Stalker several interesting stories about the native Algonquin bow-maker, who was a legend around Petawawa. His bows were highly sought after the accuracy of them was legendary in this area... almost mythical. According to some, the arrows not only flew true but they would also bend around corners or obstacles and hardly ever broke.

Shin had been quite surprised when they had gone into the wigwam. The old man had bows in every space he could find, some were doubled up you had to be careful when turning you didn't walk on one. The Tianming Monk searched for a good twenty minutes; unfortunately, nothing appealed to him at all.

Shin disappointed turned to leave; unexpectedly, he stopped then stared in admiration. Propped against the far wall on the left side of the door was a bow styled almost exactly like his old one; this one was black with a carving of a pure white cross in the wood just above the grip there was one below too. The crosses had red flames curling around it forming into images of doves one on either side, both were in flight. He frowned in surprise at the hand grip it was quite unique since it had a red cord wrapped around it, giving your hand a better hold. The top and bottom both curved inward, just like his old one had. When the Tianming Monk lifted the bow the weight was less than expected, the wood gleamed with a shine he hadn't seen since leaving his homeland.

Shin tried questioned the old Algonquin bow-maker about what kind of wood he used, but the Bowyer shrugged unknowingly. The old man pointed in the general direction of the River. "Several years ago I found a log floating in the Petawawa River the idea for the bow came to me in a dream. When I took the bark off, the inside wood was black. I have never seen anything like it before or since; believe me every chance I get you will find me at the River looking, scouring the banks hoping to find another one."

Shin sighed in disappointment, but only for a moment he didn't care all that much, it was only his curiosity getting the best of him. Shadow Stalker grinned in relief, feeling that old pull of familiarity in the bow; the Tianming Monk knew this was the one for him. "I will take it how much do you want for the bow?"

The old bow-maker surprisingly turned disappearing behind an animal hide partition without a word as soon as Shin said he would buy it; several minutes later he returned with a quiver full of black arrows. The Tianming Monk could tell the fletching on the arrows the Algonquin Bowyer used were from a black and white eagle, the feathers perfectly matched the bow.

The old bow-maker beckoned for them to follow him to the back where he had a target set up; he took out an arrow before handing it to Shin with a cackle, not saying a word the Bowyer pointed at a hide wrapped around a tree. The Tianming Monk took the arrow then drew back the string, sighting carefully he let it fly. As promised the arrow flew true, seemingly effortless it embedded into the Bullseye.

Surprisingly, the old bow-maker took the bow away from Shin before handing it to Brandan with an arrow. Red Wolf frowned in puzzlement, he finally took it at the old Algonquin Bowyers insistence; he notched the arrow, the guide lifting it up and tried to pull back the string, but he couldn't budge it an inch.

The old Algonquin Bowyer laughed at the look of astonishment from the muscular Irishman; he took the bow away from Brandan, the bow-maker handed it back to Shin with a flourish. *"This bow is meant for you in all these years you are the only one who has ever been able to draw the string back. It is a gift from the Great Spirit, so take it with my blessings."*

*****

Shin tried to give the old bow-maker some money or make a trade, but the old Algonquin Bowyer refused it all. Now the Tianming Monk had his belt back in place around his waist; it was holding just a few black arrows with several of his old arrows snug against his side. Only one of the five arrows he was holding in his hand with the bow were black the rest were regular arrows. Shadow Stalker wanted to save the new ones, for now at least.

Shin had an unusual dream the night he received his new bow; it was the deepest of nights with no stars or moon visible. The Tianming Monk saw a shadow slither up from the ground even in the pitch black night it was visible to him. An arrow streaked towards it with a flame of fire following in the wake of the missile. When he woke, Shadow Stalker walked over to put his hand over the bow. "From this day forward you shall be known as Nightshade, the flaming destroyer of all things malevolent!"

Shin shook off all thoughts of his bow as he looked around at a couple of the old rundown buildings; he had been told already they were empty because the trail through this part of Quebec was finished. Brandan said they might find a logging or trappers cabin occasionally but other than that, there would be few people until they got closer to town.

Brandan predicted four days at least of hard steady traveling to get there. Shin grimaced in aggravation, it didn't matter he was sure they wouldn't get that far anyway; of course, the Tianming Monk wasn't totally sure… even his charge didn't know exactly where they were going.

Shin looked up at Cecille inquisitively the Tianming Monk was feeling sluggish right now that little snooze on the ferry had the opposite effect on him; he needed a respite from travelling but it was totally up to his charge, only she knew what time frame they were on. "How far would you like to go today, White Buffalo?"

Cecille shrugged not interested in continuing now either White Buffalo's feelings of urgency had diminished once they crossed the border. "I will leave that up to you, Shadow Stalker. Red Wolf did say earlier that there is a lake a couple of hours from here with some nice sized trout; if you would like to stop early for some fishing, it is okay with me."

Shin grinned at the thought of eating fish and his mouth watered; he couldn't help thinking of Stanley, the boy gave them two of his father's fishing poles. The Tianming Monk quickly agreed that it was a good excuse to stop early for a change. "Okay, I think that is an excellent idea."

Shin eagerly picked up the pace without saying another word. The Tianming Monk didn't want to take a chance that Cecille might change her mind; not now, anyway.

*****

Three hours later Shin leaned back against a tree with his hook in the water he had already caught two fish to Cecille's one. The Tianming Monk was feeling extremely competitive all of a sudden which was unusual for him; to take his mind off his strange mood, he listened carefully to his charge with a thoughtful frown; this was the first chance they had to discuss in depth White Buffalo's vision from the Great Spirit. Shadow Stalker smiled inwardly glad he wasn't the only one who knew the Earth was older than anyone realized.

Shin waited until Cecille finished her summary of what she figured it all meant. When sure she was finished, the Tianming Monk told White Buffalo everything he knew on the subject. "Yes, the Monks are aware of Lucifer's reign on Mother Earth before God took an interest in what was going on here. At that time humans were different, some evolved on their own or were brought about by magic and interaction with the Angels was an everyday occurrence. Many great cities were built using not only forced labour but also magic. Forbidden experiments with several magical creatures created by the Archangel were becoming the norm for the minions of Satanii; they did it to make hideous beasts of burden to build their cities for them. Lucifer was too greedy though it wasn't enough for him to be the overlord of Po... no, he wanted more. He wanted to be above the Great Spirit. He planned to build a great throne room for himself in the fourth heaven, which was directly above God's throne room in the third heaven. The Lord found out what the Archangel was up to so he sealed away all magic. It caused the great cities to fall into ruin or disappear entirely from the face of the Earth. The people magical or otherwise died some vanished mysteriously; until all that remained was Lucifer himself now dubbed Satan or the devil by an angry Shen. Still, the Archangel refused to give up his plans. When the Great Spirit confronted him here a great battle took place, God using the stars sent meteors to destroy Satan. The sun followed soon afterwards by the moon were snuffed out by a wrathful Shen then all life died as an ice age gripped the planet. It wasn't until the devil got imprisoned that things began to change."

Shin was interrupted by a wiggling fish he brought it into shore in triumph. The Tianming Monk crowing in delight gave Cecille a detailed description of his catch. Throwing the fish with his other two, he put another worm on his hook before sitting back. Shadow Stalker continued his story as if he hadn't stopped even for a moment. "Shen being a merciful God as well as lonely decided to try again. This time the Great Spirit wouldn't allow magic or his Angel's access to the Earth every day; except for his most loyal trusted Watchers who would teach only what his creations absolutely needed for survival... magic would stay forbidden forever. In seven days Po was reborn from the ashes, but of course Shen's time isn't the same as Earth's. Once the sun and moon were again allowed to warm the surface of Po; the ice disappeared from most of Mother Earth than humans again evolved, while that was happening Adam and Eve were made in the God's image. Unfortunately, the evil of Lucifer still prevails on Earth, so it wasn't long before the Great Spirit got betrayed when his creations ate the apple of knowledge. In retribution, Eden got taken away from Adam and Eve who were now earthbound. Shen being a loving God forgave his creations for eating the forbidden fruit then the Great Spirit began encouraging them to multiply. Because there was only one land mass at the time, intermixing with the evolved races was bound to happen sooner or later."

Shin was interrupted this time by Cecille's wiggling line. He let her bring the fish to shore on her own, not that he was hoping it would free itself or anything. The Tianming Monk lifted it up before frowning at the trout that was the biggest of them all; he made sure to give her plenty of praise when he described it to her. It didn't take him long to unhook her fish, at least Shadow Stalker was still one up on her.

Shin chuckled in humour at his competitive feelings as he put bait on Cecille's line. When finished the Tianming Monk continued as if he had not halted. "Satan's wickedness is never far away, though! The Watchers that were to teach humankind rebelled against God when they fell in love with then married human women, producing the Nephilim... giants that used forbidden magic. Eventually, they too turn to evil, so again the Earth was destroyed this time by water. Shen kept Noah with his three sons alive, along with their wives. Why, because Noah was a direct descendant of Adam and Eve making him a pure Israelite. Noah's wife was only half-Jew, her other half was an evolved race. The firstborn son also had a woman who was partly pure and partly Hebrew. Her Judahs father had gotten married to an evolved woman. The second oldest son, his wife was part Nephilim the other half is evolved. The youngest son, his wife was half Israelite intermixed with Nephilim. So, two of every creature got saved even the humankind. When the waters receded, the Great Spirit broke up the land to contain the excess water from the waters above as well as the waters below. The water above could be about one of the heavens having mostly water in it; maybe, the fourth heaven had been filled with water to keep Lucifer out of it. Noah's great-grandfather having written one then two of the books of Enoch gave them to his great-grandson just before the rains began. They go into greater details of the rebellions of the Watchers and the Nephilim. Noah continued to write, creating the book of Noah during and after the flood. Jesus was born to bring all humankind under God's rule with the hope that the evil of the Archangel on Po would get nullified... it wasn't! Shen and Jesus will try one more time to rid the Mother Earth of Satan's influences when they take on Lucifer again. Fire will be used this time to purge the Earth. I am so glad that I will not be alive to see that one!"

Shin laughed good-naturedly, when he was interrupted by Cecille's fishing rod bobbing again, he let her reel in her fish. They were now tied three fish each, but White Buffalo still had the largest one. The Tianming Monk put another worm on her hook before continuing the story once more. "A journal is a good idea maybe it will stop what is going to happen, I highly doubt it. Although, it might help your future descendants prepare for Armageddon. And yes, you are correct; your bloodline dates back to Noah's youngest son, he was the one cursed by his father for telling his brothers about his drunken nakedness. I am pretty sure you are wrong about the Mother Earth's well being a portal I don't think it's linked to the heavens at all. Two of the portals to heaven are unfortunately prisons, one for the Archangel Lucifer and one for the leaders of Satanii. If you remember the book of Enoch, the Lord had said he was imprisoning them here on the Earth in one of the valleys. But you are right that there is a fourth entrance, it just so happens to be my carpet. I have gotten several visits from Jesus or Angels throughout the years. I can also talk to my father who is dead plus brief time travel has been done periodically with the rug. The Tianming Monks think the magic is hidden inside one of the five heavens too. Since it managed to lift the barrier once already when the Nephilim were on Earth, I would agree that the magic is probably in the first heaven. That would explain some of the unusual occurrences that happen on Po from time to time. It would be easier to sneak through if it was near the Mother Earth. Once Jesus was born, the magic was unable to get through the barrier as often. The Monks have the same feeling as you that a piece of the puzzle is missing. They have no idea what it could be either!"

Shin yelled in triumph when his line bobbed but grumbled in disappointment when he realized it was only snagged. The Tianming Monk recast his line before continuing his musings. "I remember that dream of your father's it was the only time both of us had the same dream. I only had it once, but Edward kept having his right up until the day he walked up to the derrick then saw it for himself; afterwards, he never had it again. Your idea about the oil pockets being a resting place for the Mother Earth's well could explain a lot of things. If it is true sadly Po will end up dying, eventually; how your family is supposed to raise the Earth back to her former glory after she gets destroyed for the third time, is a mystery to me. I remember the day we disembarked from the train like it was yesterday, but I didn't know you blocked the ability to see auras, it makes sense though. Unfortunately, it also prevented your ability to feel or talk to the Mother Earth when not touching the ground."

Shin lapsed into silence as the Tianming Monk's thoughts wandered back to that day in Montreal.

*****

Edward sighed in relief as he sat across from his daughter on the train as it pulled away from Quebec City, heading for Montreal; it had taken him some time to get their horses settled. He grinned at his daughter's new attire she had decided that pants were way more preferable to dresses. She reminded him so much of his sister Raven at times, especially in her floppy Stetson with the flannel shirt.

Cecille giggled at her father she eyed Edward in approval at his new getup. White Buffalo had never seen Dream Dancer in denim's, nor had he warn his old Stetson often; he had even put chaps on, and a Colt revolver strapped to his waist. "You look more handsome in those clothes, Ni-hoi!"

Edward chuckled in pleasure at Cecille's praise, turning Dream Dancer looked over at Shin who also changed from his flowing robe to denim's; surprisingly, the Tianming Monk also had on a Stetson hat with a flannel shirt plus a vest. Instead of wearing a six-gun he devised a belt that could carry his two Oriental dragon daggers, his sword was still strapped to his back.

Michelle sniffed in disapproval eyeing the pants Cecille was wearing. The nanny had chosen a ladies blouse with a split skirt; she did get a Stetson not wanting the harsh Canadian sunlight to harm her delicate complexion.

It was not a long ride, half an hour later the conductor was walking through their compartment; ringing his bell, he called out a warning before continuing into the next passenger car. "Fifteen minutes folks."

Edward got up before gesturing towards the back compartments; Dream Dancer didn't want anyone to touch his horses, they were too skittish not liking trains one bit. "I will go see to the horses, meet me on the train platform."

Shin nodded, he helped Michelle and Cecille gather their bags before sitting again. They waited for the train to come to a full halt, not wanting to stagger around or bump into others; within twenty minutes, the Tianming Monk had his charge standing on the platform patiently they waited for Edward to come around with the horses.

Shin saw two women coming towards them with a half dozen men behind them. The young men were making lewd comments as they nudged each other playfully daring each other to approach one of the ladies. The Tianming Monk dismissed them; they were a bunch of young men going to college, no threat to his charge.

A husband followed closely by his wife with six daughters ranging from ten to five in age, was next in line. The girls all clutched tickets to get on the train as they waited quietly for the passengers to finish disembarking so they could go to Quebec City. Shin couldn't help noticing immediately that the kids didn't seem happy; most girls their age would be giggling as they chatted excitedly.

"Uuggghhhh!"

Shin looked down at Cecille in confusion she was bent retching uncontrollably; the Tianming Monk dropped the bags he was holding instantly, he knelt in front of White Buffalo in concern.

Michelle had a hold of Cecille by the shoulders trying to give her some support; the nanny was totally baffled. "I'm not sure what happened she was fine just a moment ago?"

Shin waited until Cecille was done getting sick then gathered her close. He chanted softly looking towards the people waiting to get on the train before whispering in her ear knowingly. "White Buffalo you must learn to bury others auras when they are beyond your understanding. Evil lies in all of us but some embrace that wickedness wholeheartedly, allowing it to stay close to the surface of their lives; which eventually affects all those around them you must see past these people, they can't hurt you!"

Edward came rushing up in fear; Dream Dancer saw his daughter bent over getting sick, but he had to secure the horses before he could come to her. "What's the matter?"

Shin lifted Cecille he handed her to Edward; the Tianming Monk waved for them to go on without him. "Take her White Buffalo will be alright once away from here I will explain later."

Edward nodded without argument, Michelle followed the two with the bags the Tianming Monk handed her; they hurried to where Dream Dancer had left the horses.

Shin watched them go then when they were safely away from here he jumped off the platform. He went passed the women before the Guardian gave the college group a wide berth; not having time for mischievous pranks as they impatiently waited for the train. Once behind the man with the six girls, Shadow Stalker spun around unexpectedly before pulling out one of his daggers as he turned. He kicked the back of the man's knees dropping him into a kneeling position. The Tianming Monk put his knife under the big sweating chin then leaned close as he whispered a fatal warning. "If you ever touch one of your daughters again, I will hunt you down and kill you... do you understand me!"

The black-haired, black-eyed, five foot two three hundred pound man squeaked out in shock. "Yes sir I swear, never again!"

Shin made sure to put enough pressure upwards on the dagger so that a thin, shallow line of red occurred. It wouldn't need *stitches, but it would scar the man for life; now, every time he looked in a mirror he would be reminded of his vow. Stepping back, the Tianming Monk disappeared just as silently as he had attacked.*

In a rage, the mother gathered her daughter's close then turned back towards the station; she marched away from the sobbing man who was pleading for forgiveness.

*****

"Nneeiigghh!"

Shin was jerked from his contemplation by the sound of a loud, angry, defiant squeal of rage and pain from a horse; the Tianming Monk quickly pulled his fishing line back in before jumping up he ran towards the fire.

Cecille hearing it too quickly reached over grabbing hold of Misfit; she knew her dog being the curious type would want to investigate White Buffalo made sure to keep a tight grip on her. "Stay here with me, girl!"

Shin rushed over to Cecille's packsaddle then grabbed Misfit's halter; returning in a hurry Shadow Stalker put it on the dog before handing White Buffalo the leash with her cane, just in case it was needed. The Tianming Monk grabbed the rifle since it was closer to him.

"Rrooaarr!"

Shin frowned that sounded a lot like a cougar! The three quickly went around the lake before slipping silently out into a little clearing. He saw a horse struggling against a rope that was attached to its halter it got caught between two rocks. It only took the Tianming Monk a minute to process the scene; he knew immediately he was looking at a stallion, the horse was quite a beauty too. A cougar was trying for a meal as it impatiently paced trying to find an opening to get at the stallion, but the stud was in his prime. If it weren't for the rope holding him captive, he would easily fend off a full grown cougar.

Shin gave Cecille a full description of the scene as the cougar crouched readying itself for another attempt at taking down the stallion; the Tianming Monk readied the rifle but paused waiting for the go ahead from White Buffalo.

Cecille knelt, promptly she consulted the Mother Earth first; if it were meant to be, they would turn away without interfering allowing nature to take its course. Edward's dire warning to his daughter that long ago day on the ship that brought them to Canada from England had made a huge impression on the young ten-year-old. White Buffalo, jumped to her feet after only a few seconds. "Hurry, shoot the cougar!"

Cecille's cry came at the same time as the cougar leaped.

Shin's shot caused the big cat to somersault in midair; it dropped dead at the half rearing stallions hooves as the horse desperately tried to strike out at the cougar. The Tianming Monk let out the breath he had unknowingly been holding it would have been a shame to let such a magnificent stallion die.

Cecille reached over for Shin's arm, White Buffalo had seen blood on the horse when she had her vision from the Mother Earth. "I will need my medicine bag the stallion is bleeding on his left side; can you go get it for me please, Shadow Stalker?"

Shin nodded, he trotted back to their camp quickly; the Tianming Monk wanted to grab something to calm the stallion down too he was just not sure what yet.

Cecille began chanting as she walked cautiously towards the horse, trying to put him into a trance so she could treat his wounds; White Buffalo didn't want to take any chances with a stallion that went wild, who knew how long the horse has free and roaming these hills.

The stallion snorted in uncertainty; the horse kept jerking his head trying desperately to get the rope loose. The stud ignored the woman trying to approach him not in the least affected by her voice.

*****

Shin grabbed his Stetson once back at camp before throwing in a few handfuls of oats he picked up Cecille's medicine bag next. Catching a glimpse of their canteen, he swung it over his shoulder on his way out. When the Guardian reached his charge, he handed White Buffalo her beaver medicine bag. The Tianming Monk put his hand over her arm to halt her advancement, which also stopped her chanting; obviously, it wasn't affecting the stallion at all.

Shin whispering in his native language calmly held out his hat to the animal, every few minutes he shook it so the oats would rattle. He walked towards him slowly letting the horse get used to his scent. He watched in satisfaction as the stallion's ears perked up, his nostrils flared at the smell of food. He must be starving, thirsty too he would imagine! The Tianming Monk let the stallion eat the oats, all the while stroking his nose slowly. When the horse finished eating, he poured a little water into the hat.

Shin was still mumbling softly; since it was keeping the stud calm. The Guardian unhooked the tangled rope now that the stallion was quieter than led the horse towards camp. Shadow Stalker quit chanting to talk to Cecille. "White Buffalo, you can treat him when we get back to camp. He isn't bleeding too badly right now. Afterwards, I will gather the cat once we release the stallion. I will skin him later, no use wasting a beautiful animal."

Cecille nodded in agreement; it wasn't long before she was putting cream on the scratches the stallion had received from the cat. White Buffalo sighed in relief, the wounds weren't that deep it didn't require stitches it would leave scars though. She gave him a little healing jolt just to keep any infection from occurring.

Shin fed the horse oats to keep him still while Cecille doctored him. The Tianming Monk stroked his sleek neck in admiration; the stallion was about four years old, fifteen or maybe closer to sixteen hands. Shadow Stalker would have to measure him to be sure, but why bother he wasn't planning on keeping him. The stud was a dark grey almost black, with a pure white mane and tail. Surprisingly he had different coloured eyes one was a light blue, with the other one being a dark brown. The Guardian saw a deep-rooted intelligence in his odd looking eyes. If he had to ride a horse, this would be the one he would choose.

Cecille finished before stepping back out of the way White Buffalo gestured with a shooing motion. "You can let him go now."

Shin chanting pulled the stallions head down one more time then put his forehead against the studs the two stood like that for several long minutes; the Tianming Monk eventually reached up to unhook the halter as he switched to English. "You are free, so go before I change my mind!"

The big grey stallion extended his neck when Shin stepped back snuffling at the Oriental's hands he looked for more oats; the horse finding none snorted, almost as if he was thanking him before turning away the stud disappeared through the trees.

Cecille smiled knowingly, feeling Shin's admiration for the beautiful majestic grey stallion she turned away without commenting. White Buffalo went to the fire to start supper she would cook the fish they had caught earlier; plus she put on a large pot of water that she knew Shadow Stalker would need for his hide. She felt the Tianming Monk leave their camp to get the cat it would be disrespectful to abandon it without at least taking the fur. Besides, they could use the skin in trade if money became an issue. Banks were not always easy to get to way out here.

*****

Shin carefully skinned the cat not wanting to nick the hide even slightly. He made sure to take all the claws, plus the teeth before he ripped open the guts. Shadow Stalker pulled out the stomach to look at it, but it wasn't big enough for his needs, so he decided to leave it. The Tianming Monk regretted having to leave the head as well; he picked up a hammer with his sharp pick to bust open the skull. It was such a beautiful cat, but he didn't have time to be delicate as he smashed open the skull to get at the brains. The horses wouldn't like the smell of the cougar at all he knew. The head would only make it worse for them, so he only needed the brains for curing the hide. As it is, they just might have to stay here one extra day to cure the skin.

Shin heard a whine behind him; he turned to look, a fox was standing at the edge of the trees with its nose held up in the air sniffing. Hearing a whoosh of wings above the Guardian looked up then saw several blackbirds, a golden eagle was circling high up above them. The Tianming Monk turned back to the cougar a coyote was sulking up ahead further back in the trees. Grinning in relief, Shadow Stalker hacked up the cougar more before throwing some meat to the fox. He knew the coyote would steal the majority of the cat; rising once done, he scattered several chunks of meat around so the other animals could have a share too. He left the clearing satisfied the cat wouldn't go to waste.

*****

Cecille just finished cooking their supper when she sensed Shin returning to camp. She had kept herself busy by making a large rack to prop over the fire so she could smoke the excess fish for later. They would also use it to drape the hide over to smoke it for a bit which would make it able to withstand the damp climate better. White Buffalo called the Tianming Monk over to eat first before he washed his skin; she knew that once he started, getting him away from it would be next to impossible until its finished.

Shin would be working half the night scraping the hide, but with both of them taking turns, it should be finished by morning. Once finished getting all the fat, tissue, and membranes of the hide they would set it over the smoking fire for an hour or two; again it would be stretched out, but a little tighter. The brain mixture would be worked in and left overnight to soak in making the hide more pliable. In the morning they would drape it over the fire for an hour before they washed it. Again it would be stretched then salt worked in to cure it because it can be air dried as they travelled along. He would need to soak it one more time, preferably overnight.

Most tanners liked to use urine for curing their hides, but Shadow Stalker preferred salt if he could get it. It was fortunate they had lots of salt since the grateful store owner in the first town gave them extra bags of the stuff for saving their baby.

Shin wolfed down his supper when finished he walked into the trees looking for a thick tree limb that was long enough to make four pegs. He needed the limb reasonably thick so he could hammer them into the ground to stretch his hide flat. He wouldn't make it too tight at first, but slowly he would continue to stretch the hide as he worked it. The Tianming Monk made sure to bring with him all his equipment for working with animal skins that he had collected over the years.

All the native men no matter what tribe of Indians considered it women's work, but Shin knew better. By the time, he was done with this hide; every muscle in the Tianming Monk's body will have had a significant workout.

Cecille, knowing Shin would be busy for a while unpacked their sleeping furs. Counting five steps from where the packs were at, she made their beds. White Buffalo never thought much of what she was doing; having memorized the camp, she didn't need her walking cane or help from her Guardian to do what needed to be done. The healer's inability to see never stopped her from doing her share. She took great pride in being able to pull her own weight when it came to chores.

Cecille walked over to Shin two hours later than took over scrapping the hide giving her Guardian a much-needed break; now he could go over and have the snack she had left out for him. It was starting to get dark when the Tianming Monk took the last turn. Thankfully, White Buffalo whistled for Misfit before running to the lake; ignoring the fact she still had clothes on she jumped in for a swim with her dog.

Shin joined Cecille an hour later White Buffalo was just getting out of the water, with an ecstatic Misfit romping around her playfully. The Tianming Monk sighed in pleasure as he waded into the warm lake cleaning the bloody mess off his clothes; he called back over his shoulder. "Done for tonight, the brain solution will keep it from drying out overnight. I will go through it again in the morning before washing and salting it just in case we miss anything that might spoil it."

Cecille nodded without commenting she took off her pants, socks, and her shirt before hanging them up to dry. She dried herself off as best she could with wet undergarments on, the warm gentle breeze helped some too. White Buffalo waited for Shin to get out of the lake to go back to camp, they both put on dry undergarments first; exhausted it didn't take the two of them long to crawl into their furs.

****

Spirit Bear went through his sparse pack again before mentally checking off everything he had accomplished the last couple days. Thankfully, he had pulled out his travelling tepee the first day to check it; finding several rips that needed mending the medicine man had immediately taken it to the women to fix it for him. They gave it back to him about an hour ago, now it was loaded on his drag poles ready to go.

Spirit Bear ate his supper then crawled into his bed, it took him some time, but finally, he fell into a restless sleep. Five hours later he began tossing and turned violently, unable to sleep anymore he got up. He estimated it to be around midnight the medicine man sighed grimly at that thought as he dressed. He couldn't sleep anyway, so he might as well go now. Thankfully, there was a full moon out; going outside he hooked the drag poles to his dog before gathering his pack.

Spirit Bear stopped to talk to a Guardian briefly before leaving the mountain pass, he didn't stay with him very long; waving goodbye, the medicine man headed out alone with only his faithful dog by his side.

*****

Powaw bolted up out of his sleeping fur in fear when the nightmare he was having let him go. Screaming in rage at the empty hollow feeling in his gut, he sat shivering as sweat-drenched him.

The last few days he had fugitively watched his brother getting ready to leave, every night since he refused to go dreams plagued him unmercifully. They were always the same he would dream of two bears fighting each other viciously until one dropped to the ground dead. One bear was white the other was black, every time the black bear would win; after giving a cry of victory, the shaman would see the white bear on the ground shimmer before his twin took its place.

Powaw envied and even hated his older brother all these years, always Spirit Bear got what the younger twin wanted. It should have been him that was named the medicine man not his older brother, it was all he had ever wanted when younger. He should be the one that was getting visions from the Great Spirit; never once had the shaman received an image from Misimanito. Unlike his brother who had them frequently. He had never let on and several times since becoming the religious leader of his people he even had to fake a vision, which made him that much more bitterly angry towards his twin.

Powaw knew that if Spirit Bear had said to kill the white-eyes, the chief would have listened to him; since it was the shaman who said that it should be done, they dismissed it with the lamest excuse. It should be him that his people listened to he was supposed to be the religious leader not his brother.

Powaw mind drifted back, he had rejoiced at finally becoming more important than his twin when he married the chief's oldest daughter; after the accident once again the shaman got relegated to second place. Deep down he knew that his brother had not let his wife die on purpose. Still, he couldn't help blaming Spirit Bear the medicine man should have done more to save them.

Powaw had always wanted what his older brother had; jealousy was not becoming in a religious leader he knew, but he just couldn't help that it was eating away at him. A tiny voice in the back of his head kept needling him to put a stop to it, which had him thinking of ways he could kill his brother. What was stopping the younger twin so far was his fear of what it could do to him since they were identical twins; there were several incidences where he felt his big brother's pain. Besides, he wanted Spirit Bear to suffer a loss first like the shaman had experienced when his wife and child died while in Spirit Bear's care. Unfortunately, no opportunity presented itself as of yet. He knew someday it would, all he needed was patience.

Powaw sighed in exasperation; he would find Spirit Bear in the morning, to find out about this so-called vision quest they had to go on together. The shaman didn't want his brother to die yet, or at least not alone. The younger twin wanted... no, it was essential that he be there to take pleasure in it.

Powaw feeling better by his decision laid back down; he went back to sleep, but even deep in slumber with no dreams an uneasy feeling began, it would continue to haunt the shaman for the rest of the night.

CHAPTER FIFTEEN

Powaw scratched at the medicine man's hide door the shaman waited impatiently outside the wigwam; when nothing happened, he growled in annoyance before barking impatiently. "Spirit Bear get out here!"

A few minutes later a sleepy mumble sounded then Spirit Bear's pupil stepped out. "The medicine man left the village around midnight; he said he wouldn't be back until after the new moon at the earliest."

Powaw without another word turned away quickly. He raced to his wigwam to gather a few necessary items; cakes, jerky, followed by a medicine bag got thrown in his large rawhide sack. A buckskin outfit was added just in case with an extra pair of moccasins, plus a ceremonial bone vest. He put a buckskin shirt on first with a plain bone vest on top. He added a pair of leggings and his headband, telling other natives he was a shaman on a quest.

Powaw picked up the black bear sleeping fur off his bed; he hurried to the front door to go back outside. Stopping suddenly, he grabbed his water bag sitting beside the fire pit and seeing his small chopping axe beside his bow he took them both too.

Powaw whistled urgently for his dog once outside before hurrying to the back of his wigwam; the younger twin picked up his tepee first to put it on his drag poles. The shaman's sleeping fur and the light pack got put on next. They too were tied on promptly without taking the time to check them.

A big brown male hound rushed up to Powaw in excitement.

Powaw picked up his dog's harness then strap the drag poles on his hound. The shaman draped his water bag on his shoulder with his bow on the left. He raced out of the village with his hound trailing.

It took Powaw a few frustrating hours to find the Guardian that Spirit Bear talked to last night; finally, the shaman was racing down a path chasing after his older twin brother. The younger twin knew he had a lot of ground to cover it was going to be a long day.

****

Shin sighed in relief; he sat back before brushing the sweat off his forehead with the sleeve of his shirt. Already it was a hot, muggy morning he was pretty sure it would be even worse by the afternoon. The Tianming Monk looked down at the hide in satisfaction. He had scraped the cougar pelt once more before smoking and washing the brains off it. Shadow Stalker just finished curing it by rubbing salt into it good he would leave the salt on for the rest of the day. Hopefully, he would be able to soak it tonight.

Shin lifted his head his nose twitched sniffing at the air in appreciation as a strong smell of bacon wafted towards him when the wind shifted directions. The Guardian found a ducks nest with six eggs in it, but he only took three when Cecille promised him a breakfast feast. Shadow Stalker didn't want to take them all then have no chicks to supply eggs for travellers in the future, besides White Buffalo would only eat one egg. The Mother Earth and Shen didn't like it when you killed animals for no reason; wasting food was also forbidden in the Tianming Monk's Monastery at home too, the leftovers get taken to the needy.

Shin sniffed again at the enticing scent remembering that Cecille had promised him bannock as well, he could hardly wait he was starving. The Tianming Monk looked at the sun he estimated the time to be around nine o'clock, still plenty of time for him to wash up before eating. It was early enough they could continue their journey for a few hours at least; he would discuss it with White Buffalo while they ate.

"Breakfast is ready!"

Shin jumped up at Cecille's call; he rushed over to the fire eagerly. Shadow Stalker took a plate before helping himself quickly! He sat uncaring that he was full of gore from the skin. The Tianming Monk looked at White Buffalo inquisitively. "The hide is salted already, so it just needs to air dry now. I will wash it later tonight, so we can leave here after we clean up the camp if you want. I will secure the hide on the packhorse; it can continue drying as we travel along."

Cecille nodded, but didn't comment as they ate quickly; White Buffalo was now more than eager to get moving again.

****

Spirit Bear stopped it was around noon he figured, it was a bit hard to tell with the cloud cover. He was quite pleased with his progress so far, with nothing hindering him the healer was making excellent time; he had left the trail into the village several hours ago, so was now on the main trail going west. The path here was a little wider so easier going, which helped him to keep up a steady ground eating trot. The medicine man called his dog closer before sitting on a log he rummaged inside his pack looking for food.

Spirit Bear took out jerky followed by travelling cakes, which the women made with animal fat, berries, ground up rice or corn, nuts, sometimes even squash was added. The cakes kept for a long time once they were cooked slowly in underground ovens, he had brought hardtack too just in case; the medicine man ate half a cake, he gave the rest to his dog and some jerky.

Spirit Bear was giving some to his dog when he paused and caulked his head listening intently. Frowning grimly he looked up through the trees, the healer was sure it was thunder he just heard to the north; quickly, he lifted his water bag off his shoulder. The medicine man gave some water to his dog first before taking a few swallows himself then he put the rawhide strap back over his shoulder. Afterwards, he jumped up to continue on his journey.

Spirit Bear kept up his comfortable pace for two more hours; he stopped suddenly when a fork in the trail appeared. He looked to the right the medicine man knew this path would stay straight for another three hours before turning back on itself. It would end up leading him deeper into the foothills then north into the mountains. Soon after the trail would disappear, so another path would have to be made. Lots of bears up there, it would be the logical choice. He knew that Misimanito their Great Spirit was not always rational though! The Cree healer could not help chuckling at that thought.

Spirit Bear looked to the left this pathway slanted upwards; it looked like it was going up a steep rise, which should take you further up the mountain trails; the older twin knew the path was misleading. It was really going down, so would take you south for a ways then it turned south-west. Eventually, it would bring you to another path that leads west towards a town called Kipawa before it reached the Quebec and Ontario border. The medicine man knew that there were more white towns in that direction with only a few stubborn bears that refused to leave their territory.

Spirit Bear sighing in aggravation sat down at the fork in the road right in the center of the trail before pulling out his pipe; he filled it with his ceremonial leaves. Once done he put it down to gather dry leaves lying on the ground, with a few branches. He put them together in a pile to make a small fire so he could light his pipe. Opening the pouch hanging at his side he pulled out flint with a rock, striking them together he bent to blow on the spark that flew into the kindling. Humming, the medicine man sat back up with a twig to light his sacred pipe. Inhaling deeply on it, he closed his eyes asking the Great Spirit where he should go next.

Spirit Bear quit chanting in mid-chant his eyes popped open after only a few seconds. The older twin doused the little fire before he emptied his pipe, next he put his stones away in his pouch; all the while, he was mumbling irritably under his breath at Misimanito surprising unexpected directions. The medicine man rose then turned left he followed the fork that headed towards Kipawa.

****

Shin looked up at Cecille in concern he lowered his voice in caution to give her a warning; he kept walking, not wanting to let on yet that he knew anything was amiss. "White Buffalo, someone is following us there is at least one horse behind us!"

Cecille chuckled in humour with a knowing nod she didn't bother to whisper, there were no human ears anywhere around except their own; White Buffalo was just surprised it had taken Shin so long to mention it. "Yes, I'm well aware of that already!"

Shin looked up in consternation, he halted instantly in shocked surprise; the Tianming Monk's irritation with Cecille was pretty evident in his angry tone. "How long have you known about it, I also want to know why you didn't say anything to me?"

Cecille shrugged not in the least upset that Shin was mad; she knew the Tianming Monk would get over it sooner or later he usually did. White Buffalo opened her mouth to justify her actions, but closed it as the reason walked up beside her which made explaining unnecessary.

"Neeighh!"

Shin swung around in astonishment, he stared at the grey stallion in amazement speechless for several minutes; eventually the Tianming Monk waved his hand in a shooing motion towards the horse. "What are you doing here Grey, go on leave you are free!"

The horse shook his head as if denying that statement he snorted before stepping closer to Shin; the stallion dropped his head, resting it against Shadow Stalker's chest. When he didn't get a scratch, the stud nudged the Tianming Monk insistently.

Cecille laughed aware that the stud was supposed to be with them, but even animals had free will; it needed to be the horses choosing to join them. White Buffalo had known since she touched Mother Earth yesterday this horse was special, so she was instructed to save him at any cost. "The stallion is meant for you, Shadow Stalker."

Shin sighed in surrender he scratched the studs forehead between his eyes. Reaching down, he lifted the horses head until their eyes met; the Tianming Monk stared intently into them searching, it was not long before the Guardian nodded in defeat. "Fine come along then just don't expect me to ride you anytime soon!"

Grey woofed air out of his nostrils as if laughing at his master; the stallion pushed his nose against Shin's chest, nudging him.

Shin pushed the stallion's head away with an exasperated snort of his own he turned before picking up the trot once more. Cecille's mare was now on the Tianming Monks left side Grey was now on his right; the packhorse wedged her nose in-between the two older horses, so they had to keep a discreet distance from each other. Precious was behind the Guardian it was a strange sight to see with no halter ropes on any of the horses, they stayed in a diamond formation. White Buffalo did have a bridle without a bit on her mare, but the reins were tied together lying on Saya's neck in case of an emergency.

*****

Shin came to a halt four hours later when they left the dense woods on either side of them behind. He was thankful the road crew had come before them clearing this trail there was no way they could have gotten through such a thick tangle forest otherwise. He looked around in interest at the beautiful landscape below the Tianming Monk looked up at Cecille as he described the scenery to his blind charge. "We are about to go down into a valley the trail is not too steep. The trees thin out as we get further down until they practically disappear; there is an area further back by a creek that has a small grove of trees for shade. The water looks deep enough to bathe in, so I think we should camp there for the night even though it is a bit early. It might even have catfish and crayfish they would make a nice change in our diet. I need to soak my hide anyway for the night, who knows if there will be any more streams or a lake further on."

Cecille grinned in delight; she loved crayfish. They reminded her lots of the lobsters that they used to collect at the bottom of the cliffs not far from her home in Wales. The only difference was that crayfish were slightly smaller. They lived mostly in freshwater some even burrowed in the slimy mud along the banks of creeks. At home, the cook always made lobster by boiling them. The natives here slowly cooked the smaller crayfish in underground ovens. Either way, White Buffalo loved the taste of them so didn't have any preference. "Good I could use a cold dip right about now this heat has me drenched in sweat!"

Shin lifted off his Stetson. Using his sleeve, he wiped the sweat off his forehead. It wasn't often the Tianming Monk resorted to wearing his hat. Thankfully in this heat, it kept most of the sweat from dripping into his eyes. Shadow Stalker replaced his Stetson eagerly they trotted down the hill; another early day with a cold dunk would be welcomed.

*****

Shin was lying on his stomach at the edge of the creek with his hand in the water waiting patiently. Suddenly, he felt a flutter brush against his fingertips. Fanning his fingers slowly, he allowed the fish to rub against him until it swam further up; now he could feel the gills. Quickly the Tianming Monk closed his hand before pulling the fish out of the water. With a quick flip, he threw it on the ground behind him with a grin of triumph.

In the Ojibwe Indian village where Cecille had trained this was a favourite sport of the young warriors coming of age; wagers were known to happen even though they were frowned on by the elders. This time of the year was best since fish were more dormant because of the heat making them easier to catch.

Shin now had two big catfish he had already given Cecille several crayfish to cook in the underground oven he had built for her; he had dug them from the mud first since it took them a little longer to cook. The Tianming Monk turned he put his hand back in the water wanting one more catfish. The extra would get smoked so that they could take it with them to eat at a later date.

Shin could see quite well in the crystal clear mountain stream, which allowed him to choose his next victim two small catfish swam away unmolested. Then the Tianming Monk saw it; a huge granddaddy of a catfish, compared to the others behind him it was twice their size. Calmly he waited in anticipation, keeping his hand still.

The catfish paused enjoying the tickling sensation of Shin's fingers. The Tianming Monk showed great restraint as he waited patiently for the fish to swim up just a bit more; he needed to be able to get a good hold on the gills.

Splash! "Neeighh, phfft!"

Shin looked up in surprise it was just in time for the wave his new horse generated to swoosh upwards, it caught him full in the face; with water dripping down his nose the Tianming Monk watched in disappointment as a tail fin disappear back up the creek with a furious swish.

Splash… splash, splash.

Shin looked up angrily at his stallion before the Tianming Monk pushed himself back into a kneeling position; he put both hands onto his knees prepared to vault to his feet if his suspicions were even remotely confirmed. Shadow Stalker stared at his horse in contemplation, watching Grey's antics for several long minutes he was almost positive it was on purpose.

Grey was standing in the creek up to his knees instead of lying in the refreshing water like the two mares further to the left were doing. The stallion was using his left leg to hit down into the water causing it to splash up under the belly. Shin could see steam rising from the studs coat as the icy mountain water hit his over hot underbelly; when his leg got too weary, he switched to the other one. When that one began to get tired he would rear up before dropping down, causing small waves that swamped the banks of the creek.

Grey quit rearing and stood quietly in the water staring at his new master in demand. The stallion struck at the water before throwing his head up and down as if laughing at Shin; he snorted again as he neighed teasingly. "Pfft, nneighh, pfft!"

Shin leaped to his feet in indignation now he was entirely sure it was intentional; the Tianming Monk wasn't going to let a mere horse win even if it was only a water fight. "Is that a challenge I hear, well I accept you will be sorry that you provoked me, Grey!"

Shin vaulted over the bank before landing in the creek. The Tianming Monk ended up on the left side of his horse. Grey once again snorted in a challenging manner then struck the water. Shadow Stalker squatted quickly he proceeded to splash the stallion unmercifully; the stud half rearing playfully splashed him back.

*****

Cecille having heard the splash of water and challenges between the two antagonists promptly knelt letting the Mother Earth show her what was taking place. She laughed in delight this was the first time she ever felt Shin let down his guard so completely; she heard the Tianming Monk chuckle lots over the years even laugh outright a few times, but never this unrestrained unguarded laughter that he was exhibiting now. It helped White Buffalo to comprehend just how much responsibility Shadow Stalker always showed when around her.

Cecille stiffened when she felt the vibration of several horses galloping down the other side of the hill; she knew they wouldn't be able to see her here, being cautious White Buffalo backed into the trees taking Misfit plus the rifle with her. "Shh, now girl be quiet!"

*****

Grey's head jerked up fearfully; his nostrils flared angrily at a scent he hoped never to smell again. It preceded the half dozen men trotting down the steep embankment on the opposite side of the hill that the stallion had followed his new master down only two hours ago. The stud's neigh now was quite aggressive, but if you listened carefully, a deep-rooted fear was evident.

Shin stiffened, he looked towards the bank where he had been laying earlier; it just figures that the only time he removes his scabbard during the day, he might need its contents. Unfortunately, his sword with both of his daggers was still there. He had several stars on him, but they would only wound because he never dipped them in poison like they did in his homeland. At the same moment, the Tianming Monk also knew that Cecille was gone. He relaxed knowing he had someone to guard his back. Shadow Stalker turned to the men approaching then studied them intently.

The two mares lying in the water got up instantly at the stallions angry challenge. Saya quickly jumped out of the creek before heading towards the camp; Precious so use to following her mother stayed close to her. The older mare was instantly ready to bolt towards the grove of trees if her mistress called for her; getting to the edge of the tree canopy, she curiously turned to stare at the strange horses now riding up the creek towards Shin and the stud.

Shin crossed his arms in front of himself then waited he could feel Grey's fear even from this distance. A few minutes later, he heard the stallion move directly behind him. He was so close the Tianming Monk felt the studs uneasy breathing on his left shoulder, which was coming in short spurts from his nostrils. It was as if his horse was trying to hide behind him; it was a good indication to the Guardian that the men were known to the stallion and feared.

Shin assessed the six men carefully when they slowed their horses to a walk. Looking at the three in the back, he dismissed them instantly they were just ordinary townspeople nothing unusual about them; the Tianming Monk figured that they were probably just here for some extra money, possibly as witnesses if the law happened to catch up with them.

Shin turned his attention to the three leading instantly he knew that the one in the centre was the leader of the group. It was easy to tell because of the silver Spanish spurs with the fancy bridle his horse was wearing. The horse would have been a beauty if it wasn't for the gouges out of her sides from old plus new scars from those cruel spurs he wore. Even from here, the Tianming Monk could see the mare's muzzle flecked with dried blood from the sizable unneeded bit in her mouth. The man had light brown short hair when close enough the Guardian could see brown eyes. He had a long moustache that hung below his chin on either side of his mouth with no beard; having been to court Shadow Stalker could spot a dandy anywhere. The immaculate hand tailored fancy riding outfit, glaringly portrayed him as one.

  Shin turned his attention to the man on the left of the fancy man he was the most dangerous one of the lot. He had black hair with no moustache or beard; his eyes were black as coal, emotionless. The hired gun slouched to make his employer seem taller. He had a cruel downward curve to his lips that was permanent. The Tianming Monk knew instantly that the man was a hired gunman, so would do almost anything for a few coins even kill! He was the dandy's personal guard he would be paid handsomely to keep his employer alive.

  Shin eyed the third man on the dandy's right in surprise, not expecting to see one such as him here. Usually, they never left their towns unless on a stagecoach. He had to be a lawyer in his black business suit; the string tie was also a dead giveaway. He reminded the Tianming Monk of Edward's lawyer in England with that serious face. His hair was blonde, with deep-set grey eyes. His forehead crinkled in worry, looking around uneasily out of his element here in the middle of nowhere.

  The men all halted the leader leaned forward with a smirk of disdainful amusement as he eyed the soaking wet Oriental. He looked over at the two mares that were standing close to the trees, neither had ropes nor halters with no hobbles that he could see either. Looking beyond them he saw smoke from a fire, but the man didn't notice any others around. He gestured making introductions; himself first then pointed to his left before finishing off with the lawyer on his right ignoring the ones behind him because they were unimportant to him. "Evening mister, my name's Denis this here is Bill and Sam."

  Denis waited, hoping the man would introduce himself as well. After a strained silence, he decided to ignore the Orientals rudeness by continuing to talk; the dandy gestured inquisitively with a wave of his hand to indicate the horses. "Are all these horses yours, sir?"

  Shin kept his face expressionless he had been right, it was for witnesses. If he said yes, they could bring him up on horse thieving charges. What they didn't know was that the Tianming Monk had his own witness hiding in the trees; they didn't need to know that she was blind.

Shin unfolded his arms before pointing at the mares first. Next, the Tianming Monk jabbed his thumb over his shoulder indicating the stallion behind him. "The two mares are mine; the stud I found hooked by a rope between two rocks, a cougar was trying to make a meal out of him. I killed the cougar then released the horse; as you can see he decided to stay with me of his own free will!"

Denis snorted in disbelief as he sat back not believing that for a moment, the Oriental must have some magic about him to keep the horses here. "That stallion was mine, so I can attest to the fact that he has never stayed anywhere voluntarily, ever. He is as mean as they come nobody has been able to train him; this is the fourth time we have had to go searching for him. If I hadn't sold him already as a stud to Sam's employer, I wouldn't have come looking for him again. If I were to keep him, I would castrate him I already advised the lawyer to tell his employer that."

Shin turned to the stallion he pushed against his neck to turn him sideways so the men could see the results of the cougar attack for themselves. "I really don't care who owned him before; I saved his life, here is the proof if you need it. He is quite scratched up I treated the wounds, but they are deep and will scar for sure!"

Sam rode closer to get a better look he turned around in his saddle grimly as he looked back at Denis in anger; the lawyer chopped his hand down in decisive action. "My employer will not want him now he is damaged goods!"

Denis shrugged grimly he already had the money, so he didn't care what the lawyer wanted now. "A deal is a deal; not my fault you let him get away from you!"

Shin quickly interrupted before the angry lawyer said something stupid signing his own death certificate; the Tianming Monk knew that Grey would not go back voluntarily. "How much do you want for him Sam, I will buy him from you?"

Sam turned back he looked at the soaked bedraggled Oriental in disbelief before snorting in contempt. "You don't have that kind of money mister; my employer paid five hundred dollars for this stallion because his bloodline is from premium British racing stock I can't take any less!"

Shin frowned pretending to be disappointed as the Tianming Monk rubbed his chin thoughtfully. "Well, that is an awful lot of money for a horse. I have been saving for years to buy a parcel of land near

Kipawa, five hundred dollars is what they want for it. Last week, I managed to earn the last dollar needed to buy it. It is all the money that I have in this whole world. Not sure, I should be spending it on a stallion. It doesn't mean anything to me what kind of bloodlines he has a horse is a horse. I can pick one up for fifty dollars or less most places!"

Sam perked up instantly he gestured eagerly seeing a way out of this unfortunate dilemma. He knew his employer would fire him for sure for this fiasco, so he better fix it now. "You can always race the horse yourself in town. I bet you can double your money in a week. If all else fails you can trade him for the land later if the stallion doesn't meet your needs in the future; you can take him to Ontario they are always looking for prime racing horses there."

Shin nodded thoughtfully still, pretending to ponder the situation. He was trying to be careful not wanting the hired gun or the dandy to think he might have more money hidden somewhere; it would give them the incentive to come back looking to hold him up afterwards. The Tianming Monk nodded hesitantly giving in reluctantly before allowing his voice to gain in excitement as he contemplated making more money. "That is true enough maybe I can even win enough to buy my land and a herd of Herefords. Okay, I will go get it be right back."

Shin turned with a whistle of command for Grey to come with him. He waded back to shore then thankfully he collected his knives plus the sword scabbard with his dragon Samurai sword inside, his fish, and his belt. The Guardian strapped them back in place in relief before trotting to the fire that was almost out all three horses followed him into camp. The Tianming Monk made sure his back was to the six men watching him as he bent pretending to rifle through his things; it gave him a bit of time to converse with Cecille. "Did you hear everything White Buffalo?"

Cecille standing behind a tree answered quietly, White Buffalo made sure to keep herself hidden from the men; she didn't trust them at all. "Most of it, the money is in my pack on the left side; be careful the Mother Earth has sent me a strong caution. They might come back, or this has been done before then the lawyer or the person with them would end up dead. Now that you are involved things have changed, so not sure what they might do!"

Shin gave a little snort in agreement; the Tianming Monk already thought of that scenario. "Yep, I figured that so keep the rifle handy."

Shin found the money he counted out five hundred; he hid the rest before standing up and turned to the stallion the Tianming Monk put his hand over his horse's nose. "Stay here Grey, stand!"

Grey snorted agreeing with a bob of his head.

Shin turned away then headed back to the six men, he left his bow and arrows behind. They wouldn't do him any good right now anyway before moving his belt that held his two daggers into a better position; his sword was still strapped to his back because he never went anywhere without it, it was his responsibility. The Tianming Monk also made sure his six stars were in easy reach. They might not kill outright most of the time, but they would still hurt like hell, he knew.

The six men had taken the opportunity of getting out of the water while Shin was gone. Sam was now by himself, with the other five huddled together. The Tianming Monk knew Cecille was right they would go after the lawyer as soon as they could get him alone; the other possibility was the outlaw gang might go after Shadow Stalker first followed soon after by Sam, but not until the money got exchanged.

Shin walked ahead about thirty-five feet before stopping he beckoned for Sam to come to him. He could go a bit further, but he wanted to make sure Cecille could hear everything. The Tianming Monk knew that White Buffalo's keen sense of hearing weakened after about forty-feet; this would also keep the Guardian in the shade of the trees. With the sun now sinking it would be harder for the other men to see, so would give him an advantage.

Shin waited for Sam to get closer before the Tianming Monk held out the money; he waved it enticingly. "The money is yours if you have a bill of sale for me?"

Sam frowned in surprise not having expected that from an Oriental. He remembered the one the rancher had given to him yesterday. Thankfully, the name had been left blank; Denis said it was so his employer could put his name on it himself. He had thought that was odd since it was perfectly legal to have your lawyer sign a document for you.

Sam nodded that he did, he looked down at the Oriental with a touch more respect. Earlier the lawyer had thought the man was a little simple; he hadn't paid much attention until now. The lawyer dismounted before rummaging inside his saddlebag.

Shin moved so Sam would have no choice but to come around his horse to give him the paper; it would provide the Tianming Monk with a chance to warn the lawyer of his immediate danger without the others knowing what he was doing. It effectively kept the horse between the two groups in case they needed cover to hide behind.

*****

Cecille waited for Shin to leave; stealthily she made her way to the edge of the trees. White Buffalo stopped periodically to consult the Mother Earth. Reaching a good position she knelt then put a hand onto Po and one on Misfit. Using the Mother Earth she showed a vision to her dog, sending her on a critical mission.

Misfit licked her mistress's cheek before turning into the trees, she raced away.

Cecille hoped her message was explicit enough for Misfit to follow. She didn't like to ask her dog to do things this way because it was done by showing her an image of what was expected. Once before she had tried this, it failed miserably although, she was a pup at the time. White Buffalo figured there was no harm in trying it again, because she was older now it just might work better.

Cecille turned back to the conversation she heard Shin ask the man for a receipt to get him off his horse. The healer turned her attention to the five people huddled closer together; through images that the Mother Earth sent to her, White Buffalo watched the gunman split away from the others.

Cecille jumped to her feet immediately then gave the prearranged whistle to Misfit. Chanting, she released White Buffalo quickly so she could see before revealing herself. The healer rapidly pushed down on the lever of the rifle allowing a bullet to enter the firing chamber; promptly, she lifted it then pointed it at the unsuspecting gunman, everything happened in slow motion suddenly.

*****

Bill already having pulled his revolver to take down the Oriental shifted his aim to shoot towards the trees when he caught a glimpse of movement. Unfortunately, at that moment his horse squealed and tried to buck him off as an animal came out of nowhere then attacked his horse. He brought his gun down trying to aim for the dog, but a sudden excruciating pain in his head had him toppling backwards off his horse; he walloped the ground hard enough that an exploding whoosh of air got forced from his lungs. Continuing to convulse for several more minutes the nerves in the gunman's body finally stilled when realizing that he was dead.

Four identical expressions of shocked disbelief turned towards the woman that came out of nowhere killing the most notorious gunmen

Twin Destinies

in Kipawa Quebec. The border of Ontario was only a few miles from town because it was a border town it was a haven for outlaws and gunmen... just like Bill; usually, they were hiding from the law.

Shin trotted out from behind the lawyer's horse he had Sam's rifle aimed at the four; the Tianming Monk waved the gun towards the ground in command. "Get down off your horses now!"

Sam followed the Oriental, confused. "Are you sure about that?"

Shin nodded matter-of-factually the Tianming Monk gestured towards the leader of the small gang of thieves. "Yes Sam, the stallion you bought was trained when he was just a foal to untie himself; once loose, he would run away from whoever bought him. It is only logical that the barn where the stud is raised would be the first place the new owners would think to look for the horse. Then Denis, with his gang would offer to help the new owner locate the missing stallion. Once here, they would kill the unsuspecting man after finding the horse before burying him somewhere. Since most can't read or don't bother checking the entire contract because it's left blank, they miss the part that gives the outlaws ownership of their horse. Once they kill their victim, they put their name on the paper. Now they have another horse, with hopefully a lot more money stashed in the victim's saddlebags. Unfortunately for Denis, his stallion didn't stop here this time for some reason but continued to run until his rope got caught between some rocks. When I saved his life, it earned me his loyalty."

Denis looked at his three accomplices from town in accusation; with a growl of rage he took a menacing step towards them but stopped when the Oriental stepped closer to halt him. Instead, he made do with pointing an accusing finger at each of them in turn, trying to decide who the guilty one was. "Which one of you has been opening their big fat mouth there is no way he could have known that not without one of you telling tales!"

The three men looked at each other in confusion, but each one shook their head baffled before they murmured their innocence. Shin grinned in wicked satisfaction as his guess was confirmed; the Tianming Monk stared intently into Denis' eyes. Giving him the bad news with pleasure before turning, he handed the lawyer his rifle back. "Actually, you just told me Denis, up until now I was guessing. Sam, hold your gun on the other three while I tie this sorry excuse of a human being up."

Shin grabbed Denis' arm he marched him to the back of his horse. He rummaged inside the leaders saddlebag; just like the Guardian figured he found the rope with a gag waiting. The Tianming Monk bound the dandy's hands together and put him up on his horse before tying him tight to the saddle. Shadow Stalker did the same to the other three.

Once done, Shin fastened the reins of each horse one to the other, so they were all following the lawyer's horse.

Shin handed Sam his horse's reins; afterwards, he went over to the dead gunman then picked him up. He put the outlaw on his stomach over the saddle of his horse Shadow Stalker tied him there. The Tianming Monk tied Bill's horse's reins to the back of the last horse.

Shin walked back to Sam before the Tianming Monk used a shooing motion with his hands to get the lawyer to mount. "There you go take them straight into town, don't stop anywhere for any reason. Make sure you give them to the Sheriff to hang; tell him you are unsure how many other victims there are neither do you know how many might be buried out here. You keep all the credit for bringing the outlaws to justice."

Sam mounted he put his rifle back in its carrier before turning; the lawyer looked down at the Oriental inquisitively. "You are not coming to town? I thought you were buying land in Kipawa?"

Shin shook his head with a grin of sarcasm; the Tianming Monk rolled his eyes at the daft lawyer in disbelief, Sam should have guessed it was a ruse. "No, I said that to be able to go get the money and talk to my partner to make sure she could hear. You have your money for the stallion I have a bill of sale from you, good luck!"

Shin reached back as soon as he gave his farewell; without another word, the Tianming Monk slapped the lawyer's horse on the rump sending him on his way before Sam could say anything. He didn't want anyone to know where they were going especially that group.

Cecille met Shin partway still holding the rifle just in case; White Buffalo had remained in hiding not wanting anyone to be able to identify her or see that she was blind. "Do you think we should find another place to camp tonight Shadow Stalker, maybe there is a better spot up the stream a bit?"

Shin snorted in denial; the Tianming Monk had no worries the outlaws would get away. "No, they will not be coming back; there is no way they can get out of those ropes without cutting them, I made sure of that. If they manage to get loose, with their hired gun dead they will run for the hills to hide until the hunt for them dies down."

Cecile smiled in relief before nodding in agreement. White Buffalo went back to their camp to restart the fire to finish supper. The crayfish are done, but the catfish needed to be cooked. She also wanted to smoke some for later; the fish would last longer that way.

****

Powaw growled in frustration when the black clouds directly over top of him opened; he ended up soaked within moments. He could hear lots of thunder. It was getting closer by the hour as he tried to catch up to his brother. One delay after another slowed him enough he was falling behind. The shaman slowed when he reached a clearing; he knew his brother had been there, but was long gone.

Powaw was debating on whether he should erect his shelter now so he could sleep for a couple of hours or continue. With the cloud cover blanketing the late day sun it was making it quite hard to see. Sighing resignedly the younger brother shrugged in aggravation the spiritual leader was already really wet, so he might as well continue.

Powaw stayed at a walk, needing to give his eyes time to adjust from dusk to dark so he didn't step in a hole and break his leg. He pulled out jerky than a travelling cake; he ate half his meagre meal before feeding his dog the rest. Once done, the shaman picked up the trot again trying to gain on his older twin.

Powaw struggled for another hour and a half to see the trail as the sky darkened; finally, he had to stop. He couldn't go any further anyway, not without possibly going in the wrong direction. The shaman could sense his brother here since it was an intense feeling he knew Spirit Bear spent time trying to decide which way to go.

Powaw turned from the split trail, he whistled for his dog to follow him into the trees before unhooking him so he could get water. The trees on either side of the shaman gave him lots of shelter. Again he took out his travelling food to eat; after feeding his dog, the younger twin pulled his hide off the travois. He wrapped it around him too tired to care, not wanting to sleep long he lay down under the trees.

*****

Spirit Bear stopped when the rain caught up with him; it was so muggy the cold moisture was a relief, but he didn't like lightning in these dense trees. Ahead was another fork in the trail the medicine man turned into the trees then made himself a shelter, it was too dark to see, anyway. Hopefully, in the morning he would have a sense of which way he was to go. Eating another cold meal, he fed his dog before curling up to him and slept.

CHAPTER SIXTEEN

Powaw jumped up quickly he folded his hide then put it back on the drag poles. He only slept for about two hours, so was optimistic he could catch up to his brother before dawn. The shaman got back on the trail after hooking his dog up to the drag poles; he looked up in relief glad the rain slowed down now it was just a thick mist. He figured it would be finished by late morning or so he hoped.

Powaw stopped at the intersection and knelt. He was quite pleased his eyes had adjusted so well to the darkness; he could see a lot better than last night.

Finding a black partially burnt twig Powaw knew his brother built a fire here, which meant he must have had trouble deciding which way to go. Spirit Bear would have lit his pipe before meditating here; the shaman felt around the ground, just as he hoped a faint indent was apparent from the drag poles. Shuffling further along, he followed it until it turned veering towards the left fork.

Powaw satisfied he found the trail his brother took stood up. He promptly settled into a steady ground eating trot; he could feel himself drawing closer to his twin with every step he took. Now the shaman's confidence that he would reach his brother in plenty of time grew into a certainty.

****

"Rrooarr!"

Cecille bolted upright in her sleeping fur she held onto her chest as her distressed breathing continued for a bit before eventually, it finally calmed down. "Ahhhk; ah, huh, ahu, huh, ah...!"

Shin rolled over and sat up he had been aware for some time that Cecille was having a nightmare. The Tianming Monk looked up at the dark sky, a tinge of colour was starting to lighten it a bit; he turned back to his charge. "Are you okay White Buffalo?"

Cecille nodded, she brought her knees together then drew them up she wrapped both arms around them before White Buffalo laid her left cheek on top. "Yes I am fine, I just keep dreaming of two animals fighting each other and people dying around them; at least I think they are animals sometimes it is hard to tell. They are only shadows, so I never get to see them. I'm pretty sure they are not the ones killing the people that are dying, only each other. I haven't been able to figure out what exactly is causing the others to die or how the two fighting each other is linked to the deaths!"

Shin smiled in sympathy before the Tianming Monk reached over he patting Cecille's shoulder consolingly. "You will find the answer White Buffalo I have no doubt about that. It is early, but I think we should go. Especially, if it gets as humid as it did yesterday that way we can stop if it gets too hot; hopefully, we will find another stream or a lake to stop at even if it is earlier than we usually camp."

Cecille nodded in agreement, but didn't comment as she rolled out of her sleeping furs and stood up; she closed her unseeing eyes before she began to chant softly to get her bearings. Once confident White Buffalo knew which way she was facing, she turned almost ninety degrees until she was facing the grove of trees. Counting her steps, she walked straight ahead humming as she went, just to make sure she didn't walk into anything.

Once in the trees, Cecille counted ten steps then stopped lifting her nightshirt the healer squatted to relieve herself.

Misfit discreetly followed Cecille to make sure her mistress didn't get too close to anything.

Cecille finishing, promptly she stood up before turning left again she counted her steps as she hummed until reaching twenty-five; now free of the trees White Buffalo turned right, she walked another twenty steps to the creek.

Cecille had washed here yesterday, so knew the hill was not too steep; carefully, she walked down the slight mound. She knelt at the edge of the creek to splash water on her face to wake herself up more. It was icy cold very refreshing. Finished, White Buffalo walked back up the embankment. She counted her steps to get back to camp before dressing. Afterwards, she started breakfast.

Misfit turned before disappearing into the trees; she knew that her mistress wouldn't need her now.

Shin packed up their bedding; thankfully it wasn't long before it was ready to be put on the packhorse. He looked around for the horses but didn't see them anywhere around the camp. The Tianming Monk turned to his charge inquisitively. "White Buffalo, did you by chance happen to hear the horses at the creek?"

Cecille shook her head negatively she hadn't paid any attention, closing her eyes she opened her other senses searching for her mare; White Buffalo had a special bond with Saya that went beyond horse and rider, it wasn't long before she pointed west towards the trees. "They are on the other side of the water further down the creek."

Shin mumbled thanks irritably and left to go find them. It would also give him a chance to gather his cougar hide; Cecille could drape it over the fire for a while, at least until they were ready to leave. He needed to bring Precious here to load her up the Tianming Monk always liked to have at least the packhorse ready to go before he ate breakfast. That way they could leave after they got done eating.

Cecille stayed behind she rummaged inside her pack for the last of their bacon. She would make biscuits with bacon; there was still some fish leftover from last night too. If she made a pan of bannock, which is what the natives called their biscuits, White Buffalo could pack some for them to munch on as they travel. This way there would be no need to stop for lunch if they ate on the go. She would talk to Shin about maybe getting supplies in town before they headed into the mountains.

Misfit trotted back into camp she rubbed up against her mistress with a pleading whine; her nose was going none stop, the enticing smell had drawn Cecille's dog away from the exciting squirrel that had caught her attention.

Cecille laughed, she knelt then stroked her dog's head before giving Misfit a treat; White Buffalo knew how much her Dog loves bacon. "Yes my darling one, I am making breakfast here have a piece of this, I will feed you after."

"Bloody hell, Grey!"

Cecille stilled instantly in concern when she heard Shin screaming in the distance; she listened intently trying to decide if there was a threat of some kind, but the Tianming Monk only yelled out his horse's name. White Buffalo pushed her dog away. "Go see what the problem is Misfit, go help Shadow Stalker!"

Misfit took off running instantly.

Cecille put her palm on the ground searching for danger, finding none she let the Mother Earth show her what was happening. She couldn't help bursting out into uncontrollable laughter when White Buffalo figured out what had upset Shin. The Tianming Monk's British accent always returned when he cussed, which wasn't often; she got such a kick out of her sober Guardian when he lost control like this, but seldom did Shadow Stalker allow it to happen.

*****

Shin walked around the edge of the trees towards the creek looking for their wayward horses; the Tianming Monk knew they wouldn't be far because Saya would never leave her mistress voluntarily their bond was that strong. He was surprised the mare even wandered this far off, which was highly unusual for her.

The sun was beginning to peek over top of the hill which caused Shin to squint to see across the water; he put his right hand up to shade his eyes before whistling in demand when he saw all three horses together. In satisfaction the Tianming Monk watched Saya's head lift, she turned towards him. Immediately, she broke away from the other horses to cross the creek at his call. Shadow Stalker stopped to wait knowing Cecille's filly would follow her mother.

Shin stiffened in surprise, he couldn't help inhaling in astonishment before his mouth dropped open in shock. It took several minutes for the disbelief to wear off enough for him to break out into a headlong run. The Tianming Monk racing towards the horses was screaming as loud as he could at the stallion when Grey chased after Saya. Biting the older mare, the stud drove her back to her daughter. "Bloody Hell, Grey; get away from those mares this instant!"

Shin running full out looked down at a noise he grimaced in relief when he saw Cecille's dog run up beside him; the Tianming Monk pointed across the creek in command. "Misfit, get that stallion away from the other horses... go!"

Misfit raced away ecstatically; it wasn't often she was permitted to chase one of the horses even though Cecille's dog was always more than willing to do so.

Shin screamed out again; unfortunately, he was still too far away to do anything except watch incredulously as the stallion tried to mount Saya. "Damn you, Grey I am going to bloody well kill you get away from that mare this instant, you mangy mule you!"

Saya not in heat yet squealed angrily when Grey knocked her down onto her front knees trying to rape her. A stallion in the wild used this tactic to force dominance over the herd mare. Cecille's horse for all that she was a passive mare was still the biggest and strongest out of the horses; furiously, she vaulted back up refusing to stay down. Once able to, she kicked back at the stud in a rage.

Misfit ran up then bit at the stallions back leg; the dog made sure it wasn't hard enough to draw blood that was not allowed she knew. She did make sure it pinched enough to sting, which got the stud's attention away from her mistress' mare.

Grey reared back to get away from the dog which saved him from a nasty kick as Saya's back hooves just grazed him. The stallion twisted before dropping onto all fours he curled his upper lip back then charged at the dog in a raging temper; unexpectedly the stud had to come to a sliding halt.

Shin eventually reaching the opposite bank jumped between the stallion, Misfit, and Saya. The Tianming Monk pulled out one of his dragon daggers. It is all he had thought to grab this morning before leaving camp. Shadow Stalker held it by the blade so he could give the stud a good whack between the eyes with the handle if need be. A stick or a whip would have been preferable; the Guardian pointed it at the stallion furiously. "You bloody well better stay there Grey!"

Grey shook his head frustrated with a loud snort, he blew through his nostrils angrily; the stallion lifted his right front leg before stamping his hoof on the ground in a striking action trying to drive Shin away from the mare. "Pfft!"

Shin held his ground not giving an inch as his stallion tested him; the Tianming Monk knew if he gave in now, the stud would be unmanageable afterwards. Getting an idea the Guardian sheathed his dagger, taking a running step he grasped Grey around the neck before twisting it; the stallions head was almost flush against his left side leaving him with no choice but to drop on the ground. Shadow Stalker straddled his horse keeping him down.

Grey squealed angrily, struggling he tried to get his new master off his neck this had never been done to him before and he didn't like it one bit either. The stallion threw his head upwards trying to rise again, but he couldn't move. The stud breathing heavily for a long moment gave up trying to get back to his feet; still, it took some time for him to calm down as the horse waited for the beating that always followed his acts of defiance.

Shin feeling Grey shudder in uncertainty laid flat on top of him then crooned soothingly to him, he stroked his horse's neck until he began to relax. The Tianming Monk keeping the stallion pinned ran his hands all over him. He needed the stud to see him as the dominant male or this fight would be an everyday occurrence. Finally, feeling the time right the Tianming Monk stood up; he straddled his horse before pulling up on his mane insistently Shadow Stalker clicked his tongue against the roof of his mouth for him to rise. "Up you go, Grey!"

Shin held on tight to Grey's mane the stallion stood up with the Guardian sitting on his back; once his horse was standing fully, the Tianming Monk leaned forward on Grey's neck to continue stroking him as he praised the stud. Mindful of his horses scratched up sides, he turned him then nudged him to walk up the creek to the edge of the trees where his hide was soaking. Once he pulled it out of the water, they got out before going towards camp.

Shin halted Grey just before rounding the grove of trees; he jumped off him and walked around to face his stallion. The Tianming Monk put his hand onto the stud's nose bringing his head down so they were eye to eye. "I will tell you this only once Grey, you will behave there will be no mounting the mares until I say it is okay; if you try that stunt again, I will castrate you myself. Afterwards, I will give you to the first person interested in you do we understand each other!"

Grey softly snorted through his nostrils before bobbing his head as he respectfully gave his new master a nudge of affection. This man had saved his life not once, but unknowingly twice. The stud knew his other master would have given him a severe beating for taking off. He had taken a big chance running away knowing that. Neither had there been a whipping from this man after the stallion defied him; the horse was sure he made a wise choice when deciding to befriend the man even though he was given his freedom after the cougar attack.

Shin sighed in relief as he stroked Grey's nose; the Tianming Monk didn't want the mares bred right now, not until they were settled in one place that is. The Guardian turned to go back to camp, Misfit stayed beside him they were followed by the horses.

Cecille trying to hide her twitching lip from Shin turned away so her Guardian couldn't see her face. She had used the Mother Earth to watch the outcome of the incident White Buffalo was glad the stallion picked now to show his defiance. Who knows what perils were in store for them yet; they still had a ways to go she was sure.

Shin hearing a little snicker from Cecille chose to ignore it. He had his charge help him wring out the hide then she draped it over the fire, he went back to cleaning up the camp; the Tianming Monk had the filly packed up and Saya saddled by the time White Buffalo called him for breakfast. They dished up their meal then ate quietly, both immersed in their thoughts.

****

Powaw halted at another intersection with a frown of anger he missed his brother again. Thankfully, he was catching up to him but which way to go was now the question. The shaman would have caught his brother here if it wasn't for one of the straps on his dog's harness letting go; it had stalled him for almost two hours as he repaired it.

Powaw sighing in frustration dug out a cake and a piece of jerky. He only had two of each left so would have to hunt tonight, it would mean stopping early whether he caught up to his twin or not. The shaman was glad the rain quit, a misty sun was drying things up fast but not too quickly; he gratefully noted when he saw two indents where Spirit Bear's dogs drag poles dug into the ground.

Powaw fed his dog then followed the left fork in the trail with an irritated shake of his head. They were only two-and-a-half days from the white town known as Kipawa why his brother was going this way had the shaman totally confused. If Spirit Bear was searching for a place to have a vision, a white eyes town would be a poor choice to have it at; even close wasn't a good idea.

Powaw stopped to have a drink of water he was getting low on that as well; the shaman knelt then gave some to his dog before rising. They continued searching for his wayward twin, his confidence unshaken earlier was eroding by the minute... would he make it in time now or not?

*****

Spirit Bear was jogging at a good clip now that the trail was better travelled; unexpectedly, he halted abruptly. An irritating itch on the back of his neck had him turning entirely around facing the way he just came. Something wasn't right; the medicine man was going the right way he was sure he needed to go down this path so what could be causing his unease.

Spirit Bear shook his head in aggravation when the feeling disappeared just as fast as it appeared; shrugging, he turned back around before continuing onward. That momentarily unsettled feeling though continued to gnaw at the medicine man.

****

Shin halted as he looked around speculatively letting his eyes adjust to the brightness again. Their day had been a real long one; the sun was just beginning to go down, but they hadn't found another lake or creek to stop at. Cecille having made fresh buns to go with the leftover fish so they could eat on the go hadn't wanted to stop for lunch. The Tianming Monk could tell they were closer to town since the dirt used to fill the holes from the removal of stumps was only days old; he knew that sooner or later they would meet up with the crew removing the stumps or find where they had left off.

The two of them had been in and out of the trees most of the day since they stayed close to the edge of the road. Thankfully it gave them shade from the intense sun; unfortunately, the trees were thinning out now. After they reach the bottom of this hill, there won't be any protection from the sun. The trail was wider below so there were no trees for at least a half mile on either side of the path they were on, neither could he see stumps. For several miles, it was a barren, hard rocky terrain before more trees were seen further in the distance, maybe five or six miles.

Shin looked up at Cecille in question when he spied a trail going right; the Tianming Monk knew it would keep them in the trees for much-needed shade if they went that way. "Do you still want to go into town? We will get there sometime tomorrow if you do or should we head further into the mountains. There is a well-used trail here going north, deeper into Quebec. Either way, we will have to stop soon. If we stay on this path, we have about three hours to find a camp before dark. If we turn here, I would say maybe two hours. The trees will block out the late day sun giving us less daylight."

Cecille frowned thoughtfully but couldn't decide, so she jumped down off her horse before kneeling to consult the Mother Earth; when White Buffalo's hand touched the ground, two shots were fired rapidly, in quick succession.

Shin gasped in shock; the Tianming Monk grabbed at his chest before toppling backwards.

Grey reared in fear at the loud gunshots; when his new master fell at his feet, he spun around before racing off in a panic.

Cecille gasped in horrified denial when the Mother Earth showed her the two bullets entering her Guardian; one in the left chest and one just above his right eye. As the Tianming Monk fell, White Buffalo shrieked his name in disbelief. "Shhiin..."

Cecille's scream got cut short when something hit her on the head; she dropped to the ground groaning dazed by the blow. White Buffalo shook her head trying to get rid of the dizziness, stubbornly refusing to blackout. The healer tried to chant, but all she managed was a whimper of protest when she heard her dog howl in agony.

Cecille could vaguely hear a man's voice as unconsciousness tried to claim her, he was standing right above her yelling at someone else in anger; it was the last thing she heard before another hit to the head knocked her out cold!

"You idiot, you weren't supposed to kill him!"

****

Powaw sighed in defeat; he halted as his belly again rumbled hungrily, there were only a couple hours of daylight remaining. Still, his brother was nowhere to be found. The shaman didn't have a choice now he had no food at all; with only a few sips of water left his brother was going to have to wait.

Powaw turned left and he frowned thoughtfully at a narrow overgrown trail that veered off to the north. He knew this place at the end of it was a creek he could use to refill his water bag. The only problem was that it's an extra five miles out of his way, but he didn't have a choice. The shaman shrugged then turned picking up the trot he headed north.

Powaw was already making plans as soon as his camp was ready, he would hunt. In the morning, he would again try to catch up to his brother. He would make sure to have lots of leftovers to eat. There would be no stopping tomorrow to make up for time lost.

It didn't take long for the younger twin to reach a small clearing near the creek; once there the shaman removed his dog's harness so he could have a drink. It had been exceedingly muggy today, so most of the puddles had dried up quickly.

Powaw decided against putting up his shelter now since water and food were more important right now. Grabbing his water bag, he walked to the creek to fill it; bending, he saw two nice sized trout. The shaman rose he looked around for the right sturdy tree limb, not too thick. What he needed wasn't hard to find in the thick woods that surrounded this brook, the youngest twin quickly pulled out his small hatchet. He cut the limb before pulling his knife out to shave it into a point as he walked back towards the creek.

Powaw waded slowly into the water he stood quietly waiting patiently. Suddenly, he threw his makeshift spear then jumping ahead trying to grasp the shaft before the wiggling trout could take off with it. Missing it completely his foot slipped on a moss covered rock at the same instant causing him to fall into the creek face first with a shriek of outrage. Scrambling up quickly, he chased after his bobbing stick frantically trying to catch it. Just as it was about to disappear over an embankment, the shaman lunged forward. Lying halfway in the water; he managed to get hold of the spear, keeping it in a death grip the younger twin pushed down with all his weight until the fish quit wiggling.

Powaw jumping to his feet, promptly he lifted the stick high with the trout impelled on the end of it; the shaman thrust the fish up towards the heavens three times in quick succession giving thanks before he yelled out a loud whoop of victory. It shattered the quiet of the peaceful hidden sanctuary.

Powaw soaking wet trudged back up the creek towards his camp, mumbling irritably at having gotten his bone vest wet. He threw the offending fish on the shore once close to his drag poles; his bone vest and shirt soon followed, it was too hot for them anyway. Within half an hour he had four more fish laying on the bank lucky for him none of the other ones was quite as eventful. Wading back to dry land, he jumped out of the creek before picking up his garments. He gathered his fish too and went over to his drag poles to take off his tepee. The shaman's hunger got the best of him, so he left the shelter partly erected. Impatiently he gathered wood as well as several rocks to build a fire.

Powaw, waiting for the fire to become better established made himself a small drying rack before draping several pieces of fish on it. Smoking the excess trout would keep the meaty portions from spoiling if kept longer than a day; it would give him several days of food to eat on his travels. Afterwards, the shaman chopped off the head and tail of the last fish, skewering it he put it over his fire to cook. He didn't bother cleaning this one; he would eat it off the spit, already his mouth was watering. The youngest twin gave his dog half a fish plus all the scraps.

While Powaw's supper was cooking, he dug in his pack searching, finding what he was looking for he pulled out his snare. He took it a ways into the trees away from his camp then set it. He was hoping to catch a rabbit by morning giving him more to eat as he traveled. The shaman turned to go back to his camp but stopped listening as his dog barked before growling in fear. The youngest twin blanched when his dog gave a painful yelp then there was silence; suddenly, a distinctive growl erupted one he knew well.

"Rroarrr... grrr!"

Powaw pulled his knife before racing back to his camp, but he was too late to save his dog. The shaman stood staring in disbelief at an enormous ancient silver grey bear she must have been blonde at one time he couldn't help thinking; it was highly unusual to find a bear that has survived to such a great age, especially a female.

The old bear hoping for an easy meal gave the dog another savage shake before throwing him across the clearing. Food was getting harder to come by for her the older she got, her slower reflexes even made fishing hard which was one of her favourite meals. With most of her teeth missing now, berries with an occasional fish was all she could handle these days. The smell of food cooking had drawn her to investigate, seeing only a dog she attacked it; if she got hungry later, she would eat the dog too.

Powaw took a step back towards the safety of the trees to hide. He would wait for the beast to eat its fill before salvaging what was left.

He froze in fear when the bear turned and charged him as if she knew he was there; the shaman lifted his knife in defence. Unfortunately, his hatchet was still sitting beside his fire pit with his bone vest. Screaming in challenge, he braced himself.

*****

Spirit Bear stopped in surprise at a prickling sensation running down his spine it was a shock to find it here.

Instantly, he knew his twin brother was nearby; the medicine man ignored his uneasy feelings most of the day, but after eating the last of his food he surprised himself by turning around then went back.

Spirit Bear was now standing beside a path that was familiar to him; when they were boys before their mother died and the white man built a town close to the border, the twins came here often with their parents. It had been one of their favourite fishing places; shaking off his fond memory, the medicine man eagerly turned. He trotted towards his brother hoping he was here to come with him.

Spirit Bear was almost into the clearing when his dog growled a warning beside him; he stopped when he heard another dog in the distance screaming out in pain. Promptly, he knelt to unhook his hound; the medicine man knew what was occurring. He put his hand under the male dog's muzzle before lifting it in concern. "Distract the bear Maska, but please try not to get yourself killed!"

Spirit Bear took off his water bag then pulled his knife out before jumping back to his feet. He looked down longingly at his bone vest, but not having the time to fuss with it he turned away racing after his dog. The twins had to kill the bear with their hunting knives he couldn't use his bow or his axe. He knew everything had to be done just like in his vision. Screeching a war whoop hoping to confuse the bear; the medicine man rushed into the clearing just as the old behemoth turned to attack the dog biting her back leg.

Powaw took the opportunity to attack the bear from behind, but he was ignored; the old silver grey bear went after Spirit Bear instead. It wasn't until the shaman's knife entered the bears left shoulder that she turned catching the younger twin by surprise.

Spirit Bear, knowing the bear was fainting and planned to go after his younger brother, ran up to push the now defenceless Powaw out of the way. The older twin screamed in agony when the bear's claws raked his left chest tearing open his flesh with one vicious swipe. Unfortunately, he took off his buckskin shirt with the bone vest earlier because it was too muggy out; now he wished he had left it on, it would have given him some protection. The medicine man didn't let the excruciating pain stop him. Taking a wild lunge towards the bear, he buried his knife in the monsters right eye.

Powaw getting to his feet jumped on the silver-grey behemoths back then pulled his knife free from its shoulder before stabbing it into the side of her neck. The shaman was hoping to sever the main artery; unfortunately, he only nicked it.

Screaming the old silver bear tried to reach behind her shoulder to get the clinging man off her back. The bear was growing really tired now; she could no longer see properly because the blood covering her face was dripping into her one good eye. The easy meal that she had envisioned earlier was fast turning into an unexpected struggle for survival.

Spirit Bear rushed in now that the silver grey bear wouldn't be able to see him; pulling his knife free of her eye he thrust it under the bear's jaw when she reared back up a bit to get away from him and into its throat. The medicine man desperately twisted the knife sideways with all his remaining strength. He ripped it to the side hoping to sever the bear's juggler. In triumph, he crowed in delight when gore sprayed everywhere drenching him in blood.

Powaw jumped off the bears back as she toppled backwards dead, the shaman stood there breathing heavily. He stared at the medicine man in disbelief before an ironic curl in his lip expressed his unwilling thanks. "Well, looks like you saved my life!"

Spirit Bear drenched in blood smiled back; he opened his mouth to answer, but all he managed to get out when a dizzy spell hit him was an exclamation of surprise. He dropped ungracefully onto his backside, losing his breath in the process. "Harrumph..."

Powaw rushed over in astonishment he looked Spirit Bear over carefully. He assumed all the blood was the bears until he saw his twin brothers torn left chest; the shaman promptly helped the medicine man up. "Come, we need to get all the blood off you so I can see how badly you are hurt!"

Spirit Bear nodded, he put his uninjured arm around Powaw's shoulder and let his brother help him. Trying not to put too much pressure on his left side, he allowed the younger twin to steer him towards the creek. The medicine man sat before lying back full length in the water allowing the strong current to clean most of the blood away. Staring in fascination, he watched rivulets of dark red blood flow down the creek. His whole left side was numb now he couldn't believe how much blood he was losing. Fortunately, the icy cold water eventually slowed the bleeding to a trickle.

Powaw left Spirit Bear then immersed himself to rid himself of the bear's blood, but not for long; he didn't have much on him, unlike his twin. He jumped out of the water before rushing over to look at the medicine man's shredded flesh; the shaman frowned as he helped his brother to sit up he needed a closer look. After examining him carefully, the younger twin realized he didn't have what was needed in his bag because he hadn't been prepared to go on this journey. "Where is your medicine bag?"

Spirit Bear pointed behind him back down the trail, he didn't want to leave the water now that the bleeding had slowed. The medicine man was praying the cold mountain stream had cleaned the wound enough no infection would result, but he wasn't holding out much hope on that one; even one small scratch from a bears nasty disease carrying claws was lethal depending, on what their last meal was. "It is partway down the trail, I unhooked Maska when I heard your dog scream hoping he would help distract the bear, till I could get here. Take my dog and hook him up, I need my herbs before the infection gets further into my bloodstream."

Powaw immediately jumped up he rushed down the path with Spirit Bear's dog following him; it didn't take long for the shaman to reattach the dog to his harness. Afterwards, they raced back.

****

Cecille came too slowly in confusion, not quite sure what happened to her or where she was. She inhaled deeply and knew instantly she was draped over her mare's back. Both hands were tied together before being secured to her saddle as were her feet, which effectively kept her from falling off if she unexpectedly moved. She also had a gag in her mouth making her utterly helpless because she couldn't chant, so was unable to bring White Buffalo to the surface to see; not only that, but without being able to touch the Mother Earth she was completely blind.

Cecille emptied her panicking thoughts she needed to stay calm right now, giving into her fear wouldn't help her one bit. Taking deep breaths, she searched for Shin but felt nothing she couldn't feel their bond at all; White Buffalo caught back a sob quickly when she realized she could hear voices in the distance. Hoping for some information on who was holding her captive, she caulked her head listening to what was being said."

I told you everything Sheriff, we were trying to get the stallion back from the thieving Oriental. The stranger slipped into the lawyers camp during the night taking Thunder, Sam immediately

Twin Destinies

came to my ranch thinking the horse had just wandered off. When we caught up to the missing stud Bill decided to take only the lawyer with him to negotiate. His hope was that with just two of them the Chinese man wouldn't feel threatened. Suddenly, she came out of nowhere shooting them both down in cold-blood; we had no warning at all I swear to you!"

Cecille groaned quietly in despair at the familiar voice from the creek. Denis, how did he manage to get loose before apparently killing Sam? White Buffalo's thoughts were interrupted when another man began talking; he didn't sound familiar, so he must be the sheriff. She stilled listening carefully then frowned maybe she had heard the voice for a second right above her, he must be the one who hit her knocking her unconscious.

"You are trying to tell me this slip of a girl managed to get the drop on one of the most notorious gunmen in Ontario and Quebec; I examined both men's wounds, they don't match up at all. Bill was shot by a rifle the lawyer was killed by a pistol!"

Cecille grinned in relief apparently the sheriff wasn't stupid; White Buffalo had high expectations of getting out of this in one piece as Denis sputtered for a moment... until!

"Yes, well um, hmm we didn't stop to examine Sam because we needed to get you right away before they disappeared. I guess the Oriental could have shot him. We all assumed it was her too, but it isn't the issue; all four of us saw her shoot your brother so she should hang for that at least!"

Cecille stiffened in shock, she blocked out the rest of their conversation, she knew now she would hang for sure; White Buffalo unknowingly shot a sheriff's brother, even if he were a hired gun it wouldn't matter in the least!

****

Powaw looked at his brother before shaking his head in exasperation, he thought back to earlier. His twin treated his own wound then the shaman helped wrap his chest. Now they were both skinning the large old silver grey bear since the medicine man insisted they do everything like his vision had shown him. The older brother was trying to do his share even though he could hardly stand; the younger twin tried to get him to lie down while he did the skinning, but his wounded brother steadfastly refused.

Spirit Bear knew how important it was to have everything exact, look what happened when it wasn't he had argued vehemently; because Powaw wouldn't come with him at the beginning things changed. In the medicine man's vision at the village neither of them was hurt, but now the older twin was; in the first vision he saw both dogs lying by the tepee door, now one of them is dead.

Powaw not able to argue much over that logic nodded resignedly. Spirit Bear wasn't looking good though, so the shaman had taken over as much of the skinning as possible; luckily, they didn't have to cure the hide too his brother assured him.

Spirit Bear moved further away, he sat on the ground to dig his hole for the meat he had taken from the bear. Powaw was now cutting open the bears stomach to remove the liver. The medicine man put in his kindling and grabbed a branch out of the central fire to light his underground cooking pit. Carefully, he put in several rocks not wanting to smother it before letting them get red hot. He put the piece of haunch in with the leaves he had taken from his medicine bag, now he was able to cover it up; the meat would slowly roast making the stringy greasy bear meat more palatable.

Spirit Bear paused as he knelt there with both fists pressed to the ground; his arms were locked it was all that was keeping him from dropping to the ground. He waited for the dizziness to settle before he was able to sit back up. The medicine man lifted his right arm then wiped the sweat off his forehead the older twin was getting weaker, but he needed to hold on a bit longer.

Powaw taking pity on Spirit Bear walked over and helped him up, he still could hardly believe what the medicine man had told him. The details of the vision his older twin had while in the sweat lodge after they buried their father was quite unbelievable. The shaman shuddered at the thought of eating it raw he needed to get this done quickly. "Come on we need to put the tepee up, I finished skinning the bear before cutting the hide in two; the liver has been removed, it is unfortunately waiting for us."

Spirit Bear nodded, it didn't take long to put the two tepees together before putting it around the carcass of the blonde bear and the fire pit; effectively, enclosing the twins in together. They did everything exactly as the medicine man remembered from his vision, he hoped. It seemed like a lifetime ago, but in reality, it had only been a couple of days ago.

Once all the rituals were complete the twins sitting across from each other began chanting, rocking it wasn't long before Spirit Bear was pulled into the future. The medicine man saw a young woman with raven black hair bent doctoring a man in a wigwam that was familiar to him; he could feel himself helping her as she chanted in a strange language, unknown to him. She was the healer needed to help his people, but who was she? Just as she was lifting her head so he could see her he was yanked away from his home.

Spirit Bear was taken down the path he used to get here before going passed this place. He continued until he was on the outskirts of the border town, the older twin felt the healer here. The medicine man kept walking forward until he came upon a crowd of white people that surrounded a platform, a woman was standing on top of it. She had a rope wrapped around her neck, her head was bowed with her long raven black hair covering most of her face; suddenly she stiffened sensing him, she lifted her head.

Spirit Bear stared in horrified fascination; she had no eyes at all how was she supposed to help his people without them. The older twin shook his head in denial before closing his own eyes. Opening them again hoping he imagined it all he stared again at the woman with black holes where her eyes should have been. She reached out her hand beseechingly to the medicine man. "Help me!"

At first, it seemed to Spirit Bear that she was talking directly to him. He turned to flee in fear but was unable to move from that spot. It wasn't until then that the medicine man saw a shadowy image rushing passed him, beside it was his younger twin brother; surprisingly, the shaman seemed to be helping the shadow.

Spirit Bear cried out in denial when he felt a tug he wasn't ready to leave the vision just yet; now that his brother was involved the older twin wanted... no he needed to see more of it. He tried to resist the pull, but the medicine man's subconscious was jerked back to his body with a violent jolt.

*****

Powaw sitting across from Spirit Bear stared at him he could tell his older brother was getting a vision, but again the shaman wasn't having one; when his twin brother's eyes open, he watched them roll in their sockets before the medicine man fell over out cold.

Powaw getting up in a fit of temper pulled off his bloody bear hide before stalking to his brother. He yanked the one off Spirit Bear; turning, the shaman threw them in disgust. Seeing the older twins bedding in the opposite corner, he went to gather up a sleeping fur he returned and threw it on the medicine man.

Powaw stormed out of the tepee mumbling irritably under his breath. Unfortunately, he couldn't kill his brother tonight not until he found out what that vision was all about. He jumped in the creek to wash himself clean, now more than ever he was determined to find a way to kill Spirit Bear and soon. Of course, not until after the shaman found out how to cure his people; once he had that information, he would be free to do so.

Powaw's mind now set left and marched to the back of the tepee he uncovered the bear haunch then quickly the younger brother ate. Going back inside the shaman crawled in his sleeping fur, but his brain refused to let him rest. It kept playing over and over again all the likely scenarios on how to accomplish his goal; until, he was just about ready to bash his head against the ground in frustration. It was the wee hours of the morning before he finally slept.

CHAPTER SEVENTEEN

Powaw stared incredulously at his fevered twin before the shaman shook his head in disbelief. "You aren't really serious, are you?"

Spirit Bear nodded decisively before wiping the sweat from his forehead; he was quite befuddled, the older twin never thought to wonder why Powaw was questioning him the shaman should have had the same vision. The medicine man wasn't faring well his wound was infected badly already. His brother helped him remove the bandages, but he had to pop several pussy sores before he could put more herbs on them; afterwards, they wrapped his chest with the last clean rawhide bandage.

Spirit Bear didn't know how he was going to get to town in this condition. He was sipping a tea that was helping numb the pain, but how long he would be able to run before it wore off was the burning question. He should make a lot more and put it in his water bag so he can sip on it throughout the day, as soon as he was finished with Powaw he would get more water.

Spirit Bear turned back to his incredulous twin. "Yes, I'm sure Powaw we need to go into the town called Kipawa to rescue a black-haired woman who has a rope around her neck. If we don't get there in time, she will die, and the cure for our people will go with her to the grave. The only other way to know her is that she has no eyes but is a healer. When we get to town, there will be a shadow trying to help her too. We have to team up with whatever it is, I have no idea who it is or even if it is human; all I could see was a shadowy blur, it was there for a moment then disappeared just as quickly."

Spirit Bear frowned into his tea; he was a bit confused by the vision. He had seen the shadow, as well as Powaw, but hadn't felt himself there at all. Unless he was the shadow, did that mean he was dead? If so was he helping his brother from the spirit world? The medicine man shook his head mentally to himself. No, the older twin was sure he would have still felt something if he had been the shadow. Besides, that made no sense at all since he had seen himself in his wigwam helping the woman later in the future. Could he be wrong, maybe it had been the shaman assisting the woman, not him.

Spirit Bear hearing a warning growl, but too late; looked up in a bewildered daze. The medicine man saw the large club coming towards him in disbelief as if from a long distance away, but couldn't do anything to halt it. The wooden weapon struck him solid with a resounding, thwack!

Spirit Bear's skull split open instantly spraying blood everywhere; the medicine man dropped to the ground, soundlessly.

Powaw lifted the club to give Spirit Bear another whack just to make sure but stumbled back when Maska jumped between them with a menacing growl. The shaman eyed the dog wearily he could kill the dog too of course. Finally, he shrugged before dropping the stick when he saw blood leaking from the older twins head; his brother would be dead soon anyway, so why bother.

Powaw looked down at all the items he needed to carry now that his dog was dead; it took him several minutes to decide the best way to pack everything. Just before leaving he grabbed his bow then draped it across his chest, it would help to keep everything on his shoulders in place. He kicked dirt over the fire... finally ready, he left in a hurry.

Powaw grinned relieved now that he was back on the trail leading to town, he felt no remorse whatsoever for leaving his brother to die. The shaman was just glad he hadn't felt any pain after hitting his twin; unlike their younger years before they had been separated to find their adult names and their purpose in life. When they were kids, the two were inseparable they even felt everything the other one did, which is all that kept him from killing his brother sooner. If he had known he wouldn't feel anything, he might have been tempted to end his brother's life years ago.

Powaw sighed grimly then couldn't help chuckling in delight at accomplishing his heart's desire. He had always wanted to get rid of his pesky perfect twin who seemed to be able to do nothing wrong in the eyes of their people. He would go to town, rescue this eyeless black haired healer before taking her back to his tribe so she could heal them. For once the shaman would be the hero, he was confident everyone would finally start listening to him.

Powaw feeling a twinge decided that on his way back this way he would stop just to make sure Spirit Bear was dead. He might even bury his twin; feeling better after that thought the shaman picked up his pace. When he got to the main trail, he turned right before following it.

****

Clang, jangle, clump, clump, clump... jingle, bang!

Cecille quietly groaned in fear trying not to let them hear her; she bit at her bottom lip hard to stifle the noise. Listen to the cell door slam shut with finality, followed by the keys hitting the bars on her door didn't help either; involuntarily making her flinch uneasily.

Cecille was in the furthest cell, so the sounds of retreating footsteps made her shudder. The keys hitting together as they were hung up by the far door leading into the sheriff's office made her cringe. Finally, in relief, White Buffalo heard the door bang loudly as it got closed tight sealing her in.

The absolute silence caused Cecille to shiver in dread. White Buffalo had continued pretending to be unconscious when they carried her in here so she didn't have to look or talk to anyone. None of them even knew yet she was blind, she managed to hide that from all of them.

Cecille rolled off the hard lumpy cot the sheriff put her on; thankfully, he took the rope and gag off of her once she was in the cell. White Buffalo dropped to the floor before putting both her hands onto the Mother Earth searching frantically. She groaned in denial when she felt nothing.

Cecille frowned in fear then she began chanting lightly before trying a little louder; her voice grew stronger in panic, but again absolutely nothing happened. White Buffalo couldn't feel her eyes change colour either nor could she bring her power to bear so she could see where she was at. The healer deep down hidden even from herself had felt overwhelmed by her power all these years. Over time, she had managed to block so much of it trying to shield herself because of her feelings of unworthiness.

Cecille curled her legs up; she wrapped her arms around them before burying her face between her knees sobbing uncontrollably. White Buffalo felt abandoned not only by her Guardian, but also by the Mother Earth and the Great Spirit.

Cecille opened her unseeing eyes before staring blankly at the far wall. Her eyes were not a dark green now, but an empty coal black; White Buffalo was now completely blind not only physically but mentally too as she built an unemotional wall around herself keeping all out even the Mother Earth.

*****

Grey stood still shivering in fear even though his instinct was to flee as far as he could, he didn't budge for a long moment. The stud ran for half the night until exhausted the horse needed to stop; why he turned back once rested was a mystery only the stallion knew.

Grey snorted uncomfortably, the smell of blood was strong here; taking a cautious step, the stud lowered his head before putting his nose closer to his master's face, he waited for a sign of life but nothing happened.

Grey blew hard through his nostrils then suddenly jumped back in fright when he heard a whine further to his right; turning he walked over before nudging the dog trying to get her to rise too. When that didn't work and only produced a pitiful painful cry, the stallion went back over to his master. Lowering his head he once again snorted, the stud nibbled at his master's nose insistently. "Pfft."

****

Maska whined pleadingly; he had just re-entered the tepee, for an hour he sat by the door guarding it against his master's twin. Thirst eventually drove him outside to the creek for a much-needed drink. He walked over to the corner before nudging Spirit Bear urgently; the dog dripping icy water licked more blood from his master's temple trying to rouse the medicine man.

Spirit Bear moaned when he felt his dog's wet slimy cold tongue on his face. He pushed Maska off him before the older twin sat up holding his head in confusion. The medicine man rose unsteadily, he staggered outside calling for his brother; unsure what had happened... was his brother dead? He couldn't remember anything except excruciating pain after pushing his brother away from the bear, saving his twins life.

Spirit Bear was burning hot, clawing at the bandage on his chest he staggered to the creek. Just as he succeeded in pulling off the confining restraint, he dropped to his knees into the icy brook, which helped to cool him off. The medicine man drank some water before falling sideways. Fortunately, onto his injured left side, several sharp jagged rocks dug into his skin popping several sores; he never felt a thing though as he lost consciousness once again.

Maska followed Spirit Bear discreetly, watching him carefully in concern. When his master passed out, the dog rushed over to push him onto his back so his face wasn't in the water. He carefully grabbed the medicine man's buckskin leggings with his teeth, to pull him a little at a time out of the creek. His left foot and arm were still in the water keeping him cooled off, but he was out enough for his dog to lie on him; he tried to keep him warm that way. The white hound with only a little black on his chest, made sure to stay off his master's injured left side. Periodically, he would sniff at the wound before licking it with his rough tongue busting the rest of the blisters. It allowed puss to escape, which helped to let fresh clean blood flow.

Maska finished cleaning the wound put his head on Spirit Bear's chest; he whined anxiously before dozing in the hot sun. He would stay with the medicine man until his master was dead then he too would die, loyal to the end the dog would never willingly leave him.

****

Cecille heard the door in the distance opening. She turned around on her lumpy cot, so her back was all the sheriff would be able to see. A few minutes later she heard the jingle of keys hitting together when they were taken down off the wall; next, the clumping of familiar booted feet echoed down the corridor before stopping at her cell. White Buffalo closed her dead black eyes, pretending to be asleep.

Clank, creek, bang!

Cecille ignored the lock being opened as well as the creaking of the door; a moment later, she heard the sheriff drop the tray of food he had brought her to the floor. She could smell the stew and biscuits even from across the room, but White Buffalo refused to move. She could feel the sheriff standing beside her bed waiting for her to turn around, again she refused to react. Why bother, she was dead anyway.

The sheriff stared at the woman's back in annoyance he could tell she was awake just by her posture. "I'm Sheriff Cooper and I want to know your name as well as why you killed my brother; I also brought you some food you need to eat!"

Cecille refused to turn or give the sheriff an answer White Buffalo almost laughed hysterically at his notion that she needed to eat; why, she was to die soon what difference did it make.

Sheriff Cooper took the last step bringing him closer to the cot then grabbed the woman's shoulder forcing her onto her back. He inhaled in surprise as he stared down at the delicate flawless pixie face she was stunningly beautiful! Suddenly she opened her black, unseeing eyes; he staggered back in shock with an oath of disbelief before leaving the cell in a hurry.

Cecille completely ignored the food; White Buffalo turned back to face the wall.

*****

Shin's eyes popped open in shock when he felt something wet on his nose; it was just in time for Grey to snort in his face before trying to bite his nose. Jerking into a sitting position the Tianming Monk grabbed his chest in agony. Everything went black for a moment as unconsciousness threatened once more. Taking slow even breaths Shadow Stalker managed to stay upright, thankfully the dizziness calmed after a few minutes.

Shin lifted his hand weakly to feel the crease above his right eye it went all the way across his temple into his hairline; fortunately, it hadn't left too big of an indent in the Tianming Monk's head it had bled profusely, though.

Shin cautiously moved his left arm experimentally before probing around the small bullet hole. There was only a thin rivulet of red on his shirt where a bit of blood initially leaked out. Carefully the Tianming Monk reached back hoping the bullet had gone all the way through. Feeling a bigger ragged hole in his back, the Guardian sighed in relief; lucky for him the bullet hit at an angle, so the back exit wound was far enough up he could reach it. He couldn't help feeling grateful the trajectory hadn't been too high it didn't quite reach his collar bone. The slant told Shadow Stalker the shooter was lying down on the ground in the shade of the trees to his right, at the bottom of this hill. The exit wound bled a lot since it was four times the size of the bullet entry, which was why he felt so weak.

Shin turned himself slowly before getting on all fours, but tried not to put too much pressure on his left arm; he had to stay there for several moments when his head throbbed, it felt like his skull was about to burst open. Unfortunately, his shoulder began bleeding again too. The Tianming Monk groaned in denial he had to push back the black void trying to pull him under again.

Shin's breath caught at the sound of a distressed cry coming from the trees on his left it helped him to stop the blackness from creeping in. Slowly he crawled towards it before dropping onto his right side; tenderly the Tianming Monk stroked the soft ball of fur soothingly, until comforted Cecille's dog stopped crying.

Misfit hushed when she felt someone touching her lovingly; instantly, the dog knew it was not her mistress she lifted her head and licked Shin's hand before her head dropped back down. She panted in exertion even that little movement caused her excruciating pain.

Shin felt along Misfit's body looking for a wound Cecille's dog whimpered painfully when the Tianming Monk pressed on her ribs; they were severely bruised or broken, someone must have kicked the dog pretty hard.

Shin laid his head down on the ground weakly, thankful that Cecille's dog was still alive. All that was missing was the two mares with their precious cargos; the Tianming Monk allowed the black void to overtake him, he passed out only because his body refused to obey him.

Grey reached down then sniffed the two before turning towards the trail to keep watch.

*****

Cecille was just beginning to doze off; it was so quiet now that the insistent banging from the hammers building her execution platform had halted ten minutes after the sheriff left. Just as sleep was claiming her, White Buffalo's eyes popped open involuntary at the slamming of the door down the corridor. Closely followed by several angry voices as well as booted feet shuffling to her cell. The clanking of the key before the squeaking of the cell door opening made her stiffen again, she didn't turn to look.

Sheriff Cooper stormed over to the cot he pulled the woman around before grabbing her by the hair; he yanked her up into a sitting position so that the four men could see for themselves. "Open your damn eyes woman, or I will gladly force them open!"

Cecille having no choice now reluctantly opened her unseeing eyes. White Buffalo heard an in-drawn breath of shock even that brought no response from her; what did it matter, without her Guardian or dog she was useless. Without the help of the Mother Earth or the Great Spirit, she felt powerless.

Denis frowned in shock, how had she managed to kill Bill Cooper when she was blind! He looked at his three accomplices, they all shrugged just as confused as he was before all blabbered ways that she could have accomplished it; the leader eventually held up his hand in a silencing motion as he turned to look at the sheriff. "We don't know how she did it, but we all saw her shoot him what does it matter if she's blind that doesn't make it impossible!"

The three accomplices nodded vehemently in agreement.

Sheriff Cooper scowled thoughtfully remembering a circus that came to town about two years ago. They had a blind woman who did stunts; she also walked a tightrope before being thrown between two men as they swung her high above the crowd and she never missed. He looked down at the young woman again his anger getting the best of him he savagely pulled back on the woman's hair. He tilted her head further back so he could see her expression. "What is your name, why did you kill my brother?"

Cecille felt the sheriff's sharp breath close to her face; she curled her lip up in the right corner, the smirk was unquestionably unremorseful. She closed her eyes refusing to give them her name or speak a word in her defence. Denis held his breath in trepidation then released it slowly in a sigh of relief when she refused to say anything to clear her name. With the Oriental dead which he made sure of there were no other witnesses; as long as she kept her mouth shut he would get away with killing the lawyer.

Sheriff Cooper growled in frustration before shoving the woman back on her cot savagely. He spun away, at the same time he waved for the four men to leave the cell. Seeing the untouched tray still on the floor by the bed, he picked it up then stormed out of the cage; he locked it with a swift flick of his wrist. "She is obviously a witch!"

Cecille listened to the men retreating before curling up on the cot she faced the wall forlornly. Self-doubt, loneliness, and self-pity began rolled down her cheeks in rivulets. White Buffalo paused, but only for a moment when she heard the hammering start up again in the distance as the gallows continued being built; closing her black eyes, she tried to ignore the noise. She sobbed uncontrollably for quite some time until exhausted she tried again to sleep.

****

"Neigh, pfft!"

Powaw halted in astonishment; effortlessly he pulled his bow over his head. He had an arrow notched within seconds before aiming it to his right when he heard a horse in the trees. He was almost at the fork in the trail that would lead him into town, so meeting other travelers was bound to happen. The shaman had another two hours to go then he would be turning west. Cautiously, he waited several minutes for the horse and rider to reveal themselves. Getting impatient when nothing happened, he slowly advanced keeping his bow at the ready.

Powaw stopped then lowered his bow before chuckling at the white and black mare as she turned to stare at him forlornly. She was caught in a tree by a wood box that was attached to her rump. Eyeing the things on her back, he grinned thoughtfully. It would give him an opportunity to get rid of some bulk on his shoulders. Taking pity on the poor thing, who knew when she got stuck there. The shaman put the bow back over his shoulder; carefully he walked around the mare hoping she wouldn't kick at him as he crooned soothingly.

Powaw thankfully got to her other side with no mishaps. Grasping the large tree limb, the shaman pushed against it until it snapped. The mare instantly spun around she raced out of the trees back on the trail before she turned left heading down the road at a dead run.

Powaw frowned in disappointment after the retreating mare. He should have held on to her, but she had no rope on her. He scratched his head baffled that she would bolt so quickly. The shaman shrugged turning he trotted to the trail it was getting pretty late dusk would soon be over. He would have no choice but to stop to sleep pretty soon; he was hoping to wait until he reached the other path then the spiritual healer could get some much-needed rest before getting an early start in the morning. The younger twin figured he could get close to the town by tomorrow afternoon sometime.

Powaw turned left once out of the trees now back on the trail he picked up the trot again; the shaman sighed in disappointment again when he caught a brief flicker in the distance of the retreating mare before she disappeared completely.

****

Shin woke again with a splitting headache his throbbing left shoulder was in even worse shape, but at least now he was clear headed. He sat up slowly before looking behind him and saw quite a bit of blood on the ground. The Tianming Monk pushed himself up off the ground. Shadow Stalker had to slap his stallion on the rump to get him to move out of the way. Misfit was awake panting heavily, she needed water and so did he; his stomach growled angrily at him... food too!

Shin was about to take a step, but suddenly froze when Misfit lifted her head as far as she could to growl a warning. Grey heard it too, so arched his neck before neighing a challenge. The Guardian eventually heard what the other two could hear; it was the sound of a horse galloping full out, surprisingly it was coming from the trail that led into the mountains. The Tianming Monk weakly pulled out one of his daggers. Although, with all the blood he had lost Shadow Stalker wasn't sure he could hold off an attacker at this time. He wouldn't go down without a fight though.

Grey's nostrils flared again searching for a scent, unexpectedly he started prancing in place before nickering a greeting. Cecille's packhorse with her precious cargo leaning precariously on the left side of her rump but thankfully still in one piece, barrelled around the corner; she came to a skidding halt when the stallion raced to her. The stud put his head over her neck to comfort the distressed mare that kept bugling out in fear.

Shin looked up in relief; the Tianming Monk gave heartfelt thanks knowing the Great Spirit was watching out for him. "Thank you Shen, merciful God of all living things!"

Shin slowly walked to the distressed mare every step he took was excruciating, but he buried the pain determined to reach the packhorse without passing out. The Tianming Monk pulled off the water bag first, he rummaged inside the right saddlebag; finally, he pulled out the last two buns; the rest of the jerky, and he grabbed his medicine bag too.

Shin turned back before pausing to stroke the mare's neck consolingly. "I'm not sure where you ran off to Precious, but I am definitely thankful you came back!"

Shin slowly shuffled back to Misfit he carefully sat before crossing his legs. The Tianming Monk poured water into his cupped hand letting the dog drink first before having a drink himself. The Guardian split up the last of the meat then they each had a bun, he gave Cecille's dog another drink of water; as he was putting the cap back on his water bag Shadow Stalker saw a dark brown familiar object on the trail to his left.

Shin got up slowly he walked down the path to retrieve Cecille's Stetson that had been left behind. He walked back to the horses; pouring water in the hat he gave the stallion and mare some then the Tianming Monk walked around to the opposite side. He took out the rest of the oats it would have to do until they could forage.

Shin finished with the horses went back to sit with Misfit; the food and water had helped him tremendously. Thankfully, he didn't feel quite as weak now; he pulled down his shirt in order to take out his left arm. He rummaged in his medicine bag until the Tianming Monk found a container of cream, he pulled it free. It was quickly followed by a small bottle of whisky, a bandage, a bowl then finally a needle with a long thin rawhide sinew already attached. The Tianming Monk poured some whisky into the bowl and he put in the needle. He took a couple generous swigs of the rotgut before dumping a substantial amount over his shoulder, he hissed painfully as the alcohol hit his bleeding shoulder front then back.

Shin seeing stars ground his teeth in determination not wanting to pass out again. After an excruciating few minutes, the pain dulled. He picked up the needle then biting his lower lip to keep himself from making any noise, he sewed closed the bullet hole in his upper left shoulder. Lucky for him it was not a big hole, so it only required three stitches; unfortunately, the Tianming Monk couldn't sew the larger hole in his back. He would have to make sure to wrap it tightly once he put his cream on, the ointment would help to keep the bleeding to a minimum. At least he wouldn't have to worry about losing more blood from this side, it would just have to do for now.

Shin put the needle in his mouth when he was finished and pulled the rawhide thread tight he used his dagger to cut it. Afterwards, he threw the needle back into the bowl with the whisky; instantly, the rotgut turned blood red. The Tianming Monk put a little whisky in his right hand, taking a fortifying breath he pressed it to his temple; he allowed his breath to escape in a hissing sigh before the sting of the alcohol dulled, the throbbing in his head calmed a bit too. Shin reached for his jar of cream then opened it now that everything got disinfected he could use his healing cream. He brought it to his nose before inhaling deeply it always reminded him of home. It was an ointment the Tianming Monk's made only a few were permitted to know the recipe; it was entirely different than the one Cecille made. He was getting low, so would have to make more.

Shin pulled out a generous handful before reaching back he put a generous amount on the hole in his shoulder, it was still seeping blood. The Guardian tried pushing as much as possible inside the wound and the rest Shadow Stalker spread around it as best he could. He grunted in pain as the movement pulled on his new stitches, but they held; grimacing, the Tianming Monk brought his hand back in front he spread the rest of the salve on his stitches.

Shin picked up his bandage, holding one end in his teeth; he wrapped his shoulder tightly then tied it the best he could. Afterwards, the Tianming Monk put more cream in his hand and put some on his temple before singing in his native language he spread the rest between his two hands. Shadow Stalker rubbed them together vigorously as he chanted; feeling the heat begin, he continued to rub his palms together till they were as hot as he could stand.

Shin pulled his palms apart then reaching down he laid both hands onto Misfit's ribs, his chanting intensified for several long minutes. The Tianming Monk could feel the heat transferring into Cecille's dog it wasn't long before her breathing became less stressful; when he was satisfied he helped ease enough of the pressure that the dog would recover now on her own Shadow Stalker took his hands away.

Shin quickly placed more cream in his palms, again he rubbed them together hard. This time he put one hand over his own temple, with one on his upper chest allowing the heat of the ointment to penetrate deeply; lastly, the Tianming Monk reached over his shoulder and put his hand as far back as he could reach until it was over the bullet's exit wound. Chanting he held his hand there for as long as heat was entering his shoulder.

Shin sighed relieved after he got finished. The pain was now half what it was earlier. Pouring the last of the whisky on his hands than a little water he washed the ointment away before repacking his medicine bag. The Tianming Monk put everything back on the packhorse, walking over the Guardian carefully lifted Misfit; there was about another hour left of the fading daylight, they needed to find a better place to camp. Somewhere a little more private to be able to use his carpet, gently putting Misfit over the packhorses withers he slowly made his way down the embankment.

*****

It took two hours for Shin to find a good camp since he needed to get past the open rocky, barren ground. It was on the edge of the northern tree line, which he planned on staying close to not liking how open this road was now. He took out only what he figured he needed for the morning before unpacking his carpet the Guardian made sure to set it up away from the firelight. He took it deeper into the trees, so shadows were hiding it; just in case anyone happened to go by. Shadow Stalker didn't want anyone to see the uniquely designed Japanese carpet since others killed for it in the past it was best to keep it hidden. The Tianming Monk humming knelt in the middle; he put his longest finger and thumbs against each other than laid his hands onto his knees facing upwards. Quietly he meditated searching for Cecille but in vain.

Shin got up in frustration and repacked the carpet before locking the trunk once more. When finished, he crawled into his blankets with a troubled frown the Japanese rug hadn't helped him at all, which was highly unusual. The Tianming Monk's concern was rising steadily; something wasn't right. He would try again tomorrow morning. Curling up to Misfit, he slept a heavy healing sleep as the ointment continued to penetrate deeply.

****

Maska whined in anxiety; the dog lifted up, his master's breathing had gotten shallower as the day moved into the night until it was all but non-existent. He growled in confusion when Spirit Bear started twitching all over having a seizure of some kind. It lasted several minutes before once again the medicine man lay quietly. Maska got up he went to the water for a drink; thirstily, he lapped up as much as his belly would hold it also helped to calm the hunger pains he was now having. The dog returned to his master then licked his wound clean again before lying back down on Spirit Bear forlornly he kept watch.

*****

Powaw slowed as he got closer to the end of the trail before cautiously he walked out onto the main path. He almost stepped in a pile of horse's dung. He looked down frowning speculatively there was blood everywhere, the tracks were very confusing. Horse's tracks were coming and going, dragging marks, several different sized boots, as well as dog tracks. The shaman walked towards the trees; he found more blood with scuff marks of something getting dragged or maybe it was a person pulling himself forward trying to reach the trees. No bodies were evident, but the blood was relatively fresh.

Powaw shrugged it had nothing to do with him he decided to go into the trees a little way to sleep for a couple of hours; the shaman didn't go far in before dropping his black bear hide on the ground, he sat on it. He ate quickly, too tired to think about anything he wrapped himself in his fur propping himself against a tree he was instantly asleep.

****

Cecille had to jerk herself awake again when the nightmare she was having refused at first to let her go; they were getting more disturbing each time she closed her eyes, but White Buffalo needed sleep badly. Without it, she was becoming more unresponsive, or maybe it was resigned to her fate.

The sheriff had brought her food again, but still, she refused to eat anything. He tried one more time to find out her name but to no avail. Getting frustrated he tried taunting her with ugly descriptions of what her last day on Earth would be like tomorrow; he was hoping to trigger some kind of response from the woman who seemed to be dead already. White Buffalo was to be hung by the neck until deceased at sunset tomorrow for killing Bill Cooper in cold-blood.

Cecille sighed grimly every time she closed her eyes all she could feel was nothing, which scared her more than the images of her dangling from a rope. White Buffalo felt a tingle before a throbbing in the back of her head; she pushed back against it as more pain jolted through her skull until finally, it eased. That too was becoming a constant occurrence today. Come to think of it that pressure had been with her since they came to Canada, but it was so light most of the time it never bothered her. Only once could she remember it getting worse than this; it was just after her eighteenth birthday it didn't last long, so she forgot about it until now.

Cecille cleared her mind then welcoming sleep slowly began creeping in. Unexpectedly, her black eyes sprang open again. She gasped and cried out sorrowfully when she felt Shin die before hearing Misfit yelping in pain; her dog must have been hurt pretty bad or was dead because she hadn't been able to come help her mistress. White Buffalo concentrated needing to block that out too. Unfortunately, it took her a long time to erase that feeling of helplessness she had felt.

Cecille groaned in frustration taking a chance she reached into her shirt before pulling out her medallion. Thankfully, the men hadn't found her necklace or medicine amulet hiding under her shirt. Even she had forgotten about them until the sheriff forced her head back so far, causing the chain to pinch her neck painfully. White Buffalo clutched the Celtic medallion in her left hand hard until indents from the dragon formed on her palms; she wiped all thoughts from her head then humming, she eventually drifted off into a restless sleep as dreams of the past started to haunt her...

*****

Cecille turning seven in the middle of a blizzard was ecstatic to receive a mare as a combined birthday and Christmas present from her father; she named her Saya. Unfortunately, a late spring made it impossible to ride much, so only now was she able to take her mare out. Having been cooped up because of the harsh winter, White Buffalo felt rejuvenated today, almost as if she could fly.

Cecille, wanting to amaze everyone on how well she could ride planned a surprise for today. The difficulty of getting away from her father throughout the winter had been a real challenge. Every time Edward went away on one of his business trips, White Buffalo would sneak into the barn; she was trying to learn to somersault off the back of her horse.

Shin was the worst of the two rarely could Cecille get away from him since he followed her everywhere. Most of the time, she had to pretend to be sick so wanted to stay in bed. Once the Tianming Monk was busy, White Buffalo would stuff her blankets with a decoy before taking the opportunity to disappear into the barn.

Saya extremely gentle, plus having been well trained was exceedingly tolerant of the child that kept standing on her while she tried to eat. The mare became quite good at ignoring her mistress's repeated attempts to land on her feet. Several times, Saya had to stop eating to nudge Cecille just to make sure the groaning child wasn't hurt too badly. She would try to help White Buffalo up from her sprawled out position on a pile of hay; thankfully the girl had the foresight to spread it on the dirt floor of the barn on both sides of the mare in case of a fall.

Cecille giggled in anticipation today was the day. She carefully stood up on her horse's back balancing there precariously. They were now travelling at full gallop across the lush emerald green grass of the back gardens at their castle in Wales. It was way faster than Edward usually allowed her to go, she could feel her father's fear for her even from this distance. Like usual she ignored it; the seven-year-old knew if she didn't she would never have any fun around here, Dream Dancer was such a worrywart. White Buffalo held out her arms before throwing back her head ecstatically, she counted to ten silently. Suddenly jumping upwards off her horse, the young girl did a somersault through the air.

Cecille ended up landed at Shin's feet in a crumpled heap, having miscalculated. She remembered having some pain, but it was her father Edward screaming at her Guardian that White Buffalo recalled the most; Dream Dancer always seemed to be angry with the Tianming Monk. "She is too young she isn't ready yet!"

*****

Cecille left that scene and more images of Edward trying to hide who she is flickered through her dreams until she was standing on the platform of that ship. White Buffalo watched herself draw in the lightning the ecstatic look on her face scared her even now. She could still distinctly remember the thrill she felt. It ended up terrifying her later that night when a dream had shown her exactly what she looked like at the moment the lightning was entering her.

Thankfully it wasn't the act itself that caused Cecille's fear; she was born to serve the Mother Earth. No, it was the feel of glee... the wanting more that guaranteed she would never try it again. Not even realizing she had done it, White Buffalo shut that ability off instinctively. She ended up doing the same with the auras after leaving the train in Montreal that long ago day.

Cecille's thirst for knowledge, plus her need for new experiences over the years served her well when she was young; she hadn't been able to get enough of either in those days. Things began to change for White Buffalo as soon as she had hit puberty at thirteen, which is when she first began to bleed. As her body started becoming more womanly, her emotions also began to change. Once they began transforming she wanted something different, a home, love, plus an existence away from the higher powers that seemed to be in control of her. It got worse after she had her womanhood ceremony at eighteen and was allowed to braid a strip in her hair now that she was the age to marry. The maidens in the village had their ceremony at the age of fifteen. It was way sooner than her, but again her father held her back insisting the legal age for a British woman was eighteen.

Cecille began watching Silver Fox through images from the Mother Earth with envy. She was her stepmother's older daughter she was also White Buffalo's only real friend. Her step-sister was two years older than her; she lived only to please her intended husband, who had been chosen for her when she was just a child because she was the chief's only grandchild.

Cecille spent many hours with Silver Fox listening to her describing her future husband; plus her plans for the two of them once they were married as well as how many children she wanted to have. White Buffalo's step-sister was ecstatic her intended husband lived only a few doors down from her mother. This way she would always have someone around to help her when needed.

Cecille over the span of many years ask Silver Fox a question curiously; the older Ojibwa girl answered the same even on the day of her wedding. White Buffalo couldn't fathom why anyone would willingly let someone dictate how their lives were to be lived or even remain in one place their entire life.

Cecille shook her head dumbfounded; she again asked the same question she wanted to know from before, but this time White Buffalo threw in something extra trying to shake Silver Fox out of her compliance. "Don't you think there is more to life than just kids or a husband, why are you letting them force you into marriage? You were born in this village if you stay you will die here as well why not go out into the world to see something exciting first? What if I was to tell you that you will die in childbirth, would it make any difference to you?"

Silver Fox would laugh in her tinkling giggle, which always annoyed Cecille even to this day. White Buffalo hadn't grasped until now how true her step-sister's words would become for her; she had always silently scoffed every time the wise older Ojibwe girl tried to warn her. "Of course not my little sister, I am quite content with the Great Spirit's plans for me. I was born to live and love right here this is where I'm meant to be it is my destiny. We are all bound for different things as the circle of life revolves you must accept yourself to become content in this life. If you don't embrace who you are or continue to fight against it, you will never be at peace in your soul. That is when an evil heart manifests itself turning us into something we aren't meant to be as evil pulls us into despair. Someday you will be faced with a hard decision on who as well as what you want to be. Always remember, it is only you who can make that crucial choice. You are not me, your Guardian, your Father, the Mother Earth, or the Great Spirit; you are unique, you must embrace your differences because they are what make you who you are! Even though all of us do influence you in some way or another, only you can make the final decision on whether to listen to us or not. You are too reliant on others, and someday you will have to stand on your own to become that which you are meant to be!"

An unknown female voice kept repeating insistently in Cecille's mind as dreams of her life flickered from one moment to the next; it was a voice White Buffalo didn't remember ever hearing before. "Who are you? Only you can accept yourself you must have faith! Believe in yourself... **WHO ARE YOU!?**"

CHAPTER EIGHTEEN

Powaw rose after he ate then donned his sleeping fur before putting his bow over top his head and across his shoulder. He was really missing his dog now having to carry everything himself was aggravating as well as exceedingly hot; he hadn't wanted to leave his sleeping fur because the black bear hide was the first kill he made on his own, bringing him into manhood. The shaman planned on taking his brothers dog but he hadn't cooperated, maybe on his way back Maska would be approachable with a bribery of food.

Powaw shrugged resignedly then picked up his pack and water bag he stepped out onto the trail. He turned west, it was still quite dark out with a faint light distinguishable in the distance; it did not take his eyes long to adjust. The shaman frowned grimly before shaking his head angrily at all the soft stump holes he kept stepping into once past the hard barren strip. They hadn't bothered filling them all the way nor did they pack them down making it dangerous for animals. At one time this forest was thick, overly lush. White-eyes were always destructive why could they not live in harmony with Mother Earth instead of always trying to bend her to their will.

Powaw didn't look forward to having to deal with a white woman but he had no choice; the shaman wondered if he should kill her after she was done healing his people. Shrugging in indecision he figured it was best to wait to decide until later, he could sell her back to her people so they could finish hanging her. He shuddered in revulsion at the thought of having a rope around his neck squeezing the life out of him; his people believed dying in such a way would trap one's spirit in the body, trust the white-eyes to come up with something that despicable

****

Shin groaned as he rolled out of his sleeping fur, he stayed on all fours not wanting to get up yet before reluctantly rising. He looked up at the sky; the Guardian grimaced at the pink in the far distance beginning to lighten up the horizon it was early yet. The Tianming Monk looked around then saw Misfit walking around looking for a place to do her business, he sighed glad to see her mobile; distractedly, he rubbed his aching left shoulder sympathetically.

Shin turned he walked over to stir up his coals before throwing in kindling with a few larger pieces on top. He pulled over his skillet so he could add water to it; afterwards, he put it over the fire to boil.

All he had left to eat for breakfast was porridge, it would have to do. Twenty minutes later, the Tianming Monk scraped out the pan giving the leftovers to Cecille's dog. Pulling out his cream, he doctored himself and Misfit once more. Thankfully, the cream had worked its usual magic he hadn't lost any more blood. Once done that, he cleaned up his camp getting everything ready to go.

Shin hooked his bow to the packhorse he wouldn't be able to use it with his injured shoulder anyway, so he kept out the rifle instead. The Tianming Monk frowned down contemplatively at his locked wooden box; he wondered if he should try his carpet again, suddenly he stiffened before turning quickly with his rifle ready when Misfit growled a warning.

Shin stared in aggravation at the Indian standing only a few yards away from him, distracted by his lost charge was no excuse for his inattention. He looking the man over carefully; he had on a long buckskin shirt that was covered by a decorative animal bone vest. Accompanying it, which made it a typical native outfit were fringed leggings with moccasins. The Indian had shoulder length black hair with a thick rawhide headband encircling his head. Different feathers with porcupine quills decorated it in a unique pattern. A bear fur was hanging over his left shoulder, with a bow going from the right hip across his chest before draping over the top of his head and left shoulder. It effectively kept the hide in place while he was in motion leaving his hands free to pull his knife or axe. A rawhide quiver was strapped around his waist on his left side instead of attached to his back. This way he could keep his water bag as well as his two other pouches against his body by the belt holding his quiver in place. The Tianming Monk had never seen the unique quill-work on the man's buckskin leggings; the bone pattern of the vest was quite different too, so he had no idea what tribe he was with.

Shin had missed the whisper of sound that preceded the Indians arrival, which annoyed him to no end his sarcastic tone clearly portrayed his irritation. The Tianming Monk switched to Ojibwa, he also used the universal sign language of the natives out here; in the hopes the Indian would be able to better understand him now that it was light enough for one to see. "You could get yourself killed sneaking up on people like that... who are you?"

Powaw frowned, he stared in surprise not having expected anyone to be out here; he looked closer at the mare then grunted in humour he jabbed a finger against his chest before pointing at Cecille's packhorse. "I am Powaw, Shaman to the Spirit Bear Clan of the Cree. I saved that horse she was caught in trees by the wood thing on her rump. You speak funny, you are different looking white-eyes too what are you called?"

Powaw noticed the blood on the strange man's shirt, he looked at the dog that gave his presence away and remembered the clearing he stayed in last night; the shaman looked around suspiciously checking for others before turning back to the small man grimly. "Lots of blood with many tracks where I camped last night, was it you? I don't see more white-eyes here!"

Shin's tone turned ironic as he let go of the trigger on his rifle; the Tianming Monk was now glad he hadn't pulled it back all the way, or he would have had to spend precious time reloading. The Guardian didn't like having bullets in the chamber of his rifle that is how accidents happened. "I am Shadow Stalker an adopted Ojibwa, I learned the language from them; they live by the three big waters, many days journey from here. I am not, a white-eyes but an Asian from a different land. I came here on a big canoe many... many moons ago. My people are like yours, they live to serve the Mother Earth and the Great Spirit."

Powaw gestured towards the town inquisitively being careful, the shaman hid his hopeful expression; he didn't want the strange man to read too much on his face, it might give away his plans. "You are going to the town called Kipawa?"

Shin nodded his head grimly the Tianming Monk jabbed a finger angrily towards the town. "Yes, I am going there to rescue my sister they took her yesterday, so I have to go get her back from them; why would a Cree Shaman be heading that way?"

Powaw kept his face expressionless inside though the shaman was crowing gleefully. Maybe this was the shadow his brother had seen, the name definitely fits; if so, he was in luck no searching would be needed. "I have vision of a woman who is a healer with no eyes. She wants help to get away. I need her to come to the village to save my people, who are dying. If I help her, she will help me in return."

Shin chuckled, but there was no humour in it. The Tianming Monk knew Cecille wouldn't like being called eyeless. "White Buffalo can't see; although, she does have eyes!"

Powaw frowned curiously, the shaman was unfamiliar with a lot of the words Shadow Stalker was using; although, there were quite a few easily translated the sign language was helping a bit too. "What is the word, gagiibiingwe?"

Shin grinned he put his gun strap over his left shoulder before bending he picked up his wooden box to secure it to the mare. The Tianming Monk wouldn't be able to use the carpet now that Powaw was with him. "Gagiibiingwe is a word that the Ojibwe have for a person who is blind; blind is a word that the white-eyes uses to describe someone who has a film over their eyes so can't see anything."

Powaw nodded in understanding the shaman gestured inquisitively. "I will help get sister back if you bring her to village to help my people?"

Shin done with the mare, whistled for Misfit; carefully he lifted Cecille's dog then draped her over the packhorses withers, the Tianming Monk turned before looking at the shaman speculatively. "Where is your tribe located?"

Powaw turned before pointing north-east; the shaman looked back at Shadow Stalker earnestly. "Up in the mountains is a secret path where my people anxiously wait for my return, she is our only hope. Even our medicine man wasn't able to help the Spirit Bear Clan we are the last of our band of Cree."

Shin nodded knowingly that was the direction Cecille was being pulled too; the Tianming Monk knew White Buffalo would want to help the shaman's people he didn't even need to ask her. "Yes, I will bring her to your people."

The two men clasped arms to seal their agreement.

Powaw watched Shin finish packing up the mare in interest, his people didn't know anything about horses they always used dogs; turning he eyed the stallion speculatively, wanting to get rid of some of his bulk. He unhooked his quiver before putting his pouches and water on the ground. The shaman took his bow from his shoulder next so he could pull off his sleeping fur. He walked over to the stud then threw his bear hide high on the horse's withers.

Powaw walked back to his quiver, reaching down he picked it up before strapping it to his back; he grabbed his two pouches next, draping them over his left shoulder. He picked up his bow it went back across his chest, which would keep the straps secure, so his water pouch and food were handy. The shaman turning around frowned when he saw his sleeping fur on the ground, the stallion was eating the grass he found not far away from it.

Shin standing beside the mare had watched the incident in amusement but made sure to keep his face expressionless, not wanting to embarrass the shaman. The Tianming Monk waited to see what would happen next; hoping, he could keep his stoic expression intact.

Powaw mumbling irritably that his bear hide must have fallen off; marched over to his fur he picked it up before walking back to the stallion, the shaman again draped it across the stud's withers. Beginning to turn away, he caught movement from the horse out of the corner of his eye. Turning back quickly, he stared in stunned disbelief when the stallion nonchalantly reached back then pulled the fur off his back dropping it. Casually, he moved further away from the offending garment lying on the ground.

Powaw rushed back over to his sleeping fur, angrily he picked it up all the while he was mumbling about stupid animals; grimly the younger twin took it back over to the stallion before throwing it on his back this time. Maybe, the horse just didn't like anything up quite that high. The shaman barely got it in place this time when the stud reached back… again he pulled it off his back.

Grey turned away with the sleeping fur in his teeth, this time he ran off with it. Squealing dramatically; the stallion playfully jumped around throwing his head back and forth shaking it like a dog. The hide was swinging from side to side he made sure to keep the fur out of the reach of the infuriated shaman who was chasing the stallion.

Powaw was screaming angrily at the stud tried to get his sleeping fur back from the teasing horse, he wasn't amused in the least.

Shin couldn't help a snort of laughter from escaping, but promptly he smothered it before Powaw could hear him. Once back in control, he whistled in command for Grey to come to him. The Tianming Monk took the bear hide away from his stallion when he obediently ran up to his master. Turning away, which thankfully gave Shadow Stalker a chance to hide his amused expression; he put the bear hide on the packhorses withers then turned an expressionless face to the upset shaman. "The stallion is not a pack animal, only the mare is. She will gladly carry your bearskin for you or anything else you wish to add to her load."

Powaw gave the stallion a wide berth; he angrily went around the horse that was staring at him balefully. He put his two packs on the mare but kept his water with him before marching ahead. The shaman refused to comment not wanting Shadow Stalker to send him away now that he was so close to finding the cure to his people's illnesses. Shin chuckled softly so Powaw wouldn't hear him; he gave Grey a passing pat of affection. The Tianming Monk had a feeling there would never be a dull moment with his new stallion around, he was full of surprises. He never met a horse who had such a love of pranks before if nothing else he would be laughing a lot from now on, he was sure. Rapidly, Shadow Stalker caught up to the angry shaman neither of them said another word on the subject as they silently hurried towards Kipawa.

****

BANG! "Neeighh... eek, pfft!"

The stableman cursed in aggravation before hurrying down the ladder from the loft where he had his sleeping quarters he didn't even have time to put on britches. It was an hour or two earlier than he usually got up, but the squealing mare the sheriff brought him last night was having a fit. He needed to calm her down in a hurry, or she would upset the rest of the horses; already, he could hear several of them moving around uneasily neighing in alarm.

The black and white mare had been fine at first. Unless you tried to take off her saddle or bridle, then her ears pinned back before she would rear or bite at you. The stableman wisely left them on her; the bridle didn't have a bit so it wouldn't hurt her to keep them on until she became more familiar with her surroundings. He still wasn't sure what he was supposed to do with her yet, it probably wouldn't be decided until after the hanging.

The stableman winced at another bang as the unruly mare kicked at the stall door. He wasn't sure what had set her off, but it wouldn't be long before she had that door busted as large as she was. He turned rapidly into the tack room and grabbed his long whip, not often did he have to use such extremes; unfortunately, sometimes he had no other choice.

Bang, bang... carrack!

The hefty stableman was breathing laboriously; he ran towards the mare's stall. He didn't run often, but at the sound of splintering wood, his steps quickened. He raced down the corridor as fast as his chubby legs could go. "Hey there, ya stop that this instant!"

Ssnaapp!

The stableman flicked the whip causing a loud cracking sound to reverberate down the long barn.

Saya instantly turned around when she heard the stableman coming; non-threatening she backed up further into the stall. The mare dropped her head before bobbing it up then down with a soft neigh of greeting calling out sorrowfully to him.

The stableman walked closer to the stall once the mare quit showing so much aggression, he looked over the door before shaking his head as he tsked irritably. "Well, looks like I will have to put ya in the bigger pen this door will need to get fixed; oh, I see you're out of water is that what's got ya so riled up?"

Saya bobbed her head before blowing softly through her nostrils, waiting patiently.

The stableman glad he hadn't needed to use the whip on the beautiful mare, propped it against the wall before opening the door. He grabbed one of the dangling reins that were tied around her neck and led her outside the smaller stall. He took her down the passageway to a larger pen at the front of the barn; these were for a stallion that is why these stalls were enclosed with more massive doors, there was one on each side of the corridor. This way the stableman didn't have to worry about a mare getting pregnant by a rogue stallion getting loose.

Saya docilely followed the man with a quiver of anticipation she waited until the stableman was unhooking the big stall door; seeing the sun peeking over one of the buildings in the distance she knew the double doors at the front of the barn were open. She reared up before lashing out sending the stout man flying. Now free she barrelled outside, running full tilt down Main Street the mare flew as fast as she could go heading back the way she had come.

The stableman ran to the doors before hollering after the horse indignantly. He would have to remember to give his son a beating for leaving the doors open again; a few minutes later he bent holding onto his side in obvious pain, he eventually gave a weak wave of anger. "Damn... well go on with ya then!"

Saya charged through the early morning streets of the town, lucky for her not many people were about yet. She knocked a cursing man over that didn't move out of the way fast enough, she veered at the last second managing not to trample him; another man tried to grab her, but she twisted and sent him sprawling. A wagon getting unloaded by the store lackeys was sitting in the middle of the street, the mare jumped over it effortlessly before making her escape.

****

Shin pointed across the road at a trail that would hopefully lead them to the clearing up ahead on the left; they would have to make a run for it leaving them visible for a bit. The Tianming Monk didn't want to stay on this side anymore the trees were too dense now, hiding in them would be difficult. The glade on the other side would be perfect to eat lunch at, the trees thinned out further down on that side too giving them more hiding choices. "We will stop for a brief rest there, but I don't want to stay for long. We need to get to town quickly so that I can scout it to find out what is going on before we can come up with a plan."

Shin quit talking instantly he caulked his head listening before waving Powaw to the right. The shaman hearing it too disappeared into the trees without argument. It took the Tianming Monk a few extra minutes to find a big enough hole in the trees to hide the horses in; finally, he managed it as a horse barrelled past them. He kept his rifle at the ready as he waited letting whoever it was get further away. Unexpectedly, Shadow Stalker twisted grabbing his stallion, but he was too late.

Grey jumped out of the trees he bugled a call to stop the mare.

Saya came to a skidding halt before turning when her daughter also exited the trees in excitement.

Shin grumbling under his breath followed the horses out; the Tianming Monk ran his hand through his hair in frustration he sighed in resignation before scowling in disapproval at his stallion. "Damn it, Grey... you are going to give me a heart attack yet. I think I need to buy you a halter with a lead rope while I'm in town."

Powaw followed Shin out before shaking his head in wonder; the shaman pointed at the mare. "Shadow Stalker, are you powerful shaman where you come from, you have many animal friends who is horse?"

Shin walked towards Saya crooning soothingly, wanting to check Cecille's mare over when he saw blood on Saya's feathering; he walked behind her, carefully he felt down her leg she quivered but didn't move away. The Tianming Monk picked up her right back foot first before checking her hoof then her hock; he didn't see anything wrong with either there were a couple of dry blood stains on it nothing serious, so he let her foot go.

Shin walked to Saya's other side; he ran his hand down her left leg giving her lots of warning that the Tianming Monk would be lifting her foot up. It wasn't wise to grab a horse's leg without the proper preparation; they have a tendency of kicking when frightened or unsure.

Immediately Shin saw the problem, a large splinter of wood was protruding just above her hoof. It wasn't bleeding now, but it would when the Guardian took the sliver of wood out. The Tianming Monk checked it carefully, but it didn't look deep nor did he see any veins nearby that would cause him to take out his medicine bag. Quickly he pulled the sliver out he held his finger on the hole for a good five seconds before taking his hand away; satisfied he let go of her leg when no blood formed.

Shin stood back up slowly he couldn't help a groan as he held onto his left shoulder when it pulsed painfully.

The Tianming Monk walked around Saya again but didn't see any more wounds or blood. He joined Powaw before answering his earlier statement. "Only the stallion is mine, the two mares and the dog belongs to my blood-sister who is a medicine woman plus a shaman of the Ojibwa; she has powerful big medicine."

Shin turned away from Powaw, looking across to the trees in the far distance he mapped out the route that was best to take to the other side. There were lots of tree stumps visible ahead now that they were getting closer to the town the Tianming Monk planned on using them for cover. He looked towards Kipawa he could see lightning in the distance. A big storm was coming from the Ontario side, which is why there were no crews out digging up the stumps. Shadow Stalker was glad because it kept them from being seen then possibly identified by whoever had shot him. Shaking off his need to wrap his bare hands around the neck of the shooter; he trotted out of the protection of the trees before making a quick dash towards the opposite side.

The horses, immediately getting in position followed Shin closely.

Powaw brought up the rear with an incredible shake of his head; he had watched the horses expectantly, waiting for them to run off in every direction since none had ropes. The shaman was flabbergasted when they stayed in a formation willingly following Shadow Stalker.

It didn't take long to reach the other side, thankfully undetected.

Powaw got the food ready while Shin fed and watered the horses. The shaman frowned once he finished, he was now able to sit down to eat. Thoughtfully, he continued to give quick fugitive glances of awe towards the horses. Well killing the woman later wasn't going to happen anytime soon, especially with that much big medicine. The Cree spiritual leader knew his tribe would be cursed forever if the younger twin tried it. They could use a medicine woman now that their healer was gone so keeping her as a slave was still a possibility; if he could get rid of Shadow Stalker, that is. The two men ate in silence both immersed in their thoughts.

*****

The five foot eight, blonde haired, brown eyed barkeeper looked up in annoyance at a man in an over-sized floppy Stetson that

Twin Destinies

effectively hid his face. He had a beautiful cougar pelt draped around him, but he refused to sell it. The stranger banged his glass insistently on top of the mahogany bar. He tilted dangerously to the left, but righted himself promptly; the man had a thick British accent making it hard to understand him especially now that he was drunk. "Anoder whisky sir!"

The barkeeper sighed irritably, he took out his cheapest watered down rotgut; he always served it to outsiders trying to make some extra cash. "You have two hours left before the tavern gets closed for an hour because of the hanging, you can come back later!"

Shin pulled out a silver dollar and put it on top of the bar; he put a dirty hand over it wanting information. The Tianming Monk weaved side to side needing the barkeeper to continue with his impression that he was drunk. "Hiccup! Well, beder bringed me anoder glass den. Who is unfortunate one dat is being hanged? No been here for a while, jus got in from me traps in Ontario an da furs were da best!"

The barkeeper brought the stranger another shot glass before pouring some whisky into both glasses; he smirked in glee, it was the most excitement they have had in years. He hoped a lot of the townsfolk would show up here afterwards for a drink or to gossip the tavern was too quiet lately. The hanging was the talk of the town right now, so no secret. "Some blind woman who killed the Sheriff's brother, there are four witnesses to the shooting. Nobody has come to her defence yet; the sheriff was some mad when the other witness was killed by his brother's friend while being apprehended. It's too bad since the woman refused to be cooperative so far. Between the two of us, its good riddance to that no good scoundrel he was a mean hombre. The only thing that kept Bill from a noose all these years was because his brother is our Sheriff."

Shin stiffened then released the coin, when the barkeeper turned away the Tianming Monk emptied one glass under the counter but drank the other one in shock. He left quickly remembering to stumble against a table on his way out. The Tianming Monk weaved out of sight of the tavern before straightening. He hurried to the store at the end of town where he left Cecille's packhorse; once supplies got bought Shadow Stalker stored them quickly leading the mare he raced out of town. Shin passed the gallows with a shudder he scowled grimly already an eager crowd was gathering; it was highly unusual to see a woman hang, especially one that was also blind. The Tianming Monk picked up his pace he only had an hour or so to come up with something.

*****

Cecille groaned pitifully; she tried again to wake herself up, but the medallion wasn't finished with her yet. Most of the night had been spent remembering her life up till now then she spent quite a while in the past; she watched individual family members make their choices, which ultimately led to her. White Buffalo could feel herself now rushing forward to the present again.

Cecille saw herself standing on the platform with a noose around her neck she didn't feel threatened by it. Instead, she felt the rope was a turning point in her life; a critical decision loomed before her when two pathways opened in front of her. White Buffalo knew that throughout one's life choices had to be made. Each one would lead you to the same outcome in the end but in a different and usually a more painful way.

Cecille frowned when a third path formed directly in front of her; it moved the other pathways over reluctantly. It was weaker so faded before solidifying again as if it wasn't supposed to be there.

Cecille scowled grimly unsure which one to choose, taking a chance she kept her left foot on the platform hoping it would ground her in this time; she prayed that it would give her an opportunity to view all three paths without having to pick one right away. Choosing the right path first, she tentatively put her foot on it since she noticed it was the shortest pathway out of the three. White Buffalo felt the noose tighten around her throat; her eyes remained dead black before nothing. She died without knowing or even caring who she was. Almost instantly she felt the Mother Earth die too, why it happened so fast she couldn't figure out. Was there another link between them she was unaware of that her death would affect Po so drastically or was it a coincidence?

Cecille jerked her foot back as she shuddered if she chose that path not only would she be doomed but also so would the Earth. White Buffalo looked at the other two pathways unsure if she wanted to know more; feeling compelled, she kept her right foot on the platform this time before putting her other foot on the path that veered sharply to her left. It was longer than the other two she also felt especially drawn to it.

Cecille heard the infectious giggle of a child first; immediately, she couldn't help smiling fondly at the sound. Next, she felt love before finally she realized she could also see here her eyes were green with no film over them. A shadowy man with a little girl holding his hand stood in the distance beckoning to her insistently.

White Buffalo could feel so much love coming from the two she almost took another step reflectively but paused when she felt Mother Earth dying beneath her feet; slowly as time moved on the Mother's wells gradually diminished until Po and every living creature on the Earth also died.

Cecille quickly stepped back up on the platform; her breathing was coming in short distressed outbursts. If White Buffalo chose the left path, her life would be a paradise with a husband as well as a child. Her sight would eventually get returned to her she would have everything she ever wanted. Her life would even be a long one so she would die of old age. The price tag would be the gradual death of every living thing when evil wins. Eventually, all life will be snuffed out.

Cecille stared down the pathway that again shimmered trying to disappear. She sighed knowingly she didn't need to go down this one. The healer knew this path was the one she would take if she accepted what she was born for. This pathway was longer than the first, but half as long as the left path. Down this road she would find love too; a baby would be born, but White Buffalo would never see the girl child who would also be born blind because she would die in childbirth. On this pathway was acceptance of her blindness as well as the magic within her. If she continued on this road all the generations to come would have to live with her decision. It would ultimately seal her family's ties to the Mother Earth, the Great Spirit, and the Asian Guardians.

Cecille frowned grimly when that strange voice again echoed through her head, still asking the same question who was she! Looking down the three paths again she paused for a moment on the trail to the left; she was so tempted, it was the life the younger girl had dreamed of after Cecille Summerset hit puberty. Unexpectedly feeling compelled, she lifted her foot to take that step. White Buffalo was jerked out of her dream by the loud slamming of the door before the distinctive sounds of booted feet clamping to her cell. She quickly tucked her medallion into her shirt.

CHAPTER NINETEEN

Cecille sat on her cot with her medallion clasped in her hands. She had gone back to sleep after the sheriff brought her breakfast, but dreams continued to plague her throughout the day; until at last, she sat up on the cot. It hadn't helped, only intensified them making them more real. She was chanting lightly, swaying as images of past, present, and future continued to taunt her. White Buffalo quit rocking when a woman appeared in front of her.

Crystin smiled at her daughter sadly then reached out beseechingly, but unfortunately, she couldn't touch her. "You have grown into such a beautiful young woman inside and out. I so wish I could be with you now to hold you as you struggle to find your way. I can feel your fear of the magic within you and how over the years you have suppressed so much of it because of that fear. You have much strength in you that I never had; you inherited that from your Father. Whatever path you choose, I know deep in my heart it will be the right one for you. Be strong my daughter have faith in yourself. I will love you unconditionally, no matter your decision."

Crystin flickered twice before her form again solidified her voice deepened a bit hardly noticeable. "I urge you to choose the left path it would be best for you, my daughter; no longer would you need to worry about magic than your sight will get returned to you, I'm only looking after your best interest, my dear..."

Cecille whimpered in disappointment at the banging of the door in the distance it pulled her reluctantly out of her trance. Quickly, White Buffalo put her medallion inside her bodice out of sight when she heard the sound of the sheriff's booted steps coming closer; he stopped in front of her cell. The key made more of a screeching sound this time around when it was turned to unlock the door. She shuddered grimly, knowing it was her overactive nerves.

Sheriff Cooper stood in front of the woman with a scowl that was a confusing mixture of anger, uncertainty, and bewilderment. He couldn't figure out why she wouldn't say anything in her own defence. He knew his brother was a scoundrel and on several occasions, he came close to being hanged. Thankfully evidence would disappear, or new evidence would conveniently appear that would save his hide at the last minute.

Sheriff Cooper shook his head sorrowfully beginning to regret this; she is such a beautiful little thing what a waste, but if she refused to say anything nothing could be done to stop this. The law was the law, without someone or something to counter the four accusing her she would have to hang; unless a clause only he knew was invoked! He shook off his unexpected remorseful feelings where that surprising thought came from he couldn't figure out. Reaching down, he pulled her up. "Come, it is time now!"

Cecille never struggled even for a moment as her disordered thoughts kept her enthralled; she was spinning around in circles unable to stop this roundabout or merry-go-round as they called it in Canada. Meekly, head bowed with her hair hanging over her face she let the sheriff lead her through the door then down to the office before going outside. White Buffalo was directed to the left of the sheriff's office, down the street towards the gallows at the end of town. As her foot lifted to go up onto the first step, a brilliant streak of lightning struck the ground not far from the platform bringing much-needed rain. Unexpectedly, she stopped dead refusing to move as an image of her father sprang into her consciousness. It seemed to her that for a moment he was standing right there in front of her directly in the brilliant flash.

*****

Shin watched the sheriff lead Cecille to the platform, but suddenly she halted refusing to budge. He stared in consternation at the whipped I am giving up posture she was portraying, it wasn't like his White Buffalo at all; not until that moment did the Tianming Monk feel the unexpected absence of their bond, now it all made sense she thought he was dead.

Shin pushed his way up to the front of the crowd closer to the execution platform; he made sure to keep his hat low, so it hid most of his features. The Tianming Monk inhaled in shock as the sheriff lifted Cecille giving Shadow Stalker a more unobstructed view of his charges face and eyes, they were empty black! Now he knew that it wasn't his death causing her reaction there was something more sinister happening here.

Shin looked around frantically who or what's responsible for this? Turning, he slowly searched not even sure what he was looking for at first. The monk went almost full circle before he spotted movement in the shadows beside the general store. All the Tianming Monk saw as the man stepped back further into the alley was a hand holding a large cross then the darkness swallowed him up; it was all that the Guardian needed to see to know. Shadow Stalker pushed his way through the crowd and pursued the dark robed Priest.

*****

Cecille felt herself being lifted into muscular arms, but her father refused to relent. "Where is my daughter, you aren't my little girl! You must fight don't let them win; I know you are stronger than this fight White Buffalo... FIGHT!"

Cecille blinked... White Buffalo's eyes lightened just a little. "Father who am I!"

Edward's hand reached out lovingly Dream Dancer couldn't physically touch her, but just the motion reassured them both. "You are what you wish to be, I have always taught you that nothing is impossible if you believe in yourself. You are, 'SHE'; the beginning, the first Mother of many generations of Mother's to come until the end of time itself! Your destiny is to help the Mother Earth, keep the evil at bay, as well as bring peace to those searching for something more. Be strong my Daughter, never let anyone or anything stop you from fulfilling your destiny. You are still my little girl, and you are now ready...! "

Cecille whimpered in denial when her father disappeared, just as she felt the sheriff set her on her feet. White Buffalo pushed the man away. She dropped to her knees on the platform before rocking herself back and forth. She pressed her two hands together in prayer as she chanted, looking towards the heavens through the rain she didn't let it stop her; the chant started softly but quickly gained in power then volume reaching to the back of the growing crowd of people. Flashes of lightning preceded by loud crackling rolling thunder accompanied the chanting, keeping the townspeople rooted to their spots in awe.

Sheriff Cooper backed away from the woman he waved the hangman back. "Let her have her moment with God the Lord knows she will need forgiveness."

Cecille ignored everything around her; White Buffalo's chanting again brought the insistent irritating tingle in her skull to the forefront. Quickly she blocked it which helped her to settle the chaotic disoriented thoughts that were spinning out of control.

Cecille clearing her mind of all else began pushing back against the ache. She felt the pressure ease in her head, which allowed all three pathways to solidify in front of her not just the right and left ones. White Buffalo now clear headed lifted her foot, without any hesitation at all she stepped onto the middle pathway. Never would she question or doubt herself again as she made her choice willingly. Instantly her power surged through her body; in relief, she felt her bond to her Guardian first before she felt the Mother Earth's pleas to come back to her.

*****

Shin whistled the prearranged signal sharply, hoping Powaw had seen him run off. The shaman thankfully appeared beside the Tianming Monk, so he pointed ahead as they raced after the man in the distance. "I need to stop that man; he is a Priest with an evil spirit inside him. I need you to go back to the execution platform then make some kind of distraction to help White Buffalo when she wants to get away. Here take the rifle, but don't kill anyone or the town will be hunting us!"

Powaw obediently took the gun before veering off. Getting an idea, he ran back to the edge of the crowd; going to the sheriff's office, he went to where the big mare was waiting. The shaman pulled off his black bear fur, which he had brought with him not trusting that nasty stallion one bit. He wrapped his hide around himself. He tucked the rifle beneath the robe, rummaging inside the saddlebag he grinned when he found a bottle of whisky.

Saya turned her head she stared balefully at the man that just joined their group before shifting; otherwise, she ignored him. The mare was patiently waiting for Cecille or Shin's call, neither would she move until one of them did so.

Powaw backed away from the mare with an incredible shake of his head; Shadow Stalker told the horse to stand she hadn't moved an inch since, even with them both gone. The shaman had been told not to touch her, but he was allowed to take off his sleeping fur, nor was he to tie her in any way. Shrugging he turned before going to the back of the crowd waiting for the right opportunity to cause some excitement.

*****

Shin picked up his pace then saw the man run towards an alley. He knew it went behind the Tavern since he had carefully examined it earlier when trying to find the quickest escape route from the town possible. The Tianming Monk changed directions promptly before barrelling through the batwing doors of the building. Thankfully, no locks were on the entrances he had checked that on his way out earlier.

Shin raced across the empty barroom to the door at the back of the room this area was called the parlour. It's only for women no men were allowed in; they drank tea here while gossiping waiting for their men who were usually drinking in the bar. The Tianming

Monk ran across the room; not paying any attention to the beautiful cream and red artfully decorated room that was laid out to provide the most comfort for their female guests.

Shin reached the door leading to the back alley. He threw it open violently, hoping the man hadn't gotten this far yet. Hearing a grunt of shock then feeling the door shudder as something hit it the Tianming Monk grinned in satisfaction. He stepped around the door before straddling the dazed man on the ground. Shadow Stalker pulled out of the top of his boot a small thin dagger it looked like an innocent letter opener. At the top was a thin golden open circle suspended inside the ring with nothing holding it in place was a pure white dove; its wings were open a bit as if about to take off.

Shin using the razor sharp dagger sliced open the man's robe to just below his ribcage; he was careful not to touch the black gem in the middle of the Priest's cross. He used one of his dragon knives to lift the necklace out of his way before putting the little dagger flat in the middle of the man's chest. Making sure the dove was facing upwards slowly the Tianming Monk brought the necklace back down positioning the jewel on the cross over the top of the dove. He tipped his dagger so the gem would drop on top of the encircled dove. Quickly, Shadow Stalker got up and stood back waiting expectantly.

The man convulsed then tried to scream, but no sound could be heard; the smell of burning flesh and a sizzling noise with some smoke caused the Priest to turn his head before retching uncontrollably. Shin waited for the sound to fade as well as the smoke to lift before walking over to make sure it was done; the gem sitting on top of the dove had turned a pure white. The Tianming Monk now satisfied reached down taking the cross of the encircled dove since it was safe to touch now. Shadow Stalker moving the necklace out of his way picked the little dagger up off the black Priest's chest.

A permanent image of the blade with the dove was now burnt deep into the man's chest it would never fade. The image would appear to be a tattoo; anyone seeing the long thin knife with a dove about to land on top of it would not know the difference either.

Shin stood up straight, chanting he closed his hand loosely so that the tip of the dagger nestled inside his closed fist. He checked making sure the point wasn't visible on the other side of his fist either, it must be completely enclosed. Turning his right hand back around his left hand went above the other and covered the rest of the blade. He lifted it up high, so it pointed towards the sky then both hands tightened around the blade. Red blood dripped down his arms; when the Tianming Monk was ready he brought the dagger back down then removed his left hand and waved it in front of the now glowing dove. At the same time Shadow Stalker turned his hand upright, there was no blood visible anywhere now.

A live pitch black dove mysteriously appeared on Shin's index finger cooing at him. The white dove suspended in the circle of the dagger was gone. The pure, unblemished black dove spread its wings before flying straight up until it disappeared from his sight. Shadow Stalker smiled up as he watched it go; once the dove was gone he looked back at the dagger. Suspended inside the circle with no glow apparent at all was the white dove.

Shin shoved the little knife back into his boot top. He looked down at the man in sympathy he couldn't help feeling sorry for him. The Priest wouldn't die but would have no memory of his past life. The once Catholic Bishop would forever search for the truth of his existence. None would ever be found, but the burnt image on the man's chest would keep him looking. The Tianming Monk sighed grimly; incidences like these would become more prevalent as the magic and the evil of Lucifer tried to get free now that the Great Spirit was preoccupied elsewhere.

Shin had been quite surprised by Cecille's interaction with God at the cave. It was the first indication the Great Spirit hadn't abandoned them even though no other prayers or miracles had occurred for some time. The Tianming Monk's had not felt Shen's spiritual presence for years now. Unless White Buffalo was wrong, maybe it was Jesus or one of the other messengers of the Lord that was used to talk to her. The Guardian shrugged it wasn't something he needed to worry about now; he knew when it was time Shen, the God of all living things would again let them feel his unconditional love which radiated out intensely from the Creator.

*****

Cecille heard a curse reverberated through her skull from far away then a thud before her Guardian's satisfaction. The unknown threat was now gone completely, and no pressure in her head could be felt. Even the one that had been present when they first come to Canada was gone. White Buffalo felt her power peek inside her; she closed her green film covered eyes to rejoice when her full power became available to her; no more was any part of it hidden or locked away now that she willingly embraced it.

Cecille reassured that she was back in control quit chanting and stood up. She opened her dark green eyes staring at the sheriff's aura. No more would she need to touch someone to see beyond them. Neither would a nimbus be able to overpower her or cause her to get sick. He wasn't evil like his brother, but had been duped by him for years. White Buffalo took a step closer before reaching up she forcefully brought the sheriff's lips down to kiss him.

Sheriff Cooper gasped in shock when the woman forced his head downward with ease. Unwillingly, his lips met hers just as a bright flash of lightning hit the ground close to the platform before a boom of thunder quickly followed. It echoed through the streets of the town. As soon as their lips touched, images of his brother's life flickered in quick succession through his mind; until the day of his death then it slowed showing him the whole truth.

Cecille released the dazed sheriff with a shocked look of her own; the sheriff was shown his brother's life while she got to see a life of sight she gave up. At the last second, Sheriff Cooper would have stopped the hanging before marrying her to save her life they would have had a child together. Shaken, White Buffalo turned away and whistled shrilly for her horse, she could feel that Saya was close.

Cecille turning at the last second dived under the hangman's arm; she came up behind him then kicked the back of his knee so he dropped into a kneeling position. As he fell forward, lightning flared hitting the post on the left side of the gallows causing it to shatter. The execution platform leaned precariously to the left as the main supporting beam broke, the sheriff dropped to his knees still dazed.

The thunder this time was deafening, several townspeople shrieked in fear before covering their ears in reaction. Cecille put her arm across the man's fat neck, jerking him back hard. "No longer will you deal out death or you will meet your own end swinging by a rope on the gallows!"

Cecille chopped her right hand down into the side of the hangman's neck before letting him go. She didn't want to kill him, it was just a warning; she hoped he would heed it. White Buffalo hearing her mare pushed the unconscious man onto the wooden boards; jumping up, she sprinted to the edge of the platform.

*****

Powaw staggered around at the edge of the crowd; every time a white eye looked at him with a frown of disapproval, he would lift his bottle pretending to drink. Once they lost interest in him then turned away he would continue walking. The shaman hoped nobody looked closer they would see the rifle sticking out of his robes. Thankfully, the dark angry skies with the rain were helping him a bit.

Powaw watched the woman in confusion when she jumped up then kissed the sheriff; he wondered if she was putting a curse on the poor man, the unexpected lightning, with the booming thunder made him confident that is what she was doing. The shaman saw the sheriff stagger back disoriented, he heard her whistle loudly for her mare before knocking down the barrel chested hangman. He stiffened in apprehension when the execution platform tilted, hoping it would stay upright.

Powaw saw the black and white mare racing towards the back of the gallows; knowing it was now time he screamed out his war whoop as loud as he could before shooting off several shots into the air. Thankfully, he saw the woman drop onto her horse everyone else dove for cover figuring an Indian attack was immediate. The shaman raced around the crowd shooting at nothing, he ran behind a building and chased after the mare.

*****

Shin turned from the man on the ground without further thought before hurrying towards the end of the alleyway; Cecille had gotten away, the thunder almost hid the sounds of a horse galloping closer. Thankfully though, he could feel her getting nearer now that their bond was re-established no longer were sounds or sight needed. The Tianming Monk would have to lead White Buffalo to his hiding place or she would never find it. He scowled in humour with a shake of his head; of course, she would, her dog was there.

Cecille feeling her Guardian ahead of her slowed then sat back letting Saya and Shin lead her to safety. Once in the camp she jumped off her mare before rushing over him; she gently cupped his face in concern. "Are you okay I am sure I felt you die?"

Shin took Cecille's hands; he put one on his right temple before putting the other on his left chest where he was shot. "It was a close one White Buffalo, here feel for yourself. Quickly, we must leave!"

Cecille nodded chanting, she released White Buffalo; she saw everything up until this point, while the medicine woman was at it, she healed her Guardian before backing away

Misfit whining butted up against her mistress, her second favourite pack member had made her stay to watch over the other two horses. She had not liked that, but the dog obeyed Shin nevertheless. Besides, she was in too much pain to keep up.

Cecille dropped to her knees; she hugged Misfit in relief glad she was okay. At a painful whimper, she healed her dog. She tensed before getting up when she felt the presence of their companion.

The healer caught a brief glimpse of him while looking through Shin's memories. It wasn't a pleasant feeling the woman was experiencing, but surprisingly she felt herself blush. White Buffalo looked at the man's aura in confusion as the Tianming Monk introduced the Cree Shaman, explaining how they met.

Powaw stared at the woman in awe she was even more beautiful than his late wife had been; the shaman clamped a lid on his wayward thoughts. "You will come to my village to save my people I have travelled many days searching for you!"

Cecille felt an attraction but at the same time, she was also revolted. There was a strange darkness in him she could not figure out. White Buffalo also saw a cord that was so thin it looked about to break; occasionally it would pulse since it was uneven and went interval without pulsating, she figured it couldn't be a heartbeat.

Cecille blinked she shut off her ability to see auras because it was too much right now; later she would try to unravel what it all meant. White Buffalo felt the Mother Earth's push towards the shaman which she didn't need already having guessed that is where they needed to go next. "Yes, I will help your people."

Shin nodded in satisfaction then turned to Cecille's young mare and the stallion. He untied his stud before putting Precious' halter back on her. The Tianming Monk had attached Grey to the packhorse when he left, knowing the stud would happily stay with the mare. The Guardian had bought a halter, a lead rope, a bitless bridle, as well as a saddle. He also added a rifle scabbard for his stallion because the monk had known they would need to make a run for it. Shadow Stalker prided himself on his speed, but even he couldn't keep up with a galloping horse.

Quickly, Shin saddled his stud while explaining things to Cecille. "Powaw can ride the packhorse, White Buffalo. I bought riding gear for Grey plus more supplies earlier in town, so let's mount up we need to get out of here; a posse should be showing up here soon!"

Shin beckoned to the shaman after he finished helping Cecille mount. The Tianming Monk took his rifle back then put the bear fur in front of the box on the mare's rump; it would give the Indian something to lean back on. "Have you ridden a horse before?"

Powaw shook his head negatively; the shaman grimaced uncomfortable with the notion of having to get on a horse. "No, we have dogs to carry loads; our trail up the mountains isn't good for horses unless you can find the path in the back, which is hidden. It too is steep, but a horse can climb it easier."

Shin nodded already having figured the shaman had never been on a horse before; the Tianming Monk cupped his hands to help Powaw up. "Just step into my two hands and get on all you have to do is hold onto the big horn in front of you. The mare is well trained; she will follow her Mother just hold on tight."

Powaw frowned in trepidation but didn't want to show fear to the woman. He carefully stood up in Shadow Stalker's hands before lifting his leg he straddled the mare uncomfortably. The younger twin held onto the saddle horn with a death grip while Shin put his feet in saddle rings that were hanging down; the shaman had this feeling that he wasn't going to like this, not one bit!

Shin walked up to his stallion then pulled his head down the Tianming Monk chanted lightly; he felt Grey relax in gratification. "You will behave, my friend, we must hurry!"

Grey bobbed his head as if agreeing.

Shin satisfied walked around Grey and vaulted into the saddle. The Tianming Monk sat still waiting, but when his horse didn't act up, he turned him before going to Cecille. "I don't want to stop until we get to the turn off that goes up into the mountains; you will ask Mother Earth for her assistance to help the horses make such a demanding ride."

Cecille nodded before beginning to chant she held her arms up for her dog while she was doing that; once Misfit was settled in front of her, and the Mother Earth had agreed White Buffalo quit chanting. "It is done, Shadow Stalker!"

Shin took the lead then Cecille was second, Powaw followed; the shaman, white as a ghost was clinging to the saddle horn for dear life; most of the time his eyes were closed while he prayed to Misimanito for deliverance from this torture.

*****

Shin halted waiting for the other two to catch up, eight hours at a dead run was more than most horses could endure. Thankfully, with Cecille giving them energy from the Mother Earth, they were foam-flecked, but their breathing while ragged wasn't dangerously stressed. The Tianming Monk turned to Cecille. "We are at the turn off; I think it would be best if we trot for fifteen minutes before walking for an hour to cool down the horses. When I feel they are no longer exhausted, we will camp."

Cecille nodded in relief, glad they didn't have to stay where all the trouble had begun. She felt Saya turn and pick up a light trot White Buffalo put her hand down feeling her mares heaving side in concern before chanting she gave the horses a healing jolt. Yesterday, she would have had to get down off her horse in order to put her hands on the Earth to do this. Now that her powers were restored she no longer needed to.

Cecille lifted her arms when Misfit whined wanted down.

Shin eventually slowed to a walk he leaned forward listening for any stress in Grey's lungs; sitting back up the Tianming Monk sighed in relief, already the stallion was breathing more comfortably. Powaw called out to Shadow Stalker, hoping they would be stopping soon the shaman's legs and backside were both numb. "There is a small creek a little further up the trail good water to fill water bags; it comes down from mountains till late summer."

Shin waved back in acknowledgement before continuing on; the Tianming Monk didn't answer he had hoped to ride a little further yet oh well, they were all in need of a break.

*****

An hour later an exhausted trio dismounted.

Cecille was a lot more concerned about the horses than her growling belly she checked each one carefully even though she hadn't eaten in two days she could wait; White Buffalo sighed in relief, only Saya being the oldest needed extra attention.

Powaw stood massaging his aching backside, the inside of his thighs felt overused like he had done too much squatting. He could hardly believe how fast and far the horses had brought them, he would have to talk to his chief about getting a few horses; the valley was large enough to keep a dozen of them. The shaman watched the two curiously as they fussed over the exhausted animals. Finally, he turned away before building a fire. He could not understand anything they were saying anyway it made him angry, wondering if they were talking about him.

Powaw periodically found his gaze wandering to the woman, he frowned grimly. She was a white-eye so how could he marry her? Would his people even accept her, his idea to keep White Buffalo as a slave wasn't possible now either not with such big medicine. The shaman knew her blood brother would never permit it; killing him would be a hard task to accomplish that he knew for sure.

Powaw watched White Buffalo turn away from the horses. She mumbled something to Shadow Stalker that he didn't understand.

Trying to be as inconspicuous as possible, he watched her fugitively when she walked down the pathway away from them. She turned to come back, but unexpectedly crossed to the other side. Again the healer walked up a ways before across to the other end of the path, turning she came back this way again. The shaman scratched his head in puzzlement; the dog was following her closely, occasionally she would push up against her mistress causing the blind woman to stop or turn around.

Shin walked to the fire pit with the skillet and one of the food saddlebags. The Tianming Monk squatted; he pulled out beans with a slab of pork fat the Guardian got in town. The store clerk assured him the pork was fresh today it would keep for a few days. He was glad the rain quit after they turned up this trail.

Shin looked over at the silent shaman he saw him taking quick peeks of bewilderment in Cecille direction. He was trying to hide his interest of course. Shadow Stalker grinned knowingly; he pointed towards his charge with the knife he was holding then went back to cutting up chunks of pork before letting them drop into the sizzling pan. "White Buffalo is memorizing the camp her dog will keep her going in the right direction. Misfit will also make sure she doesn't run into anything or go past a certain point. By morning my sister will be walking around here with no cane or dog, nobody outside this camp would even know she can't see anything."

Shin opened a can of beans he dumped it into the pan with the crispy bacon fat. He pushed the pan further into the fire to heat it faster. While that was cooking, he made coffee since he restocked their sugar the Tianming Monk couldn't stomach the hot beverage without a little sugar or honey; he set it on the fire before pulling out a can of peaches for dessert. Shadow Stalker also found canned pears, so he grabbed as many as he could. They made such a nice treat, plus they kept for a long time.

Cecille done, walked over... she sat beside Shin. White Buffalo leaned over the pot to sniff in appreciation before sitting back. The healer nudged the Tianming Monk in thanks for cooking; she didn't need to say much. "Mm, that smells heavenly I'm starving!"

When the beans were dished up, the three ate without a word; all that could be heard was the scraping of spoons on tin plates. Silently they clean up the camp, so they were ready to go after breakfast. Too exhausted to talk they dropped into sleeping furs. Promptly they fell into a dreamless sleep accompanied by the sound of frogs croaking then the crickets joined in chirping their nightly songs.

CHAPTER TWENTY

Shin walked over to the fire he squatted down beside Cecille when he saw Powaw leave camp to do his business. The Tianming Monk frowned as he watched him go before turning to White Buffalo his tone was uncertain and thoughtful. "There is something not quite right with that Indian he makes me nervous; although, he hasn't done anything to cause my suspicious feelings so far I just can't seem to help it!"

Cecille nodded agreeing with Shin; she stirred the porridge preoccupied before she sighed in aggravating frustration. She tried reading Powaw's aura this morning, but she could not figure out what was upsetting her about it. Every time she looked there was something completely different about it, why it was continually changing White Buffalo couldn't figure out, it was unlike any aura she ever saw.

A nimbus varied in people of course, but there were three basic ones. There are the good ones with dark strands here or there where something terrible happened in their lives, or they veered from their paths for some reason. Some were neutral you could say they were boring like Cecille's step-sister had been. They went through life with no surprises, unexpected deaths, or any variations in their lives.

The final one was mostly evil with some good mixed in; seldom could you find a purely evil person because nobody is born evil. At least once in their lives even as a child, they would have done something good. The patterns in the aura itself should stay the same throughout one's lifespan it is what makes the person who they are.

Cecille remembered Stanley's Aunt her nimbus was just as chaotic as Powaw's was. Her pattern had stayed the same only her colours changed inside the structure, depending on her mood. The shaman was opposite his colours didn't change, which was unusual in itself. His pattern was always shifting though, especially around the thin little thread White Buffalo noticed was getting smaller; she felt it was an indication that they were getting closer to whatever was at the other end of the cord. "I feel the same, but because his aura keeps changing regularly, I am having a hard time reading him; he also has an extra thread that is confusing me because it's so weak... really fragile."

Shin grimaced thoughtfully, a moment later he grinned in satisfaction before gesturing towards Cecille. The Tianming Monk was pretty sure he had one too it connected the two of them, but White Buffalo probably hadn't noticed it. "You have two extra strands you know; those who have mated with their soul mates have an additional thread when kids are born more threads will branch out from it."

Cecille looked towards Shin's voice in surprise White Buffalo had forgotten all about that. "You think he has a twin somewhere close?"

Shin shrugged unknowingly the Tianming Monk couldn't say for sure, they had not gotten close enough to share confidences. "Or maybe a soul mate! There is also another possibility because he is a shaman the thread could be his connection to his people. We have one that links us together I am your Guardian; a spiritual bond connects us to one another, but the thread is different thinner just barely noticeable. You have always had thousands of these little threads until yesterday, now it's even more since your power is now restored so reading you is all but impossible."

Cecille removed the pan she dished out three bowls of porridge as she pondered the possibility of Powaw having a direct lifeline to his people. It would explain why the thread was so thin and only pulsed periodically, since it was shrinking in length as they travelled further up this pathway, White Buffalo assumed they were getting closer to them. They needed to get to the village promptly before that thread disappeared completely; this was now a much more serious concern. "We will need to hurry Shin time is limited for the shaman's people if it's true!"

Shin nodded without comment, already aware of that; the Tianming Monk held out a bowl of porridge to Powaw, quickly the three ate before the camp got dismantled, within an hour they were mounting up.

Shin helped the shaman to mount first before going to Cecille to assist her up on her mare; the Tianming Monk put his hand onto White Buffalo's knee to get her attention. "Let Powaw ride beside you to keep an eye on that thread the shaman informed me his tribe was still two days away. If the thread gets close to breaking, we will have to ride straight through the night we will need the Mother Earth's help if we do."

Cecille nodded before riding up to the shaman; Shin mounted then they were off. The Tianming Monk kept them at a comfortable ground eating trot, one that wouldn't tire the horses out too much.

*****

Powaw fidgeted a few hours later then frowned in indecision the trail leading to the creek was ahead, but he wasn't ready yet they had gotten here way too soon. The shaman was struggling with the decision on whether he should stop to bury his brother or if he should take the healer to his people first; he could always come back later. At the rate these horses were going, they could be in the village before nightfall. If they stopped, it would take a while to dig a hole deep enough for his brother, so they would have to camp out another night.

Powaw shrugging mentally to himself and the shaman continued riding ahead, what did it matter his brother was dead; he wouldn't care one way or the other.

Cecille sighed grimly Powaw had told them it was two days to his village, but he never travelled by horse before. She figured they could cut that time in half at least or maybe even more. That little thinning thread had gotten smaller than had unexpectedly veered, now it was pointing behind them; once it changed directions, it began getting longer. White Buffalo was totally confused unless this trail turned somewhere up ahead. If so, they could end up circling around and possibly entering from a different place. She could feel the shaman's disquieting feelings with quite a bit of hesitation. Suddenly, it was gone as he continued riding beside her.

Cecille stopped her mare quickly than White Buffalo frowned puzzled when the Mother Earth sent her a distressed message.

"Go back... he must not die!"

Cecille chanting instantly let White Buffalo come to the surface so she could see. She spun her horse right around without taking the time to explain since the thread was about to snap at any second. White Buffalo galloped back before turning onto a small trail heading north. She raced down an overgrown path praying that she arrives in time; the healer kept low over her mare's neck hoping she wouldn't get knocked from Saya's back by overhanging branches.

Powaw was almost unseated when the packhorse he was riding unexpectedly spun around, chasing after her dame; all that kept him in the saddle was the box behind him. The shaman desperately tried to stop the horse but she refused to halt, not wanting to leave her mother.

Shin hearing horses whinnying behind him before galloping away spun his stallion around in surprise, wondering what that was all about; rapidly, the Tianming Monk flicked his reins on the horse's side he bent low racing after the retreating mares. "Ayah!"

Twin Destinies

Cecille almost out of the trees heard a dog howling in sorrow, she grimaced was she too late! As soon as White Buffalo's horse lunged into the open, she was off her horse; grabbing her beaver medicine bag, the healer raced towards the creek. She promptly came to a stop before backing up a step at a growl of anger. Quickly, she whistled at her dog. "Misfit hurry get him away from there, but don't hurt him he is only protecting his master!"

Misfit rushed ahead before springing at the male she easily knocked him into the shallows of the creek; the dog weak from lack of food stayed down, he whined pleadingly when the female straddled him refusing to let him up.

Cecille already chanting rushed to the dying man as fast as possible she dropped to her knees beside him before laying her hands over the bear claw marks; she transferred as much power into him as she could. White Buffalo wasn't even sure if she made it in time, but she didn't let that stop her as she pulled more power from the Mother Earth. Pleading to the Great Spirit to allow the healing she thankfully felt her eyes change to black.

Powaw sitting up on the mare scowled angrily, how did his brother manage to stay alive this long? He was even more confused on how the woman knew Spirit Bear was here? The shaman's face became expressionless when he heard Shadow Stalker ride up beside him, things were beginning to deteriorate at an unpleasant rate; if the medicine man went to their chief with what he did the younger twin would be stripped of his status and banished from the tribe forever.

Shin caught a quick flash of changing expressions on Powaw's face, but he didn't comment on it. He jumped off his horse before rushing over to Cecille. The Tianming Monk knelt beside the dying Indian so the shaman who was trying to get off the mare couldn't see what White Buffalo was doing. Feeling for a pulse, he looked up at his charge in regret. He was about to shake his head sadly when suddenly Shadow Stalker felt a faint flutter.

Cecille feeling the flicker too continued chanting, not relenting even for a second. Thankfully, it was not long before she felt his heartbeat become a bit stronger. White Buffalo didn't quit right away, not until it was beating properly in rhythm; afterwards, she gave him just enough energy to stop the infection. It also helped to speed up the healing process she stopped just before the wound started closing though. Pulling out the necessary items, she stitched the deeper claw marks then put her healing salve on the rest finally she was able to put a bandage.

Spirit Bear groaned he turned his head before opening his eyes for the first time since falling in the creek; the medicine man didn't feel any pain now and seeing a woman bent towards him in concern he reached up tenderly stroking her cheek. "Have you come to take me to the happy hunting grounds of Misimanito?"

Cecille chuckled as her eyes changed back to green before they filmed over; she cupped the hand over her cheek for a long moment feeling a warm tingle from the contact. White Buffalo reluctantly moved the man's hand back to his chest, she smiled in pleasure. "No I am sorry to disappoint you, but you are not dead yet!"

Shin laughed knowingly; the Tianming Monk reached out before patting Powaw's brother's shoulder in consolation. "Believe me you aren't the first one who thought White Buffalo was an angel."

Spirit Bear turned his head he looked at Shin in confusion; the medicine man turned back to stare in bemusement at the woman. "You both talk funny who are you?"

Cecille sat back; White Buffalo could feel the strong connection between the twins now that they were together. "Do you remember anything your name or how you were hurt?"

Spirit Bear sat up slowly thinking furiously, spying his younger twin brother it brought back some memories; the medicine man grimaced when the last few days came rushing back with a vengeance. "I am Spirit Bear, a medicine man of the Spirit Bear Cree we got attacked by an old silver-haired bear; all I remember is jumping in front of Powaw to save him. I also recall seeing a woman with no eyes, a healer who can help my people then nothing after that."

Cecille chuckled ironically yesterday she would have taken offence at that description of her impairment. White Buffalo couldn't help reaching up reflectively feeling her eyes. "Sorry to disappoint you, but as you can see I do have eyes; although, I am blind your brother helped save me from being hanged in Kipawa."

Powaw now standing in front of his brother shook his head in amazement; glad his twin didn't remember the incident in the tepee. Hopefully, Spirit Bear never would. "I thought the bear had killed you!"

Cecille hearing a pleading whine whistled at her dog to come so that the male could go to his master; White Buffalo turned to Shin afterwards, she didn't want to stay here too long. "Misfit let him go! Shadow Stalker since we are here we might as well eat before continuing on."

Twin Destinies

Shin nodded with an uneasy frown troubled when he saw Spirit Bear's dog curl his lip with a growl then give a wide berth to the younger twin; the Tianming Monk saw Powaw smirk nastily at the dog before he turned away to hide his expression. Shadow Stalker helped set up the camp but continued to monitor the shaman as his disquieting feelings continued to plague him.

Animals were a great judge of human character; if a dog would not go near someone, usually there was an excellent reason for it.

Cecille cooked a quick fish stew with the trout Shin caught and the provisions he got in town. While White Buffalo was busy with that the three men took down the two tepees; Spirit Bear's was strapped to Maska's drag poles before they left Powaw's would be fastened to the packhorses saddle to get dragged behind her.

Spirit Bear walked over to sit beside Cecille then frowned in confusion when Powaw rushed over; rudely, the shaman pushed his way between them. The medicine man shrugged resignedly before turning he sat beside Shadow Stalker instead. Thankfully, this put him straight across from White Buffalo in a much better position, now he would be able to watch her too. "You speak differently, some words I find hard to understand."

Cecille smiled before pointing vaguely to the south-east; White Buffalo could follow most of the twin's words because even her father's people, the Cheyenne used a similar language. "We learned language from Ojibwa, which is the universal Algonquin Indian language of Canada and in some other countries far away. Although, it does vary by quite a few letters or words depending on whether you are plains, central, or an Eastern Indian tribe."

Spirit Bear remembered the night of his coming of age as well as the tale of his family's tragic background. The medicine man wondered if the Ojibwa were his great grandmother's people. "My Father's, Mother's Mother was found several days from our village; nobody could understand her words at first I believe the two languages mixed, we adopted a lot of her words over time."

Cecille filled a bowl for each of them before passing them one. White Buffalo hadn't taken long to understand the Ojibwa since their languages were so similar to Edward's Native Indian family. "Yes, most languages evolve that way. My Father is mostly Cheyenne with some white-eyes mixed in, but I lived with the Ojibwe for many, many moons; when I speak, it's only natural for me to use Ojibwa, English, and Cheyenne words depending on which one expresses what I am trying to say better."

Spirit Bear lifted his right eyebrow in surprise, were they natives too; the medicine man shrugged in confusion. "Cheyenne, we are very isolated out here I don't think I know who they are? Our ancestors come from a faraway land that was frozen year round I don't think they had many visitors there either."

Cecille grinned she pointed towards the border of the states; White Buffalo knew he wouldn't understand what a boundary was, but it wouldn't matter. "Many moons of travelling to the south-west before you cross into another territory, is a place called Montana. That is where my Cheyenne ancestors live they are Indians too just a different kind of tribe."

Cecille lapsed into silence so she could eat, White Buffalo was confused by her mixed feelings she didn't think she would ever figure out what it meant. The healer felt an attraction to both men, which didn't surprise her since they are identical twins. What had her so uneasy about it was a surprising feeling of revulsion she kept experiencing; especially when they were standing close to each other and she was nearby. Reading Spirit Bear's aura was as confusing as his twins, but when they got closer to each other their nimbus blinded her, it was quite intense. She had to look away before suppressing that ability for the time being.

Once done eating the camp was quickly cleaned up; Spirit Bear was doubled up with Cecille even though Powaw argued vehemently then finally, they were off once more.

*****

Spirit Bear couldn't believe how much faster they could travel with a horse. It had taken him a day and a half to get to the creek by foot, but only eight hours to come back by a horse. Of course, the trail he had taken was still a few hours away. This path led to the back entrance, which is the one they needed to be on because of the horses. The medicine man leaned against Cecille he pointed north over White Buffalo's shoulder to give directions forgetting she couldn't see. "There is another path coming up soon, you will need to turn onto it; the trail going up will gradually get steeper until we enter the valley it's the easiest way for the horses, halfway up we will have to lead them."

Cecille nodded, she whistled for Shin to wait for them before nudging her horse closer; White Buffalo relayed the medicine man's message.

Spirit Bear leaned passed Cecille with another caution for the Tianming Monk; the medicine man could not see anyone yet, but he knew one would be nearby. "Shadow Stalker when we turn onto the path you must halt we have sentries that will stop us on the way up."

Shin nodded without comment before continuing on; ten minutes later, the Tianming Monk was turning up a small pathway Shadow Stalker stopped as instructed.

Spirit Bear whistled a prearranged signal before jumping off the back of Cecille's horse with a groan of pain when his legs almost buckled beneath him; rubbing the inside of his thighs, he walked around White Buffalo's horse. The pathway from here was winding it would become harder to climb later, so he decided thankfully to walk now. The medicine man turned slowly sensing the brave. He spoke to the sentry that appeared silently beside him.

Powaw got off the pack mare before joining his brother in giving reassurances to the guard who didn't want the outsiders to go in until blindfolded; the shaman laughed in disbelief he pointed towards Cecille incredulously. "The woman can't see anything, White Buffalo doesn't need a blindfold I will also personally vouch for Shadow Stalker he is not like the white-eyes."

Shin dismounted before walking around his horse when he heard the argument. Shadow Stalker had no objections to being blindfolded, it wouldn't be his first time or the last he was sure; the Tianming Monk's spent six months training in a dark root cellar under the monastery back home it was part of their mental exercises. "I don't mind having something over my eyes Spirit Bear as long as you lead my stallion."

Spirit Bear shook his head angrily. The medicine man gestured grimly, in finality. "No, it is not right you are honoured guests; White Buffalo is here to heal our people, you are not prisoners. We will go ahead you will follow us you can ride for now."

Shin nodded before going back to his horse he remounted when the twins took the lead; the Tianming Monk followed with Cecille beside him, the packhorse as always followed her mother.

*****

Dusk was just beginning when they reached the village, one of the sentries ran ahead of them to inform the chief outsiders were coming; a curious crowd gathered they weren't used to visitors here.

Spirit Bear held up his hand halting them; the medicine man turned then mumbled a caution to his guests. "Wait here, I need to speak to my Chief first."

Shin nodded as Spirit Bear and Powaw left. The Tianming Monk looked around curiously being isolated there was no signs of smallpox or any other white man diseases here. There was also no white man's clothing, tools or weapons. Most of the men were topless they wore a breechcloth that was shorter than the Ojibwa's with moccasins; their loincloth wasn't quite as short as Dream Dancer's Cheyenne ones. There were several men with long buckskin shirts with bone vests over top of the buckskin shirt which displayed their hunting skills. Shoulder length hair was the most popular, but there was quite a few with long braided hair.

The women all wore buckskin shirts with skirts of various lengths as well as styles. They were fringed or colourful quills were added to make unique patterns. Their hair was long with a single or a double braid in the married women; the younger ones wore their hair loose if they were of age to marry they sported a small single braid on the left side of their foreheads. Cecille had a similar braid, but hers was on the right side.

No horses were evident, but there were at least two dogs for every person. Misfit's hackles were raised defensively, she growled slightly in warning towards the dominant male and female when they tried to get close to her; she stayed near her mistress refusing to be drawn away.

Cecille had her cane out, not wanting to trip on anything first impressions were everything when dealing with a new tribe of Indians. White Buffalo had to show these people as much confidence in herself as she possibly could; if she showed any weakness, they would never trust her no matter what Spirit Bear said in her defence.

Cecille watched Spirit Bear's interaction with his brother Powaw when they were ahead of them leading. It gave her an excellent opportunity to view their auras from a distance it wasn't quite so blinding that way. She was more confused by what she saw now that they were staying close to each other. An image of a white bear glowing appeared between them with each having one thick strand connecting them directly to it; over a hundred pulsating strands veered away from the bear. Once they were in the village, White Buffalo could see the strands connected to individual Indians in the crowd. Periodically, one of the strands would snap then disappear as soon as it did the bear's rhythmic pulse would hesitate before its glow dimmed. Afterwards, each strand connecting the white bear to the spiritual leaders would get thinner.

Cecille frowned perturbed when she heard a wail of grief it followed soon after one of the strands disappeared; White Buffalo stepped closer to Shin as a suspicion began to gnaw at her thoughts. "Shadow Stalker how many children can you see around here?"

Shin looked at Cecille in surprise before figuring out what she was thinking; the Tianming Monk looked around grimly as he counted. "I don't see any babies at all I can see about ten or so five-year-old's, with maybe another dozen ten-year-olds. There are about thirty young adults here, but there could be more in the village."

Cecille nodded sadly when her suspicions were confirmed, these people were dying. For some reason, their deaths were directly connected to the medicine man and shaman. She had been in several different Indian villages over the years never had she felt such a powerful connection from the people of a tribe to their totem. Nor for that matter their spiritual leaders, even the chief had less influence than the two men. White Buffalo was puzzled, in all her years of being a part of the native spiritualism; never had she heard of any people dying out because of their spirit totems anger or disinterest. She would consult the Mother Earth later, maybe long ago they did, and because these people were untouched by outside influences, they relied exclusively on their totem.

Spirit Bear turned before coming back to them the medicine man pointed down a hill behind them showing Shin the trail. "Come we are putting you in the sweat lodge since it is away from the village close to the creek with lots of grass for the horses. Two boys have already been assigned to collect grass twice a day for them, so they don't have to forage far. The sick will come to you tomorrow, but I will take you to my wigwam after you have settled so you can help the ones needing care tonight; they are the worst, none of them can walk."

Cecille went around her mare before pulling off her dog's harness to put it on Misfit; once White Buffalo was ready, she turned to Spirit Bear. "Shin will go set us up I want to see the ones that need me, immediately."

Spirit Bear murmured agreement before giving additional instructions to Shadow Stalker; the medicine man turned back when he was done, he took Cecille's arm. "Come White Buffalo I will lead you."

Cecille sat on the ground beside the fire when they got inside Spirit Bear's wigwam, she put her palms on the Mother Earth; sadly, there was nothing she could do for the two that were in here they were already being called to the Great Spirit, so she wouldn't interfere. White Buffalo turned to the medicine man unhappily to give him the news. "I can make them more comfortable, but I will not be able to heal them it is their appointed time!"

Spirit Bear nodded with a sigh of resignation; he had taken too long. The medicine man had high expectations that White Buffalo would be able to stop the spread of the disease after tonight. Shaking off his thoughts, the Cree healer turned his attention to the medicine woman.

Cecille went over to the two warriors and eased their pain; when White Buffalo was finished, she walked over to Spirit Bear. She knelt before gesturing for him to sit down in front of her. "When did this sickness start try to remember as far back as you can, don't leave anything out even if it seems unimportant to you?"

Spirit Bear stared at Cecille grimly as unpleasant memories sprang instantly into the medicine man's head; he sighed sadly before telling White Buffalo the sad tale of his brother's wife. "It is indirectly my fault I think."

*****

Spirit Bear sighed in defeat staring at his persistent sister-in-law in resignation he shook his head grimly; the medicine man knew his brother wouldn't like it. "You should wait until the Warriors get back from the hunt Powaw will want to go with you, why the rush all of a sudden Little Sparrow?"

Little Sparrow waved away the medicine man's concern she also chose to ignore his apparent reluctance. "Father has agreed to come too, and several of the elders would also like to go. We are tired of being cooped up here Spirit Bear the winter will be early this year that is being predicted by many. It's time to begin harvesting before the snows come, soon I will be too big with the child to help the others; your Father will not go with me unless you do, please my brother!"

Spirit Bear stared at the determined wife of his younger brother then gave in unwillingly; he took a dozen women his father, a couple of older braves plus two elders with them.

*****

It would be a decision that Spirit Bear would regret for the rest of his life; the medicine man talked for two long hours giving Cecille every sordid detail he could remember of the death of Powaw's wife and son. Unknowingly, as the story unfolded, he was also healing himself.

Cecille patiently listened when Spirit Bear finished his tale she got up before calling for her dog; White Buffalo beckoned for the medicine man to rise. "Please take me to the sweat lodge I will need to meditate to ask the Great Spirit for help. I'm not sure if what you told me is the real reason, but hopefully, I will find the answers."

Spirit Bear sighed solemnly then took Cecille's arm before leading her from his wigwam. He took her directly to the lodge knowing she must be pretty tired after her ordeal in Kipawa. Seeing Powaw standing by the door of the sweat lodge, the medicine man smiled in greeting. He was about to ask his brother what he needed, but snapped his mouth shut angrily when the younger twin furiously brushed passed him without a word of explanation; the shaman disappeared back into his wigwam.

Cecille frowned grimly feeling Powaw's anger; she didn't need to see the shaman's aura to know, White Buffalo patted Spirit Bear's arm consolingly, feeling how upset the medicine man was becoming. "Your brother has an evil spirit inside him. Unfortunately, it will take many years with much praying for you to overcome it."

Spirit Bear sighed before he changed the subject, the medicine man didn't want to discuss it. "I know, goodnight White Buffalo; oh, the Chief's daughter will bring you breakfast in the morning."

Cecille nodded in acknowledgement before opening the door and went in. White Buffalo stopped inside, her head tilted so she could get a better whiff; sniffing in appreciation, she grinned in delight. "Mm, smells heavenly beaver tail stew if I'm not mistaken!"

Shin laughed not surprised in the least that Cecille identified the smell since it was one of her favourite meals; the Tianming Monk dished her up a generous helping. "Ten steps straight ahead; afterwards, take one step to your left White Buffalo."

Shin gave a detailed description of their new home to Cecille while she ate; it wasn't long before exhausted the two crawled into their beds to sleep.

*****

Cecille wandered the dream world the healer wasn't sure what she was looking for or why she had been pulled here as soon as her eyes closed. Was she supposed to be searching for the answers here? If so, hopefully when White Buffalo saw what was needed it would be obvious. She was a bit confused the dream world wasn't a very reliable source of information most of the time; unless, a doctor was dreaming about curing a disease that was similar.

Cecille saw a familiar glow ahead unable to resist, she headed for it then entered her father's dream. Edward was dreaming of her when she was little; she could tell that they were still in Wales just by the looks of the room he was in. His worry for her was hard to miss. She gave Dream Dancer reassurances that she was okay; White Buffalo felt a lot of relief from him before she exited his dream.

Cecille wandered again for quite a while, searching for what, still had her completely baffled. She halted suddenly as a pull to her right had her turning towards a pulsing dream that was black one moment and white the next. White Buffalo frowned troubled it was highly unusual to see colour here. Unless it was not a dream, sometimes a dreamer with the potential of reaching this place became trapped here. They either died trying to find their way or went crazy, which kept them locked in the dream world for the rest of their lives. Dreamers always had a touch of colour it is how one can get identified. The stronger the radiance, the better trained they are to come and go; which is why it was unusual to see colour because not many could reach here on their own?

Cecille turned not having time to waste knowing that dawn was only an hour or so away, she kept going. She went from one spot to another until she found another coloured dream this one was black before it went red. White Buffalo frowned grimly; she hadn't seen this much activity here for a long time, but then she stayed away from this place once her journey started. Not since her training with the Ojibwa Shaman had she spent this much time here.

Cecille stopped abruptly; turning rapidly she raced back towards the white and black pulsing dream. She hurriedly stepped inside before dropping into a kneeling position by the bed; White Buffalo took the hand extended. "My beautiful Daughter, I have so longed to see you one last time, and I thank the Great Spirit for allowing it. My time has come at last. Gitche Manitou is calling me to the happy hunting grounds. Although you were not born of my body, you have always been the Daughter of my heart. I fear there is a great deal of sadness with much pain down the path you have chosen, but I am proud of how you have grown. You will become stronger as time moves on, may the Great Spirit and the Mother Earth watch out for you child. Go to the Medicine Man he has great need of you, but you must go to him in the flesh; you can't help your sister in the world of dreams. We will meet again one day White Buffalo in the hunting grounds of Gitche Manitou."

Cecille lifted her hand to put it against the shaman's cheek. Although, she knew he couldn't feel it physically; it made them both feel better. Rising, she quickly left the dream before the shaman's spirit left his body or she would be trapped. White Buffalo promptly woke herself then stood up. "Shin, I need the carpet hurry, please!"

Shin jumped out of his furs instantly awake he rushed over to his trunk; he took the carpet to Cecille before unrolling it. Nobody would ever believe by looking that at one time this rug was full of his father's and a Baptist Pastor's blood; nor that it was over a thousand years old it looked brand new. Neither the flowers nor the symbols on it had faded over the years, not even a little. Chanting, the Tianming Monk knelt in the middle; White Buffalo crooning also dropped into a kneeling position in front of her Guardian.

Shin reached out he took Cecille's hands suddenly they were hurtling down the pathway then through the mountains before crossing the Quebec border into Ontario. The Tianming Monk didn't need to ask where they were going, he just knew; he held them at a steady gut wrenching speed until abruptly they were in the village rushing towards the medicine man's tepee.

Cecille stepped inside, the first thing she saw was her father Edward; he was with the medicine man, they were bent over Dream Dancer's wife. White Buffalo stepped closer to her former teacher before putting her hand onto Manitou Ogimaa's shoulder; silently, she asked for permission.

The medicine man feeling Cecille's spiritual form beside him, sighed in relief their message had gotten through in time; gladly, Manitou Ogimaa opened himself letting White Buffalo who was his former pupil in.

Cecille entered the medicine man before chanting she brought his hands up to feel her father's wife's aura; this also allowed White Buffalo to see what had taken place yesterday. While out walking along the trail to the creek her step-mother fell; she felt a wrenching pain along her right side. After a while she had risen then went back to her wigwam, Edward had made her tea to help ease some of the pain. Dream Dancer had examined her, but couldn't find anything wrong with her.

Edward woke up to his wife's scream of pain just after Cecille's midnight visit to his dreams; his Ojibwa wife was only a little over eight months pregnant, but already her water broke, and she was fading fast. The shaman had used the last of his strength to contact White Buffalo giving up his life to help bring in a new one.

Cecille chanting brought her power to bear she pleaded with the Great Spirit for guidance as she laid her hands on her step-mother.

White Buffalo could feel that the baby wasn't even close to being in the right position, so she needed to be turned first. Dream Dancer was trying, but her umbilical cord got tangled; it was wrapped once around her thigh before it went up her back then around her right shoulder, which kept her leg and right arm in an awkward position. It was making it impossible to move her without possibly dislocating one or both of them. She pushed her father out of her way then sat.

Cecille's chanting intensified, she drew more power from the Mother Earth; slowly the healer pushed the baby girl back up as far as she could before turning her until the babies feet were pointed down towards the birth passage. Her head was now up by her mother's rib cage. White Buffalo cautiously moved the little one around onto her stomach, being careful she continued pushing the baby girl until she was again facing upwards.

Thankfully, the umbilical cord unravelled so Cecille was able to allow the baby to rotate counterclockwise. The medicine woman helped the tiny infant turn until her head was towards the birth canal. Eventually, White Buffalo was able to help the baby girl go back down until she was in position.

Cecille could feel her step-mother dying, but there was nothing she could or would do to stop it. To save the baby, the mother had to be sacrificed; it was her designated time to join the Great Spirit anyway, White Buffalo's half-sister's time was far from now.

Cecille got up, allowing her father to kneel between his wife's legs again. The healer continued to chant helping the baby girl down the birth canal and out into Edward's waiting hands just as her step-mother drew her last breath; White Buffalo quickly bent towards her father, she whispered a hurried regretful message to Dream Dancer. "Her name is Black Rose goodbye ni-hoi I wish I could have saved them both for you."

Cecille returned with a sickening lurch before White Buffalo opened her eyes; for a second she stared in bemusement at Shin but didn't actually see him. Her eyes rolled back in her head as she fell to the carpet in the Cree sweat lodge out cold.

Shin stood up before gathering Cecille into his arms then carried her to bed; tenderly he put her down on her blankets. Afterwards, he covered her up. Standing back the Guardian sighed, so much power in such a little package she had matured so much since they began their journey here. Still White Buffalo hadn't used nearly half of the power coursing through her veins. He hoped she never did either, now that she went from reluctant participant to wanting to save the world the healer would be tempted by evil. How she would react in darker days to come would depend on her will to resist temptation. The Tianming monk had prepared her as best he could it was now up to her.

Shin would always stand by Cecille no matter what path she chose. For now, it was time for him to back away and watch from a distance. What happens in the days ahead must be White Buffalo's choosing as much as it would pain him to see her hurt. The Tianming Monk knew that he must stand fast!

Shin turned away with a sigh of resignation he gathered his carpet then put it back in the trunk. The Tianming Monk knew in the morning Cecille would regret the choice she had made tonight, so he must be there to help her through it. This would be the last bit of help he would be able to give her for a while. He went back to his sleeping pallet; sleep though was a long ways away for him.

CHAPTER TWENTY ONE

Cecille dropped down beside her fire pit with a sigh of relief now that the sweat lodge was empty once again. Tomorrow would mark a full month they had been here. A wigwam made especially for them would be ready to move into soon, maybe even today if all went well. It was a hospital not just a sleeping place with six beds plus plenty of room to add pallets for the sick or injured if need be. White Buffalo with the help of Shin designed it so it was as efficient as they could make it, with lots of shelving. There were two hanging racks suspended over a small fire pit to dry her herbs on in the far right corner. It also had a central fire pit for cooking big meals or just for extra heat. A smaller fire pit was in the backroom which was their personal space; it gave them a little privacy, especially when they dropped the white buffalo fur down to cover the entrance.

Cecille was quite exhausted both emotionally and physically. It seemed that for every two people White Buffalo helped another would then die. Unfortunately, no amount of pleading to the Great Spirit for assistance to stop the disease helped; her powers seemed useless at times, especially when Shen refused to allow the healing.

Cecille and Spirit Bear needing to spend so much time together had grown closer, and love was beginning to blossom. As it did she could feel Powaw's hurt feelings becoming a lot more powerful; regrettably, that meant the bad spirit inside him was growing stronger too. It seemed the more furious he became, the faster the disease progressed. White Buffalo couldn't even read his aura now he had found a way to hide from her becoming secretive before secluding himself in his wigwam; more than once she had felt the shaman's baleful glances towards the medicine man when she was with him.

Cecille pushed thoughts of the troubled younger twin away she dispiritedly reached over to stroke Misfit's soft fur when she whined for attention. Her thoughts turned to her Guardian Shin too was distancing himself from her the closer she got to Spirit Bear the more the barrier grew; the Tianming Monk had found solace in the arms of one of the chief's daughters, so most of the time he was with her now. White Buffalo could feel a change coming she wasn't sure she liked it.

Cecille shook off her reflective mood when she heard a giggle just outside the sweat lodge before turning. She smiled in welcome as

Red Dawn opened the wicker door for Shin who was carrying a pot of rabbit stew for her. White Buffalo highly approved of Shin's choice the tiny plump Cree woman was one of the first to be widowed by the disease; her big heart, infectious giggles, and her love of life promptly endeared her to the both of them. She was the youngest of the chief's daughters, so had been assigned to look after them when they arrived.

Shin put the pot on the hot coals in the fire pit. He looked over at the far empty bed before sitting beside Cecille he put a hand over her knee consolingly. White Buffalo's calm look didn't fool the Tianming Monk, he knew she was blaming herself for his death; he switched to English solemnly. "Running Buck didn't make it?"

Cecille shrugged forlornly, with a sigh of deep regret; White Buffalo, lifting her hands rubbed her face tiredly before dropping them back into her lap in frustration. "No, he didn't! Spirit Bear with the help of a friend took him to the Shaman to ready him for burial the Medicine Man said he would be back shortly."

Shin nodded grimly he squeezed Cecille's knee affectionately; the Tianming Monk needed to keep her spirits up. "You can't save them all White Buffalo."

Cecille scowled with an angry nod of agreement as she chopped her hand down for emphases before gesturing in exasperation. White Buffalo couldn't help this feeling of responsibility every time one died she just knew it was something she was doing or not doing. "I know that but what is the good of having healing abilities if I can't use them; my power has waned since the night I saved my half-sister's life. It feels different… I feel unsettled!"

Shin made a quick suggestion knowing the problem wasn't Cecille's powers it was her balance. The healer's emotions were so chaotic right now until she found her equilibrium it would continue to be unpredictable. The Tianming Monk reached out he took White Buffalo's hand before squeezing it in encouragement. "Maybe, it's time to bring out the carpet for another spiritual cleansing. You haven't been doing your dance lately either, nor have you had time to meditate with Mother Earth. I will start moving things into our home tonight; afterwards, we will fire up this sweat lodge and have a vision to see if the Great Spirit will reveal how to help the people."

Cecille nodded in relief; she accepted a bowl of stew from the petite but plump Red Dawn before turning back to Shin. The healer was glad he understood her feelings of frustration; White Buffalo's smile was calmer now. "Okay, I think that is an excellent idea!"

Shin smiled tenderly in thanks when he took his bowl from Red Dawn before turning to Cecille once more; the Tianming Monk needed some time alone too, he needed to do his soul searching in private without White Buffalo distracting him. "I will be going hunting with the braves tomorrow at dawn you will stay in the village while I am away?"

Cecille nodded distractedly hearing a knock White Buffalo could tell just by the way the medicine man tapped on the door that it was him. "Come in Spirit Bear!"

Spirit Bear entered with a chuckle of disbelief; once facing them, the medicine man threw his hands up dramatically in bafflement. "How does she do that, I can't figure out how White Buffalo always knows when it is me at the door?"

Shin laughed teasingly; he got up before moving to the other side of the fire to sit beside Red Dawn so Spirit Bear could have a seat beside Cecille. The Tianming Monk switched to the Assiniboin language so everyone would understand. "Better get used to it White Buffalo is never wrong. I even tried masking my smell once it doesn't help."

Cecille chuckled in delight thinking back to that long ago day before life had gotten so complicated for her; White Buffalo almost walked right past him, an unexpected shift in the wind had tattled on him. "I remember that day he rolled around in horse dung then tried sneaking up on me... I almost fell for it too!"

Spirit Bear sat down he nodded in thanks as he accepted the bowl of stew from Red Dawn before turning with a laugh to Shin; the medicine man wrinkled his nose pretending to catch a foul smell he sniffed towards the Tianming Monk playfully. "I will have to remember not to try that one."

Everyone laughed before quiet descended as everyone ate.

Cecille finished scraping out her bowl before she lifted the spoon halfway to her mouth; suddenly, she paused as a scratching sound on the door was heard. White Buffalo sighed resignedly she called out knowingly looking towards Spirit Bear grimly. "Come in!"

A brave staggered inside holding onto his stomach White Buffalo dropped her spoon into the bowl rapidly she got up to help him when duty called once more; Spirit Bear was right beside her, at least they had almost finished lunch this time.

*****

Cecille sighed in relief three hours later when she stood up. She went to her wall shelf while Spirit Bear helped his friend up. She put together her tea ingredients and gave it to him with instructions that his wife was to prepare one cup in the morning, another in the evening; she assured him that he would be brand new by the third day. White Buffalo's tea was becoming quite the legend in the Cree village. They didn't need to know it wasn't the tea responsible for them getting any better, but the healing jolt she gave them before they left.

Cecille said a hurried goodnight to Spirit Bear almost pushing the medicine man out the door in her haste to get rid of him. Shin had taken the rest of their things to the new wigwam but left the special soap he made just for her. The Tianming Monk also added everything she needed for a bath; plus, he brought out her Chinese robe which she hadn't been able to wear since leaving the Ojibwa village. White Buffalo grinned at the thought of her silky night robe in anticipation it caressed her naked skin in ways that were downright sinful she was sure.

Cecille scooped up her items, promptly she left the sweat lodge with Misfit following her dutifully then raced down to the creek. She made sure to count her steps carefully as she ran, knowing that she had one crucial turn coming up. When White Buffalo reached twenty-five, she turned left before following the path the rest of the way to the women's secluded bathing area.

Cecille stopped standing quietly White Buffalo listened carefully; there was nobody else around now that dusk was falling because it was getting too dark to see, so the women went home to cook supper for their men.

Cecille put her bundle down on a tree stump used for this purpose, rapidly she stripped before gathering her soap; White Buffalo waded into the lukewarm sun-kissed water, although now that the sun was lowering it was beginning to cool off.

Cecille counting her steps again, walked straight ahead for the count of ten. She turned left to a floating watertight basket anchored about waist deep to hold soap root, which the youngsters collected for the women to use. The root once crushed in your hand released a soapy substance used to clean oneself with. White Buffalo didn't need it though she threw her special soap inside the basket to free up her hands.

Cecille soaked for a good ten minutes. Afterwards, she swam around until she could hardly lift her arms. She flipped around to float on her back enjoying her time alone, not wanting to get out yet. When she was ready she collected her soap before scrubbing herself vigorously with it she loved the smell of the violets and roses Shin used when making it. Finished, White Buffalo threw the soap backup on the shore; she drifted on top of the water for another fifteen minutes.

Cecille finished her bath, gathering a root before wading closer to shore she whistled for Misfit to come in the water. White Buffalo crushed the soap root, so she could scrub her dog down good with it. Finally, they got out of the water; she wanted them both to smell fresh for the move to their new wigwam.

Cecille gathered her long waist length hair, she twirled it around until it was in a long rope; the tighter she twisted the more water she was able to wring out of it, when she was done she draped her hair over her shoulder. Reaching down White Buffalo picked up a soft buckskin cloth then dried off as best she could.

Cecille turned she whistled for Misfit she knew her dogs keen sense of smell would help her find the flowery soap a lot faster; if White Buffalo had to search for it on her own, she would get full of dirt making her bath useless. "Where's my soap at girl?"

Misfit ran over to Cecille before leading her mistress to the object.

Cecille gathered the soap up even with the dirt on it she wrapped it in the buckskin cloth she had dried herself with; when next she used her soap, the gritty sand embedded in it would give White Buffalo a much better scrub. Her step-mother taught her that trick sadly she looked up sending a prayer to the woman who had been like a mother to her all those years.

Cecille shook off her sadness and went back to her things she reached down to pick up a rawhide strip to tie her hair back. Pausing in suspicion she sensed something or someone watching her. Tying her hair, she tried to appear casual as she promptly donned her robe covering herself. White Buffalo allowed her senses to broaden outwards searching but since Misfit wasn't acting funny or barking, she shook off her feelings of unease before gathering everything; she hurried back unsettled.

Cecille cleared her mind of everything as she entered the sweat lodge she inhaled deeply when incense tickled her nose she knew Shin was ready for her. The Tianming Monk materialized beside White Buffalo before taking her dirty doeskin dress, he threw it in a corner; Shadow Stalker handed her a pair of silk pants with a flowing silk shirt he turned his back allowing his charge her privacy.

Cecille gave Shin her robe when she finished he threw it into the corner with her clothes. The two went to his carpet they both knelt chanting the Tianming Monk settled himself in the middle, while his charge sat cross legged in front of him. She had both hands pointed upwards with her middle finger touching her thumb; White Buffalo went on a mental journey of self-healing as she looked for much needed answers to the many questions swirling around in her head.

Shin feeling Cecille relax, got up to light the central fire pit; they were not in any rush, so he hadn't lit the wood yet. The Guardian knew that White Buffalo would require more time alone to search for her inner peace. He added lots of rocks before letting the fire burn down to make the stones get red hot. Reaching up he pulled on a rawhide cord that closed the hole above, so no smoke was allowed to escape. The Tianming Monk dumped quite a bit of water onto the hot rocks so a cloud of vapour filled the wigwam.

Shin squatted then reached over to pick up his tea pot when he heard a hiss of steam escape from it. The Tianming Monk poured tea into two Oriental cups he placed them on the matching tea tray, next Shadow Stalker picked up the waiting pipe. He lit it with the twig he had waiting. Afterwards, the ornately designed peace pipe got added to the tray.

Shin picked up a fistful of sage before holding it towards the fire to light it, he threw it into the hollowed out clay container made for this purpose; it would hold several types of dried medicinal plants. Sage was the most prevalent since it was used by women for strength, wisdom, and clarity of purpose. He also put in cedar which is suitable for purification, plus it added a lot more clarity. Of course, sweetgrass also got included because it was the fourth medicinal plant given to the people by the Creator. The monk threw several pinches of tobacco to the mix the natives believed it holds open the door between the worlds of Spirit and Earth so is sacred. It also helps smooth the inhalation of the acrid medicines.

Shin done his preparations picked up the tray he took the tea to Cecille then knelt in the middle of his carpet. He gave his charge the bowl first, the Tianming Monk watched in satisfaction when she put it down in front of her before leaning over it a bit. Using two hands she pulled the smoke towards her as if scooping it over her head and around her ears. The natives believed the rising smoke would lift your prayers directly to the Great Spirit; pulling it towards ones ears would be done to hear the spiritual truth from the Creator. When the healer pulled smoke towards her eyes then mouth it was so she would see the beauty of Mother Earth and talk truthfully. White Buffalo scooped smoke towards her heart next so she would feel the truth then grow in harmony plus balance. It would help her to become pure which would assist in her ability to show compassion, caring, and gentleness towards others.

Cecille brought more smoke towards her feet then washed them too so she would walk the true path. It helped with balance plus her harmony so she could be closer to family or loved ones but most importantly the Creator. Shin knew it would help prepare her to flee her enemies, as well. He gave White Buffalo the drink next and handed her the pipe last. The Tianming Monk had done his smudging earlier, so he only needed to drink his tea which was way more potent than the healers; afterwards, he took the pipe from her before inhaling deeply. Satisfied at his light-headed feeling, Shadow Stalker put the pipe beside him.

Shin reached for Cecille's hands; chanting powerfully he allowed himself and his charge to drift letting the vision take them where it will, with no directions from either of them. The Tianming Monk was pulled down the now familiar path out of the mountains, back across the Quebec border to Ontario. He frowned in surprise as they got close to the Ojibwa village, but suddenly they veered passing right by it. They picked up speed unexpectedly until they entered Perth, which was the closest town to the Indian village before halting on Main Street. The Guardian glanced around puzzled he heard White Buffalo's in-drawn breath of shock, followed quickly by a horrified cry of disbelief.

Shin spun around in trepidation; he saw Edward standing fifty yards away holding out his left hand towards them as blood trickled from the right one pressed to his left chest. The blood couldn't be halted though it squeezed out between his fingers slowly before running down his hand and his arm.

****

The blonde five foot three, blue-eyed, hefty barkeep watched the former earl stagger towards the bar. He had tried ignoring him for the last couple hours he instructed his girls to do so as well. In all the years he had known Edward, he never once refused to give him a drink in his establishment; although, most Indians or half-breeds were not allowed in his saloon because they became unpredictable when drunk. Dream Dancer was different... until recently that is.

Edward, after a week of unsuccessfully trying to look at his newborn daughter without raging at the unfairness of it all; gave up before leaving the village. It was now going on three weeks since Dream Dancer had stumbled into Perth grief stricken at the loss of his second wife in childbirth. He continued to try drowning his sorrows at the bottom of a whisky bottle or between the thighs of one of the dancing girls. The older red headed, green eyed dancer took pity on him allowing the former earl to stay with her; even though keeping a gentleman in their rooms for an extended period was usually prohibited.

The owner was more than happy to accommodate Edward, considering how much money he was wasting in here. Twice now, they had to remodel the tavern when the drunken Dream Dancer had started a barroom brawl over some imagined or real slight. Sometimes, it was hard to tell which one it was; lucky for him nobody wanted to press charges yet. The owner was beginning to enjoy the changing scenery in here, thanks to the half-breeds generous over-payments when he paid for the damages.

Edward leaned heavily on the bar he was beginning to sober up having had a nap at the far table; Dream Dancer banged his empty glass on the bar insistently. "Anoder one Daniel, please! Did I ever tell ya about a pastor friend of mine, who ended up marrying my Aunt? His name happened to be Daniel too…?"

Daniel sighed resignedly as he half-heartedly listened to the tale of the doomed pastor who died by a magic sword which also took the life of its wielder. The barkeep didn't believe a word of it, but it did not matter now since he could recite the story by heart; having heard it at least once if not twice every day for the past three weeks. If he ever had kids, it would make a good bedtime story he couldn't help thinking, because of his profession though children were the furthest thing from his mind.

Daniel wandered to the other side of the bar, filling glasses as he went it was beginning to pick up now that supper was finished; he went back to Edward, who was still rambling on not even realizing the barkeep had left, or maybe the former earl just didn't care.

Daniel hearing loud voices looked up at the stairs going to the rooms the barkeeper frowned grimly watching the two strangers coming downstairs; brothers they were, the youngest one had shown up two days ago he was scruffy with brown shoulder length greasy hair and bearded with a moustache. He was about five feet eleven inches, skinny as a rail awkward looking with his big feet. He sported a black eye after calling Edward a dirty half-breed.

The older black haired brother also bearded, but neatly trimmed was about six feet burly with cold, emotionless brown eyes. It only took one quick glance at those empty fathomless pits to know the stranger was a hired gun, a man killer. He had shown up early this morning then slept the whole day away according to a disappointed Jasmine who happened to be their youngest dancing girl; he hadn't even touched her once.

The younger brother was pointing Edward out to the older one as they paused on the steps to look around.

Daniel waved one of his girls over sensing trouble. "Rose you better run and fetch the Sheriff, quick now!"

Rose spun around promptly, Edward's red-headed bed partner hurriedly left in concern.

The two newcomers walked to the bar then physically pushed two of the regular patrons out of their way before the older brother slapped the counter insistently. "A whisky for brother and me; best to get one for the breed besides me it will be his last!"

Edward turned a baleful drunken eye on the black haired Frenchmen before grinning insolently seeing the younger brother cowering behind, the older one. Dream Dancer opened his mouth to answer but snapped it shut when Sheriff Cranmer came into his line of sight he had a rifle cradled in his arms; the former earl didn't want to end up in a prison cell it would sober him up and that he did not want to happen.

Sheriff Cranmer touched the brim of his hat he stepped forward to eye the brothers before looking at Edward in warning. "Evening boys, not planning on busting up the tavern again are ya; I didn't arrest the two of you last time since nobody wanted to press charges. I won't let that stop me this time if you give me a reason I will throw the lot of you in a cell!"

The older brother gulped down his whisky before turning insolently he stared at the older grey haired sheriff assessing him in one quick glance; at one time he might have been quite good, but a quiver in the old wrinkled hand gave away the fear he couldn't hide. The gunman's eyes narrowed dangerously before giving the sheriff a disdainful look, one of his eyebrows arched up in disbelief. "Who will stop me old man... you!"

Edward rapidly pushed away from the bar then grabbed the gunman's arm, but he was way too late. The echo of a gunshot exploding caused the tavern to still in stunned disbelief as their sheriff dropped to the floor dead with a bullet between his eyes. Dream Dancer grappled with the hired gun, he had the advantage of height, but the stranger was ten years his junior; neither was he slowed by alcohol.

Edward got thrown across the room, he promptly staggered to his feet before lurching badly he blundered out of the tavern. The former earl tumbled down the stairs, quickly getting up he weaved drunkenly as fast as he could towards the barn and his horse in the distance; he needed to sober up fast. Dream Dancer halted then turned with arms raised above his head at a shot of warning behind him until he was facing the sheriff's killer.

The outlaw spun his revolver completely around in his hand before catching the butt of the gun. Everyone that had piled out of the saloon to watch could tell he had a great deal of skill. All the townspeople on the streets gathered around as well waiting in anticipation. The gunman was eyeing the half-breed insolently; he holstered his revolver with one fluid motion and fanned his fingers out readying himself. "You will draw the gun, or I shoot you down now!"

Edward dropped his arms a bit before rubbing at his face vigorously giving himself a few extra minutes trying to sober up more, good thing he had a nap earlier. Dream Dancer put his arms down, he unhooked the strap holding his gun in place, slowly he fanned his fingers out; he focused his blurry gaze on the gunman ignoring the crowd that gathered to watch as the minutes ticked by his eyesight thankfully righted itself.

Edward nodded that he was ready; he carefully watched the man's eyes hoping for a flicker that would precede his hand movement; Dream Dancer almost missed it, everything seemed to happen in slow motion when they both drew their revolvers. The outlaw was a second faster as the two pistols fired one after the other.

The gunman with a bullet hole between his eyes fell backwards with a stunned look on his face. Edward grinned thankful to be still standing, sometimes when you are too fast accuracy can be sacrificed. Suddenly, Dream Dancer gasped then grabbed at his chest when another shot rang out; the younger brother screaming in rage held a smoking pistol out towards the former earl.

Edward turned in disbelief feeling a familiar ethereal presence behind him; immediately, he could sense Cecille with Shin. His smile was both loving and sad, he held out his left hand to White Buffalo before mouthing I love you both then dropped to his knees.

*****

Cecille screech of anguish pierced the fabric of time... instantly she stepped through space before rushing to Edward; dropping to her knees in front of her father White Buffalo began to chant in desperation. The healer felt a shiver of foreboding as she reached out for Dream Dancer, but she ignored it.

Edward inhaled in fear he held up his red bloody hand keeping his daughter away from him; Dream Dancer emphatically shook his head in denial. "You can't do this White Buffalo it is my designated time, if you do the evil will be released. Please remember our conversation on the ship, only the Great Spirit can stop death. You must let me go sweetheart, look behind you see who is waiting for me!"

Edward looking into the distance as his sight faded showed Cecille her mother. Crystin was waving at him to join her, gladly giving up his physical body before White Buffalo could stop him Dream Dancer toppled sideways; Edward Summerset's spirit rose high above his body, taking his wife's hand they both disappeared and he never looked back once.

Cecille felt two familiar arms wrap around her in comfort as she sobbed pitifully; thankfully, it drew her back to herself. White Buffalo screamed in denial one last time before being wrenched back into her body with a sickening lurch. The healer's sobs were heart-wrenching now, but also accepting. She rocked herself shocked beyond words at what she had almost done.

Shin with tears of grief pooling in his dark brown eyes, tenderly cradled Cecille in his arms. The Tianming Monk stroked White Buffalo's hair soothingly as they shared their sorrow together while the fire died down.

Shin knew that going hunting tomorrow wouldn't happen now because staying close to Cecille as she grieved was more important. The Tianming Monk helped his charge up; he took her to their new place making sure to drop the white buffalo hide down in front of their private quarters. Now she would have more privacy than he tucked her into bed. Shadow Stalker headed back to the lodge to gather their things, he gave the inside one final look to make sure he hadn't forgotten anything. The Guardian closed up the sweat lodge before going to their new wigwam, which was only about a hundred yards east of where the lodge was at.

Shin entering the hospital walked over to their private area he shouldered aside the white hide before putting everything away. The Tianming Monk locked his carpet in the box that was now being used as a table. Shadow Stalker stared down at the inconspicuous box with a frown of dread at what transpired tonight, what kind of repercussions would result he couldn't imagine. Shadow Stalker was glad Cecille hadn't used her power to stop her father's death; he had no idea what would have happened to White Buffalo if she had. The Guardian just knew it was best for all concerned if they never found out either.

Shin crawled into his own bed and allowed a few tears out as he grieved for his foster father. The Tianming Monk had noticed when putting the carpet away that another symbol had been added to the many others; it gave him hope that someday, they would meet again. Shadow Stalker whispered into the dark, making a solemn oath to the now deceased Edward Summerset. "I promise you Father I will always watch out for White Buffalo!"

Shin felt a sense of well-being he knew Edward was now at peace, he didn't always need his carpet to communicate with the dead. Eventually, the shock of Dream Dancer's death subsided then his grieving took on a tone of acceptance before it finished; the Tianming Monk tried to sleep, he knew that it would be a difficult night with White Buffalo across from him crying periodically, while she slept.

*****

Cecille tossed restlessly before whimpering softly in her sleep she wandered the dream world searching desperately for her father's dreams, but of course, there was none. Turning in circles White Buffalo sobbed until suddenly she felt a comforting hand cover her shoulder and a whisper in her ear from behind, which halted her. "I will always be with you my precious Daughter, know that I will love you forever; your half-sister is in good hands with her older Ojibwa sister who will love her as her own. Do not despair even though my time on Earth is finished one day we will be together again. Try to be happy for me since I have been reunited with your Mother!"

Cecille sighed in relief her sobs finally subsided before her sleep deepened; taking White Buffalo out of the dream world then into her own dreams, not surprising they were of her father.

CHAPTER TWENTY TWO

Cecille helped Red Dawn up she smiled in relief glad it wasn't the sickness coming back; this would be the first time a baby was conceived in the Cree village in over five years. Hopefully, the disease is waning. White Buffalo handed her a pouch of tea leaves before leading her to the door, giving instructions as they walked. "You drink this tea in the morning, when you get low come see me I will refill it. It isn't the same tea that I gave you for the Spirit Flu. This one will help your baby stay strong as it develops inside you it will keep your nausea down to a minimum. Plus, it helps to promote a rich supply of vitamins with lots of essential nutrients in your breast milk. I am happy for you both, have you told Shin yet?"

Red Dawn shook her head negatively as she accepted the pouch from Cecille before smiling shyly. "No, but I will now I wasn't sure at first then I got that sickness, so it slipped my mind; thank you White Buffalo for all your help I am feeling much better already."

Cecille put her hand out she stroked Red Dawn's belly in affection; she was about three months pregnant so not showing yet. White Buffalo gave her one more healing jolt, to make sure. "You will have a healthy son I will make sure of that!"

Red Dawn smiled at Cecille's earnest promise before leaving.

Cecille looked around she sighed in relief the hospital was empty for a change; the village was quiet the last couple weeks with everyone hunting or gathering preparing for winter. Shin built these people an underground storage cellar where food could be butchered and left for more extended periods of time with less chance of spoilage. They were now trying to fill it before the snow came even though it was a bit early.

Cecille went to her private room and knelt to stoke up the smaller fire pit. She put her teapot on the hot coals since their coffee had run out last month it meant she was now back to drinking tea. White Buffalo sat back letting her mind wander; she could hardly believe three months had passed since her vision of her father's death, much had changed after that night.

Shin watched Cecille like a hawk for a month before he packed up his things, it didn't take him long to move in with Red Dawn. The Tianming Monk knew the worst part of his charges grieving for Edward was finished. Although, Shadow Stalker was aware that neither of them would ever stop missing Dream Dancer.

Twin Destinies

Two days after Shin moved out of Cecille's hospital, Spirit Bear showed up at her door with his dog harnessed. Maska was pulling his master's tepee, which was loaded already with supplies. The medicine man informed her that he was leaving the village; for how long he wasn't sure yet, but at least a month. He didn't seem to know, or maybe he just did not want to tell her why he was going. The Cree healer did mumble some nonsense about needing plants for his medicines that could only be found at this time of the year up in the mountains.

Cecille with a restless Misfit both moped around the hospital; it wasn't long before White Buffalo figured out her dog was pregnant.

Cecille could hardly believe Misfit let a male cover her; for years every time a male got close to her, she would sit so they couldn't mount her. The fact that she was staying inside, plus upset implied to White Buffalo it must have been Spirit Bear's dog that impregnated her. The healer knew most female dogs would let multiple males mount them, but not her dog; she was too loyal just like her mistress.

Powaw showed up at her door a day later helping one of the Braves to the hospital for treatment; the shaman stayed to help Cecille out, since then every day he would arrive before offering to assist her while his brother was away. White Buffalo at first was highly suspicious because she still couldn't read his aura, which made her wary of his motives. As the weeks passed she couldn't help warming up to him they even became friends... until!

*****

Powaw lifted the white hide that partitioned off Cecille's private area before walking in he knelt down beside her with a weary sigh; the shaman accepted the cup of tea she handed him. "They are all sleeping now thankfully!"

Cecille nodded in relief as she handed him a bowl before sitting back; White Buffalo eventually gave the sickness affecting the village a name, she called it the Spirit Flu. "We have not lost a single person this month maybe we have this disease beat!"

Powaw smiled accepting the warmed up deer stew from Cecille that Red Dawn brought to them earlier, but they were too busy at that time to eat it. The shaman finished his food hungrily before he turned to Cecille. He couldn't help chuckling in delight when he pictured one of the young Guardians who had shown up here earlier; thankfully, he didn't have the flu. "Do you think Running Dog will take your advice?"

Cecille snickered when she thought of the poor brave that came here at least once; sometimes twice a month needing stitches or a place to sleep for the night. He had two wives who hated each other they fought constantly, but every once in a while they would gang up on him. White Buffalo suggested that since there were empty wigwams because of the flu maybe he should talk to the chief about using one for his second wife. If they had their own homes to stay in, she was sure the fighting would stop. The healer laughed in humour, finally able to relax now that her belly was full. It was nice to have something to smile about too. "I sure hope he does, it would solve a lot of his problems... some women just can't live together!"

Powaw stared at Cecille in longing she was so beautiful when she smiled. It took him lots of talking then arguing with Spirit Bear to get him to leave for a month so he had a fair chance with White Buffalo. His attitude towards her changed a lot since he found out she had native blood in her; even though it was only a quarter, it made marriage to her possible. The shaman had a week left before his brother was to return. He needed to make something happen soon or he would lose her to the medicine man, taking a chance he leaned over and kissed her longingly.

Cecille stiffened in surprise as their lips met; she didn't push him away at first, wanting to be absolutely certainty there was no feelings present before saying anything. White Buffalo felt a little thrill for a moment then nothing as an image of Spirit Bear came to mind. She broke away from Powaw with a sad shake of her head. "I'm sorry, it's nice that we had time to get to know each other and I will always be your friend, but my heart belongs to your brother!"

Powaw jerked back as if slapped; angrily he jumped up before storming out of Cecille's private quarters. The younger twin exited the hospital in a rage without saying another word to anyone. The shaman quickly ran to his wigwam then shut himself inside, refusing to leave it until the day Spirit Bear returned. He wouldn't budge even with White Buffalo's desperate pleas that she needed his help.

*****

Cecille returned to the present, but her contemplation continued. Spirit Bear arrived three days later Powaw waylaid him as soon as he stepped into the village causing a heated argument to take place. It wasn't long until the younger twin stormed off once again.

Twin Destinies

Promptly, the shaman disappeared back into his wigwam. White Buffalo had no clue what the dispute was about; although, she did have a sneaky suspicion it had something to do with the medicine man's disappearance for a month.

Cecille felt Powaw's angry disappointed stare for about two weeks, even though she never saw him. It made her so uncomfortable she refused to go out after a while, becoming a prisoner at the hospital. Spirit Bear confronted his brother, but the shaman swore to the medicine man it wasn't him. White Buffalo knew better; it was the younger twin, she was sure of it.

Cecille had been quite shocked a month later when Powaw suddenly showed up at her wigwam apologizing profusely for his rude behaviour. The shaman had been a model brother afterwards helping them here at the hospital almost every day; he tried his best to assist them now that the Spirit Flu had strengthened again. Several more warriors died, but thankfully only one woman. It kept White Buffalo and the two men busy, so the bickering was kept down to a minimum.

Cecille scowled disgruntled when her thoughts were brought back to the present by Misfit's whine of discomfort; she stroked her dog soothingly until she settled. The healer wasn't sure why her thoughts were so chaotic, spinning out of control they went over every detail since her father's death. White Buffalo wasn't sure when her edginess started or why she couldn't concentrate on her patients, it's a good thing she only had one today.

Cecille's thoughts wandered off again she frowned at first thinking of the scare Red Dawn had given them all; the scowl only lasted a few minutes before White Buffalo smiled in pleasure when she remembered the first week of Spirit Bear's return...

*****

Shin, carrying a limp Red Dawn stumbled wearily into Cecille's hospital; the Tianming Monk took her to a hospital bed then gently laid her on it before turning to White Buffalo agitated. "She collapsed a few minutes ago she has been unwell for at least four days now, but my love refused to come see you. She said you have enough to worry about without her upset stomach taking up any of your time!"

Cecille rushed over to examine Red Dawn; White Buffalo looked up at the Tianming Monk in concern. "She has the Spirit Flu I promise to do what I can for her. Can you get Spirit Bear for me please, Shin? I know he just returned, but I need his assistance again. The flu has returned with a vengeance and all my beds are full already!"

Shin followed thankfully by a concerned Spirit Bear rushed in ten minutes later. The three spent five gruelling hours treating before sending all home except for Red Dawn.

Cecille was having a bit of trouble bringing her back from the danger point; at long last after another two hours of working on her with the Tianming Monk also lending his strength, the petite Cree woman opened her eyes. Shadow Stalker gathered her close in relief before accepting the medicinal tea from White Buffalo. The Guardian lifted his mate tenderly refusing to let a protesting laughing Red Dawn walk he carried her back to their wigwam.

Cecille with her first real smile of the day closed the door after the retreating couple she turned before leaning back against it in relief. The healer not realizing it was extremely exhausted now that she stopped for a moment she was unable to move even a finger. Standing like a statue with only her eyes moving she felt paralyzed; the amount of energy White Buffalo needed to use today to be able to draw that much power from the Mother Earth left her empty emotionally and physically.

Spirit Bear rushed over then tenderly lifted Cecille into his arms before carrying her to her private room he gently laid her on her sleeping furs. The medicine man rushed back into the main hospital to the central fire pit where a large pot of beaver tail soup was cooling down; now that nobody was tending to the fire, it was almost out.

Spirit Bear dished up two heaping bowls he carefully went back to Cecille's sleeping nook. He shouldered his way around the white hide draped in front of the entrance. The medicine man put the two bowls beside the fire. Afterwards, he added wood shavings to the coals to build up enough of a blaze to heat the soup.

Spirit Bear looked over at the sleeping Cecille, he couldn't help giving a tender smile of love; he moved the soup further away from the flames before scooting over the medicine man gently lifted the covers to gather White Buffalo close to him. He would only hold her for a few minutes until the soup was finished warming up enough to eat. Not meaning to, he fell asleep with her in his arms.

*****

Cecille's nose twitched enticingly before her stomach growled softly at the smell of her favourite food; beaver tail, whether made into a soup, stew or fried the healer could smell it a mile away. She didn't want to get up to get herself some because she was still so tired. White Buffalo wasn't entirely sure what woke her up already after only a couple hours of much-needed sleep.

Cecille stiffened suddenly when she heard a soft whistle and felt a breath of air against her cheek; instantly, her eyes sprang open in shock. She inhaled deeply, which told her immediately it was Spirit Bear beside her. White Buffalo's sightless eyes were staring in stunned confusion at a sleeping medicine man. He gave a bit of a snort before he inhaled more air again another gasping breath escaped his lips.

Cecille's shock disappeared quickly before her expression turned to one of wonder. She lifted her free hand then tenderly stroked Spirit Bear's smooth baby face he didn't seem to have much facial hair; although, now she could feel some whiskers coming to the surface. The healer could feel that the medicine man had an indent in his cheek, not far from his lip. It told her that he had one dimple on the left side. Moving her fingers to the opposite side, she noticed he had two on the right side of his cheek it made White Buffalo smile tenderly.

Spirit Bear feeling someone touching him opened his eyes, he grinned sleepily at the tender expression on Cecille's face. His breathing deepened so she would feel him getting closer to her. He made sure she had lots of time to back away if she didn't want this. He leaned forward to catch her lips with his. The Cree healer kept the kiss light, undemanding at first before finally deepening the kiss when she didn't protest or move away from him.

Spirit Bear tentatively brought his free hand down stroking Cecille's back, he went down to her hips to pull her closer; now White Buffalo would be able to feel his arousal the medicine man didn't want any kind of misunderstandings between them. He wanted her desperately his fully erect manhood rubbing against her enticingly, made that abundantly clear.

Cecille groaned in pleasure before reaching up she entwined her arms around Spirit Bear's neck drawing him closer, which gave him her unvoiced permission to proceed further. She moved back when he tried to take off her doeskin dress then helped him remove it. White Buffalo also assisted him in pulling off his buckskin leggings with the breechcloth. The medicine man was already bare-chested, she could feel the hard muscles in his chest bulging. Her hand caressed the deep claw mark running down his left breast; promptly, she thanked the Great Spirit silently for allowing her to save his life.

Cecille shaking off her distracted thoughts went back to contemplating Spirit Bear's powerful physic; the only hair he had was a few single strands right around his nipples. White Buffalo running her hands back up and down his arms shuddered in pleasure at the muscular feel of the medicine man's enlarged biceps. They bulged outward when he lifted her closer. Getting a lot braver, she let her hand continue downwards to touch his manhood experimentally. Being a doctor she had no shyness at all when it came to the human body whether hers or anyone's. His manhood was hard, unlike the soft flaccid ones she usually dealt with. At the same time it was silky smooth causing her to shiver in excited awe. She would need to use both hands to cover him fully from base to tip he was quite a handful.

Spirit Bear chuckled in satisfaction at Cecille's look he gently pushed her onto her back. He lifted himself to move on top of her before parting her legs so he could settle between her thighs. The medicine man kissed her lips, he travelled down to her neck kissing then nibbling as he went; slowly he moved down to her breasts, lavishing a lot of attention on them. Stroking, he bit down gently then sucking he drew the nipple into his mouth as deep as he could unable to get enough of them. White Buffalo had beautiful lush breasts, which were well hidden by her modest buckskin dresses. When he first met her, she was wearing pants like Shin but once in the village she changed into her native attire.

Cecille squirmed in pleasure, she never realized how sensitive her nipples were until now; the more Spirit Bear teased and played with her breasts the more she squirmed as a funny pressure built between her legs. She tried to close them, but couldn't since the medicine man's lower body was there keeping her immobile. White Buffalo gave a squeak of shock when he lightly bit at her nipple. It wasn't until then that the pleasure she felt exploded before a tingling sensation travelled throughout her body causing her to groan in ecstasy.

Spirit Bear grinned in gratification he had never met a woman who had such sensitive nipples. He would have to remember that in the future, tenderly he moved back up as he positioned himself at Cecille's opening; the Cree healer just couldn't wait any longer, it had been a long time for him he was about to burst at any minute. The medicine man looked down at her before he stroked her cheek tenderly asking for permission first, he would not take her by force. "White Buffalo I need you!"

Cecille pulled Spirit Bear's head down, she smiled sweetly; wordlessly, she gave him a nod of permission. Finally the healer pulled the medicine man's head down further for a deep demanding kiss before opening her legs as wide as she could to accommodate him. White Buffalo lifted her hips invitingly with a groan of need wanting more, no she insisted on having it all.

Spirit Bear reached down, he pulled Cecille's left leg up over his buttocks to get a better penetration. He groaned in approval when she lifted her other leg of her own accord to wrap it around her left ankle, she squeezed her thighs together in demand. The medicine man couldn't wait another second, but biting his lower lip in concentration he entered her as gently as he could. It was her first time so knew White Buffalo would feel uncomfortable at first; there would be a lot of pressure before her body would adjust to his size. He wasn't small, but not overly large either he had been told in the past. Still, he knew she would need a few minutes to get used to having him inside her.

Cecille felt apprehensive as Spirit Bear's manhood stretched her opening, it wasn't painful only unpleasant. Suddenly, the medicine man gave a quick thrust. She gasped in surprise when she felt him enter her fully, at first White Buffalo felt completely invaded! Thankfully, there was no real pain. Being a doctor, she was aware that most girls wore out their hymens when doing various activities; especially riding a horse. Because she rode her mare a lot and she did splits in her exercise routine, her hymen was probably none existent. The healer also knew that not all women had the stretchy piece of tissue that most baby girls were born with. The ones that do, by four or five years old the hymen was becoming thinner or beginning to even disappear.

Cecille's feeling of invasion only lasted for a few minutes. Quickly pleasure overrode it so now there was more ecstasy in it than any real discomfort. Spirit Bear moved tentatively inside her again; now White Buffalo felt only rapture.

Spirit Bear waited patiently for Cecille to relax even though it was killing him not to move; he continued to hold on wanting her to feel as little pain as possible. Feeling her squirm a bit, he knew she was ready. Unable to hold back another second he groaned as he ground his hips against her. When White Buffalo cried out in pleasure, the medicine man couldn't hold back any longer he exploded with a yell of delight mixed with disappointment. The Cree healer wanted to give her more pleasures, but it wasn't to be.

Cecille cried out in gratifying shock before exploding deep inside; it was really intense more so than the one she felt earlier when Spirit Bear was playing with her breasts. White Buffalo seeing stars convulsed at the same time as the medicine man; she could feel him ejaculating deep inside her it caused the healer to have another small orgasm.

Spirit Bear broke their kiss he dropped his head onto Cecille's shoulder before turning it so he could kiss her neck letting her body calm itself. White Buffalo giggled before squirming in pleasure, her nerve endings being quite sensitive was causing her to be ticklish. The medicine man chuckled in satisfaction, now knowing he had done an excellent job; he leaned closer and whispered in her ear lovingly. "Will you marry me, my love?"

Cecille turned her head; she lifted her free hand stroking the medicine man's cheek affectionately. She could feel the lines in his face beginning to deepen as he frowned earnestly waiting. It told her how vulnerable he was feeling right about now. White Buffalo nodded jerkily as tears filled her eyes. "I will gladly marry you, Spirit Bear."

Spirit Bear happily cuddled against Cecille for a bit, they both even managed to sleep for another hour; neither of them was used to having anyone in bed with them though. Eventually he roused her, now more hungry than tired he re-heated their cold soup before their discussion turned to Powaw. The medicine man promised White Buffalo his brother would be okay with them getting married. Wanting to get off the depressing discussion of his twin brother he tackled his wife-to-be. Getting frisky again he proceeded to make passionate love to her once more, but this time it was a lot slower with even more intensity.

Cecille settled back against Spirit Bear staring up at the ceiling in contentment while he snored gently beside her; sleep was far away for her as thoughts of Powaw kept intruding on her blissful moment. White Buffalo couldn't get the thought out of her head of the last baleful look she felt from the shaman before he stormed out of her wigwam. The younger twin would cause her more than one wrestles night in the days to come she was sure...

*****

Cecille frowned grimly when she again brought herself back to the present. Still, she couldn't keep her mind focused on anything.

Unfortunately, her thoughts inadvertently returned to Powaw. She couldn't fault the shaman for his reaction to her rejection; she had tried to be as gentle as possible. The healer knew being spurned is hard to take no matter who you are; she was glad he got over it quickly, but once in a while, she would feel the shaman staring at her intently. White Buffalo couldn't interpret the feeling she got from his look and when he noticed her looking towards him in return; he would shut off his thoughts then relax before turning away.

Powaw surprised them all yesterday with a suggestion that Spirit Bear, Shin, and of course himself should go with the hunting party in the morning. It would give the Tianming Monk a chance to hunt for his adoption combined wedding ceremony; he was to marry Red Dawn once he proved his worthiness. A hunt was necessary to show he would be able to contribute to the welfare of the people. The most crucial aspect of this hunt was to prove to the other Cree warriors that Shadow Stalker wouldn't be a burden to them.

Spirit Bear decided he should hunt for their wedding feast next week too, this way nothing from the winter storage would need to be used; the medicine man always went on the hunts anyway even though he didn't really need to, it never failed that someone would end up hurt or dead.

Powaw would go too in order to help give all the hunters a much-needed spiritual boost. It was believed a shaman could draw animals to the hunters giving the people enough meat to survive the winter. The religious leaders didn't need to hunt themselves since the village provided for their needs; although, having the shaman there always helped them to become more focused.

Cecille having saved many lives would be adopted without the need to help gather food. White Buffalo already showed her value; once adopted she would be considered a religious leader, after that everything she needed would be provided by the people.

Cecille was glad she hadn't needed to go even though she was more than capable of providing meat or forging with the women. Misfit was getting close to her time now, so she didn't want to miss that. The healer sighed then laid down for a much-needed nap, she was not feeling all that great either. To tell the truth, she hadn't been well for at least a week or so. White Buffalo sure hoped she wasn't coming down with the Spirit Flu; she had no worries that she would die from it but it would make her extremely sick, unable to help others while her body recovered.

Within minutes, Cecille was sound asleep, exhausted beyond what an average person was expected to endure.

*****

Shin cautiously took another step the three of them had broken away from the main hunting party earlier. He stayed with the two brothers for the first hour. Eventually, the Tianming Monk left the bickering twins not able to handle their constant fighting.

Shin was tracking a buck that he caught enticing views of from a distance, what he could see in those brief glimpses was a five-pointer. It didn't have a big rack plus it still had some separation between its shoulder and neck. It had quite a bit of muscling to his chest with lots on his rump too; these signs told the Guardian it was probably a three or at the most a four-year-old and hopefully he hadn't mated yet. It was the perfect age because it would have enough muscling for lots of meat, but thankfully it shouldn't be so much the meat would be tough.

Shin preferred doe meat; unfortunately he hadn't seen any females at all. If he wanted to get married at the same time as Cecille the Tianming Monk had to make his kill today. Afterwards, he would be adopted then married to his Red Dawn.

Shin hearing a rustle to his left lifted his black bow then turned smoothly, sighting on the buck that was watching him curiously. Calmly with no jerking movements he effortlessly released the string; he tracked the black arrow knowingly in satisfaction. He watched it bury itself in-between the fifth and sixth rib it was a perfect lung shot. The Tianming Monk sighed in smug gratification when the buck only took a couple lunging hops before dropping to the ground dead. Thankfully it didn't get out of the clearing into the trees, which would make it tough to track.

Shin ran forward with a whoop of triumph; the Tianming Monk pulled out his hunting knife then kneeling he cut the buck's throat letting him bleed out. Chanting loudly, he sent up a prayer of thanks to the Great Spirit for providing food for the people to eat. Knowing he would need to find the twins to help him the Guardian uncoiled the rawhide braided rope from around his shoulder. He threw one end up into the branches of the nearest tree to hoist the deer upwards to keep it away from scavengers while he was gone. He bent to tie the other end of the rope to the base of the tree. The unsuspecting Shadow Stalker was just standing back up when something hit him hard in the back of the head. Instantly he dropped to the ground... out cold!

CHAPTER TWENTY THREE

Cecille sat straight up on her bed... White Buffalo screamed out in disbelief. "Shhiin!"

Cecille immediately jumped out of her bed; in her haste, she almost stepped on Misfit. White Buffalo bent before gently stroking her dog in apology. "You stay here girl you are in no condition to go anywhere!"

Misfit whined plaintively, but obediently she dropped back down. Cecille's dog was so close to giving birth she wouldn't be able to leave the wigwam; already a puppy was making its way down the birth canal, she gave a grunt as a contraction rippled her belly.

Cecille disappointed she wouldn't get to be with Misfit when she had her first litter of pups made a mental note to stop at Red Dawn's; maybe she would be able to stay with her dog. Chanting so she could see, she ran to the corner where the healer kept all the gear for her horses. She grabbed her mares saddle, which had the bridle hanging off the horn then rushed out. She went to the back of their wigwam where a small lean too had been put up to give the horses a place to go. Quickly, White Buffalo saddled her mare before jumping onto her back.

Cecille quit chanting before stopping her mare as soon as she saw Shin's mate thankfully walking towards her; White Buffalo's eyes instantly changed back to green within minutes she went blind again.

*****

Spirit Bear cautiously walked ahead, bow at the ready. He was so glad Powaw left him fifteen minutes after Shadow Stalker did; he didn't blame White Buffalo's blood brother for going one bit, his own brother had become unreasonable lately. Nothing the medicine man did seem to be enough, not one of the sacrifices he made for the shaman recently appeared to matter to him at all.

Spirit Bear felt a twinge in his left breast; remembering how he pushed Powaw away before taking the old silver grey bear's swipe that almost killed him, but would have killed the shaman for sure. Saving his twin's hide didn't seem to make any difference to his brother at all.

Spirit Bear paused he knelt staring grimly at a bear print it was quite a large paw track too. On closer inspection, seeing the deeper claw marks with the toes touching pointed to a grizzly. The medicine man rose before turning away he went in the opposite direction; he was not here to tangle with another bear especially a grizzly, one bear in a lifetime was one too many.

Spirit Bear's thoughts went back to his younger brother; his latest, most excruciating sacrifice hadn't helped ease the rift between them either. Powaw had shown up at his wigwam the night Cecille had her vision of her father's death. He pleaded with his brother to allow him a month with the doctor since the shaman couldn't get close to her when his twin was there. The medicine man refused outright he loved her too much to give her up.

Spirit Bear had a dream that night of Powaw getting married to White Buffalo. The shaman had such a look of love and contentment on his face, which hadn't even been present with his first wife; it made the older twin stare in shock. The medicine man watched as he stepped into the background before his love married another. His heart slowly died, but he knew his younger brother's happiness made it all worthwhile.

Spirit Bear approached Powaw the next day; he agreed to leave only on the condition that if White Buffalo chose him, his younger brother would abide by that decision. Afterwards, whatever debt his twin figured he owed him for not being able to save his first wife and son would be paid in full. The shaman agreed readily enough, so the older brother left. The medicine man went back to the creek where the old grizzly ambushed his younger brother, to restock his dwindling medicines.

Spirit Bear lonesome for his people finally packed up then made the trip back, he still felt good about his decision to allow Powaw time to court Cecille. Even though it would kill him inside to watch the two of them together, he still felt he made the right choice. The medicine man arriving a couple days earlier than he planned ended up having an angry bitter shaman waylay him. He made sure to keep his face expressionless; although inside he was crowing in glee when he found out White Buffalo chose him over his twin brother.

Spirit Bear moved into the hospital just over a week later, and now they were to be married next week. The medicine man could hardly believe his good luck; his brother had settled down eventually before helping them at the hospital, but occasionally the old Powaw would rear his ugly head. The shaman couldn't seem to help argue with him over the stupidest things like today!

Spirit Bear shook off his wayward thoughts then studied the ground carefully so far he had no luck at all finding any suitable animal tracks. The healer was about to turn to go another way when he spotted the tracks of a wild pig further to his right. He hurried forward before kneeling to examine them more closely, what luck to find one here. Partway back to his feet the medicine man froze fearfully when he heard a distinctive grunt followed by a growl that he knew all too well; promptly, he spun around.

*****

Cecille waited till Red Dawn had agreed then left for the hospital before she reached down, she put her palm flat on her mare's neck. Chanting the healer connected with her horse, so she was able to see through Saya's eyes. She had tried this union once or twice as a child, but since Shin was always with her, it became unnecessary. Unfortunately, White Buffalo had forgotten all about it until now because it was one of the abilities inadvertently blocked with her gift to see auras. Wow, how she had missed being able to look through her mare's eyes it was a thrill that was indescribable.

Cecille wouldn't be able to do this with just any creature it didn't quite work that way. It was only possible if there was a deep connection with the animal like White Buffalo had with her horse or Misfit.

Cecille raced out of the village and down the trail leading out of the mountain with Grey following too. He wouldn't leave the mare unless given a command to stay. White Buffalo didn't send him back they might need the stallion even though he wasn't saddled. Saya's daughter was with the hunters, so she could be used to carry meat back. At the bottom of the hill, the healer turned left going east; Spirit Bear had given her a vague description of where they would be hunting just in case she needed to send someone for him.

Cecille was a bit confused by her vision; she hadn't felt Spirit Bear or any of the other hunters anywhere around Shin. All she had seen was the Tianming Monk leaning over a dead deer. White Buffalo watched him slit its throat before pain exploded in her head just after he hoisted the deer up into a tree; now she couldn't feel her Guardian at all.

Cecille feeling compelled halted her mare before dismounting; she walked off the trail towards a small meadow that preceded a thick forest of trees. The animals would be okay here there was lots of feed for them to forage. White Buffalo turned to the horses when they followed her; she held up her hand to keep them from advancing further. To be on the safe side, she gave them both a verbal command and a visual one. "Stand!"

Cecille severed her connection to her mare before kneeling she put her hands flat on Mother Earth asking Po for directions to Shin; she didn't need to touch the ground anymore, but old habits were hard to break sometimes. Surprisingly, she didn't receive any communication at all from the Mother Earth; White Buffalo stood up grimly.

*****

Spirit Bear unable to get his bow up in time looked up in trepidation at the towering black bear in front of him. He screamed in stunned shock when he felt a burning pain across his left chest, crisscrossing the old scar that only just finished healing. The medicine man's first thought was why he let Powaw rush him this morning, which unfortunately caused him to leave his bone vest behind. He fell backward in an agonizing stupor, as he was dropping the bear rippled unexpectedly; the Cree healer saw flesh, but only for a moment before his head hit the ground with a resounding thwack, and he knew no more.

*****

Cecille suddenly doubled over grasping her left breast in agonizing pain it was so intense she almost screamed out. The healer catching her breath fearfully she stood up straight; she went back to her mare before pulling her cane out of its sheath. That pain was not from Shin she knew neither was it far away. White Buffalo carefully followed the Mother Earth's directions glad that Po had answered her this time she went deeper into the trees.

Cecille froze when she heard a rustling to her left; she could smell old blood first then the stench of the grizzly. Chanting she sent out her thoughts through the Earth, thankfully the bear turned away when she asked it too. White Buffalo had a special affinity with Po's animals, but a grizzly was unpredictable at the best of times.

Cecille cautiously walked ahead again allowing all her senses to broaden. The huge bear gave White Buffalo a picture of another male bear in the vicinity, which it was hunting because this was his territory; no grizzly would allow a lowly black bear access to his hunting grounds.

Cecille exiting the trees gave a low cry of fear when she was shown Spirit Bear on the ground through images sent to her by the Mother Earth. Chanting so she could see White Buffalo felt her eyes turn black; she ran ahead and dropped to her knees beside him. She put her cane on the ground before reaching out to lay her hands over the bear claw marks on his chest. The healer looked around in confusion when she received an unexpected vision of a bears head with a skin lying on the ground hidden by tree branches not far away. It was meant as a warning sent by the Earth.

Cecille frowned uncomprehending at first, what exactly was Po trying to tell her? White Buffalo looked down grimly it wasn't until that moment she noticed the claw marks on the medicine man's chest were different too. They were at an odd angle, not deep so more like scratches; although, they were swollen grotesquely already.

Cecille grunted in shock when unexpectedly she was hit in the back of the head, it was hard enough to immobilize her but not knock her entirely out. Stunned, she dropped on top of Spirit Bear. Unfortunately, two arms wrapped around her pulling her backward away from the medicine man now she wouldn't be able to heal him. White Buffalo was thrown to the ground before a body dropped on top of her, a surprising vision from the Mother Earth crystallized in her blurry mind. She was shown the leering face of Powaw; he was drenched in blood from the black bears carcass.

Powaw grinned down evilly he brought up a long sharpened eye tooth from the old silver grey bear the twins had killed together at the creek. He put the bears tooth in Cecille hand for a moment so White Buffalo could feel it. He chuckled in pleasure before lifting it away in preparation. "Well, I must say it is really sweet of you to come join us so unexpectedly; it saves me a trip to the village to go get the healer for her to come help Spirit Bear who was attacked by a black bear. I have carried this sharpened tooth with me all this time. At first I had planned on using it on the medicine man, but then I got a better idea when you rejected me."

Powaw took the tooth away then brought it down as hard as he could manage towards Cecille's left side; with all his considerable strength he jabbed the sharpened eyetooth down into her as far as he could go. All the while the shaman watched White Buffalo's face in grim satisfaction. He could hardly believe his good luck in her finding them here, soon it would be over. Thankfully, he would be rid of Spirit Bear forever.

Cecille screamed in painful denial when she suddenly realized that the reason she hadn't felt good lately was because she's pregnant. The healer could feel the tooth as it entered her abdominal cavity going down at a sharp angle, lucky for her it missed her large intestine. It did slice open White Buffalo's left suspensory ligament attached to her uterus, but it didn't completely sever it. It nicked her fallopian tube next before the point embedded itself between her ovarian ligament and the ovary. Sooner or later, it was bound to work its way further down until it completely cut through that small ligament. Thankfully it kept the sharpened tooth from getting to her uterus or her bladder. For how long would depend on many factors like how large the baby would get or maybe it was meant to be the instrument of her death; she passed out involuntarily when her body took over to heal itself.

*****

Shin struggled against the ropes holding him desperately, he hadn't seen what hit him, but he had a good idea who it was; the Tianming Monk was a bit confused about why Powaw hadn't killed him outright why go through the trouble of tying him up.

Shin eventually managed to wiggle his hands closer to his right side where a star was hidden; if he could just get to it, he could cut the ropes. The Tianming Monk had to twist his wrist at an awkward angle to reach it, straining as far back as he could he felt the bones rub. Shadow Stalker bit his lower lip not wanting to cry out not sure if the shaman was still close by or not.

Shin crowed softly in triumph he grasped the star just before he had to break his wrist. Of course, he would have done so if given no other choice. Elated the Tianming Monk pulled it free, while he was busy painstakingly cutting the rope he couldn't help but stare up at the towering trees above him. Shadow Stalker sighed in aggravation; how many times was this going to happen to him before the nightmare that the Guardian had on the ship coming to Canada was done with him.

At least Cecille wasn't here and safe in the Indian village so this couldn't be the nightmare of him losing White Buffalo. Besides, he was sure that dream was a warning for when he had been shot.

Shin was halfway through the rope when abruptly he stiffened in shocked denial. All of a sudden, he could feel Cecille getting closer. The Tianming Monk went back to frantically sawing at the ropes, desperately trying to get free as he mumbled grimly. "Damn it, why couldn't she stay where she was at; just once, I wish White Buffalo would do as she is told!"

Shin thankfully broke free he immediately jumped to his feet. Abruptly, he dropped to his knees before falling back to the ground on his back in excruciating pain; Shadow Stalker stared up grimly at the towering trees above him then knew he had been wrong all this time... it was today! The Tianming Monk called out feebly in desperation. He could hardly breathe as he held onto his left side. "White Buffalo!"

Shin stunned laid there for an agonizing minute before he was eventually able to block Cecille's painful, desperate thoughts of her unborn baby. The Tianming Monk had suspected for about a week now since he had felt two heartbeats lately instead of just one. Quickly, he managed to jump back to his feet and raced through the trees. Shadow Stalker pulled out his two daggers in preparation, he was unsure what kind of situation the Guardian was running into; it didn't matter, they would be his best defence because of the thick woods. If need be he could always switch to his sword if the trees thinned out ahead, his only hope right now was to reach White Buffalo in time!

*****

Powaw jumped up in triumph he couldn't help laughing insanely in satisfaction. His plan was progressing almost exactly as he intended. The shaman looked from Spirit Bear to White Buffalo before his gaze was drawn back to his twin. The medicine man should be coming too soon; his older brother would find the woman he loves dying right beside him. If the tooth didn't kill her, the poison he had dipped it in would.

Powaw went over and uncovered his hide. He put it there to distract Cecille once he got her here so he could give her a stunning blow. He knew she wouldn't be able to see it, but her extraordinary sense of smell would alert her to it. If not he would make sure to mention the smell, which would give him the time he needed to get behind her. The black bear head had done its job, the blood still drenching him had thankfully helped to mask his smell from White Buffalo since it was pretty fresh; even though she had shown up here unexpectedly everything worked out perfectly.

Powaw was using the paw he had taken from the old silver bear; he only took one, but he also declawed the other three and took those as well before leaving Spirit Bear to die on that long ago day. The hide he wore to fool the medicine man was his own sleeping fur. He used it instead, knowing he wouldn't have enough time to skin the black bear properly. He would throw it away now because there was too much blood on it, but he could go back to the black bear he killed earlier than skin it. The shaman had left it hanging in a tree, just in case he wanted the hide later.

Powaw smirked in satisfaction one last time when he looked over at Spirit Bear. He used a potent neurotoxin on the razor-sharp bear claw he racked across his twin's chest. It is known only to a shaman because it causes paralysis before slowly poisoning the body... death occurs, usually within a day or two. If used in minute doses prepared another way, its powerful enough to visit the spirit world, but the antidote needed to be close in case of mishandling. He made sure to pick one that was agonizingly slow, not wanting his brother to die without feeling the torment of his love dying first. The medicine man would only be able to move his eyes to watch; there was no way he could move any other body part to help his beloved White Buffalo as she suffered an excruciating death within arm's length of him.

Powaw gathered everything rapidly he didn't want any evidence of his involvement left behind; he would be banned from his tribe for life if they ever found out. He already had a strategic hiding place all picked out; from there he could watch his brother go through the same agony he lived through when the shaman's wife and unborn child died in Spirit Bear's care. Shin should have come too by now, hopefully he would get loose before the older twin died; Shadow Stalker would attest to the fact that Powaw wasn't anywhere near when the two died.

Powaw was almost out of the clearing when he halted in fear then had to back up at a grunt and a growl of anger from a huge grizzly. The immense, dark brown silver tipped bear with the distinctive hump had swung back around looking for the other male encroaching on his territory. He wasn't used to having a smaller bear come willingly into its area because black bears are nowhere close to aggressive enough to challenge a grizzly; they tried avoiding the monsters at all costs. As soon as Cecille had passed out her connection to the silver tipped behemoth had disappeared.

Powaw lifted the black bear head he was holding; the shaman threw it as far as he could. His hope was that the monster would go after it, but he forgot he still had the blood of the black bear all over him. When that didn't work he threw the claw in the grizzly's face; the shaman dropping his bear hide before pulling his knife out, he backed up more.

*****

Spirit Bear eventually came to the first thing he saw when his blurry gaze focused was Powaw full of blood. The shaman was standing a ways away with a knife held out towards a huge dark grizzly. The medicine man's eyes frantically searched trying to make sense out of what happened to him. He was sure it was a black bear that attacked him or was it; he remembered seeing something strange for a moment, but he couldn't recall now exactly what it was!

Spirit Bear's eyes swung to his right when he heard a moan of pain beside him; the medicine man tried to cry out when he saw Cecille laying in a pool of her own blood. Paralyzed the Cree healer couldn't get to her since he was unable to move any of his muscles. Where did White Buffalo come from why was she on the ground had the bear attacked her too?

Spirit Bear's eyes were drawn back involuntarily to the struggle happening in front of him. He was completely powerless unable to help his brother. All he could do was watch in horror as the grizzly knocked the knife out of his twin's hand with a casual swipe of his immense paw; the silver tipped brown behemoth pulled Powaw into a bear hug. The medicine man would have winced if he could have moved when he heard a loud snap as the shaman's back broke.

Powaw's agonizing scream of terror was cut short abruptly when the immense bear ripped off the shaman's head before throwing him negligently aside. The huge silver tip grizzly dropped onto all fours; he eyed the two lying on the ground curiously. He took a step forward to see if they too were a threat to his territory, one smelt familiar to him.

*****

Shin stopped at the edge of the trees when he caught the distinctive smell of a grizzly. The Tianming Monk put his dragon daggers away before pulling out his sword. Hearing Powaw's scream, Shadow Stalker charged out yelling at the bear trying to get him to come after him; he could feel Cecille here, but her heartbeat was slow irregular.

The big grizzly turned in surprise with a roar of rage at being interrupted before charging the insignificant man running towards him.

Shin leaped to his right just before the behemoth got to him. He continued his forward motion all the while spinning on his left foot until he was facing the side of the grizzly bear. The bear's momentum had him charging right past the Tianming Monk, the sword flashed wickedly when the late day sun caught it coming downwards. It severed the grizzly's head in one clean swipe, Shadow Stalker stopped with legs spread apart and sword extended in a stance that showed he was ready for more. The silver tipped brown grizzly not realizing it was missing something at first, continued to run ahead a few more steps; twitching, it eventually dropped to the ground dead!

Shin turned, he saw Spirit Bear trying to crawl to Cecille it was taking him an excruciating amount of time to get to her, but he was determined; the medicine man gathered her in his arms in fear, whispering soothing words of love he clung to her. The Tianming Monk walked over then cleaned his sword on the bears hide giving the two lovers a few minutes of privacy. He sheathed his Oriental sword before going to White Buffalo to see what the problem with her was, Shadow Stalker had no worries that she would die; her body would automatically heal her. He was aware the higher powers would never allow that, especially when she was now pregnant.

Cecille opened her eyes when she felt Spirit Bear holding her, the first thing she saw was blood dripping down his chest; she lifted her hand and put it on the medicine man's breast over his heart before giving him a healing jolt. She was too weak to heal him completely, but she was able to take away the poison eating at his system. White Buffalo's hand fell against her body feebly; the healer passed out having used all of her strength to heal her lover.

Shin dropped to his knees, he pushed Cecille over so he could examine her wound better. The Tianming Monk could feel something in it, but didn't know what it was. Thankfully, White Buffalo wasn't bleeding anymore since her body was already working to heal itself. Shadow Stalker took her from Spirit Bear. "Go collect your brother, we need to get back to the village; everything I need is at the hospital, I have no equipment here to dig out whatever is in her side."

Shin whistled shrilly, knowing Saya would be close by. A few minutes later the mare rushed into the clearing, fortunately for them with his stallion following her. The Tianming Monk had left the packhorse in camp a few miles away with the hunters he would collect her later after seeing Cecille to the hospital. Shadow Stalker put White Buffalo down then took Grey over to Spirit Bear, he was moving around better now; although still a bit slow and awkward. The Guardian helped the medicine man load his brother's body, which they wrapped in the younger twins sleeping fur. It helped to keep the head with the body because the stud didn't have a saddle or saddlebags.

Grey pawed the ground nervously he nickered uneasily at the smell of the grizzly; he stood fast though, impatiently waiting for his master to mount.

Twin Destinies

Saya stepped back nervously before standing; still little tremors of fear were quite visible all over her body, but except for the first hesitation she stood refusing to move. The mare lowered her head sniffing at her mistress, nickering softly in concern she nudged her. Getting no response she lifted her head looking towards Shin, she waited for her precious cargo to be lifted onto her back, although every instinct said to run.

Shin walked back to Saya, Grey followed him with Spirit Bear holding his dead brother on the stallion's back. The Tianming Monk picked up Cecille then turned to the medicine man. "Get up on the mare Spirit Bear, I will pass White Buffalo to you I will make sure to keep the shaman from falling off, I promise. We need to hurry I have to get whatever is in there out before it's too late, the wound will close fast making it impossible to retrieve it."

Spirit Bear nodded without arguing he went to Saya and mounted awkwardly before tenderly taking Cecille from Shin. The medicine man kissed White Buffalo on the forehead lovingly while waiting for Shadow Stalker to mount; praying to Misimanito, he cradled her carefully trying not to put any pressure on her wound.

Shin jumped onto Grey bareback. He wrapped his right hand in the stallion's mane to keep himself steady before he put his left one on the headless shaman to keep him in place. The Tianming Monk kicked the stud into a trot, once out of the trees he turned west. When they got back on the path; Shadow Stalker picked up his pace, but was careful not to leave Saya too far behind him.

*****

An hour later they halted in front of the hospital. Instantly Shin jumped down turning he lifted the dead shaman off Grey then put him on the ground beside the wigwam. He rushed over to Saya next, reaching up he took Cecille from a reluctant Spirit Bear. Once the Tianming Monk had her cradled in his arms, he rushed inside before putting White Buffalo on a hospital bed. He hurried to the shelf with all the instruments; Shadow Stalker took down a scalpel, long tweezers, antiseptic, and a needle that was already threaded to close up the wound.

Spirit Bear followed Shin closely; he took the opportunity to take Cecille's buckskin shirt off, while Shadow Stalker's back was turned before putting a hide discreetly over her breasts. The medicine man scrutinized the wound completely baffled by the events that he couldn't entirely recall. "There is some kind of hard object deep in her side I have no clue what it could be I am so confused by what happened. I distinctly remember leaving White Buffalo safe in the village, so how is it possible she ended up hurt then lying beside me after the black bear attack? I know I gave her a vague description of where the hunt was going to be at, but she was in the village when we veered off. How did she know we were five miles further away from the hunting party?"

Spirit Bear stroked Cecille's cheek lovingly, hoping for any absent memory to resurface. He remembered the look of terror on Powaw's face as he tried to hold off the grizzly, his twin would forever remember the shaman's sacrifice. The medicine man looked up at Shin once more in confusion. Talking out loud, he tried to piece together what had happened. "It was a black bear that attacked me I'm sure of it; where did the grizzly that killed my brother come from and when did Powaw show up? He left me soon after you did, believe me, it was a shock to see him trying to protect us with a hunting knife. My twin has never been the type to be self-sacrificing!"

Shin let Spirit Bear ramble on; The Tianming Monk was too busy concentrating on finding what he needed to help Cecille.

Shin brought everything he needed to the bed; the Tianming Monk grimly shook his head at Spirit Bear as he knelt beside the cot on the other side of Cecille. Shadow Stalker decided not to say anything to the medicine man until he talked to his charge, she might not want him to know everything. "I won't be able to tell you anything we will have to wait until White Buffalo wakes up for her explanation."

Spirit Bear stared down at Shin, thoughtfully; the Oriental had his head down studying Cecille's wound intently. The medicine man frowned grimly that's right Shadow Stalker had gone off before Powaw had. How did the Tianming Monk just happen to show up at the right moment too? He shook off his suspicious thoughts they needed to concentrate on White Buffalo now. Once she is awake, they could exchange information, he would have to wait patiently.

Shin poured antiseptic on the wound cleaning the blood away he needed to be able to see what was in there; the Tianming Monk looked up at Spirit Bear before pointing at a candle, Cecille always had one on hand for extra light. Shadow Stalker went back to probing at the wound when the medicine man got up. "Can you light the fire pit for me and bring me the candle that's beside it, I could use more light!"

Spirit Bear picked up a match that was sitting beside the candle he had been utterly flabbergasted when Cecille first lit a candle with the little stick; the medicine man was utterly amazed that such a thing was possible it only took him a few minutes before he rushed back to Shin with the candle.

Spirit Bear shook off his wayward thoughts grimly he turned his attention to Shin. The medicine man watched Shadow Stalker closely; since the two strangers had entered their village, he had learned how to use many wondrous things that White Buffalo had brought with her from the white-eyes. Shin decided to try the tweezers first he didn't want to cut Cecille any more than necessary. He carefully inserted the tweezers if this didn't work the Guardian would have to resort to using the scalpel on White Buffalo; already the hole the object made was half its original size it was closing up fast. The Tianming Monk frowned intently in concentration pushing the long thin forceps further inside searching Shadow Stalker went in a little deeper.

*****

Cecille floated as her body worked to heal itself; she could feel the poison attacking her system. She was semi-conscious the whole time; entirely aware of Shin's rush to get her to the hospital. White Buffalo listened to their conversation, glad the Tianming Monk didn't tell Spirit Bear anything. She felt the tweezers enter her side causing the tooth to move further in getting closer to severing the membrane keeping it from getting to her uterus. The forceps pushed against her fallopian tube causing a slice that just begun to heal.

Cecille silently screamed at Shin to try stopping him. Of course, the Tianming Monk couldn't hear her; White Buffalo desperately sent out a vision to her dog, hoping that Misfit would understand her. The healer's baby depended on it.

*****

Shin with sweat running down his face crowed suddenly in triumph. "I almost have it!"

Shin looked up in surprised shock at an intense growl from Misfit, which was all the warning he got as Cecille's dog jumped at him. The Tianming Monk fell backward with her on top of him. The tweezers went flying; quickly, she jumped off the Guardian going after them. The dog picked the forceps up in her mouth before she raced to her bed then dropped them on her blanket. Promptly she dropped on top of them.

It was not until then that Shin noticed the brood of puppies on Misfit's bed. The Tianming Monk had been so intent on White Buffalo he hadn't even noticed anything else.

Spirit Bear rushed over to Cecille's dog but her lip curled menacingly; Misfit growled a warning, which caused the medicine man to step back in surprise. White Buffalo's dog had never shown any aggression towards him before! Why now, was it the puppies?

Shin sat up slowly before eyeing Cecille's dog grimly; the Tianming Monk called Spirit Bear back. "Leave her be I will bandage White Buffalo's side for now, we will just have to wait for her to come around. She is bleeding some I must have caused more damage Misfit would never attack me without good reason."

Spirit Bear nodded as he walked back over to Cecille before putting his hand over her forehead lovingly. He bent kissing her gently on the lips the medicine man stood up; he looked down at Shin who was kneeling beside White Buffalo's bed. "I will prepare my brother for burial I will also send a party to collect the meat."

Shin nodded, he gave Spirit Bear directions to the deer he had hoisted into a tree. When the medicine man left, the Tianming Monk finished bandaging Cecille's side before sitting back. Shadow Stalker knew it was going to be a long wait.

Shin went to the back room to get his carpet, he put it beside Cecille's bed; kneeling on the Japanese rug the Tianming Monk went deep into meditation. The Guardian reached up pulling his charge into his arms he cradled her gently with the hope that the carpet would help her to heal faster.

CHAPTER TWENTY FOUR

Spirit Bear stood in the doorway of their wigwam with his arms crossed resolutely; four months had passed since that dreadful day. Again he was trying to keep the fear out of his voice he was even more unsuccessful this time around. The medicine man stared at Cecille grimly he ignored Shin standing behind his wife knowing the Tianming Monk would be no help. Shadow Stalker's Cree wife was even closer to giving birth. "No, you are five months pregnant White Buffalo I forbid you to go! Look what happened the last time you were in a white-eyes town, they put a rope around your neck. If you die that way, we will never find each other in the spirit world of Misimanito. My people believe if they hang the soul gets trapped in the body, for all eternity."

Cecille reached up to cup Spirit Bear's face lovingly; her husband's people were such a simple, easygoing group thankfully still untouched by outside influences. White Buffalo pulled his head down but had to stand on tiptoes to get around the medicine man's crossed arms; she gave him a deep kiss before moving back. "I'm sorry love I have to go, the Mother Earth demands it. Shadow Stalker will protect me with his life as he always has. The Great Spirit will also protect me from being hanged by the white-eyes I was assured of that when I had my vision. I will be as quick as possible it should only take us about forty-two days my Guardian figures. If we don't have too many problems maybe less, I will be back before my eighth month... I promise."

Spirit Bear sighed forlornly before dropping his arms knowing that his angry, demanding tone wouldn't get him anywhere; when the Mother Earth or Great Spirit called for Cecille to help, he had no choice but to let White Buffalo go. The medicine man gathered her close as a ripple of fear shivered down his spine, he didn't know why but he continued being a bit afraid. "Maybe I should go with you I can ride the mare now since Shadow Stalker taught me!"

Cecille felt Spirit Bear's shiver of fear she sighed grimly. She also felt uneasy about this trip, but the Mother Earth insisted pregnant or not she had to go to New Brunswick. A man was going there who was extremely powerful he was full of the Mother's magic. White Buffalo needed to give him his spirit name or the magic within him would die, eventually so too would he! This man was important in the future for some reason, making it imperative that she go. Po had given her a reassuring vision of herself in the Indian village having her daughter, so even though she felt this trip would be her last; she would make it back here for the birth of her child, it was the most important thing to her right now. That she would die in childbirth was already known to her, she kept that from the medicine man knowing he wouldn't understand. "No, one of us must stay here the village can't afford to lose two healers at the same time."

Cecille reluctantly disentangled herself from Spirit Bear with a smile of confidence. Getting an idea since she was so sure of her return she reached inside the bodice of her fringed doeskin shirt and pulled out her Celtic medallion. She detached the chain from her medicine bag before pulling the rawhide string back out of the bag then put it around her neck and under her shirt; it seemed so much lighter now. White Buffalo stepped forward she took the medicine man's hand to put the medallion in it she closed his fingers over it. "Keep this as my promise that I will be here for the birth of our daughter. This dragon cross has been in my family for many generations past it has never gotten left behind. When our daughter is born, you will put it around her neck with the silver one that I always wear they are both important family ties."

Spirit Bear reached out the medicine man tenderly stroked Cecille's cheek. "I promise to do that for you my love, thank you White Buffalo for understanding my feelings. I am positive now you will return; safe journey, but be quick I will miss you dreadfully."

Spirit Bear dropped to his knees kissing Cecille's distended belly, only recently had the baby's kicks became strong enough for him to feel them. White Buffalo insisted it was a girl, but he didn't care as long as she was as beautiful as her mother; the medicine man felt a kick, he smiled lovingly and whispered sadly. "I will miss our nightly songs my little Dove take care of your Mother for me."

Spirit Bear feeling another vigorous kick grinned before standing up he gave Cecille one last kiss of farewell; reluctantly, the medicine man stepped back letting White Buffalo go without him knowing she was right, he had to stay to look after his people.

Cecille turned from her husband; she couldn't help a tender smile of love from surfacing. White Buffalo let Shin help her into the saddle.

Cecille waved farewell to Red Dawn, who was standing by her wigwam with a forlorn expression on her face. They said goodbye to the expectant Cree woman earlier, Shin's wife would probably have her baby before they got back. White Buffalo made sure to

Twin Destinies

give her another healing jolt, wanting Shadow Stalker's son to have a smooth birth.

Once Powaw died, it was like an epidemic of pregnancies in this village, ten for sure that Cecille knew of all within a few weeks of each other; hopefully, White Buffalo would make it back here to help out some of them. A week after the shaman got killed the Spirit Flu vanished as it had never been.

Shin as always was in front riding Grey. He was enjoying his unpredictable stallion these days, so no longer put up a fuss when it came to being on a horse. The packhorse was on the Tianming Monk's left; Precious had a halter on with no rope attached. Cecille's mare was on the right her nose was close to his leg; it didn't matter which way Shadow Stalker went the horse would follow, used to this routine. Saya's reins got tied together before being draped loosely around her neck she didn't need White Buffalo's guidance.

Misfit stayed close beside the mare loping along if she got too tired she would jump up on Saya's neck to rest. Every once in a while Cecille's dog would look up adoringly at her mistress; once reassured she was still close the last Indian Bear dog and Staffordshire Bull Terrier cross continued to follow. She ended up having five puppies amidst White Buffalo's life and death struggle; her pups too young to travel such a long distance got left in the care of Red Dawn.

Cecille hearing a bark in the distance opened her senses so the Mother Earth could show her the runt of the litter chasing after them. A boy was trying to catch her, but she refused to be left behind. White Buffalo called out a warning to Shin before halting letting the exact image of her mother catch up. She smiled as the determined pup ran past her; the runt attached herself to the Tianming Monk like an ever-present shadow. He called her Little Miss because she liked to get into trouble.

Shin jumped off Grey in aggravation before walking over he lifted the pup up; the Tianming Monk stared intently into her eyes, grunting in resignation Shadow Stalker turned to the boy. "It's okay let Red Dawn know we are keeping Little Miss with us."

Shin marched back to Grey grumbling in aggravation about a female never doing as they are told human or otherwise. The Tianming Monk went to the front of his stallion before holding up the tiny puppy to introduce the newest member. "This is Little Miss you will be nice to her; get used to the fact that she will be on your back most of the time with me since she is too small to keep up!"

Cecille bit down on her lower lip hard trying not to laugh knowing that Shin wouldn't appreciate her humour; White Buffalo knew the human comment was directed towards her and his wife who hadn't taken the Tianming Monk's leaving well.

Grey snorted before nuzzling the little runt playfully; the pup whined she licked the stallion's nose in greeting.

Misfit gave a little bark of demand before rubbing up against Shin wanting to see her puppy.

Shin put the pup down with her mother. "Okay Misfit, Little Miss can stay with you until she gets tired; make sure she doesn't wander off."

Shin remounted Grey, a few minutes later they were again on their way; the Tianming Monk would pick up the pup once they were out of the mountains by then the horses should have warmed up a bit. Once they turned east, they would pick up the pace. Shadow Stalker knew Little Miss would never keep up with the galloping horses.

Cecille sighed resignedly it would take at least three weeks to get to where they were going she figured; depending on the weather and barring any unforeseen mishaps that is. They would also have to go through a few white towns too White Buffalo grimaced grimly. Hopefully, there would be no repeat of what had taken place the first or the last time they had ended up in a white town. Unfortunately, Spirit Bear had reminded her of the previous unpleasant encounter with the whites. The healer hoped there would be no wanted posters out on them because of it.

Cecille couldn't help but grin when her thoughts turned to Spitting Badger he lived in the first town they had been in. White Buffalo walked in the boy's dreams not long ago. She felt his satisfaction when he testified that his step-father was the culprit who set the fire at the hotel, not them which killed three hotel guests. The healer also felt his joy when he got reunited with his birth parents; lucky for him they were still alive.

Cecille sighed in relief glad that they had gotten cleared of any wrongdoing in Ontario; there shouldn't be any wanted posters out for them because of that incident.

Cecille shifted with a grimace as she was rudely brought back to the present by a jabbing pain in her left side; it made her lean a bit more to the right putting pressure on her opposite side. Even after four months the tooth embedded in White Buffalo's side from Spirit Bear's twin continued to remind her of the unpleasant grizzly bear incident. It was also a bitter reminder of her husband's brother who tried to kill her. They kept it a secret from the medicine man only because the shaman died inadvertently saving his twin from certain death by unintentionally sacrificing himself at the end.

Cecille still didn't understand why the tooth couldn't get extracted; although she had a sneaky suspicion, it would be used to kill her in the end when she was delivering her daughter. How else would it be accomplished since her body could heal itself death would have to be instantaneous?! Lately, White Buffalo could swear the tooth was touching her womb at times which was a constant worry to the expectant mother. Could it pierce the uterus and kill the child growing inside her, it would be the shaman's last revenge against a brother he hated. Shin assured her that the Great Spirit wouldn't allow it.

Cecille knew Shin was right neither the Mother Earth nor Shen would let that happen; if the baby inside her died, the prophecy would also die so who would protect Po then! White Buffalo shook off her unpleasant thoughts as they continued on.

*****

Spirit Bear watching Cecille go clutched the medallion tightly in a fist; so hard, in fact, the dragon left deep imprints in his palms. Never had he seen White Buffalo without this necklace, the fact that she gave it to him reassured him immensely. The medicine man put the silver chain with the medallion around his neck then put it inside his shirt and under his medicine bag to lie against his chest; not far from his heart. He turned away forlornly as the woman he loved disappeared.

Once around Spirit Bear couldn't help his glance from stopping at the shaman's tepee. A man was walking inside. It wasn't his brother, of course; the chief asked White Buffalo if she was interested in being their shaman since she's trained already, but she refused.

Spirit Bear still couldn't believe he survived two bear attacks in his lifetime. He put his hand over his left breast, feeling the odd marks on his chest. The first attack was by an old silver grey blonde bear she raked his left side; the marks halted just below his nipple. If it weren't for White Buffalo finding him when she did the medicine man would have died. His brother had sworn he thought his twin was dead when he left him there.

Spirit Bear couldn't remember much of the second attack, only that it cost him his twin brother; sometimes he swore there was a black bear too, but Cecille and Shin assured him there was only one. The dark brown silver-tipped grizzly ripped his claws from just below the medicine man's right shoulder crisscrossing the old scar before going past his left nipple.

The monster had also bitten Cecille before Shin could stop it, leaving a tooth embedded in her side. They tried to remove it, but it just went deeper in threatening their unborn child. It didn't seem to bother White Buffalo much, so they eventually left it alone.

Spirit Bear's wife always insisted the bear had bitten her but try as he might to find the other tooth mark he couldn't; the alternative was one he didn't want to contemplate, so the medicine man shook off his suspicion and continued to remember his brother's sacrifice.

Spirit Bear turned away, going to the far wigwam he scratched at the flap to be let in. Red Dawn pulled open the door then the medicine man disappeared inside; they would give each other solace as the days turned into weeks before they turned into a long, excruciating month.

*****

Cecille reluctantly got off her mare when Shin halted. She immediately turned to the exhausted horses giving each of them a jolt of healing while he set up a camp. The Tianming Monk refused to go any further until they had something to eat. Already they went over thirty miles, which is usually what a horse can do in a full day. White Buffalo was using the Mother Earth again to give the horses enough stamina to continue galloping straight through; she was feeling a bit light headed though.

Shin kept giving Cecille surreptitious glances of concern. About fifteen minutes ago he unexpectedly almost fell off Grey at a severe dizzy impression. The Tianming Monk stopped instantly; it wasn't often White Buffalo's emotions were so strong that he could physically feel them unless she was in immediate danger. Shadow Stalker dished her up a helping of beaver tail stew that Red Dawn sent along with him. He knew that his charge would never say no to her favourite meal.

Cecille dropped down beside Shin she gladly accepted a bowl of food; quickly she wolfed it down, so hungry she hardly took a breath between bites. White Buffalo put the dish down when she finished before taking the canteen of water the Tianming Monk passed her. The healer gulped down half of it she hadn't realized how thirsty she was either.

Shin took the container from Cecille, he took a long swig himself before reaching over he took her bowl to use; he divided the leftovers between Misfit and Little Miss. When they were done eating he emptied the rest of the water in the bowls, he would refill his water bottle in the creek before they left. The Tianming Monk looked over at his charge intently; his tone had a chiding cautionary sound to it. "You are pushing yourself too hard White Buffalo! I want to get this done with just as fast as possible too; remember I have a son on the way but if you over do it, it might halt us longer. Having to recuperate from exhaustion could take up to a month!"

Cecille nodded knowing Shin was right, she got up before slipping behind a tree for privacy then helped to break camp afterwards. White Buffalo waited until she was in the saddle then looked down at the Tianming Monk intently. She continued the conversation from earlier. "I know Shadow Stalker, but Spirit Bear said this trail will only take us so far. He wasn't sure exactly where it ends if it runs out we will have to take time to find another route. The medicine man is sure his great, great grandmother was found further to the east, if we find her tribe maybe they will help us; I want to go as far as possible today, it will give us extra days if we get stuck somewhere or need more time."

Shin sighed resignedly knowing that Cecille wouldn't let up anytime soon, regardless of what he said to her. The Tianming Monk would just have to keep a close eye on her. White Buffalo could be so stubborn when she wanted something. He picked up his pup before mounting, next he tied the canteen he refilled back on his saddle horn trying to stall a little; eventually, unable to wait any longer Shadow Stalker kicked his horse into a trot to warm him up. It was not long until they were once again galloping full out.

*****

Shin jumped off Grey; he quickly put his pup on the ground before rushing to Cecille. He reached up for her just as she dropped exhausted into his arms. The Tianming Monk tsked in disapproval. He knelt and sat her on the ground. He had known she wasn't going to make it much further even though she insisted they keep going. "Bloody fool woman you are going to kill the baby or yourself this way; unless it is an emergency, there will no longer be extra energy given to the horses. Your mare is pregnant too and so is Precious. Please, try to remember that you are taking a big chance on losing both foals! I know you want to get back as soon as possible, but the extra days you are giving us won't be worth everyone's health!"

Shin looked up at the full moon that was beginning to lower now that the midnight hour had come and gone; it was the only reason they kept going this late.

Cecille refused to stop this time, so they chewed some jerky before she dug out a few pemmican cakes to munch on. With White Buffalo giving the horses more energy from the Mother Earth they went an unheard of hundred miles today, but at what cost. The Tianming Monk shook his head in exasperation, getting up without another word he went to the packhorse to gather their bedding. After putting his charge in her blankets, he stripped the stallion and Saya last.

Shin sighed thankful to be finished, now that the horses were seen too he built himself a small fire. He pulled out the rabbit soup Red Dawn had given to him she put it in the stomach of a moose so it wouldn't drip over everything. Pour it into a pot the Tianming Monk left it to heat. He went back to Cecille with a canteen of water, holding her head tenderly he helped her to drink a good portion of it. Laying her back down Shadow Stalker went to the fire before pouring the broth out of the pot into a cup; going back to White Buffalo he helped her to sit up in order to give her the warm broth, neither of them said a word.

Shin got up with the empty cup he went back to the fire to eat his share of the soup before whistling to Misfit and Little Miss; the Tianming Monk gave them the rest, after extinguishing the fire he was able to crawl into his bedding completely exhausted they all slept.

*****

Cecille sat up in stunned shock when a drop of water splashed on her cheek. A moment later a loud boom of thunder sounded far off in the distance. White Buffalo winced as another drop fell on her nose this time; she listened intently, but couldn't hear anyone moving. "Shin?"

Shin materialized beside Cecille, he reached out touching her shoulder in reassurance not wanting her to use any of her power right now. The Tianming Monk already had the horses saddled. "Come on White Buffalo the wind is picking up pushing a storm towards us. We need to get out of here before the lightning gets any closer. The horses are quite spooked already wanting to get out of this gully, unfortunately there is still a lot of trees to get passed ahead. Once we start going down this mountain we should be out of the trees for a while, at the bottom is a large lake. The old chief gave me a rough map; regrettably he never went any further, so couldn't tell me what is beyond the lake. I am hoping we can rest there for a few hours."

Shin helped Cecille up before directing her to Saya, Misfit's pup was the reason he was awake already. She tried to burrow into the Tianming Monk's blankets when a crash of thunder scared her; although, the storm was quite a ways in the distance there was no use going back to sleep afterwards. Shadow Stalker needed to gather White Buffalo's furs before they could leave here. He was beginning to get a bit uneasy himself as the lightning drew closer to them it was travelling fast. "Your mare is five steps in front of you, be careful though Little Miss is between the two of you... she is absolutely petrified of the thunder."

Cecille still more asleep than awake got an image from the Mother Earth of where Little Miss was before veering around her. She did manage to climb into the saddle on her own, without her Guardian's help this time. White Buffalo was clear headed now, but still weak from her overuse of Po's magic; feeling the horses need though she didn't even hesitate to give them each a boost. The healer looked down at Shin grimly when she heard him walking towards her. She gave him a warning even though she knew the Tianming Monk would be angry with her. "Shadow Stalker you will need to tie me to the saddle, I have given the horses all that I have left. I'm not sure if I will even be able to stay in the saddle for long!"

Shin grumbling irritably about a foolish woman who never listens to anything she is told, he fastened Cecille's bedding to the packhorse. He made sure it was piled up in front of the wooden box that his rug was in forming a cushion. He quickly rummaged inside one of the packs for rawhide rope. The Tianming Monk marched to White Buffalo grimly; he pulled her none too gently off her mare and took her to the packhorse. Shadow Stalker lifted her onto Precious' back, while tying his charge to the saddle he was giving her instructions too. "I put your bedding behind you to make it possible for you to rest while I find a way out of the mountains. Now you can sleep without having to worry about falling off we might need the Mother Earth before this is over!"

Saya nickered uneasily; Shin looked back at the mare, but didn't have time to waste on reassurances. The Tianming Monk picked up Little Miss before mounting Grey; Misfit jumped up on Saya, which thankfully calmed her down. Even though every instinct in Shadow Stalker said to run, he nudged his horse into a fast walk. With the moon now hidden by the blackening cloud cover, he needed to make sure the horses didn't step into a hole possibly breaking a leg. The Guardian calmly kept them at that speed as lightning drew closer.

*****

Shin winced two hours later when a lightning bolt flashed to his right. It was so bright he couldn't see for the count of ten that he got to before thunder crashed right above them, making him cringe; it was too close. He looked past his shoulder at Cecille, but even the noise didn't wake his exhausted charge. Taking a chance, the Tianming Monk nudged the quivering Grey into a trot. Every muscle in the horse's body was strung tight. He reached down soothingly to stroke his stallion's neck. They both could hear a distinctive sizzling sound then smell the strong scent of sulphur from the lightning bolt hitting a tree. "Easy big fella, there is no need to panic just yet we are going down now. Hopefully we should be out of these trees soon and rain is beginning to fall, it will help."

Grey nickered uneasily, he did settle down at his master's calm reassurances. He refused to slow any; now that they were going down the path was getting rougher with more rocks to contend with. It wasn't long before the stallion had no choice but to slow to a walk, the ground was becoming too treacherous. He picked his footing carefully since the rain was coming down harder now making the rocks slippery. He could no longer smell the sulphur with this heavy rainfall it reassured him.

*****

Cecille was dreaming of her father, which she hadn't done since his death. Edward brought their golf clubs with them from England, once a month he would take her golfing with him to the outskirts of Montreal. It was a three day trip to Fletcher's Field, which was part of Mount Royal Park where the first Canadian golf club was founded in eighteen seventy-three. Dream Dancer would line his daughter up before giving her the yardage needed; twice she had a hole in one. White Buffalo couldn't see it happening, but she could hear it as the ball hit the bottom of the cup with a loud clutter.

Cecille remember with fondness that Edward always grumbled good-naturedly that he would never get a hole in one before he died. Although, his blind daughter already had two as young as she was. She recalled the day it all changed for her father; she could still feel the excitement in the air when White Buffalo heard the crack of the club hitting the gutty golf ball. Without having to be told she knew Dream Dancer finally made his dream come true!

Cecille frowned in surprise, puzzled when the loud sound of the club hitting the ball continued for way too long. It seemed to take several drawn-out, agonizing minutes before she eventually heard

Edward screaming at her in elation. No wait, it wasn't exhilaration she was hearing but fear; Dream Dancer was shrieking at her, insistently. "Get out, White Buffalo... rrunn!"

Cecille's eyes sprang open instantly; as fast as she could the healer undid the bonds holding her in place. Lucky for her Shin hadn't tried to keep her from getting loose, she easily untied the ropes. She jumped off the packhorse since she was picking her footing carefully and going slow before running to Saya. All the while she was screaming at the Tianming Monk above the sounds of rocks and mud gaining ground on them. Finished with her warning to Shadow Stalker, she chanted bringing White Buffalo to the surface so she could see. Vaulting onto her mare; she connected to the Mother Earth as well as her horse in desperation then galloped ahead of her Guardian taking over the lead.

Cecille carefully followed Po's instructions around several obstacles that she couldn't see even while joined to her mare. They raced as fast as possible off the side of this mountain.

Cecille still exhausted mentally was having difficulty with keeping her focus on the Mother Earth; it seemed to her that the faster they went, the closer the mudslide got to them. White Buffalo cringed as a massive rock to her left rolled past them gaining momentum it rapidly outdistanced them. All she could think of at this moment, was how was she going to get back to Spirit Bear now!

Shin clutched his pup close to his chest, trying to keep her from falling off the madly galloping horses. To give Grey more stability, he was laying back as far as possible on the stud's hind-end trying to keep the stallion's nose up. He didn't want to end up tumbling head first down this hill. The Tianming Monk prayed that Cecille would hold out because he couldn't see a thing in this driving rain; they were getting closer to the bottom, but so too was the mudslide as several large boulders tumbled past on his right. Shadow Stalker couldn't help thinking when the sound of the rushing mud was directly behind him, overpowering all else... they weren't going to make it!

CHAPTER TWENTY FIVE

Saya slowed to a walk when she felt Cecille wobbling dangerously to the left. White Buffalo fell into a semi-unconscious state as she slumped over her horse's neck. The mare eventually came to a stop now that the danger had passed; she heaved air into her lungs with a cough of exertion. She could still hear the loud rumble of the mudslide behind her, but she ignored it. Thankfully, her daughter came to a halt close to her; a few minutes later, she heard the stallion walk up beside her before her mistress was lifted away.

Shin leaned down as far as he could then let go of the pup so she could walk with her mother before sitting up in the saddle. He reached over to pull a limp Cecille into his lap; holding White Buffalo close in concern, the Tianming Monk nudged Grey into a walk to cool him down.

The other horses followed with heads drooped in exhaustion. They couldn't stay here there was too much mud piling up behind them, it would get to this point sooner or later maybe even beyond it.

Shin needed to cool off the horse's anyway because they were all sweating profusely and winded; if he stopped now Saya especially would die, being the oldest and pregnant the Tianming Monk could hear her laboured breathing from here.

Shin followed the edge of the lake hoping to find the right place to camp, but no opportunity presented itself; dawn began lighting up the sky before the rain quit altogether. The Tianming Monk letting the horses find their way dozed, still holding Cecille protectively. Shadow Stalker heard the distant bark of dogs and Misfit growling protectively, even that didn't rouse him thoroughly as Grey came to an uncertain halt.

*****

Cecille drifted in a void, unable to wake herself; she felt Shin gathering her into his arms so she snuggled close to the Tianming Monk before allowing the emptiness to pull her further in. White Buffalo felt the Mother Earth whispering soothingly, Po was cradling her as she fought a battle within. The healer took in too much of the Earth's magic it was consuming her relentlessly, but she couldn't seem to stop it.

Cecille felt others take her from Shin. She whimpered in denial when she heard the Tianming Monk cry out her name pleadingly. Still, White Buffalo couldn't wake up as she felt herself moving

Twin Destinies

with many hands holding on to her before she was put down on something soft. Suddenly, a chanting began niggling at her consciousness. The words were unfamiliar at first; it didn't take her long to realize it was a different version of Spirit Bear's Cree language. They pronounced several words differently than the medicine man's people did, with quite a few extra syllables. It wouldn't take her long to learn it since she was only partially unconscious as she listened to them talk. Thankfully, she still had an affinity for languages.

Cecille felt Shin several minutes later when he too was carried in. She didn't feel any distress from the Tianming Monk now, which would point to their immediate danger; relieved the healer allowed herself to continue drifting. Through the Mother Earth, she checked on the horses Saya had a cough that White Buffalo would have to heal as soon as she could. Otherwise, they all were surprisingly healthy despite their ordeal.

Cecille checked on her baby next, but she was okay, not stressed any; comforted she allowed herself to continue drifting letting the Mother Earth cradle her, lovingly. White Buffalo frowned in concentration, the loud chanting from the medicine man or shaman couldn't drown out the Earth's whispers. What Po was trying to say she didn't understand, surprisingly it was in a language unknown to her it sounded foreign. It seemed to be more of an incantation, one she was unfamiliar with.

Cecille felt time slipping away, how much she wasn't entirely sure of; in relief, she finally felt Shin beside her. The Tianming Monk was also chanting now trying to draw her from wherever she was at, back to the living. The healer was beginning to feel uneasy the Mother Earth didn't seem to want to release her. Every time she tried to wake herself Po's chanting would increase, which calmed White Buffalo enough that she would continue to let the Earth cradle her as she drifted.

*****

Shin frowned down at Cecille in concern over twenty-four hours had passed. Still, she refused to wake up. He had used his carpet earlier but was told by his master to leave her be; this was necessary because she had taken in too much magic. The magic she had stolen shouldn't have been hers to command it was supposed to be held in trust for another hundred and fifty years or so. The Mother Earth needed to withdraw it slowly before it damaged White Buffalo forever. Unfortunately to take it back his charge would have to be stripped of all her powers becoming an ordinary human. The Tianming Monk was well aware that they would have to be careful now since she would no longer be able to heal herself after this.

Shin knelt on his carpet again; he had placed it beside Cecille's bed so he could be close to her. The Tianming Monk found out this Cree village was on the outskirts of a town called Timbrell it had maybe ten houses he got told; it did have a hotel with a tea room that took in weary travellers, with a Catholic church. It also had its own trading post that trappers took their furs too, which is what was keeping the village from becoming a ghost town. Lucky for them the natives in these parts were a friendly bunch they didn't have much to do with the town Shadow Stalker was reassured by the chief. Except when a trader came then they would sell goods for modern white-eyes conveniences.

Shin also found out that long ago the shaman of these people had an unusual vision, even to this day the story survived. It was of two bears fighting over one of their woman that had gone out alone to pick berries; one was an unusual pure white the other was black, when the fighting finished the woman was taken away by the black bear never to return. The Tianming Monk smiled knowingly before telling them about Spirit Bear's great, great grandmother who was found close to the lake. After much excitement that Cecille was related by marriage to them, Shadow Stalker got subjected to many introductions of possible relations to White Buffalo's child.

Shin hearing a bark, turned with a smile and gathered Little Miss into his lap Misfit followed her in a few minutes later. The Tianming Monk was glad that all the animals survived relatively unscathed. Saya had to get treated for a cough the medicine man of the tribe had taken her into the sweat lodge and treated her there; now thankfully there were no problems with her breathing.

Shin looked up he smiled in thanks before putting his pup beside him. He took the plate of cornmeal mush the toothless excessively wrinkled old woman handed him for breakfast. The Tianming Monk obediently ate while she tidied up; these people were fairly short ranging from four foot five to five foot six at the most. The older married woman had short to shoulder length hair the younger ones had long hair some all the way past their buttocks. Most of the younger men shaved or plucked their hair, leaving at least half of their scalp bare. The older men had braided hair most down to their shoulders; since it was so close to a white town, their clothing was in-between traditional with a lot of white-eye outfits.

Shin ate hungrily afterwards he laid down for another sleep he was still trying to recuperate himself. Dawn was two hours away, plenty of time later for the Tianming Monk to decide what his next move was if Cecille didn't wake soon. It took Shadow Stalker several minutes to fall asleep with the shaman still chanting loudly it made it difficult to settle down. The old man was shaking a rather long rattle with feathers hanging off it over White Buffalo's body; the monk figured he was trying to revive her or maybe it was keeping her in the world of the living. He was a bit unsure what it was all about not having understood everything that was said.

*****

Cecille stared around her in amazement; she was standing in that field of wildflowers with mountains in the background and like the first time she was able to see. The Great Spirit's presence wasn't here this time she was utterly alone. Smiling in awe, she walked around admiring the different coloured flowers. Bending she drew in a big whiff of a heavenly fragrance from the purple one before turning she sniffed a deep yellow one enjoying its scent too. Giggling in delight, White Buffalo continued walking looking around in excitement.

Abruptly without any warning, the flowers disappeared when Cecille entered a valley that was bare of everything; except, for a huge rock right in the middle White Buffalo didn't recall this place from before.

Cecille stopped in shock; she stared at the stone in surprise unable to look away. It was ebony black and just as tall as her and twice as wide until she took a step into the valley. Instantly the rock began changing colour from the bottom it seemed to be turning green. She blinked her eyes then rubbed them, maybe she just imagined it was black or it could be a trick of the light; it was no ordinary rock. The nearer she got to it the deeper the colour seemed, amazingly at first she could see clear through it. The gem reminded her of the green malachite that got used for the eye of the dragon on her medallion. She astonished herself by giggling in wonder; maybe it was the dragon eye! White Buffalo shook off her irrational thought before walking towards it curiously. She wasn't sure if being here was such a good idea, but the gem was calling out to her compelling her closer.

Cecille stopped in front of it in delight; now that she was closer to it, she could see herself in the looking glass. When did it change into a mirror? Frowning in bemusement, she scratched her head in confusion before shrugging distractedly unable to remember it changing. White Buffalo didn't dwell on the difference very long, too excited to see what she looked like for the first time.

Cecille saw another image appear behind her abruptly, she spun around quickly in fear but she couldn't see anything around her. She turned back to stare grimly at the presence behind her; jerking her head around rapidly just to make sure there was nothing physical there, she checked one more time. Turning back, White Buffalo noticed that her own image was gone only the other remained.

Cecille reassured that it was just a false image, wondered how the deep red and black dragon on her medallion had ended up in this gem. She had left her necklace with her husband she was entirely sure of that, no wait; White Buffalo leaned forward in awe, the dragon inside was a pure white when had that happened?

Cecille reached out curiously to feel the smooth crystal she still couldn't help wondering where her image disappeared too. She was beginning to think the rock was connected to her in a mystical way; when she walked into this open valley, she was wondering if the beauty of the field of flowers was a reflection of her own image. Afterwards, for a minute White Buffalo saw herself in the crystal.

Cecille's next thought as soon as she saw the rock changing colour was the eye of her dragon; it wasn't long before the dragon from her medallion showed up behind her. The mythical creature could have turned white because of her namesake. If that was so why had she not seen a buffalo yet, unless the colour white was the most crucial part of White Buffalo's namesake?

Cecille, unable to contain her curiosity laid her left hand onto the rock until her palm was flat against it. All she could feel at first was a momentary heat, with just a slight humming vibration. Unexpectedly, she screeched in shock before pulling her hand away she shook it, bringing it in close she blew on the red burn on her palm. White Buffalo scowled in astonishment when for just a quick moment, she saw the image of the crystal imbedded in her palm; it was only a brief impression. Afterwards, the pain then redness disappeared as if it never happened.

Cecille looked back at the offending rock, but it was nowhere to be seen; she spun around in circles, all she could see again was hundreds of wild flowers at least one of every description. Until abruptly the flowers with the field disappeared, White Buffalo again went completely blind. Her eyes were now a dark green, a mirror image of the crystal never again would they change to black.

*****

Shin jerked awake three hours later when he heard a groan of pain from Cecille, sitting up he stared at his charge willing her to wake up. The Tianming Monk watched her face scrunch up in pain he moaned in denial wishing he could make it all better for her; his love for her hadn't diminished even a little nor will it ever. Shadow Stalker loved his wife, but it was nothing compared to his feelings for White Buffalo. Unable to help himself, he reached out to stroke her cheek.

Cecille opened her deep green unseeing eyes; instantly she lifted her hand putting it over Shin's that was still on the side of her face. She smiled up sweetly at the Tianming Monk before dropping her hand back onto the bed even that movement exhausted her. White Buffalo turned her head towards the shaman when Shadow Stalker moved his hand away the old shaman had quieted as soon as her eyes opened. Her grin this time was appreciative his chanting had kept her from losing her way. "Thank you!"

Shin waited until Cecille turned back to him; he gave a hesitant grin in question even though he knew she could not see it. The Tianming Monk told White Buffalo everything that happened after she passed out, he also told her all about the people that helped them; Shadow Stalker made sure to mention they were also related to her husband and daughter when she was born.

Shin kept talking he watched Cecille for any signs that the changes in her would affect her negatively. When the Tianming Monk hadn't seen any difference in White Buffalo's responses, he had to ask the big question outright. "How are you feeling now, you have been out for a little over twenty-four hours? Do you want to stay another night or should I go to town to pick up some trail supplies; it will take me a couple of hours at least so you can sleep a little longer if you need too?"

Cecille listening to Shin ramble on with half an ear took a long hard look at herself; the first thing she did was rub her left palm. There was no soreness or bumps on it at all she dropped her hand back to the bed in relief. White Buffalo felt a bit strange at first she couldn't figure out what was missing. She tried to connect to the Mother Earth, but she couldn't feel anything. Her ability to draw magic from Po was now gone, she felt empty before anger took its place.

Cecille's feelings ran the whole gauntlet of emotions for several long minutes, from anger to fear than to relief and beyond. It wasn't until she remembered a discussion she had with her father when the healer was fourteen that her world once again righted itself; White Buffalo had asked Edward how he managed to cope with the loss of his powers. She recalled Dream Dancer's answer with both fondness and love...

*****

Edward gathered Cecille in his arms then held her tight before sitting back. He smiled tenderly at White Buffalo's serious face his daughter's question wasn't one he took lightly. Dream Dancer's expression turned inward for several minutes remembering a time he would always wish he could forget, but he knew he never would be able too. "Your mother at first was the reason I wasn't consumed by my feelings of anger at losing a part of myself. Crystin filled the hole up until she died having you. Afterwards, you became my rock my reason to live. Even to this day, I thank the Great Spirit that you were given to me to help heal that loss. Once I allowed my love for you to blossom inside me it filled the emptiness until it disappeared altogether; replaced by a deeper love for you that kept me over full always!"

*****

Cecille put her left hand on her distended belly and felt a welcoming kick. White Buffalo instantly felt love for her daughter filling up the hole; she grinned in relief as she tenderly stroked her stomach. Her baby was all that mattered now so too was getting back to her husband. The healer looked up at Shin before smiling in acceptance. "I wish to leave as soon as possible I can sleep more while you gather supplies. I will be ready to go when you get back."

Shin stared down in astonishment at Cecille when he noticed a difference in her eyes; they were a deeper brighter shade of green, now they really reminded the Tianming Monk of the crystal dragon eye on her medallion. He never said a word about it, just glad that White Buffalo was taking this so calmly; Shadow Stalker bent before kissing her on the forehead, mumbling farewell he turned away leaving her to sleep.

*****

Shin, wanting Cecille to have a little more time to gather her strength, slowly wandered down the main street of town. He looked around in interest at the few places in Timbrell hearing about a place wasn't the same as seeing it for oneself. The hotel had a stable which the chief hadn't mentioned. The Tianming Monk didn't need to stop there for any reason, so it hadn't mattered. He was surprised such a small town had a sheriff's office. Unfortunately, the old man didn't mention that either Shadow Stalker couldn't help giving it a weary look. It was on the left side of the hotel, with a saloon across from it. He didn't have any business at either place, so he ignored his unease.

Shin looked further up the road then saw a large fort with a fence around it at the end of the street; he nudged his horse to pick up speed now wanting to get out of town quicker. The Tianming Monk looked down at Misfit, and her pup. The tone of his voice told them that he wouldn't tolerate disobedience. "Stay close now!"

Misfit looked up at Shin attentively as he spoke; when the Tianming Monk was finished giving instructions, she looked back down. Cecille's dog nudged Little Miss closer to the packhorse she followed directly behind her to keep her eye on the mischievous, playful pup.

Shin rode through the gates he continued riding straight to a hitching post to the left of the stairs leading up to the front of the porch; the Tianming Monk nodded cordially towards the four men sitting around smoking cigars but didn't say anything wanting to get his business done and over.

Shin dismounted then loosely flipped Grey's reins over the railing. Untying the packhorse from the stallion, he did the same for her. Standing between the two horses, Shadow Stalker reached in the far pocket of the pack that their clothes were in to pull out a billfold hidden in there. He stuffed it into his pocket quickly glad the four men wouldn't be able to see what he was doing. The Guardian undid the two empty packs. Lifting them, he put one over each of his shoulders.

Shin snapped his fingers towards Misfit sharply to get her attention before pointing at the ground in silent command.

Misfit went over to little Miss she grabbed her by the back of her neck before pushing her pup to the ground insistently; once the runt was laying down, she let go of Shin's puppy and dropped down beside her to keep an eye on the horses. Cecille's dog would now begin her puppies training, just like her mother did with her knowing that the Tianming Monk would expect it of her.

Shin satisfied that the two would stay put, turned then walked under the mare's reins to get to the porch. He lifted his foot to take a step up but paused before his foot touched the first step as one of the four men spat on it. The Tianming Monk put his foot back down on the ground beside his other one. The monk looked at the deputy's badge on the shirt of the grinning unrepentant lawman. Damn, it just figures the Guardian couldn't help thinking. Shadow Stalker looked at the other three men all wearing badges as well; the one to the far left was the sheriff, he had a smile on his face waiting to see what the Oriental would do next.

Shin's lip curled up on the right in a sardonic sarcastic grin, the Tianming Monk looked at the four again. He could tell right off that the four scruffy looking men were all brothers bored so were looking to add a little excitement to their day. Shadow Stalker didn't have time to waste on them. He gestured towards the front door in inquiry making sure to speak loud enough for whoever was inside to hear him. "Is the trading post not open for business, gentlemen; I can go to the saloon for a drink while I'm waiting for it to open or better yet I might head to the next town instead?!"

Shin barely got the last word out when the door was flung open by an older grey haired slim Frenchman. He rushed out in excitement gesturing for him to follow. He made sure to turn towards the sheriff with a warning look before his voice showed his displeasure at the lawman's antics. "Bonjour mon ami, we are always open. Come you must come inside now; please, you must excuse the rudeness of these men they were just leaving, my employer will not like that they are scaring off customers!"

Shin walking past the deputy that spat on the step just couldn't help his reaction. The lawman was leaning on the back two legs of his chair insolently, the Tianming Monk stumbled to the right before accidentally never on purpose, of course; kicked the leg of the chair sending the man sprawling. Shadow Stalker stopped immediately, with a mortified grin he held out his hand to help the man up. "So sorry about my clumsiness Deputy, here allow me to help you!"

Shin heard snickering behind him, but he ignored it as he cordially held out his hand to help the man up. When the deputy refused to take it, the Tianming Monk shrugged then dropped his arm; instead, the man rolled away before getting up on his own. He dusted himself off furiously taking out some of his frustration on his pant legs. Shadow Stalker turned to follow the clerk when the Frenchman pulled insistently on his arm wanting to get him away from a potentially volatile situation.

Shin listened with half an ear to the nervous talkative clerk, without commenting once. The Tianming Monk went around gathering coffee, canned fruits, beans, flour, sugar, and anything else he could find that was dried, canned or pickled; he tried to pick foods that wouldn't spoil for at least three weeks. Shadow Stalker finished with the food, picked up more matches, toilet paper, plus dog treats. He walked up to the counter with the last items, he interrupted the Frenchman. "Do you have bacon or fresh pork fat?"

The clerk nodded vigorously with a wave of his hands dramatically; he was a very expressive Frenchman his hands were seldom still, especially when he was nervous. "Mon ami you are in luck, yesterday our freshly butchered pig and cow were both done being smoked; not only do I have bacon, but ham, pork fat, beef jerky, sausages, we also have lots of smoked fish. All are guaranteed to last at least two weeks on the trail, maybe more now that the weather has cooled down some."

Shin nodded pleased by the variety he took a little of everything except fish; the village already offered him enough to see them all the way to New Brunswick. The Tianming Monk paid for all his purchases then loaded his two packs. He had problems with the last can of pears going in since they were so full. Shadow Stalker looked over the counter at the French clerk, hopefully. "Would it be too much trouble for you to open the door for me please, my hands are a bit full!"

The clerk rushed back to the front with a chagrined grin, the Frenchman dramatically smacked his own forehead with the palm of his hand at his own stupidity; he reached out for one of the satchels, but turned away when the Oriental stepped back. "Oh sacrebleu monsieur, so sorry I not think of that myself, here I will help carry one!"

Shin grimaced at the over dramatic Frenchman, he stepped away with a shake of his head before giving a lopsided grin; the Tianming Monk gestured with his head to the door. "Just open the front door for me please, I will carry them myself thank you."

The clerk mumbling under his breath in French about how stupid he was for not offering to help the Oriental didn't realize Shin understood everything he was saying. Scurrying ahead the Frenchman pulled open the door gravely with a bow he made a grand sweeping gesture. "Mon ami, please come back anytime!"

Shin took a big step to the right he was looking for any type of shadow that shouldn't be there. In satisfaction he eyed the empty porch on the left side of the doorway. He walked closer to the clerk next to look towards his horse's cautiously, they were on the right side of the porch; from this angle he could see his stallion standing with his ears straight up both were pointing forward inquisitively as he stared at the corner of the building. The Tianming Monk looked underneath the mare and saw Misfit crouched with her hackles up, also watching that corner. Shadow Stalker dropped his packsaddles on the floor before he pulled out his two dragon daggers in preparation.

Shin dived out the door at the same time he rolled himself into a ball to give them as little target as possible. Once all the way out, the Tianming Monk vaulted up into a crouch before turning. Swiftly he swept one dagger out low to bury the knife into the deputy's fleshy thigh that was waiting for him with a club. He didn't want to kill anyone then have the law looking for him. Shadow Stalker instantly jumped to his feet at a scream of pain; with a roundhouse kick, he sent the man hurtling through space to land unceremoniously into the horse's water trough out cold.

Shin dropped into a crouch; the Tianming Monk looked towards the other deputy in challenge. The younger brother, not wanting anything to do with the knife-wielding Oriental turned and fled looking for the sheriff. He needed to come up with a plausible story quickly before someone else told his brother what happened; especially, since the sheriff had explicitly told them to stay away from the stranger. Of course, once again his cocky brother had gotten him into another mess wanting to teach the Chink some manners.

Shin rushed down the stairs; he pulled the lawman partway out of the water not wanting him to drown before his brothers could get to him. The Tianming Monk trotted back into the trading post then picked up his two saddle packs; Shadow Stalker inclined his head in farewell towards the French clerk who was staring at him in amazement for once in his life utterly speechless.

Shin went to the packhorse quickly he loaded her up as fast as he could. The Tianming Monk needed to get out of here before the sheriff showed up; if the older brother ended up in the middle of this, he would take his brother's side regardless of the law. Shadow Stalker had seen it happen too many times in the past not to know what the outcome would be.

Shin tied the packhorse to the back of Grey's saddle he whistled for Little Miss to come to him before picking up his pup; quickly he vaulted onto his stallion's back. Misfit would either keep up or find them later at the Indian village. The Tianming Monk kicked the stud hard in demand; they raced out of the gates then down the main street. Hearing a shout behind him, the Guardian looked behind his shoulder he saw the sheriff running towards the trading post. Shadow Stalker leaned down closer to his horse's neck, nudging him for more speed.

*****

Cecille stretched cautiously taking her time she did a self-check to make sure nothing was injured; feeling okay, she reached down to stroke the bulge in her belly she got a nice healthy kick, which made White Buffalo smile lovingly. She paused for a moment when she felt a pang; promptly, the healer put her other hand on her stomach before bringing up a mental image of herself that she had seen in the valley. She had decided to use it to picture her daughter knowing she would look just like her when she grew up even down to being blind.

Cecille rolled over onto her hands and knees she felt around looking for her cane knowing Shin would have left it close for her. When she found it, she stood up still being a bit cautious, at least until the healer was sure everything was okay; she walked around a bit but felt no after-effects from her overuse of the Mother Earth's magic. White Buffalo heard the flap on the wigwam being opened she caulked her head inquisitively before speaking in her husband's language. "Hello!"

Misfit barked sharply in ecstatic hello she rushed to her mistress in greeting. Shin glad to see Cecille up, rushed around quickly gathering the few things he had unpacked. The Tianming Monk wasn't sure if the sheriff would come this far or not, but he didn't want to wait around to find out. "It's me White Buffalo; we need to go now!"

Cecille frowned grimly at Shin, not liking this mad rush all of a sudden. She wanted to have a bath or a purifying sweat if nothing else before they left she needed guidance that only a shaman could give her; White Buffalo knelt allowing Misfit then Little Miss to greet her. "What happened in town Shadow Stalker, were you able to get supplies?"

Shin went over to Cecille's sleeping pallet before picking up her white buffalo hide. Walking over, the Tianming Monk draped it on his charges shoulders when she stood up. "Four steps straight ahead is the door once outside turn to the left half a turn and walk three steps straight ahead; you will find the horses there waiting for us. Yes, I have enough supplies for two or three weeks, which will hopefully last us until we are right in New Brunswick. If at all possible, I would like to avoid any more white towns. I am sorry

White Buffalo for the rush, but I had a run in with a Deputy who tried to relieve his boredom at my expense!"

Cecille sighed in resignation clutching her robe she followed Shin's directions to the horses. White Buffalo was beginning to see a lot of wisdom in avoiding as many towns as possible from here on out; of course, there would be a few they would have no choice but to enter. The Tianming Monk was right, it would be best to avoid any more confrontations. Especially with the law, she would have to use Shadow Stalker's carpet later when they stopped for the night.

Cecille tied her robe onto the packhorse before she went over to Saya, knowing that Shin would have checked Precious already; she put her cane away then ran her hands over her mare checking to make sure she was up to a long ride. All her legs were in excellent shape with no heat around her ankles, knees or hooves. White Buffalo walked up to her head, she lifted her muzzle sniffing at her breath no unusual smells there. She couldn't hear any more laboured breathing, and she had felt the foal move inside her; relieved she kissed her mare on the nose in greeting. "Hello my lovely lady, are you ready for more long days?"

Saya breathed out a woof of air through her nostrils at Cecille before nuzzling her cheek in greeting; the mare would carry White Buffalo through a raging forest fire if asked. She would also take her through the devil's dominion without batting an eye; her mistress meant so much to her she would even gladly give up her own life to protect her.

Cecille chuckled and put her forehead against Saya's reconnecting with her mare. Hearing Shin she walked around her before mounting on her own, without waiting for her Guardian's assistance. The healer sat quietly while the Tianming Monk finished loading the packhorse; White Buffalo heard him mount, but stayed put when he began talking to someone about sending anyone looking for him in the opposite direction. Once Shadow Stalker was finished, she nudged her horse into a walk to warm her up.

Thankfully, it wasn't long until Cecille was nudging her mare into a gallop. They would have to be much more conservative now, giving the horses breaks whenever possible as they raced towards New Brunswick.

CHAPTER TWENTY FIVE

"Arghh, hee, hee, hoo, hee, hee, hoo... aawhh."

Cecille stroked her rippling belly soothingly as the contraction eventually eased; trying to be quiet was extremely difficult. She groaned softly in denial, she was only just into her eighth month it was too early. All she could hope for was that it was a false labour. White Buffalo could feel a constant pain now on her left side where the tooth was digging in. It continued pushing against her womb threatening to puncture her uterus.

Cecille looked around the Mi'kmaq tepee in anger, the Mother Earth promised she would have her baby in an Indian village; remembering back she realized Po never said where that would be at or for that matter what tribe of natives. White Buffalo just assumed it would be with her husband's people; apparently, she had been wrong.

Cecille groaned softly in regret she should have been home way before now, one frustrating delay after another kept her in New Brunswick. They finally left Dalhousie two weeks ago, but only made it to the border of Quebec. This small Indian village was straddling the line between the two provinces; severe weather was keeping them from going any further for the time being because of unprecedented snowstorms. One right after the other in quick succession was ravaging this little village out in the middle of nowhere. White Buffalo sighed forlornly, thinking back she tried hard to ignore the contractions that were beginning to get closer together...

*****

Cecille frowned grimly it took them three weeks to get to Saint-Siméon, Quebec, but she was thankful only one major problem surfacing in those weeks. White Buffalo hoped to be in New Brunswick before that, but they got stalled trying to get over a range of mountains; they had to wait in town for a guide who wasn't expected back for another two days. Once over them, they had made it to the ferryboat relatively quickly.

Cecille got told it was where they needed to catch the ferryboat to take them across to a place called Rivière-du-Loup, Quebec. White Buffalo frowned disgruntled remembering they were stuck on the far side for a week because of a hurricane. It kept all the boats in the harbour. The winds were relatively high at one hundred and five miles an hour which made it a storm the locals called a category two because it causes extensive damages. A storm this size usually has medium to large waves that aren't insurmountable; most of their high water barricades do manage to keep the seawater from completely flooding the town.

Cecille, having nothing better to do while they waited learned more than she wanted to know about these terrifying storms. White Buffalo was quite shocked that people would be willing to stay this close to the shoreline when it was a constant battle against Mother Nature. They continuously had to rebuild their homes. Especially, if it's a category three that storm had winds reaching up to one hundred and twenty-nine miles per hour, so was considered devastating. There was also a category four with winds that could get up to one hundred and fifty-six miles per hour; causing catastrophic damage.

Cecille shuddered then shook her head in amazement at the resolve of some people. If those weren't bad enough they had a category five, with winds of over one hundred and fifty-seven miles per hour. It could even reach higher speeds than that she had gotten told. They called this one the same as four, but it was more apt to wipe out whole villages, towns... even cities; with deaths in the thousands wherever it touched land. There had never been reports of a category six, probably because nobody ever survived one White Buffalo figured.

Cecille recalled in frustration that they finally docked one day into the fifth week of leaving home. Unfortunately, it took them another four days after that to get close to the border. Once in New Brunswick, it took them another three days to find a guide willing to usher them around to all the small towns throughout the province.

Shin told their escort that they were looking for a permanent place to call their own to set down roots before their baby was born; away from the racist people that didn't like Orientals and natives because White Buffalo was part Indian. The guide they found happened to have a skin tone that was medium brown pointing to a black ancestor but with an Irish last name. It fooled most people into believing that he was white.

Jacob O'Sullivan, he introduced himself as was more than willing to help them find a place. Even though his father was black, he had never been a slave himself the guide explained to Cecille on their journey, since he was born a free man. His father

Jacob the first had been born a slave, though. Despite the law forbidding it, his father had fallen in love with an Irish indentured servant in New Hampshire where they were living in the United States. Unfortunately, he died trying to get his wife and unborn son into Canada before she went into labour; the guide never met his late father who he was named after. Although, the guide had his mother's Irish last name because as far as she knew his father had no knowledge of his.

Jacob was extremely proud of his father because his sacrifice ensured his son wouldn't feel the touch of a slavers cat-o'-nine-tails in his lifetime; the whip could have up to seven braided tails with knots at the end of each braid, it was used for a variety of physical punishments. It was invented in the late sixteen hundreds, these days there was a lot more variations in style or length to choose from.

The cat-o'-nine-tails were not only utilized on plantations, nor was it used just on black slaves as some believed, but were deployed everywhere these days. It was used now on every skin colour to torture slaves, seaman, indentured servants, and animals. They were even in use in brothels against fancy woman, for men who enjoyed that kind of sick pleasure.

Cecille shuddered at the thought of the whip that was sometimes affectionately called the cat by the more enthusiastic users. It instantly brought to mind an image of a long lost memory. Now, White Buffalo wished it had remained forgotten; she shivered in disgust.

Edward had taken a room for them in one of the small towns they usually only passed through; having had a late start Dream Dancer figured it would be best if they stop here. It was one of Quebec's quaint hamlets there were several of them between the Indian village and Montreal where they went to play their yearly golf game.

The local sheriff caught a man who stole a loaf of bread. They tied him to a post beside the sheriff's office, which was put there for this purpose. The unfortunate thief was publicly flogged to teach him, plus everyone else in town a lesson. At the third snap of the whip, even the most hardened person there winced. It was plain cruel watching what the seven tails could do when it was hitting a man's bare back shredding the skin to pieces.

Cecille only fifteen buried her face in her father's chest when blood sprayed everywhere even to this day she remembered the man's screams. Dream Dancer having seen enough marched over, taking the whip from the deputy wielding it before paying a penalty to the sheriff for the man's release; White Buffalo never heard what happened to the victim afterwards.

*****

Cecille's shuddering thankfully brought her out of those unpleasant memories. It took her a few minutes to shake off all thoughts of the nasty torture instrument unable to stand thinking about it for another second; it helped that suddenly she was seized by another intense contraction bringing her thoughts back to the present with a vengeance, she groaned in pain. White Buffalo again began her breathing exercises, trying to stop her spasming clenching, stomach muscles. "Hee, hee, hoo... hee, hee hoo!"

Cecille closed her eyes then slowly rode out the pain trying to be as quiet as possible, not wanting Shin to know yet she was in labour. She turned her head to the right when she heard the Tianming Monk snore. White Buffalo knew if she made too much noise, he would be by her side in an instant; from this angle, the healer knew a scar would be visible running down Shadow Stalker's face he came close to losing an eye or worse his life. With no powers she had felt helpless, no longer able to heal anyone. Now she had no choice, but to rely only on her training as a doctor.

Cecille sighed wearily; she once again went back in time to keep her mind occupied and off the possibility that this was not a false labour. White Buffalo skipped passed the first three frustrating weeks in New Brunswick nothing exciting at all had happened as they jumped from town to town searching; it wasn't until they arrived in Dalhousie that things began to change, it wasn't necessarily for the better either...

*****

Cecille could feel a sense of awe then tranquillity knowing instantly she was in God's country, as Shin described Dalhousie to her in detail. The picturesque town of New Brunswick came alive for her at that moment White Buffalo could even picture it in her mind. Forested mountains that became beautiful rolling hills filled with immense trees and flowers of every description before a valley was reached leading to the sea. The Tianming Monk's descriptions reminded her quite a lot of the two spiritual visions she had received since beginning her journey in Ontario.

Cecille wouldn't find out till much later that Dalhousie according to the locals was now the shire town of the newly founded Restigouche County. She had been pleasantly surprised to find out the town site was built right on a hillside; White Buffalo was told both salt and fresh water bodies surrounded it. The town was situated around Restigouche River Valley on the tongue of the river where it discharges into Chaleur Bay. It was an arm that eventually leads out into the Gulf of St. Lawrence. The deep waters made this the perfect stopping place for massive ships needing supplies or repairs, turning this small community into a waterfront town.

They started building in eighteen twenty-six with the first significant settlement established by Scottish settlers about eighteen twenty-seven.

Cecille ended up falling in love with Dalhousie's peaceful unsullied atmosphere portrayed by the locals. As far as she could tell from the amount of time they spent there nobody got turned away, one's nationality didn't matter here at all. White Buffalo couldn't help thinking if she had no other recourse, she would have gladly remained. The healer did have a home far away with a husband that was madly in love with her; she needed to get back to it as soon as they finished in New Brunswick.

*****

Cecille's thoughts were again wrenched back into the present as another contraction hit her, this time closer than the last. She knew instantly she could no longer fool herself, she was in full labour. White Buffalo's pains were still a bit far apart, so it would be a while yet before her daughter was born; riding out the pain as quietly as possible she closed her eyes again thinking back, it was helping her to keep from panicking. She gladly let her mind wander, remembered more of the beautiful Dalhousie...

*****

Cecille shook off her wayward thoughts before turning back to the problem at hand she frowned in worry. She still had no idea, where, who, or even when she was supposed to give this person a name from the Mother Earth. She thankfully did know that she was looking for a man; White Buffalo even knew what his name was to be, but that is all she knew so far!

Cecille no longer having the power to talk to Mother Earth whenever she wanted to needed to rely on Shin's carpet now. Unfortunately, that meant they had to spend at least one full night in each town they found. It helped the Tianming Monk keep up their ruse on looking for a place to set down roots, but so far seen nothing appealing they told Jacob. White Buffalo was getting worried, she was now in her seventh month of pregnancy and getting more uncomfortable by the day; especially, with that tooth getting closer to her womb now that the baby was growing larger. She could feel a sharp stabbing pinch in her side every time it pushed through another layer of tissue, which is how she knew it was moving.

Cecille hearing a ruckus as they rode down the main street looking for a hotel turned to Jacob; Shin managed to get the question out before White Buffalo could. Saya came to an instant stop when the stallion halted.

Shin stopping Grey in concern looked over at Jacob inquiringly; the Tianming Monk didn't want to proceed until he was sure it was okay to do so, they were more cautious since his last mishap. Neither, did he want to get mixed up in anyone else's altercation with the law! "Do you know what that is all about?"

Jacob frowned in surprise at the question before halting his horse too. He listened then shrugged in confusion; he looked over at Shin. The guide could tell instantly that the Tianming Monk was quite concerned, which suggested to him he might have a problem; maybe a wanted poster was out on him or some such thing. He shrugged, it wasn't his business he was only an escort and being paid quite handsomely. "Wait here I will be back shortly."

Jacob rode around the bend and down a hill he stopped with a chuckle before turning, he rode back to his concerned travelling companions; the guide smiled at Shin in reassurance gesturing behind him in explanation. "Looks like the circus is in town, must have pulled in only recently too because the tents are just being put up. The hotel is just passed the open field where they are beginning to set up it will be a noisy night."

Shin nodded in relief the three continued to the hotel; the Tianming Monk let the guide make all the arrangements before he led Cecille to their shared room. They both dropped down on their respective beds for a much-needed nap.

*****

Cecille's groan of pain brought her out of the past, it was much louder now. Instantly Shin was kneeling beside her bed in concern. The Tianming Monk scowled in anxiety. He had suspected from the beginning that he would never get to see his son in this lifetime. Shadow Stalker prepared for that left his bow behind for his son;

since the Guardian had known he also gave his wife the boy's Oriental name. "You are in labour already, White Buffalo? Did your water break and how far apart are the contractions?"

Shin sighed in relief when Cecille shook her head negatively; she didn't speak right away too busy concentrating on her breathing. The Tianming Monk got up then turned towards his corner the first thing he grabbed was his carpet. He brought it over before laying it under White Buffalo when she moved out of the way.

Cecille felt better once the Japanese rug got placed over her white buffalo hide; she hadn't even realized until now she had been worried about it, not wanting any fluid to stain her beautiful fur. White Buffalo knew the carpet would capture all the liquid and blood her body produced keeping it trapped inside. Why it did so, she couldn't figure out even the Tianming Monk didn't know the reason for sure.

Shin pulled the covers over Cecille once she was lying back on her pallet the Tianming Monk stood up. "I will talk to the medicine woman about what herbs around here can be used in a tea for your pain; I will send her in to help you after."

Cecille nodded in relief she watched Shin go as the contraction thankfully eased; White Buffalo allowed her mind to drift once again back to Dalhousie while she waited for the medicine woman to come...

*****

Cecille sitting in front of Shin on his carpet smiled in relief when she came out of her trance; the man they were looking for was somewhere near or around Dalhousie she was told to stay here. White Buffalo got up in excitement. "Shadow Stalker if I can find him tonight or tomorrow, maybe we can head home right away!"

Shin got up then gestured at Cecille in caution the Tianming Monk needed White Buffalo to stay focused. "It could still take a week or so, don't forget this town isn't that small; with ships coming in and out, it could even be a sailor we are looking for. We still have no clue at all who it could be how do you propose going about finding him?"

Cecille frowned thoughtfully then caulked her head as she listened to music coming from the circus; White Buffalo smiled in delight having the perfect solution.

Cecille spun around in excitement till she was facing the retreating Shin who had gone to put his carpet away. "Why don't we go ask for a job at the circus, if we get something that deals with men they will come to us. Remember in England we had a lady that gave out a kiss for a shilling, it would be perfect. I distinctly recall even Father went over to sample the woman's charms before he had to knock out a fellow who refused to leave her alone. I should be able to do that, with you as my bodyguard just to make sure nobody takes unfair advantage. Thankfully I did bring a ball gown with me that was my Mother's favourite. It has a black lace mask to go with it since I wasn't sure what was needed once we got here I brought it along. It is old-fashioned, but it should work. Maybe you can wear your ninja outfit because it covers your face, which would make you a mystery to everyone; it will stop you from scare away customers too."

Shin groaned in protest; the Tianming Monk remembered that poor lady the men harassed her quite a bit, but after Edward started staying in the booth, she had no problems. Shadow Stalker wasn't looking forward to spending hours standing still in a booth. He eyed Cecille imploringly and tried to change her mind. "White Buffalo, can't we do a high wire act or something similar. What about balancing on your horses back; I do different stunts around you. That would be better than an annoying kissing stall!"

Cecille laughed at the plaintiff note in Shin's voice; unfortunately White Buffalo got her way.

*****

Cecille was brought back to the present by Shin arguing with the medicine woman as they entered the tepee. The Mi'kmaq medicine woman wanted White Buffalo to get up to move around, tea for pain wasn't permitted. Their woman never lay down to have a baby, but squatted making the passage for the infant easier. The Tianming Monk was afraid his charge would be away from the carpet making it possible they would miss the birth water and blood going on the rug; it was imperative that it do so!

Cecille propped herself up, she motioned for the medicine woman to come speak to her. White Buffalo explained about the tooth that was pushing against her uterus, which already put her baby in danger. "Shadow Stalker is right it is too risky any untold motion could puncture my womb before the baby is in the birth passage; if that happened you will have to cut the baby out of me, instead of her coming out naturally on her own. That I will die having her is the will of the Great Spirit it is already known to me."

The medicine woman frowned troubled, but eventually nodded before beckoning for Shin to follow her. "Come, I will make White

Buffalo a special blend of herbs that will relax her enough she will not feel the need to push; the baby won't be affected because it's not a tea, but inhaled from a pipe allowing the baby to come naturally in her own time. Your wife will drift in the spirit world, which will help give her an easier almost pain-free death if it's truly the Great Spirit's wish."

Cecille settled back when another contraction hit, she groaned grimly this one was more powerful than the others, they were getting even closer together now. White Buffalo again rode out the pain before her thoughts wandered back to Dalhousie again, a whole useless week they spent at the circus; she lost track of the number of men that came and went, they were all a bunch of faceless slobbering drunken sailors most of them, anyway...

*****

Cecille grimaced in disgust before pushing the offending drunken leach away he must have thrown up not long ago his sour breath reeked of it. White Buffalo heard a lot of groans of disappointment when she put up a closed sign then shut down her booth having had enough today; she heard Shin chuckle behind her, but the healer ignored his I told you so attitude that she put up with the last two days. The circus was only here for another week, so far they hadn't gotten anywhere in their search for the mystery man.

Cecille turned around promptly then grabbed her walking cane, but only after she scowled in anger at Shin; she marched out of the booth in a huff, leaving the chuckling Tianming Monk behind. The healer really didn't need him right now anyway, she knew the way by heart. He could come with her or not, right now she didn't care one way or another. She could feel time slipping away she needed to get to the main tent to change her costume. One of the ladies had been kind enough to lend it to her after the second day in the same outfit. White Buffalo switched to Japanese so nobody else would understand what they were saying when she heard her Guardian following her dutifully. "What do YOU suggest we do now Shadow Stalker, since you were right about this not working?"

Shin sighed grimly he didn't have any clue on how to find the man either. They couldn't use the carpet except at night... or could they! The Tianming Monk getting an idea rushed up to catch Cecille's attention. "White Buffalo there is a rumour going around the circus that there is a surprise addition to tomorrow's show, a magician from the United States. The strong man told me yesterday they always keep at least one act back until later, giving people an incentive to come one more time. Maybe we can talk whoever it is into letting us be the first or second act. I can set up the carpet on stage then have someone from the audience sit with you. When you are telling him his future I can stand behind you on the rug it will give me a chance to search with the carpet; hopefully, we can find the man we are looking for that way."

Cecille stopped in excitement, Shin almost slammed into her not expecting her to halt. White Buffalo turned to the Tianming Monk ecstatically. "That is an excellent idea Shadow Stalker we can wear out Japanese robes since we only have a few more days; let's go see Timothy, I am sure he can find someone to take over the kissing booth."

Shin nodded in agreement, they changed directions looking for the master of ceremonies; the Tianming Monk knew it would depend on his approval. Cecille liked him, but Shadow Stalker didn't. He was a strange individual with white skin and hair; he had shocking eye colours, one brown and one very light blue eye. It reminded him of his stallion making him uncomfortable.

*****

Cecille was brought back to the present by Shin and the medicine woman arguing again as they entered the tepee; the Tianming Monk didn't like one of the ingredients the Mi'kmaq healer used, it was known to kill. Usually, it caused a horrible painful death. White Buffalo sighed in aggravation she really didn't need this stress right now as she listened to her Guardian's concerns. "I'm telling you it is too risky using that flower!"

The medicine woman tsked in irritation she stopped at Cecille's pallet then dropped into a sitting position with legs curled to the right. Sitting with legs crossed wasn't permitted to Mi'kmaq women since this was more becoming to a woman. "I hear your worry for your wife Shadow Stalker, but I'm telling you it works differently when smoked; the healers of my tribe have been using it since time began, to help a woman who is dying in childbirth. It will relax the muscles that cause the contractions, so her womb will not clench itself when one hits. This should stop the tooth from moving any further, which is our primary concern right now. When combined with other herbs it allows the baby to move down the birth canal because the muscles are more pliable, so they stretch easier and there's no tearing."

Cecille took Shin's hand when he knelt beside her; she squeezed it affectionately with a sad knowing smile at her Guardian. She listened with half an ear when the medicine woman told her what herbs were in the pipe. It really didn't matter as long as the baby wasn't affected by the drug.

Cecille smiled at Shin knowing he would fight this till the end, White Buffalo needed his tenacity now not his unwillingness to let her go. She nodded permission at the Mi'kmaq healer to light the pipe before switching to Japanese; White Buffalo stared forlornly at the brother she felt the Tianming Monk to be. "Don't fail me now Shadow Stalker, I need your strength to help see me through this. I would like you to take me one last time to see my husband if the Great Spirit will allow it only you can help me with that!"

Shin stared down in distress at the woman he loved, but could never have. The Tianming Monk bent forward to kiss Cecille on the forehead. He closed his eyes in anguish; holding that pose for a long moment, he worked at concealing his feelings before finally succeeding. He got to his feet and nodded his face now completely expressionless. "I will go prepare myself White Buffalo, I will return shortly!"

Cecille nodded as she watched Shin go sadly, he had now shut her out; leaving the Tianming Monk with the fortitude that would now be her strength to do what needed done. White Buffalo sighed grimly then taking the pipe she inhaled deeply. She continued to puff away until there were no herbs left in the bowl before she passed it back to the medicine woman. Closing her eyes, she allowed herself to drift back one last time to Dalhousie while she waited for Shadow Stalker to return...

*****

Cecille frowned anxiously; all White Buffalo could hear was a constant noisy buzz of people, according to the stage manager, it was an over-packed tent. They hadn't anticipated two large freight ships docking during the night there was wall to wall people. He told her that unless you were one of the wealthy patrons at the front with seats or a ship's captain, you had to stand.

Cecille sat in the middle of the carpet nervously plucking at her wine coloured Oriental outfit that White Buffalo was wearing. They were the opening act, followed soon afterwards by one of the Marco Magic Company Magicians by the name of Harry Weiss; a fledgling magician, who only joined the group a few years ago. Unfortunately, they hadn't had a chance to meet him yet since he got held up by a new contraption he wanted to try escaping from. The stage manager laughed in delight even though they ended up having to come to the young man's aid earlier Harry was still determined to try it again tonight, on stage this time.

    Shin standing behind Cecille in his flowing Samurai robes from his homeland knelt when he felt his charge wanting to panic then run. The Tianming Monk put a hand on her shoulder in reassurance. "Are you alright, White Buffalo reach your hand back to take hold of my robe, we will get through this together; just relax, all you need to do is hum until it is time for the telling I will take care of the rest."

    Shin stood back up in satisfaction when he felt Cecille take a deep fortifying breath slowly she released it humming softly she began rocking, which relaxed her. The Tianming Monk stood up he nodded that they were ready towards the man waiting to lift the curtain. All the lights were shut off instantly before the crowd quieted as the squeaky curtain rose. Shadow Stalker nudged White Buffalo insistently, obediently her humming became a louder chant; his voice was added to hers as a spotlight suddenly lit the stage, the Guardian raised his arms up in preparation. Suddenly he dropped them, which was the signal for the flares to be lit sending sparks of red, orange, and yellow flying around the stage dramatically.

    Shin, ignoring the clapping of awe from the crowd brought his carpet to life asking the Great Spirit for help in finding the man Cecille was seeking. The Tianming Monk frowned when nothing happened maybe he wasn't even here; about to nudge his charge again on the other side of her hip this time, to tell her he was getting no answer; suddenly, felt someone rushing towards the back of the stage. He was out of breath in a hurry though, hoping he wasn't too late to watch his very own opening act. He was quite excited since he had always been the opening act himself.

    Shin immediately lifted his arms high with a jerk giving another prearranged signal to the stage manager before nudging his charge twice with his left foot; now she would have fair warning too. Instantly the flames were extinguished leaving everyone in the dark once again abruptly he quit chanting; White Buffalo went back to humming softly she let go of her Guardian's robes so he could gather the man they needed.

    Cecille's voice rose slowly higher and higher bringing the suspense to a peek before suddenly she felt Shin behind her once more; she gave a brief scream of victory, which was the signal for the spotlight to light up the stage once again. White Buffalo speaking in a complicated combination of languages reached out to take the young man's hands now sitting in front of her; she went back to chanting softly so that the Tianming Monk would now be able to be heard.

Shin's voice rose dramatically above Cecille's, giving his opening speech. The Tianming Monk chose his words carefully than at the end he softened his tone to a singsong chant. Hoping nobody in the audience knew Cheyenne the Guardian switched languages once his introduction was complete so only White Buffalo would understand what he was saying; this way he could tell her everything the carpet was revealing to him. "The one we have travelled long and far searching for is now sitting before Madame Cecille. The blind Oriental seeker who knows all... what message will Po the Mother Earth reveal to her today."

Cecille released the man's hands before leaning forward she cupped his face tenderly. White Buffalo's chanting quit so she could hear her Guardian; she felt the magician's brow, cheeks, hawkish nose then finally his strong chin. "You were born on March twenty-fourth, eighteen seventy-four in Budapest and you are one of seven children. In eighteen ninety-one at the age of seventeen you began your magic career becoming what was affectionately called, 'the king of cards'; soon afterwards you met a lady everyone fondly calls Bess, you married her last year."

Cecille rattled off several more unknown facts about the man that wasn't common knowledge like his childhood name as well as where he grew up; she was so accurate, it shocked the man who was now calling himself Harry. Unexpectedly, White Buffalo let go of the man's face and sat back. "The Mother Earth wants you to know that cards aren't what you are meant for; it is time to embrace your inner self to become the man you were born to be. Always take pleasure in the escape never say it can't be done."

Cecille sat forward before whispering into the astonished magician's ear. White Buffalo gave the man his spirit name from the Mother Earth. "You are Honey Badger because the badger is one of the best escape artists in the animal kingdom; a fierce Houdini of unprecedented ability able to get out of any trap, cage or enclosure man can devise."

Cecille sitting back gave him one warning that she hoped he would heed. White Buffalo threw her arms up dramatically before pointing at the other end of the stage in command. "There will come a day in your future when you will break one of your legs; don't allow anyone near you until after it has completely healed for the one who wishes you harm will deliver the final blow if you do. Begone, now another is being called to take your place."

Shin brought Cecille two more people from the audience eventually bowing they were able to leave the stage to the thunderous clapping of appreciation; the Tianming Monk gathered up his carpet himself not trusting anyone else to handle it. Promptly he locked the rug away in his trunk then hoisted it to his shoulder. Afterwards, they left the packed tent.

The two of them raced back to the hotel to change while a brief intermission got called so the next act could set up his equipment. They were both hoping to get back in time before Honey Badger started his show, wanting to see him in action. Tonight was a turning point in the young man's life. Cecille was thrilled to be a part of it. Hopefully, tomorrow they could pack up and be on their way home.

*****

Cecille was standing in the wings when she heard thunderous applause. She knew Harry was now trotting out to the middle of the stage. Shin was giving a verbal description of everything happening around them. White Buffalo turned then smiled in hello at the magician's wife who was standing further to their left; the Tianming Monk warned his charge when Bess arrived.

Cecille turned back to the stage, listening to the young man's opening speech. She couldn't help grinning in satisfaction when he paused for a dramatic moment at his stage name before suddenly, she heard him introduce himself. "Ladies and Gentlemen, thank you all for joining me tonight. I am Harry... Houdini! An escape artist who knows neither fear nor bounds, from this day forward never again will I be held captive by any man-made devices!"

Shin was whispering in Cecille's ear Shadow Stalker was trying hard to describe all the exciting drama; he added the dramatic visionary images the Tianming Monk knew she couldn't see for herself. "A woman is holding some kind of weird looking jacket towards him it's white and it will hook up behind him so it is backwards looking."

"My lovely assistant is holding out what is known as a straitjacket; I found it in one of the worst partially hidden *underground prisons I had ever seen… the Nova Scotia asylum; it is used to keep restrained the most venomous, unbalanced, psychotic individuals that are known to man. There is no way to escape this jacket I got told, but tonight you will see it done; observe as my assistant also uses huge reinforced chains with locks to keep me from getting free."*

Cecille caulked her head listening to the chains rattling dramatically then locks clicking shut, abruptly a long silence prevailed. Shin described the lights as they began to flicker rapidly before darkness unexpectedly descended. He started counting until he reached twenty-five. White Buffalo was only listening to the Tianming Monk with half an ear as she heard in extreme satisfaction, the new escape artist dropping chains and locks.

Music began rising, increasing the drama as the minutes ticked by at a sharp discorded note the music quit, instantly the lights came back on; the jacket with chains sitting on top was laying on the floor with no Harry Houdini anywhere around.

Several stunned hushed minutes later the music once again started up increasing to a suspenseful note before a grinning Harry rushed back onto the stage; he bowed to the audience that was giving him a thunderous ovation of delighted disbelief.

Cecille inhaled in shock at the sound of a loud crack as a support beam come loose from the rigging above. She screamed at Shin in warning. White Buffalo couldn't see it, but she could hear it as it fell straight down towards the oblivious Harry; who could not hear anything above the thunderous cheers of the crowd!

Shin without hesitation immediately ran towards the young escape artist; he lunged forward to push Harry out of the way, but was unable to move out of the path of the falling rigging himself. The Tianming Monk looked up then saw a shadow running towards the far end of the scaffold that was the last thing Shadow Stalker saw.

A massive beam hit Shin just above his left eye and everything went black instantly, the Tianming Monk toppled backward with blood spraying everywhere!

PROLOGUE

Spirit Bear stood up from his squatting position by the door of the sweat lodge; he had prepared himself already and he felt renewed. The medicine man was naked now except for a loincloth, this would be his third night in a row visiting the spirit world. It would be his last for at least a few days since too many trips could result in a seizure causing death.

Spirit Bear scowled grimly; he entered the lodge needing to find answers to what happened to Cecille. His wife should have been back here by now White Buffalo had promised him.

Spirit Bear had been completely frustrated in his search; the Great Spirit wasn't answering any of the medicine man's beseeching prayers so far. If he didn't get any answers tonight, he might take some warriors with him to help him search. At least up to the first white town they found; maybe White Buffalo was held up somewhere and needed help.

Spirit Bear picked up his sacred white spirit bear hide that had been in his family since before they came to these hidden mountains. He draped it over his shoulders then sat cross-legged in front of the fire. He put in front of him the medallion that Cecille had given to him; all the while he continued watching the new Powaw intently as he put water on the rocks. White Buffalo's husband accepted the tea that got handed to him. Next, he puffed on the long pipe.

Getting desperate Spirit Bear had asked their new spiritual leader for help in his search this time. His hope was that it would bring out their tribe's totem, mooksgmol the white spirit bear. That is why he had brought his hide tonight as well, it might give him the little extra help he needed. When the medicine man was ready, he picked up the necklace clutching it desperately.

The shaman advised Spirit Bear to have the medallion close to him because it was a direct link to Cecille. He was ready to try anything that might help him. The medicine man began rocking and chanting as he pleaded to the Great Spirit again. He clutched the cross with the dragon on it; desperately, he searched for White Buffalo.

****

Cecille reached up then stroked Shin's painted face tracing the scar that almost took his life. It was a four-day struggle between life and death for her Guardian; after, days of sleepless nights trying to save

Shadow Stalker's eye with no powers White Buffalo accomplished what the Dalhousie doctor said was impossible. Two days later, the Tianming Monk thankfully opened both his eyes.

Cecille's hand dropped back to her side unable to hold it up any longer it took a lot of willpower to lift it that high. She smiled up at Shin with a lopsided delirious grin; she couldn't help thinking that the Tianming Monk looked quite fierce with all that paint on White Buffalo was so stoned she could hardly move any of her muscles.

Thankfully, Cecille had no pains nor did White Buffalo feel her water break twenty minutes ago. "You are my best friend Shadow Stalker I will miss you the most my loyal Guardian. In my saddlebag with my clothes is a bible inside is a will that I had my father's lawyer make up before we began our journey. It leaves you as the sole Guardian of my daughter with full access to all funds to help raise her. My father left one estate in Wales to me, so you need to take that letter to a lawyer to have it transferred into my daughter's name. When she is eighteen, she will be able to take full possession of it. Promise me you will give her the name Pamela Cecille Luan Gweneal Summerset. Her native name, of course, will be White Buffalo. I am entrusting my most prized possession to you, my blood brother, and my friend!"

Shin lifted Cecille's upper body into his arms so he would be sitting directly on his carpet with her leaning against him. He made sure her lower body was still on the rug. He used this Japanese carpet only two days ago to watch the birth of his son, now he would use it to help his charge. The Tianming Monk made everyone leave the tepee not wanting anyone to witness what would be taking place. Only the medicine woman was allowed to come back inside, but only when he called for her.

Shin choking back a lump in his throat was finally able to answer Cecille. "I promise to guard her with my life, and I will love her as my own. I love you White Buffalo, my blood sister, and my best friend; are you ready to say goodbye to your husband now?"

Cecille nodded before accepting the pipe Shin passed her, she inhaled deeply; she wouldn't be able to drink the tea, but because of the herbs she smoked earlier it became unnecessary for her to do so. White Buffalo passed the pipe back to the Tianming Monk then began humming in time to Shadow Stalker's chanting.

****

Spirit Bear after chanting for well over an hour and nothing happening eventually stopped before opening his eyes. He looked down at the medallion angrily in frustration. Suddenly, his eyes widened in shock when he felt it getting hot in his hands. He stared at it in fascination as a flicker of an image appeared in the green eye of the dragon. Unexpectedly, it expanded until he could see Shin all painted holding Cecille up against him, the medicine man cried out in shock. He dropped the medallion in fear, which severed the connection; realizing what he had done he desperately made a grabbed for the necklace. Chanting he tried to bring the image back so he could see his White Buffalo again.

****

Cecille cried out in denial when she only saw Spirit Bear for a second before he was gone; White Buffalo clutched at Shin in desperation when the Tianming Monk quit chanting unsure if he would be able to continue. "Please Shadow Stalker try again!"

Shin frowned, noticing the tea he hadn't given to Cecille he reached for it. He drank it down in one gulp before feeling a powerful rush course through his veins, having ingested too much of the hallucinogen. He hoped it wouldn't have any lasting effects; the Tianming Monk went back to chanting powerfully, again an image of Spirit Bear formed.

Cecille reached out beseechingly staring at her husband's image sadly but White Buffalo knew he wouldn't be able to take her hand. "I'm so sorry I will not make it back home... already I am in labour, our daughter will be born away from her people. Unfortunately, it is the Great Spirit's wish that I die in childbirth. Our daughter must stay here to be raised in this Mi'kmaq village. We will meet again in the realm of the Great Spirit one day my love. Look after Shadow Stalker's wife and son, he will look after our daughter raising her like his own so too should you raise his son as yours; I charge you both with this responsibility. Keep the medallion safe my love, someone I'm sure will come for it someday."

*****

Spirit Bear cried out in desperation as he stared at Cecille forlornly. The medicine man held his hand out, palm outwards he put it as close to hers as he could. "I love you my beautiful White Buffalo, we will be together again someday; this I swear to you, not even the Great Spirit can keep us apart for long. I will gladly do as you ask my love, Shadow Stalker's Son will become a fierce warrior of the people this I vow to you both."

Spirit Bear watched Cecille fade, but suddenly without warning at all the image brightened. He watched in horrified anguish as White

Buffalo gave birth to their daughter. The last thing he heard was his wife screaming out his name before she died; even Shin was unaware the medicine man remained connected to the carpet.

****

Shin's chanting changed becoming intense; he laid Cecille on her bed then rushed to the other side of the rug. He gently spread White Buffalo's legs before pushing his hand inside knowing she wouldn't be able to feel it. He helped the baby out the rest of the way. The Tianming Monk called out for the medicine woman; he relinquished the child to the Mi'kmaq healer so she could cut the umbilical cord.

Shin rushed back to his charge, the Tianming Monk with blood dripping from his hands held on to her desperately. Shadow Stalker managed to whisper in Japanese one final parting. "Pamela is absolutely beautiful... goodbye my love!"

Cecille smiled sweetly in pleasure at Shin before abruptly she began convulsing, her back arched up as the tooth found a main artery... severing it. Blood spewed out of her soaking the carpet as she painfully screamed out her husband's name. The pain was brief though thanks to the medicine woman's herbs. White Buffalo's eyes closed for the last time; gladly she walked towards her father and mother who were standing at the end of her pallet waiting for her.

Now able to see, Cecille changed directions then went to stare down at her daughter; she lifted her hand to stroke Pamela's cheek in farewell. Turning once more, she looked sadly at the Tianming Monk as he clutched her dead body close not wanting to release her.

Edward and Crystin walked over before looking down at their granddaughter; the two smiled in pleasure at each other, glad they were given permission to see her. Together they turned and each taking Cecille's hand they pulled their reluctant daughter with them.

Cecille feeling compelled to leave turned away; they disappeared into the light now that White Buffalo was reunited with her parents.

****

Spirit Bear jumped up with a scream of anguish. His white bear hide dropped to the ground as he clutched the medallion in a death grip, now that Cecille was gone. He turned before racing out of the sweat lodge; he ran towards the remote lake trying to outdistance his raging grief. Getting to the far end, he was unable to go any further since they were hemmed in by the mountains to keep their village hidden. The medicine man having no choice but to stop had gone past the spot the women usually bathed at. The Cree healer dropped to the ground as tears streamed down his face.

Spirit Bear lifted the cross then staring down at it grimly; he shook it willing the image of Cecille to resurface. When nothing happened, he jumped to his feet abruptly. He pulled back his arm to throw the offending medallion into the lake. If White Buffalo could no longer wear it, nobody else would be able to either.

Spirit Bear paused; suddenly he eyed the roaring waterfall in the distance. If he threw the necklace in the lake somebody was bound to find it sooner or later. The medicine man, getting a better idea, dropped his arm. He raced to the water's edge before jumping into the lake. With powerful strokes he swam to the falling water, diving down he went behind the falls.

Spirit Bear resurfaced behind the water with a good-sized rock that he found at the bottom of the lake; he looked up at the cliff face then swam towards it. There were several protruding stones, which he had known having explored it with his twin brother in their youth. Using them, he climbed up still clutching the rock with the medallion. The medicine man searched the cliff and crowed in delight when he found a deep crevice that was just the right length across. Taking the rock he was holding, he pushed the necklace into the hole before hammering the stone against it; shoving the cross in as deep as he could get it.

Spirit Bear turned then threw the rock back into the river before looking up. He raised his fist towards the sky; even though he didn't have a clear view through the falling water, the medicine man did not care as he declared in a rage. "You took my White Buffalo from me, so now I will never allow another to wear her medallion. Nobody will ever find it here... this I swear to you!"

Spirit Bear dropped his arm as tears continued to stream down his cheeks; he launched himself off the rocky shelf that he was standing on through the waterfall before gracefully he dived back into the lake and swam to shore. The medicine man got out of the water. Not once did he look back as he marched purposely towards his people!

*****

The white buffalo legend and the missing Celtic medallion will get forgotten in time as the eighteenth century turned into the nineteenth, twentieth then finally the twenty-first. Except by the Oriental Guardians, who would continue to give out a dire warning to those who wished to listen!

Beware the return of the Dragon Medallion...
For THEY, are coming!

Here ends Twin Destinies
Book #2; which is my transition from western to a fantasy series...

The Curse of the Celtic Dragon Medallion

Keep watch for book #3:
Which will be the END... or could it be the BEGINNING!

The Seeker & the Shadow Hunter

Shadow Hunter, the only surviving descendant of the Oriental Tianming Monk known as Shadow Stalker and his Cree ancestor Spirit Bear who was the last existing skinwalker; finds in his youth a precious relic that remained hidden for centuries. A vision sent by the Great Spirit at his naming ceremony shows that once finished his training as a Cree and Asian shaman he will leave his precious mountains. He must hunt for answers as to why he is the only one who can seem to see the shadows rising out of the Mother Earth. What they are must also be determined. At first, the shadows seemed harmless enough with no direction except occasionally when they found a willing host. The shaman would then become the hunter to banish the shadows; hopefully, without killing the victim.

Shadow Hunter wandered aimlessly at first from town to town, city to city before crossing provinces as he searched for the truth... until he met her. The shadows seemed unwillingly drawn to her, but they weren't the only ones. The shaman couldn't help feeling a magnetic pull that he knew he had to continue to resist. Were the shadows the real danger or was it all an illusion to draw him to her, could she be the real threat! If he gave in to his deepest desires, he knew the world was doomed! As death stalked them all unmercifully, the Cree shaman found his will to resist the Seekers tested again and again; until only one remained!

A BRIEF NOTE TO MY READERS:

As I do at the end of all books that I have written so far, I am again including a list for you of where I get most of my information or if I have changed anything. Thankfully, most of what I need is now on the internet making it way easier to find everything in one spot. Wikipedia is my favourite place, but of course, I search others as well.

- https://www.warpaths2peacepipes.com/native-indian-weapons-tools/bows-and-arrows.htm
- http://www.rmgc.org/club_history
- http://www.thecanadianencyclopedia.ca/en/article/religion-of-aboriginal-people/
- https://en.wikipedia.org/wiki/Spencer_repeating_rifle
- http://www.petroleumhistory.org/OilHistory/pages/Cable/walking.html
- http://www.ottertooth.com/Native_K/jbcree.htm
- http://www.sjvgeology.org/history/
- http://www3.sympatico.ca/goweezer/canada/can1800.htm
- https://en.wikipedia.org/wiki/Stetson
- https://en.wikipedia.org/wiki/Gypsy_horse
- https://en.wikipedia.org/wiki/Iris_(anatomy)
- https://en.wikipedia.org/wiki/Beeswax
- https://en.wikipedia.org/wiki/Jeans
- http://www.dailymail.co.uk/news/article-3762905/I-did-Blind-golfer-took-game-losing-sights-hits-hole-one-36-years-trying.html
- http://www.newworldencyclopedia.org/entry/Book_of_Enoch
- http://bcspiritbear.com/spirit-bear-facts/
- https://en.wikipedia.org/wiki/Axe
- http://wleman.tripod.com/sounds/soundfiles.htm#
- https://adventure.howstuffworks.com/outdoor-activities/hunting/traditional-methods/knife-hunting1.htm

BIOGRAPHY

I was born in Dalhousie, NB, but lived most of my life in Alberta. Presently, I am living in Falher a town in Northern Alberta; known as the honey capital of Canada plus the home of the largest bee.

I married a wonderful loving man, Michel Pelletier; I have two daughters, a step-daughter, and two step-sons. So far I have four grandsons, several step-grandsons, and step-granddaughters.

I love to fish, dance, and golf but above all write. Writing has been a passion for me since I was in my early twenties; it has become an addiction over the years I find hard to stay away from for any length of time.

I was published in 2010 by a company in the US but was recently signed by Publishing House Publishing based out of High Prairie, Alberta Canada.

I have 3 series planned with at least three books in each of my series, possibly more if the writing bug continues to bite me.

The first set of books begins the journey that will tie my three series together; they start from early to mid-1800s in the USA as a western romance.

The second series is my transition from romance to fantasy, it will become a western fantasy; it's set in the late 1800's and continues into the late 2000s, which starts in England then bring you into Canada, where I will stay until the end!

My third series will be a full fantasy. It will be the beginning of a new world and reappearance of magic in its full glory; including long-forgotten creatures, different cultures, and races. With several surprises that even I am unaware of yet!